THE FAE OF THE FJELL

THE FAE OF THE FJELL

ELLE THRASHER

Ebook ISBN: 979-8-9903433-2-0

Paperback ISBN: 979-8-9903433-3-7

Hardback ISBN: 979-8-9903433-4-4

For information: elle@ellethrasher.com

Cover Designer: Damonza

Editor: Aimee Vance, Revel Books

To all the readers who have been told they were too much.
Burn bright. Be loud. Love hard.

And to Riley Jo for asking if there were Fire Fae.
Yes, yes there are.

CONTENT NOTICE

The book you are about to read contains subject matter that may be difficult or unappealing to some readers. This includes, significant violence, graphic language, on page sex, gore, death, war, natural disasters such as wildfires, house fires, brief moments of ptsd and flashbacks.

PRONUNCIATION GUIDE

Espen -- Ess-pen

Øyvin -- Oy-vihn

Alvdalen -- Alv-dah-len

Balder -- Bahl-derr

Bente -- Ben-the

Dagny -- Dahg-nee

Embla -- Emm-blah

Fjell -- Fyell

Freija -- Frey-ah

Gunvor -- Guun-vore

Halvar -- Hal-vahr

Herja -- Herr-yah

Ingeborg -- In-geh-bohrg

Jorunn -- Yoo-runn

Kjetil -- Sheh-till

Knut-Arne -- Knewt - Ahr-neh

Leif -- Layf

Oddvar -- Odd-vahr

Reuven -- Rew-ven
Salka -- Sall-kah
Skolvik -- Skoll-veek
Solveig -- Sool-vay
Torsten -- Torr-sten
Trygve -- Tryg-veh
Turi -- Tuu-ree
Unni -- Oo-nee
Veigar -- Vey-gahr
Vigdis -- Vigh-diss
Wilhelm -- Vill-helm
Ylva -- Yll-vah

1

LENNIE

That damn cruise ship was back. A year after it had abandoned me, the last ship of the season loomed large in the harbor as some of its guests sauntered past me in their tour group.

I leaned against the side of Oddvar's café, the white-painted wood siding biting into my bare shoulders that lay exposed thanks to the tank top weather that graced us today. Taking a long sip of my morning coffee, I tilted my face to the sun, enjoying the last rays of summer.

August in Norway was absolute perfection. The village was decorated with a myriad of colorful flowers spilling out of window boxes outside the main street storefronts. Signboards littered the roads and walkways, welcoming everyone to the different establishments. Wispy white clouds dotted the bright blue sky, the verdant greens on the mountainsides practically sang with euphoria, and the water—Øyvin's blessed fjord—reflected all of it like a shiny plate of glass.

"Skolvik fjord is one of the deepest fjords in the country," a little thing with an English accent said as she walked backward at the front of the passing tour group. She waved a triangular red flag, the white cruise logo emblazoned on it mocking me. "The fjord is 1308 meters deep. Or, as the locals say"—she giggled to herself—"fifty-seven trolls deep!"

I snorted. "More like fifty-seven sexy trolls."

An entire population of fae creatures called this place home, my demi-fae-self included. These tourists had no idea that two worlds collided here, living *mostly* in harmony side by side.

The group meandered on, and a bell tinkled behind me.

"Lennie?" Oddvar's gravelly voice sounded from the doorway. I spun and found the septuagenarian leaning out the door, his bushy gray eyebrows waving at me. "I need you back inside."

I gulped down the remainder of my delicious bean nectar. "On my way."

Oddvar popped back into the café, and I followed his cardigan-clad, short frame. No matter the weather, Oddvar was always in some form of knitwear—like a hardy fisherman who would never give up the lifestyle and was perpetually ready for a stormy day.

The bell above the door rang as I entered the building. Contented customers' chatter filled the air as they munched away on their lunches, and the sweet, sweet smell of coffee permeated the brightly lit room. Summer was almost over in the little village of Skolvik, but the tables at Oddvar's Café teemed with the last of the cruise ship tourists visiting the fjords like I'd done a year ago. Except now I worked here and was a demi-fae with magical powers, instead of a human tourist who missed her cruise ship.

We strolled behind the counter, and I put my used mug in the industrial dishwasher, shutting the door with a metallic clunk. Smiling softly, I donned my khaki apron and set to work.

I stroked a finger over one of the chrome knobs on the fancy Italian espresso machine. "Hello, Robertina, you gorgeous, sexy bea—"

"Stop talking to the machines," Oddvar groused from behind me.

I ignored his grumbles and winked at the machine. "Are you going to be good for me today?" I whispered, keeping my back to the surly Norwegian who was busy preparing a customer's hot tea. Robertina didn't reply, but then again, she never did. Was I crazy for talking to inanimate objects? Probably. But over the past few months working here I'd found the nicer I was to the machine, the better she performed for me. Same theory as talking to plants—keep them happy and they'll respond in kind with excellent growth and performance.

With everything on my plate this week, including my family in town, I really needed her to be kind. Said plate happened to be full of my wedding to one dapper and bubbly Forest Fae by the name of Espen Solbakke, with our partner and third member of our relationship, Øyvin Håland, set to officiate.

"One cappuccino," Oddvar said in Norwegian. My hearing juju still worked great, but this one I'd understood without the magical tinkering. Ever since Oddvar had offered me the part-time summer job at the café, I'd been voraciously studying the Norwegian language, picking up as much as I could before my employment began. There'd been a slight dip in studies while searching for the Fjell Fae heir last winter, but I'd resumed as soon as that debacle was over with. Now, I could understand most of the words spoken in and around the café, including people's orders. It was as if the more Norwegian I learned and could comprehend, the less my hearing magic stepped in.

"*En cappuccino*," I replied in Norwegian, and set to work making the hot drink. Tamping down the grinds, flicking the knobs on the machine, the steady movements of making coffees had become a rhythmic dance routine that I thoroughly enjoyed. And seeing the looks on customers faces when they sighed with contentment at that first sip made it all worthwhile.

I set the completed drink at the counter, grinning at the woman with short strawberry-blonde hair who picked it up. Her T-shirt said "I Heart Trolls" across the front, no doubt from the gift shop down the road.

"Lennie," an older feminine voice yoo-hooed from across the room. I wiped my hands on the tea towel tied in the waist belt of my apron and peered around.

Solveig waved at me from a four-person table by the front windows, two of the other seats occupied by her friends, Jorunn and Dagny.

Sauntering around the counter, I approached the white-haired trio by the sun-kissed window. "Can I get you anything else ladies? The sandwiches okay?"

"Oh, yes, my dear. Lunch was wonderful as always." Solveig smiled brightly, her short hair perfectly styled. The other two nodded in agreement, their empty plates sprinkled with crumbs. "But we were wondering why you're working today?"

"Shouldn't you be taking the day off to get ready?" Dagny pulled up the sleeves on her lightweight striped pink cardigan, the color matching the lipstick stain on Jorunn's cup.

"My mother and Espen's sister, Ingrid, have been handling all the arrangements," I replied. "I was told to get out of their way." I'd taken that wish and scampered out of Espen's cabin as swiftly as possible earlier this week. The two of them were like Pinterest on steroids. They'd even had video calls this spring to discuss wedding details. While I'd helped out here and there, and made decisions between suggested color palettes, this whole thing was down to them. And I didn't really mind.

"Well, we look forward to tomorrow," Jorunn said. She must have visited the hairdresser's yesterday as her bob was sharper than usual. "We've had our dresses picked out for months."

"Awww." I placed my hand on my heart. These three really were some of my favorite villagers. While they gossiped to no end, they'd always shown me kindness. "You're all wearing big fluffy ball gowns, yes?"

The trio snickered, leaning back in their chairs, as the bell above the front door rang.

"Solveig was considering stripper heels," Jorunn said.

Solveig's mouth fell open and her eyes widened. "I was not!"

Jorunn cackled at her own joke, wiping a tear from the corner of her eye.

"That would be dangerous considering the ceremony is outside my cabin," a familiar male voice said and a hand settled against my lower back.

My shoulders relaxed, and I leaned into the pressure, welcoming the warmth at my side.

"You know I wouldn't wear those things, Espen. I'd roll an ankle going up that hill," Solveig said.

Espen rested his free hand on the police utility belt around his waist, his usual rain jacket replaced for the season with a black T-shirt with *politi* written across the left breast in bold silver letters. "I know, I know."

Dagny pulled her glasses half-way down her nose and peered over the rim. "Would you consider carrying her if she did, though?"

Espen smiled. "For you three, anything."

The trio swooned.

"Now, if you don't mind, I need a word with the bride."

They shooed us away with little grins, lapping up the loved-up haze that'd settled over the village in the run-up to our nuptials... or maybe that was the blur of activity that was happening all around me that I could barely keep up with.

Espen planted a kiss on my cheek and steered me back behind the counter, not daring to step a foot over the bright, white line on the floor and incur Oddvar's wrath.

"I just came to check on you," the Forest Fae said. He brushed his hand through his hair that he'd recently had trimmed in preparation for the wedding. It still hung long on top and was shorter along the sides, but he'd taken enough off the front that it wasn't constantly in his eyes.

I set my hands on my hips. "I'm fine."

He quirked a brow. "When a woman says those two words, it usually means the opposite. And when that woman also happens to be you, it usually means you're thinking hard about something or preparing a prank against Øyvin."

Shaking my head at him, I reached out and brushed my palm across his neatly trimmed beard. "I'm doing exceptionally well and having a decent day at work."

"Only decent?"

I rolled my eyes. "It got better when you walked in."

He gave me a beaming smile, and something fluttered in my stomach at the sight.

"Now, is there something I can get for you or were you actually just visiting to see my pretty face?" I rested my chin on the backs of my fingers and winked.

Espen chuckled and raked his gaze across me. "No coffee order for me today." His eyes sparkled and his lips curved into another one of his signature grins. I couldn't help myself. I leaned in and pressed my lips to his. Warmth swept over me, lingering in my bones and turning them to jelly. *A hundred plus years of this? Yes, please. I do. Sign me up.*

Someone cleared their throat behind me. Reluctantly, I unlatched myself from Espen and glanced over my shoulder. Oddvar stood there in his apron, arms crossed, mouth pinched together, and a single eyebrow raised toward his thin, gray hairline.

"Sorry, Oddvar," Espen said, well aware of *why* Oddvar had painted a line on the floor by the counter this summer.

Before I could add my apologies to my boss for canoodling on the job, clinking sounded across the room. I looked for the source of the noise and found Solveig, Jorunn, and Dagny tapping their spoons against their coffee cups.

"Again!" Solveig yelled.

"Kiss!" Her two friends chimed in at the same time.

I glanced at Oddvar. He leveled a deadpan stare at me, wholly unamused about his café turning into "lunch and a show." Other customers chimed in, tapping their spoons against their cups and clapping. Jorunn and Dagny did their best to explain to the patrons around them that

Espen and I were getting married tomorrow. Within seconds, the entire café was cheering for us.

I tried to hold back the smile twisting at my lips. "Got to give the people what they want, Oddvar."

He sighed, rolled his eyes, and raised a single finger.

Espen didn't wait a second.

He grabbed me from behind the counter, spun me into the open space between tables, and dipped me. His lips crashed into mine, passion and need bubbling beneath the surface, wanting to take things much further but holding back... just. I squeezed his arms for purchase. A tingling sensation flowed through me like a cool breeze on a hot summer's day and my heart clenched with joy. Forget about one-hundred years of this, I'd gladly take a thousand.

Happiness and applause swept through the room as Espen righted me but didn't let go.

His eyes sparkled as our gazes met. It'd been an interesting—some might argue unconventional—journey to get here. But the thought of being this man's wife, committing to a life with him and Øyvin, didn't scare me away like it would've done a year ago. In fact, there was now no place I'd rather be than here in Skolvik with them.

Espen let me go and I took two shaky steps back and bumped against the counter, heat flushing across my cheeks as the applause died down.

"I'll see you at home," Espen said with a wink, stepping backward toward the front door. "Then, tomorrow..."

"Tomorrow." I grinned.

2

LENNIE

Afternoon light shone through the bedroom window of Espen's cabin, brushing across the wood-paneled walls and rustic furniture. My white dress with long lace sleeves practically glowed in the happiness and light that flooded the room. The garment was simple and refined. A lace top with some floaty tulle material on the skirt that was perfect for the warm end-of-summer day.

I reached for the crown of white flowers and greenery on the dresser and set the delicate piece atop my curled hair. It wasn't entirely my style, but I appreciated including nature, which was so important to us, in our wedding. Turning to face the full-length mirror by the closet, I fastened the circlet with a couple of pins Ingrid had set aside for me. I looked like me, but perhaps a touch more feminine than usual.

"I wouldn't be caught dead in white," Ylva muttered, her reflection appearing in the mirror as she pulled lint off the black lapel of her body-hugging suit which matched her black Converse. I expected nothing less of Espen's fearsome best friend and second-in-command.

"I'll be sure to tell Gunvor that the next time I see her."

"Please do." She patted her hair which had been braided, twisted, and pinned to the back of her head. "Mother sends her regards and regrets by the way."

Gunvor was as much of a badass as her Forest Fae daughter, and while I'd have liked to have the elder stateswoman in attendance, Alvdalen was a decent drive away and she wasn't the youngest fae in the forest.

"That's sweet. Thanks." I spun to face Ylva, the skirt of my dress swishing around the comfy hiking boots on my feet. "Is he ready?"

"He's bouncing around as happy as a dog, greeting every single person in attendance... twice." She cleared her throat. "Are you ready?"

Good question. One with an easy answer.

"Yeah," I replied. "Yeah, I am."

"Good, but also debatable." She wandered over and motioned for me to squat. I acquiesced to her request, bending at the knees. She reached over and adjusted the flower crown on my head, fussing and straightening it. A second later, a bobby pin was retrieved from her own braid and used to re-fasten the circle.

Pulling back, she examined me and gave me a nod. "Excellent. Now put on your best smile and look all bride-like. I have a sizable bet with some of my soldiers on how long it'll take before Espen tears up."

I chuckled and rose back to standing position.

She clapped her hands together in a prayer position. "I'm down for sub ten seconds. So, if you could help me out..."

"How much is the bet?"

"Two thousand five hundred *kroner*."

"I knew I liked you."

"Same here. You give that man more hell than I ever could." She grinned. "Now, let's go find the little ones and get you married to those lovesick guys."

"Guy," I corrected. "It's only Espen."

She snorted. "Don't lie. The entire village knows the three of you are an item and that this was originally for immigration purposes."

My shoulders dropped and my mouth popped open. "How'd they find that out?" It technically was still for immigration purposes. At least, the speed in which we were pulling this off. But the main reason for this marriage was because we loved each other.

"Please." She raised her brows at me and set her hands on her hips. "You three are practically glued together. Plus, do you really think Solveig, Dagny, and Jorunn would let that gossip go?"

"Yeah, there wasn't a chance of that was there?"

"Not at all. As soon as that ring hit your finger last Christmas, the whole town knew what was going on."

Small towns. What was a woman to do? Grin and bear it, really.

"Shall we find the children? Pretty sure one of your brothers gave them sweets to make today a little harder on everyone."

I rolled my eyes. As my brother Jared and his wife Jennifer had just had their own little girl and couldn't travel, and Andrew or Amanda sure as hell wouldn't give their kids candy, there was only one viable candidate. Ten out of ten chance Ryan was the guilty party. He was constantly going for the Favorite Uncle title and had always been the most gregarious of the Martin siblings.

Ylva opened the bedroom door and we strode through the tiny kitchen area into the cabin's living room.

Peals of laughter met my ears. Four young girls in white dresses with pale-green sashes around their waists sat on the small chestnut-colored sofa, two with dirty blonde hair, the other two light brown. Their locks were braided into a matching half-up, half-down hairstyle with ringlets brushing their shoulders. All four of them looked like tiny princesses.

Andrew's daughters, Abigail and Amelia had made fast friends with Ingrid's girls, Kari and Katrine, even if neither could speak the same language. Over the past week of them staying in Skolvik, they'd been inseparable. And then there was Kristoffer...

The young kid, now five years old and calling himself a big boy, stood atop the coffee table in his Norwegian *Bunad*—the traditional attire. Cream socks and a pair of black pants that cinched under his knees were paired with a red-and-green tartan vest over a white shirt. The ensemble was adorable, especially with the pieces of family silver at his cuffs and a broach comprised of two silver balls connected by a chain at his collar—the latter of which had once belonged to Espen.

"What are you doing?" Ylva's commander voice boomed across the room.

Kristoffer spun, his eyes wide as he stumbled off the table, sending the girls into fits of laughter. He righted himself and dusted off his pants, mumbling something I couldn't hear.

"We need all of you to behave today," I said in English before turning to Ingrid's kids and asking the same of them in Norwegian.

They all nodded.

"You look pretty, Auntie Lennie," Amelia said, twirling a lock of her hair around her finger.

"Thank you, cutie."

This was probably the prettiest I'd ever dressed. As the only daughter, Mom had certainly dolled me up over the years but this was a whole new level of girliness. Definitely not my everyday wear, but I didn't mind it.

A knock sounded and the front door creaked open. My parents walked in and closed the door behind them. Mom wore a lavender, beaded dress with small flowers on it, while Dad was in a black suit with a lavender-and-pale-green tie that matched Mom's dress.

"Now, now, kiddos." Mom swept into the room with her arms open wide, her dark eyes full of warmth, and her dark hair perfectly blown out and full of volume.

"Grammy!" Amelia said.

"Hello, sweetie. Don't y'all look great." The girls hugged Mom before turning their attention to Dad who gave them a massive hug each. Mom's watery gaze met mine. "And so do you."

"Did you bring tissues?" I asked.

"I have a pack in each pocket," Dad replied for her.

She glided over and set her hands on my shoulders, her lips already quivering with emotion. "I never thought I'd see you in a wedding dress."

I let out a long sigh and drew her in for a hug, squeezing her tight. "Miracles do happen."

She squeezed me back. "They most certainly do." Pulling away, she took two steps back and tilted her head to the ceiling while dabbing her pinky finger underneath her eye. "Ugh, I don't want to ruin my make-up."

"Need a tissue already, Deb?" Dad asked from under a pile of kids on the sofa.

Mom waved her hand at him before glancing at her watch. "We came to tell you it's time." She turned to the kids. "Are you ready?"

All five of them understood her and bounced off the sofa, leaving my dad behind. In quick movements, they lined up by the door per my mother's verbal and hand-motion instructions.

A hand landed on my shoulder and Ylva swept past whispering, "Less than ten seconds."

I chuckled as she crossed the room. "I'll do my best."

"I am the ring bear," Kristoffer said in Norwegian and let out a growl while taking up position by the front door.

"Now, Kristoffer," Ylva said, setting the rings in the boy's hand. "Don't drop these."

He gave her a quick salute. "I shall guard them with my life, Commander."

I grinned. Thankful that the young boy who'd crashed through the ice earlier this year was happy and healthy. Even if he was obnoxiously loud.

"Thank you, soldier." Ylva played along, and part of me wondered if Kristoffer might one day serve as a Forest Fae soldier. With the way he looked up to his uncle, I wouldn't be surprised.

One by one, each of the kids followed my mom and Ylva out the door, starting the processional. A guitar strummed a happy tune, the notes matching the children's boundless energy.

"Ope, don't want to step on your dress," Dad said, doing a little sidestep to avoid the flowing tulle hem. He smiled down at me, his eyes wrinkling at the corners, his white hair swept to one side. Daniel Martin, father of four, Ohio born and raised, friend to all, was the biggest softy—and Ohio State Football fan—anyone would ever have the fortune of meeting.

He looped his arm through mine and I picked up the tiny bouquet of lavender and white wildflowers that waited for me by the door. "I'm so proud of you, Lennie. It's wonderful to see you so happy."

"Aww." I swallowed hard, gripping the bouquet. "Thanks, Dad."

"I mean it." He patted my arm with his free hand. "While your mom and I would've loved to have you closer to home, I always knew you'd find your own place in the world, likely a little farther afield."

"Was Norway on that list?"

He tilted his head from one side to the other. "Western Europe was," he chuckled. "And you've found very nice *gentlemen.*"

I sucked in a breath, my eyes going wider than I would've liked.

He chuckled again. "Of course we know. It's a little unconventional, but like I said. It's great to see you so happy. That's all I've ever wanted for my little girl. When you brought them home for Thanksgiving and stood there in the hallway with them looming behind you, that grin on your face..." He shook his head. "We'd seen that look countless times when you were growing up. There was never any arguing with that power pose and staunch resolve. Those two were yours and no one would be taking them away from you."

My throat tightened and I took two trembling breaths. Trust my dad to get me all emotional.

"There she is, poking her head out of the sand for once."

I snort-laughed and nodded. He'd always likened me to an ostrich with my emotions, dunking my head in the sand any time things got too much. But he was right. I didn't hide from my emotions anymore. I didn't shy away from how I felt, especially regarding the two men waiting for me outside.

A lone violin began to play, the lilting tune like something from a Norwegian folk tale, rising and falling in notes that promised magic and adventure. My breath hitched as I recognized the melody, one I'd heard played countless times, but not on violin. It was Øyvin's song, the one he played on his piano when he was deep in thought. I closed my eyes, letting the music wash over me, and the tension in my shoulders eased.

"You ready, pumpkin?" Dad asked, tugging lightly on my arm as he opened the front door.

We took two steps outside, rays of sunlight dancing across the field beside the cabin, and my heart stuttered.

There, in the flat part of the field where I'd *yoga*'d with Espen for the first time underneath the Aurora Borealis, was the entire wedding congregation. As one, they rose to their feet and looked down the aisle between the mismatched chairs. And at the end, with the forest behind them, under an arch of lilac and white flowers with boughs of greenery and ribbon, wearing crisp gray suits, stood my two guys.

I smiled. "Yeah, I'm ready."

3

LENNIE

Sighs and smiles mixed with the violin's melody as Dad and I meandered down the grassy aisle. The spectacular view to my right was otherworldly, like mother nature was putting on a show and winking at us. The trees appeared greener, the sky the brightest blue I'd ever seen, and the fjord... The fjord twinkled like starlight.

At least a quarter of the village was in attendance, from Espen's boss and Oddvar to some of Øyvin's soldiers. The kids were all up front, Ylva beside the arch in her role as Best Woman. But I only had eyes for the two fae underneath the arch. Everything else seemed to fade away as we got closer.

A lone tear fell across Espen's cheek, and I caught movement out of the corner of my eye. Probably Ylva celebrating her victory.

My heart galloped in my chest and my body tingled from all the people staring at me. This was it. I was getting married. I was marrying a Forest Fae and secretly a Fjord Fae too, even though Øyvin wouldn't be calling himself my husband. This was a commitment ceremony for all three of us—today we were officially becoming husband, wife, and partners. Holy shit.

We stopped in front of the guys and my dad let go of my arm, giving it a double pat before finding his seat next to Mom.

Espen reached out taking my hands in his with a broad smile and all felt right in the world.

Øyvin's commanding voice welcomed everyone and moved on to a speech about life and the values of a partner. With a shaky breath, my focus shifted to the gathered crowd.

Smiling friends and family peered back at me. From my parents and brothers upfront in their snazziest suits, to Solveig and the ladies in beautiful traditional dresses. Leif and Torsten held hands, the former giving me a toothy grin. Even Oddvar was in attendance, wearing a dark gray suit and an expression that was far brighter than his usual surely state.

My gaze drifted back, finding townsfolk I'd come to know through work, and settled on the last row. Heidi sat beside none other than the big guy himself—Halvar had actually deigned to leave the mountain. And he was wearing a fucking suit. Black shirt with black suit and black tie—more ready for a human funeral than a wedding—but the man had dressed up.

Halvar straightened in his seat and inhaled sharply as a latecomer sat in the final chair beside him. I didn't recognize the man, but he wore a double-breasted navy suit and black sunglasses, his salt-and-pepper hair slicked back off his wrinkled brow. He looked like a more refined version of Halvar, one who perhaps lived in a gorgeous apartment in Paris and not a rugged mountain cave.

Øyvin cleared his throat. "And now the two have selected to exchange their own vows—"

My eyes widened and I whipped my attention back to Espen.

Shit. I knew there was something I'd forgotten. Vows. I was supposed to write my own vows.

Kristoffer appeared beside us, right on cue, and opened his little hands, proffering the silver wedding bands to us. We plucked the rings from his clammy palms, and Espen gave him a little wink. The young boy beamed and scampered back to his spot beside Ylva.

My gaze drifted to Espen, panic welling inside me. How the hell had I forgotten to write my own vows? Too late now. "You go first," I mumbled.

Espen smiled, gripping my hands a little tighter—having probably deduced my current predicament.

"Evelyn—Lennie—Martin," he started. "I've searched for a love like this for what feels like centuries." My heart clenched, and he squeezed my fingers. "A love that makes me dream of waking up. A love that adds buoyancy to my days, bolstering me in the moments when I feel lost. And, most importantly, a love that challenges me."

The crowd snickered and one of my brothers outwardly laughed while I lost myself in Espen's honey-colored eyes and the blanketing warmth of his words.

"Never in my most wayward dreams could I have imagined meeting a woman like you," he continued. "Someone so passionate about life, steadfast in her beliefs, and unwavering in her loyalty to family. Lennie..." He took a deep breath as if trying to quell the tears that lingered along his lashes. It felt like my heart, my entire chest was about to burst in half. "I will love you till the end of my days. And, until that end, I vow to protect your peace and bury your enemies." He scrunched his nose like it was a joke, but I knew, and so did all the fae present, that he meant every word exactly as they'd been spoken. He'd vanquish anything that crossed my path. "You have my word, my heart, my everything."

He gently pushed the silver wedding band onto my finger then raised my hand and tipped it to his lips. His kiss sent sparks of joy and comfort through my body, lighting it up from the inside. Leaving absolutely no doubt just how much he loved me.

Øyvin tilted his head in an almost imperceptible nod. His sapphire eyes met mine and extolled his agreement with everything Espen had just said. The combination of the look and the spoken words was enough to have my throat close up.

How the hell was I supposed to follow that?

Fuck, I was gonna have to wing it.

I turned my gaze fully to Espen and swallowed the gargantuan lump in my throat, desperate for a breath that wouldn't result in waterworks. "I-I... I'm sorry I punched you the first day we met."

Half the crowd laughed, half snorted, and I was pretty sure the shocked guffaw was from my mother. Before I could forget, I slipped Espen's wedding band onto his finger where it belonged.

"I don't doubt for a second that *we* were meant for one another," I added, making sure to include Øyvin in this even though the event was billed as mine and Espen's wedding. "I can vow to be a pain in the ah—butt, to make you laugh every day, and to cherish every single one of your smiles. You've brought so much light to my world." I looked between both of them and then back at Espen. "A light I never want to let go of, even if I was hesitant at first."

My guys snickered.

I straightened as the gentle summer breeze brushed tendrils of my hair across my cheeks. "I promise to love you for a thousand years and I can't wait to see what this life and world has in store for us."

I meant every word, for both of them. Based on the way their eyes hooded, they understood.

A collective awe wound its way around the gathering, and Espen practically melted on the spot as he brushed his thumbs over my fingers.

"Espen Solbakke," Øyvin started. "Do you take Lennie Martin to be your wife?"

A burst of sunshine radiated from the Forest Fae. "I do."

"Lennie Martin. Do you take Espen Solbakke to be your husband?"

I gave his fingers two quick squeezes. "*Ja.*"

Espen beamed at my Norwegian reply and took a step forward. His head tilted toward me, lips puckering, and Øyvin cleared his throat, stopping the bubbly fae in his tracks.

The crowd and I chuckled at his eagerness, and Espen pulled back, a flush of pink filling his cheeks.

"By the power vested in me," Øyvin said with a pointed look to Espen, "I pronounce you husband and wife. You may *now* kiss the bride."

Espen's lips were against mine in an instant and I entwined my arms around his neck, relishing in the steadfast promise of his kiss. Yeah, I'd gladly take a lifetime or five with these two guys.

The violin music started up again. A tune that sounded vaguely like *The* Ohio State Fight Song, *Buckeye Battle Cry*. I furrowed my brow but shook it off as Øyvin announced, "May I present, Mr. and Mrs. Solbakke Martin."

The crowd applauded and cheered as Espen led me back down the aisle. Smiles and congratulations matched the timing of my footfalls and the notes of what was either my dad's contribution to the wedding or a prank from my brothers.

As we reached the end of the aisle, Espen tugged my hand and pulled me into him. I stumbled into his embrace. "I love you," he whispered and dipped me, pressing his lips to mine.

4

ØYVIN

I grinned as Espen dipped Lennie at the end of the aisle. Seeing her happy was always a joy, and Espen brought that out in her as much as I did. Her smile only added to her beauty today. A day that was turning into a memory I'd forever cherish.

My gaze slid to their right, taking in the crowd. Everyone stood, clapping and beaming at the newlyweds. The wedding couldn't be going any—

I stilled, fist clenching around the speech in my hand.

What the fuck was the Veigar doing here?

The well-dressed man applauded like every other guest wishing the couple well, his dark sunglasses covering the black eyes hidden beneath. Despite his pleasant smile, I knew better, knew the man's fiery history and what he was capable of. Everything he touched turned to ashes. Rumor had it the last time he'd shown up to a village unannounced the place was burned to the ground by him and his minions.

Nothing good could come of him being in Skolvik.

"Are you joining us?" Andrew Martin asked with a quick pat on my shoulder.

I shook off my shock and refocused.

This was the plan. I was supposed to follow the family down the aisle and then be present for family photos. Which sounded awful, but I'd do whatever was necessary to keep my partner and her family happy.

"I'll be right there," I said, not moving from my spot.

"Okay."

Andrew wandered down the aisle with his wife and girls and I looked back at the wedding crasher.

Halvar stood beside Veigar, seeming ready to wrap his arms around the man's throat and choke him. I'd certainly jump in and help if needed. Despite my building concern, we couldn't do anything with this many humans around, or fae, for that matter.

I scanned the sunny field, looking for options as the guests started moving. My gaze locked on an onyx-haired woman walking among the crowd. I didn't recognize her from the back, but the way she moved in that blue dress looked familiar. With each step she got closer to where Veigar—

The spot where he'd been was empty, and the muscles in my jaw twitched.

Where the fuck had he gone?

Striding into the crowd, I continued surveying the scene, avoiding bumping into too many people in the throng.

Lennie and Espen were back in the cabin waiting for photos.

The family were heading that way too.

Halvar stood outside the cabin.

Oddvar was helping Heidi across the uneven terrain.

Dresses and suits mixed with *bunad* of all different colors.

But Veigar was gone.

Fuck.

The woman in the blue dress turned, her gaze landing on mine, and my stomach bottomed out. What was Salka doing here too? She hadn't been invited either. The Fire Fae Princess, now Fjord Queen should be in the Fjord Palace.

"Øyvin!" A feminine voice yoo-hooed and I spun toward the noise. Deb Martin waved from the cabin's front door. "Øyvin, we need you for photographs!"

"I'll be right there!"

As I twisted back, the crowd thinned around me, and Salka was nowhere to be found.

Shit, this couldn't be good.

LENNIE

Chatter flooded the sun-lit room and crested into rounds of applause as Espen and I entered Fisken, the local restaurant and bar where we'd had our first date. Øyvin and our families strolled in behind us after we'd taken the obligatory group portraits by the harbor. A tiny dance area had been cleared to my left near the bar and several long tables displayed a myriad of American and Norwegian dishes, set up buffet-style. The rest of the space was filled with the restaurant's usual dark wood tables and leather booths.

Everywhere I looked, I could tell Ingrid and Mom had put in some serious work. Each table was covered in white linen with hollowed birch tree tea-light candle holders. Tiny lilac and white flowers decorated the base of each adding a burst of color. It was simple, elegant, and absolutely perfect.

My ever present smile continued as we pressed into the throngs of people. Espen was practically buzzing, our fingers tangled in their own embrace as he gently tugged on my hand. I thought I'd seen him at his happiest when we'd exchanged *I love you*s, but this was something else. Something more. He radiated joy and wasn't hiding it from anyone.

My heart clenched at the sight, warmth spreading across my sore cheeks. I'd done that. I was the one making him this happy.

"Congratulations! What a wonderful ceremony," Solveig said as she stepped into our path, brushing her hands over the blue skirt of her *bunad* with a bright floral pattern along the edges.

"Thank you, Solveig," Espen said, and I matched his gratitude.

Dagny slid in beside Solveig and peered over my shoulder. "Fantastic officiating, too."

I looked behind me and found Øyvin caught in the old woman's gaze. He nodded once, let out a strained cough, and headed for the bar. Dagny, wearing her emerald green *bunad* with white blouse, eyed him the entire way and I shook my head at her antics. She really was obsessed and I couldn't blame her. For all his grumpy asshole behavior, Øyvin was a great guy.

Solveig smacked her friend's shoulder, drawing my attention back to the two older ladies. "Can we get you anything to eat or drink before you make your rounds?"

"I'm fine, but thank you," I replied and nudged Espen. "We really should go say hello to everyone."

Solveig gave us a grandmotherly grin, filled with warmth and care, and stepped aside so we could delve deeper into the crowd of guests.

From Espen's sisters and friends from Alvdalen, to my brothers chatting away with Torsten and Leif, it was amazing to see our lives gathered in one space. Peace and harmony met us with every greeting and I felt like I'd finally found the composition I'd been searching for my whole life: a home where family and friends were filled with happiness and joy, laughter and light.

The only scene that gave me pause was Heidi and the kids. All five children—both human and fae—sat at a table with her, their eyes wide, fully enraptured in whatever tale she was spinning. Knowing the Forest Fae healer, it was probably something she shouldn't be talking about to children, something that would scare the shit out of them, or that coffee was the devil's juice and should never be consumed.

After more handshakes, hugs, and smiles, my stomach grumbled, and I excused myself from Espen's side. While Espen continued being the groom and acting like a politician up for re-election, I aimed for the food.

My dress swished around my feet as I strode over to the buffet table. It hosted dishes ranging from tiny sandwiches and Buckeyes, to *Sirupsnipper* and a tower of almond-paste rings with white icing piped on it known as *Kransekake*. I found a small plate and started gathering a collection of treats for myself.

A bead of sweat trickled down the back of my neck as I grabbed a Buckeye. Someone really needed to crack a window. With this many people in the restaurant, it was going to get hot fast.

"He's a lucky man," a low voice rumbled and the salt-and-pepper-haired man in a bespoke suit and black sunglasses stepped up beside me.

"You have no idea," I quipped, turning and giving him my best smile. Was it a slightly crude answer? Yes, but I was the bride so what was anyone going to do?

The older man's face wrinkled, and he gave me a tight-lipped grin. Who was this guy again? No one had mentioned inviting their fancy-dressing great uncle to the wedding. This man looked like he belonged in Paris, sipping an espresso along the Seine, not in a tiny Norwegian village.

"Might you know what these *Buckeyes* are?" He plucked one of the little chocolate-covered treats off the platter and eyed it closely. "An American delicacy, no?"

"Ohio's finest candies. They're peanut butter balls dipped in chocolate and made to resemble the tree nut that's prevalent in my home state." Not to mention the mascot of my parents' and brothers' alma mater, *The Ohio State University*.

The man smiled and popped one in his mouth. His sharp jaw worked overtime as he chewed, his eyes widening more and more by the second. He swallowed. "My wife would've loved them. Delicious."

"Agreed." I picked one off the plate in my hand and took a small bite. The sweet and salty combo danced across my tongue. Delicious indeed.

Halvar appeared beside me, his black suit straining at the shoulder seams and his eyes locked on the man in front of me. "A little far from home, Veigar."

The man brushed his hands as if removing crumbs and pressed his fingertips together, casually pointing them away from his torso. "Always a pleasure, Halvar."

Muscles jumped in Halvar's neck as Espen and Øyvin joined our little conversation. They both sidled up next to me, angling inward like I needed protecting. I scrunched my brow at the behavior. The old man was harmless and asking about peanut butter treats not bombs.

"What brings you to Skolvik?" Espen asked, his gaze welcoming despite his tense posture.

"Visiting my daughter, of course." Veigar panned and looked at each of us. Or at least, I thought he was surveying us. I couldn't be sure as he was still wearing sunglasses... inside. Weird, but to each their own.

Halvar crossed his arms and grumbled like he didn't believe the answer. "Don't you have some volcanoes to attend to? Katla? Eyjafjalla-jökull? How is the town of Grindavik these days?"

Volcanoes?

Veigar's lips spread into a sinister smirk, like a barn cat that had been caught inside the farmhouse and didn't give a damn. "Now, now, Halvar." I flinched at the informal way he spoke to the beast of the mountain. "Now is neither the time nor place." Veigar peered over his shoulders. No one was around us and everyone else was busy chatting and eating—except Ylva. The Forest Fae's knuckles had gone white as she clutched her drink and blatantly stared in our direction from a booth.

"*Here* most definitely is not the place, Your Majesty," Espen stepped in.

My brow furrowed. Your Majest— Lead filled my stomach, and my eyes widened to the size of a camera lens. *Oh shit.*

That's what had them all freaking out. That's why Halvar had bristled when Veigar sat down next to him during the ceremony. That's why my guys were ready to launch like rockets. This wasn't just some random wedding crasher. Veigar was the goddamn King of the Fire Fae!

"I wouldn't dare interrupt such an auspicious day."

And yet here he was... in Skolvik. At my wedding.

I set my plate down behind me and took a deep breath. Everything was going to be fine. Everything was going to be abso-fucking-lutely fine.

"What do you want?" Halvar asked, his voice laden with more malice than I'd ever heard from the big guy.

Veigar tapped his fingertips together. "A diplomatic solution to our mutual problems."

"Diplomatic?" Espen tilted his head to one side, eyes narrowing at the monarch.

"That is the..." he thought on it for a second. "*Preferred* course of action."

I swallowed hard as all three local fae straightened and leaned back.

"Is that a threat?" Øyvin asked through gritted teeth.

"Gentlemen!" My Dad appeared between Halvar and Veigar, and all the air in my lungs vanished. He turned to Veigar. "I don't believe we've met." He extended his hand to the Fire Fae. "Dan Martin, Father of the Bride."

Veigar took his hand, gave it a shake, and returned my dad's beaming smile. "Veigar Eldjotnarson. Pleasure to meet you Mr. Martin."

"That's quite the last name you've got there. Where are you from, son?"

"Iceland."

"How wonderful," Dad said, sounding like the kind Midwest man my grandma had raised him to be.

"Indeed," Veigar replied. "We were just discussing what great fortune it was that Lennie missed her ship and met such a splendid partner. Life altering, one might even say."

Bile churned in my stomach, threatening to bring back up my Buckeye. This guy had done his homework. We hadn't mentioned anything about the cruise ship or how I'd met everyone. Yet with his careful choice of words, he'd not only shown what he knew, but that he'd happily start pulling the pins on the grenades in our lives.

My dad retracted his hand and turned to me, his smile never faltering. "We're so happy for her."

Heart beating faster than a camera stuck on sports-mode, I swallowed the lump in my throat. "Did you need something, Dad?" Hopefully the tone of my voice didn't betray the panic swelling inside me.

"Your mom and Ingrid said to get ready. I'm sure you know what they're talking about." He straightened his tie and lowered his voice. "I might not have paid attention last night when your mother was going over things. So, I can't give you any *exact* details."

I pushed past my guys and nudged my father away from the four fae. "No worries, Dad. I've got it." I totally didn't *got it*. In fact, the only thing I had right now was a higher risk for a heart attack and an overwhelming amount of testosterone at my back.

Sending my dad toward the throngs of guests, I turned back to the situation brewing by the buffet.

"I'm going to leave you guys to chat. Please don't break anything." I gave them a gentle jazz hands motion and skedaddled. Hopefully they could keep their cool and, in one case, not burn down the restaurant full of people—most of which were humans who had no idea what milled around them drinking beer and laughing at their jokes.

My eyes scanned the room and landed on Ylva. Perched at the end of a booth bench, she gave me a quick upward nod and I scurried toward her like she was air conditioning on a hot summer's day.

"You catch all of that?" I asked, stopping in front of her. I doubted she could hear what was being said across the busy room, but if anyone could read lips, it'd be Ylva. Espen's second-in-command was like a hawk—nothing got past her.

Ylva nodded and proffered an open flask.

"Is this what I think it is?"

"If you're thinking aquavit, then yes." She set the metallic container on the table. "Drink up. You're going to need it for what's about to unfold."

Was she talking about the wedding or the chaos that had crashed the party? With the adrenaline currently coursing through my veins, my magic rattling around inside me in a panic, and my past experiences with the fiery liquor, I doubted it would help. I shook my head and plopped down on the other bench in the booth, the supple, leather seat sinking slightly beneath me.

Were weddings always this eventful and blurry? It felt like I'd just pulled on my dress, but based on the clock above the kitchen entrance, that was hours ago.

Glassy tinkling noises started up and I peered toward the dancing area. My Mom and Ingrid stood in the center of the space, looking like pastel statues in their dresses. Mom's lilac number complemented her dark hair color, and Ingrid's pale-yellow ensemble draped across her like a Greek goddess. Their smiles radiated across the room and their eyes glittered with a mutual plan that likely included me in some way.

"It's time for speeches," Mom said in English and Ingrid translated the announcement into Norwegian.

My eyes widened. I really should have paid more attention to them when we were discussing the schedule this morning over breakfast.

"On second thought." I reached across the table, grabbed the flask of aquavit, and tilted it to my lips.

6

LENNIE

The village bobbed around behind me like a fishing boat on the fjord—up and down, up and down, up and down. The streetlights threw gentle rays across the road but were almost unnecessary. Even at this hour... whichever hour it was... the sun still graced us with her happy presence, like an operatic soprano I could sing along with.

"Silver balls—" A hiccup escaped my lips, and I wriggled in Øyvin's hold, grinding my lower abdomen against his shoulder. His grip on my legs tightened and his broad hand moved up my dress and cupped my ass. "Silver balls. It's sleepy time, in the Skolvik."

Øyvin snorted. "Those aren't the lyrics, Trouble."

Espen chuckled beside us, his tie missing, the top buttons of his shirt undone, revealing a hint of the muscles that lay beneath, and his hair rumpled. His entire being was practically begging for me to fuck him. And damn did I want to. Nay! Need to. If only the world weren't so wobbly, I could reach out and drag my hands through—

"Would you stop moving?" Øyvin groused.

I stuck out my bottom lip.

The Fjord Fae wasn't as disheveled unfortunately. He'd held off on the alcohol once Veigar made his presence known. I, on the other hand—

Another hiccup bubbled up and out.

Espen looked over and our gazes caught. His eyes were full of something... sultry, happy, thirsty. Or maybe I was projecting? "I'm so merry."

"Your merry ass is going to feel like shit tomorrow." Øyvin's words were laced with laughter as we reached the boathouse and one of them opened the front door.

"That's a problem for future Lennie. Current Lennie is merry and being carried across the threshold. Silver baaaaaalls!"

"Ancestors save me," Øyvin muttered.

The door clicked shut and the room swam as Øyvin trudged upstairs with me still draped over his shoulder. Which I wasn't going to complain about. Not at all. It'd been a long day. Who knew getting married was so exhausting? So much chatting. Lots of eating. Many, many drinking with Ylvas, and Torstens, and Leifs, and brothers. Not to mention the dancing and the speeching. Ugh, the speeching. Note to self, always include the *al* in *aldri* or it sounds like you're saying *shit*.

Øyvin grunted, the room spun, and a wayward squeak left my lips before my back landed on our cozy bed. My feet hung off the edge and the white sheets cocooned me like Princess Peach on a cloud.

"Ugh, bed, yes. Great thinking." We needed to consummate the marriage. Now.

I stuck my boots in the air, one pointed at each of my fae husbands. Partners. My fae-sbands?

They both rolled their eyes and acquiesced to my request, untying my hiking boots. Their fingers drifted to my ankles and the simple brushes of skin against skin sent goosebumps up my legs. They gently yanked off the cumbersome shoes and dropped them to the floor. A groan of pleasure rumbled through my chest as I flexed my toes. Blessed freedom.

Reaching down, I grabbed the dirtied silky hem of my dress with both hands and flipped it up over my stomach, letting it fall under my chin. "Do me!"

Espen buckled over and laughed, gasping for breath between each bout while Øyvin bit his bottom lip and brushed his hand across his forehead.

"We can't…" The blurry brown-haired blob that was my dearly beloved straightened up and put its hands on its hips. "We can't fuck you when you're this drunk."

Whaaat? My sexy turned sad as I covered a yawn. "I'm not that drunk."

"Trust me," Espen said. "I'd love to fuck you right now. I want you on all fours, screaming my name around Øyvin's cock. But you're intoxicated, Lennie."

"Now, see that's a great plan. We should do that. I want that." I really really did. I could picture it now. Me being fucked in my wedding dress. The guys so turned on and desperate to get me out of it that they ripped the bodice piece apart before claiming my tits with their mouths.

"Lennie?" Espen said, drawing me from my erotic thoughts. "How many drinks did you have?"

"Many, many drinking," I slurred.

Øyvin turned to Espen. "Silver balls, remember?"

Ugh, they were being no fun. And right now, all I wanted was fun *yoga*. The kind that lit my body on fire and had me aching the next morning.

I scrambled to the top of the bed and flipped over to face them. "I'm so glad you're my f-usbands," I mumbled through another yawn and raised my arms above my head. "I love you both, soooooooo much. Now, please fuck me."

"Trouble." Øyvin's voice was like rumbly velvet. So smooth, so yummy, so sexy. If only he could put that mouth to good use.

I rolled onto my stomach, nuzzled my face into the pillow that smelled like leather and moss, stuck my ass in the air and promptly fell asleep.

7

LENNIE

Yesterday I was the bride, today I was the Deputy Head Guard of the Fjell Fae attending an emergency council meeting with a gnarly headache. Drunk Lennie was a horny dumbass that should've known better than to do shots of aquavit. Thankfully, the only council members that'd been at the reception were Torsten and Halvar. Neither of whom were currently paying attention to me.

I leaned forward in my chair, resting my forearms on the gigantic rock slab that hosted the weary Council. Imposing stone walls arched high above us, and rugged pillars jutted from the floors in the corners of the room, seemingly holding the mountain aloft. Magical light flickered over the heads of the twelve other council members, including Halvar, who stood at the head of the table, palms flat on the surface, arms locked.

"As all of you have no doubt heard, King Veigar is in Skolvik."

Shudders ran through those gathered as the meeting began in earnest.

"He made the journey from Iceland?" One council member asked as another muttered, "We're doomed." A third, Johann, who sat across from me, clenched his fists on the table. "I heard his anger caused the Holuhraun fissure eruption in 2014. The lava flow lasted for months and by the time it ended, the lava field covered eighty-five square kilometers."

My eyes widened at the stat. I had no idea how big a kilometer was compared to a mile, but based on the weight behind the council member's words, it must be huge.

"And let us not forget the Askja eruption," Halvar said, and people around the table nodded.

A council member to my right—Bodil, if I remembered correctly—straightened in his seat. "The 1875 eruption was rumored to be caused by Veigar's immense anger and despair at losing his wife." He shook his head. "The ash poisoned the land, killed creatures, and even drifted over to our shores."

Well, fuck. If Veigar was powerful enough to cause monumental volcanic eruptions, what the hell did he want here in Norway?

Halvar stared around at the panicked chatter that arose and cleared his throat. Silence fell and everyone's eyes flicked back to the stoic fae at the head of the table.

"Did he say what he wanted?" I asked, breaking the silence. I couldn't help myself. The panic rising within me and my goddamn curiosity couldn't stop the words tumbling from my mouth. "Yesterday, at the wedding. Did he say anything else to you? Explain why he decided to show up to my wedding uninvited?"

Halvar's gaze turned to me. "He wanted more stability in the region and among the fae. As for the timing, he mentioned it was a good opportunity to get our attention."

Well, it certainly had.

Grumbles wove around the table like a crowd doing the wave at a football stadium.

"I think we can all agree that Veigar is not to be trusted," Halvar said. "With his volatile behavior once tempered by the presence of his late wife, and his history of killing anyone who disagrees with him, we must fortify our defenses and notify the fjell residents. I hope nothing escalates, but I will not be caught unprepared."

The Council nodded.

"In the meantime," Halvar continued. "We shall monitor his movements and find out what *exactly* his intentions are."

Part of me wanted to believe Veigar was just on his summer vacation, visiting family and taking in the sights of the majestic fjord. The other part of me, perhaps the demi-fae part or the Fjell Fae magic continuously warming my sternum, knew better. There was more to this than *regional stability*. Why would a powerful creature care about Skolvik's regional stability when he's not in the area?

"Why doesn't Veigar live in Skolvik, or Norway, like the other fae monarchs? Why is he in Iceland?"

All eyes around the table flitted to Halvar again who inhaled sharply.

"Well over a thousand years ago, the Fire Fae powers were no longer needed in the north, but scouts found a small island in the North Atlantic that could use their help and expertise with volcanoes and tectonic plate movement."

"So, they were sent over there?"

Halvar nodded. "They went willingly, and, as the human population on earth grew, it became a safer place for the Fire Fae to hide while still being able to train their army."

Interesting, and yet another chapter of fae history that hadn't been included in the user manual when I got pointy ears. Someone really should put together a book about that shit.

"Thank you." I leaned back in my chair, letting the meeting continue.

"Any idea where he's staying?" Johann wiped at his chin in a phantom motion that alluded to a beard having once been there.

"I sent soldiers to scour the village under nightfall," Halvar replied. "They found no easy trace, but suspect the hotel at the back of town. If anyone has a chance to find out what he's up to, take it. But be warned... The man cannot be trusted."

Another question bubbled to the front of my mind, and I cleared my throat. "Forgive me if this is already common knowledge, but why? Why can't he be trusted?"

The entire council spun on me, and I straightened in my seat, refusing to cower under their wizened gazes.

"He has a dictator-esque leadership style with a history of subterfuge and killing," Halvar explained. "Back during the Viking raids in England, Veigar installed fae among their forces. When anyone dared challenge or question an order, they ended up burned with villagers. Their heads were so disfigured you couldn't tell if their ears had been pointed or not. One of the only tells was the weapons they bore."

I swallowed hard. It sounded like he spoke from experience.

"Plus, his element is extremely dangerous and destructive." Halvar explained. "It would wreak havoc and devastation on this country if unleashed."

"Which is why he still lives in Iceland?"

"Part of the reason, yes. Tectonic plates merge there, and a Fire Fae's purpose is to protect and control the volcanoes."

A sharp inhale expanded my lungs. "That's never not going to be weird. How the hell does someone live near a volcano?"

"Beneath it," Halvar said.

"Underneath it?" I blinked twice. "Are they insane!"

"Their eyes are as black as midnight skies." Johann widened his own eyes and drew attention to them with his hands. "Said to be so to help them see in the dark beneath the volcanoes. It's why they all wear sunglasses when above the surface."

I shuddered at his use of the word *surface* as it was regarding the *earth's* surface not that of water.

Bodil piped up. "You all saw Salka's eyes when she returned to the fjord with King Reuven this winter."

Murmurs of agreement filled the room.

"I mean… I'm not going to immediately think of them as bad because their eyesight differs from my own," I said. "Seems kind of rude."

Halvar shook his head and waved his hand, dismissing the line of discussion. "Their eyesight does not matter. They're a threat when angered or provoked into attack. Veigar especially. And if he is aligned with King Reuven, then we have two powerful factions that could stand against us."

Yeah, that didn't seem ideal.

"Do you think Reuven is fully aligned with Veigar?" I asked.

"I wouldn't doubt it," Halvar replied. "Especially considering the Fjord King's marriage to Veigar's daughter."

The group nodded again, and my shoulders slumped. Fire and water aligned didn't bode well. Especially for the woods which would be susceptible to Veigar's powers. I hoped Espen and the Forest Fae Council of Elders had a plan or defensive measures they could put in place in case shit hit the fan.

"Our plan moving forward," Halvar started, his commanding tone drawing me from my fear-filled thoughts. "Garner information on his movements and true purpose here in Skolvik."

The group rumbled in agreement once more, and this time I joined them. We needed to know exactly what the Fire Fae leader was up to and prepare accordingly. If subterfuge was his usual game plan, then I needed to be vigilant.

"I'll keep my ears open for any gossip or chatter at the café. Maybe even ask Dagny, Solveig, or Jorunn if they've seen anything unusual or run into Veigar. If there's anyone in town who knows everyone's business, it's that trio." I could trust them to know the movements of a debonair newcomer.

Halvar tilted his head to me in thanks, and pride welled within me. I was doing this—a part of something bigger than me. Part of a community that took care of its natural surroundings, and a leader in my own right. I just had to see that through to the best of my ability... even if I didn't really have leadership skills.

"Meanwhile, I think we should send some soldiers to the fissure west of here and have them monitor it," Johann chimed in. The break in the mountain had been a frequent discussion point this winter and spring, with fears that snowmelt and subsequent runoff would exacerbate the fissure's size and threaten a monumental landslide. If more stuff got into that rift, it could shear the land off the mountain.

"Agreed." Halvar leaned forward again, resting his hands on the table and peering around the room, capturing everyone's gazes with his own. "I will order three soldiers to take up position there and rotate them on twelve-hour intervals. I don't want that crack growing or being manipulated by outside agitators. Now, let us all do what we can to protect our mountain."

The council members thumped their fists against the table three times, and I joined them in their usual signal for the end of a meeting. We all rose from our seats and departed, heading off to assigned duties, jobs, and lives. As my hangover headache resurged and the fleshy side of my hand smarted from being pounded against the table, I hoped I could meet the Fjell Fae's expectations. Either way, I was going to try.

8

ESPEN

Stillness ebbed through the open living space and a gentle light dappled the floorboards of the boathouse. Sat in the dining area with Ylva, I rested my elbows on the kitchen table and placed my head in my hands. In the past twenty-four hours I'd gone from positively elated to apocalyptically terrified. Because that's what Veigar was: a walking apocalypse. We Forest Fae may have been strong—hell I was the most powerful of us all, capable of snuffing out life with a flick of my wrist—but against fire, against him... I let out a long and jagged sigh.

"How dry is the terrain?" Turi's voice asked down the phone lying on the table. She was driving home and had looped the rest of the Forest Fae Council on the call too.

I swallowed hard. "Extremely. Just like the rest of the country, this summer was hotter than the last. The forest brush is kindling. It's a miracle we haven't already had a forest fire."

Grumbles of fear and agreement echoed down the line. Ylva inspected the end of her braid.

I leaned back in the dining chair and stared at the ceiling. What could I do? How could I protect my people, the village, my wife? Even if a fire did break out and I used my destructive powers to bury it under the soil, the ground lacked enough water to help smother the flames.

My damn powers that I tried to keep locked away after all the damage they'd caused these past two centuries, would be almost useless in the dehydrated woods surrounding Skolvik. But I was the only thing that stood between a Fire Fae and the Forest Fae. The only one who could stand against him and protect the Forest Fae from being eradicated like pests.

Perhaps Øyvin and his soldiers could help? Maybe we could work together—

"Espen?" My sister's voice drew me out of my thoughts. "Espen are you still there?"

"Yes, I'm here."

"What else did Veigar say to you?" Gunvor asked. The elder-stateswoman was probably fearful of the damage to the trees and the well-being of her daughter, Ylva. Yet, her voice didn't waver. "Did he say why he's in the area?"

I crossed my arms and ankles, leaning onto the table once more. "He made no direct threats but wants greater peace and stability in the region."

Turi scoffed, Ylva snorted, and I agreed with the sentiment. Veigar couldn't be trusted. Based on all the stories I'd heard from my late mentor, Mads, and even Queen Ragnhild herself, the King of the Fire Fae was much like the volcanoes he lived under: explosive and unpredictable. Not to mention, incredibly old.

"His remarks were cut short by wedding speeches," I continued. "But his main intention was to see more stability here and among the fae overall."

Several people huffed and grunted.

"I'll believe that when he's dead," Turi muttered and received more muffled agreements.

"I'd like to arrange that funeral," Ylva added, leaning so far back in her chair that it tilted onto its back legs.

I wouldn't disagree with either of them. Though Veigar had a point about the fae needing more stability after the loss of not just one, but *three* monarchs in the past twenty years—two in the last year alone—I highly doubted his altruism. I rubbed my palms across my face.

"Do you need extra patrols?" Marius asked, and I appreciated the consideration and forethought. He was an astute addition to the Forest Fae Council. The youngest by a century, but his protective instinct was as finely honed as Øyvin's.

"Not yet," I replied. We might need the wolves at some point, but it was best to keep them in Alvdalen and the mountains. I didn't need hysteria around wolf sightings on my plate too. "A small contingent of soldiers should be moved from the northern reaches of the country. I'll coordinate the movement with Ylva, but I think it's wise for us to have a larger cadre on standby, and perhaps a few extra healers." Just in case everything went to hell.

Ylva gave me a thumbs up, having received and understood the order. Shifting forward and bringing the front legs of her chair back to the floor with a smack, she pulled out her own phone and started tapping away on it.

Anxiety gnawed at my insides like a bear mauling its prey.

"I'll circle back with news, but if anyone hears anything, please let me know," I said.

Agreement flitted across the line, and we ended the call at that.

I rested my chin in my hands again and turned to Ylva.

"We're not entirely fucked," she said without looking away from her phone.

"I'm not too sure about that."

The texting stopped and she looked up at me. "I'm trying to be optimistic here."

A low and short chuckled slipped out of me. "You've never been very good at that. You're far better at getting my wife supremely drunk though."

"Well, I should get points for the attempt." She pocketed her phone and rose from her chair. "Now, I've got one of our top teams of archers heading our way, just in case Herja shows up too, but it's going to take a couple of days for them to get here. Do you think we have that kind of time?"

I nodded, but didn't feel certain. We shouldn't bring more Forest Fae into harm's way, but if there was a chance they could help in any sort of attack, even one from the menace that was Herja, then we needed them here, however long it may take for them to arrive. "I will start informing nearby Forest enclaves, tell people they need to be vigilant, and increase our scouts around the town's perimeter."

"Good, and about what Marius said..."

Scratching at my beard, I motioned for her to continue.

"We should keep it in mind. The wolves are fast, vicious when needed, and could move between lines of fighters much quicker than we can. They would be useful messengers, and more helpful than trying to call each other during a fight."

She was right. I loved that strategic mind of hers.

"I'll think it over," I replied with a sigh.

She patted my shoulder and slipped out the front door as I shoved my face back into my hands.

Hopefully the others were having a better morning than me. Especially Øyvin. With King Reuven married to Veigar's daughter, there was probably some tension beneath the fjord.

9

ØYVIN

I strode through the tunnels of the Fjord Fae palace. Cool air drifted across my face, the dampness magically removed by powerful filters at the entrances to the residence. The monstrous polished cavern system swept into the lower regions of the mountain and beneath the fjord itself—an impenetrable fortress.

With aquatic creatures carved into the smooth stone walls and magical lights guiding my path, it wasn't long before I made it to the royal wing. Guards milled about, standing at attention beside large wooden doors leading to rooms and chambers where the monarch and their family lived and entertained.

A door swung open seven paces down the hall, and I slowed to a stop. Salka, newly anointed Queen of the Fjord Fae and Princess of the Fire Fae, strode out wearing a boxy, bronze tunic with intricate embroidery around the neck. As she glanced down the hall, her black eyes locked with mine.

I dipped into a shallow bow. "Your Majesty."

She bobbed her head in thanks for the deferential display, tendrils of black hair flitting around her regal, pale face. "General."

General? I hadn't been called that in a while. Everyone referred to me by my first or last name. My title was Head Guard unless we were at war.

I schooled my features. "Forgive me, ma'am. I don't often hear that title used."

A gentle smile tugged at her lips, and she clutched her hands together at her waist. "The error is mine, Øyvin. My father has always referred to his Head Guard as General."

Had he now? I'd heard nothing but horror stories of Veigar's Head Guard, Herja—laying waste to tundra, scorching villages alongside the King during long ago battles. Hearing that he referred to her as General was unsurprising. Yet, worrying considering his current location.

"Did his General join him on his visit to Norway?"

She tensed and shook her head. "Not that I'm aware of."

Potential lie. Why would he travel without a guard? Or maybe he left his General behind in Iceland to watch over his heir? I could dig deeper, but the odds seemed high that she would report any questioning to Reuven. Best to keep things congenial.

"And are you enjoying his visit?"

"It's always nice to see family."

I forced a smile. "Indeed."

Her jaw tensed and she eyed me warily. I drew a sharp breath through my nose, refraining from any sudden movements. Silence wrapped around me like a blanket smothering a fire as we continued to watch each other. I wanted to wriggle free of the scrutiny. Escape the uncomfortable tension flitting between us.

This wasn't going well.

"How's your day going?" I asked, pivoting the conversation like Espen.

"Busy." She motioned to the room she'd just left. "There's a lot more to learn about the fjord and how things have been run by the late king."

"Making any changes?"

She stared at me, not blinking at the lighthearted but pointed remark. "Some."

She was just like her husband. Quiet, demure, secretive.

Motion behind Salka drew my attention. A member of the royal household staff wearing a long skirt shuffled out of the door. Her eyes widened when she saw me, but shot back to her boss. "Ma'am, the historian is ready for you down the hall."

"Thank you," Salka replied before turning her gaze back to me. "Have a good day, Øyvin."

"You too, ma'am."

She swept down the hall and I bowed my head as she passed.

An uneasy feeling settled in my stomach. While neither of the new monarchs had done anything wrong or unusual, my gut didn't fully trust them. They'd lived in Iceland with or near Veigar for years. The odds of them being loyal to him was high.

Shaking off that horrific thought, I walked deeper into the royal wing of the palace, aiming for the corner where my office sat, along with the Council chambers and the king's office.

A few moments later, I arrived at my destination. I straightened the sleeves of my uniform and knocked on Reuven's office door.

"Come in!"

Shoving open the heavy wooden door, I entered the room. Dark wood shelves surrounded the space, each one laden with trinkets that looked like they belonged on a ship. Long gone were Balder's books and chess set. Even the desk had been cleared of erroneous papers. Instead, orderly stacks of documents lined one edge, while the rest of the surface remained clear save for a green library lamp.

Reuven sat at his desk leaning back in the large leather chair, the sleeves of his white shirt casually rolled up to his elbows. It was a marked difference from the way his predecessor dressed and acted within this room. Where Balder ruled with immense confidence and shows of power, Reuven's presence was far more understated. He was casual and quiet with a cunning look in his eye that was more fitting with a well-traveled sailor than a power-hungry commodore. But appearances were often deceptive.

I straightened my spine, standing to attention. "Good morning, sir, may I have a word?"

"Of course." Reuven rose from his seat. "What do you wish to discuss?"

I needed to find out what he knew of Veigar's visit, figure out how concerned we should be. He had most recently been in contact with the fae and was married to his youngest daughter too. If anyone knew what the Fire Fae King was planning, it should be Reuven. My lungs expanded with my deep inhale. "Your father-in-law's arrival in Skolvik."

Reuven's light-blue eyes narrowed, the scar through his right eyebrow crinkling. "What about it?"

"Did you know of his visit?"

"I'm not my father-in-law's keeper. I dare say no one is," he said, his tone firm and considerate. He picked his words with care, noticeably not answering the question. I had to proceed with caution.

"Are you aware of his intentions with this visit?"

Reuven raised his hand to his shoulder. His shirt and beige trousers disappeared, replaced by the navy Fjord Fae uniform and the decadently detailed cape that fastened at both shoulders. "Why don't you join me at the wall? I was planning a visit today. We can check on the new fortifications and continue this discussion."

I bowed my head. "Of course, sir."

Reuven may not have been monarch for long, but I was duty bound to the fjord and would treat the man with the respect he deserved.

The sights, smells, and sounds of the human world above were gone at these depths, as was any ray of sunlight. Murky darkness owned these parts of the fjord as we swam toward the wall. Using our Fjord Fae powers, we'd both crafted air bubbles around ourselves and propelled downward to the fjordbed. Fjord Fae inhabitants nodded as we passed. Several schools of fish ignored us as we navigated around them, doing our best not to disturb the creatures. After ten minutes of swimming in silence side-by-side, we landed on the silty bottom with a dull thump. Sediment billowed around our feet as we took in the massive magical barrier.

The shimmering shield sat a third of the way down the fjord, not far from the village, and protected the inner waters from anything deemed a pollutant. Once torn apart by Balder, the two-kilometer-wide sheer structure now stretched from the fjordbed to the surface again, bolstered by Reuven's magic and power from the guards I'd mobilized down here.

"Everything looks in order, at first glance." Reuven strolled past one of the soldiers and I followed at his side, our air bubbles and special fae abilities allowing us to communicate at these depths.

"We haven't had any issues of note since your return to the fjord," I said. "But there are always threats."

"We must always remain vigilant."

I couldn't agree more.

"How is the Queen settling into life beneath the surface? It's been a few months now."

"It's not overly different from our residence on the island," he replied as we reached an unguarded stretch of the wall.

I squinted at him. What kind of housing did they have in Iceland? Did they live with Veigar or separately? He glanced over at me, and I looked away quickly.

"Do you have concerns about my wife, Øyvin?"

"I have concerns about her father."

Reuven's scar wrinkled and his lips quirked as he crossed his arms. "Like I said, I am not his keeper."

"But you are his son-in-law." I was skirting close to disrespect. I knew it. Could feel it in the way Reuven studied my every move.

"That I am. Is there a problem?"

"What *exactly* is he doing here?"

"Visiting Salka."

"I don't believe it. What do you know?"

Reuven pursed his lips. "Tread lightly, Head Guard."

Fuck the line in the sand. I was stepping over it. I needed to protect my home, my family, my everything. "Veigar crashed the wedding and started talking about more stability in the region and among the fae. Did he share his plans with you?"

Reuven raised a single brow. "I should think those are things we would all want."

They were, but we were already heading in that direction before the Fire Fae had arrived. "The fjord has already been subjected to terror this past year. I don't want more of it."

Reuven looked down the fjord, his gaze mired in thought.

Was he considering sharing what he knew with me? Or had I landed myself in trouble for speaking so boldly? Balder had always appreciated a level of candor, but I still wasn't sure where that limit was with Reuven.

With his arms crossed over his chest, he snapped his attention back to me, his brow furrowed. "Trust me. The fjord will always be protected."

My gut twisted at his non-answer.

Limit found.

"I have a few requests for you as my Head Guard."

"Okay."

"First, keep an eye on the oil refinery down the way. I heard mumblings of oil slicks near the fjord opening and don't want them coming in this direction."

That was news to me. "I'll increase our surveillance. Have soldiers swim past daily."

"Good. I also want you to report to me on all Forest and Fjell happenings."

My lungs tightened as if my Fjord Fae magic had stopped working and the water was set on squeezing every last bubble of oxygen from my chest. The message beneath his words hung over me like an anchor. He wanted me to spy on my partner and friend. He wanted me to put the Fjord first.

I swallowed hard and turned my gaze to the protective wall. I'd always put the fjord and its residents first. It was my job, my purpose. But that had all changed when a tourist breezed through town and stole my heart one troublesome act after another.

Reuven's request directly challenged me to pick a side: the fjord—which I'd valiantly served for a century—or my family. *Ancestors help me.* What would happen if I said no? What would happen if I said yes? Who was the biggest threat here? Who was most vulnerable? More importantly, what was most important to me?

"Well, will you honor my order?" Reuven asked, drawing me from my tumultuous thoughts.

Could I? Could I put my loved ones at risk? After all these years alone, would I dare to?

Images of my woman flitted through my mind. Her mischievous brown eyes always plotting and scheming. The way her hair got in her way or drifted onto her cheeks and how she flicked it aside as if it had offended her. The sound of her laughter that ignited a joy inside me that I hadn't felt in years.

"Øyvin?"

"Yes," I lied and turned to continue our walk along the wall.

10

LENNIE

The scent of herbal spices and sound of happy chatter permeated the air in Fisken as I pulled out my chair and took a seat at the large dark-wood table. Our remaining family members gathered for a final meal together. Smiles alighted everyone's faces, jokes flying between Andrew and Knut-Arne, while Ingrid and Mom corralled the young girls to their own table. My four nieces had spent every day together and were now best friends. When my side of the family departed tomorrow morning, there'd be some tears shed and frowns.

"So, Lennie, what on here do you recommend?" Dad asked from across the table as he peered down at the menu. I could now read the whole thing thanks to practicing my Norwegian and having tried everything.

"You'll like the stew, Dad."

"I do like a good stew."

Espen settled on the chair to my left, Øyvin on my right. Kristoffer sat at the end of the table between the Fjord Fae and my dad—who had earned himself a five-year-old shadow since arriving in Norway.

The waiter came and took our drink orders, swiftly returning with a tray of water, beer, and wine. As he departed to leave us more time with the menu, heat washed across my neck and I pulled my hair up into a ponytail to cool off a bit. The poor air conditioning unit in here must've been on strike after our reception yesterday.

Dad straightened and waved across the room. "Veigar! Nice to see you."

My eyes widened and my stomach clenched. This was not happening. This could *not* be happening. I twisted in my seat and found the sophisticated looking monarch ambling toward an empty table.

Mom leaned toward Dad, whispering, "Oh, Dan, is he alone?"

"I think so."

She readjusted in her seat like that simply would not do and let loose her most welcoming smile. "Why don't you join us, Veigar? We have a spot open!"

Fuck. This was happening.

For once in their lives, I needed my parents to be less of the Midwest Super Nice Neighborly Happy People that they were, and a helluva lot more like my Asshole, Øyvin. If ever there were a moment for them to sample the unwelcoming smorgasbord that was being a dick, now would be the time.

I leaned across the table to my mom. "We don't need—"

"Hush, now Lennie." Mom scolded me under her breath and beamed again two seconds later. "Everyone is welcome here."

"If you don't mind the intrusion, Mrs. Martin."

I looked up and found Veigar giving my mother a suave smile. For that alone I wanted to lunge past Øyvin and swat his face.

"Of course not. We'd love to hear about life in Iceland."

Veigar pulled out the vacant chair beside Dad and Kristoffer. "Fire away."

Øyvin cleared his throat while Espen rested his hand on my thigh. I took a deep breath and squeezed Espen's fingers. This was actually happening.

Kristoffer tilted his head and pointed at Veigar's sunglasses. "Are you blind?"

"Kristoffer Mikkelsen!" Ingrid erupted from the other end of the table, her face as white as snow, and started scolding the boy in Norwegian. "Apologize at once."

The young boy's shoulders curved as he slunk back in his seat and stared at the table. His lower lip wobbled. "Sorry."

Veigar lightly tapped the table space between him and Kristoffer. "Thank you for the apology. I have light sensitivity," he explained, and half the table bristled knowing full well that was not the whole story. "My eyes don't like a lot of light, it hurts them. So, I wear these to avoid some horrible headaches."

A tiny tear streaked down Kristoffer's face as he tilted his head up. "So, the sun is not your friend?"

Veigar smiled. "The sun is needed for all forms of life to flourish, but unfortunately, my eyes don't think so. Both of my daughters have the same thing. It's a family trait of sorts. We just learn to live with it."

Kristoffer sniffled and bobbed his head. Øyvin passed the young boy his napkin, which he took with a whimper.

"Have any of you tried *lutefisk* while you're here?" Espen piped up, mercifully pivoting the conversation.

"That's the gelatinous, fish stuff that's brined, right?" Ryan asked.

Andrew leaned back in his chair. "No, I thought it was cured in lye?"

My brothers turned their full attention to my partner. "Yes, it's usually a white fish soaked in water, then cured in lye, and soaked once more. Which does give it a gelatinous texture."

"I'm always down to try anything," Ryan piped up, exhibiting that Martin Family competitiveness that all of us siblings had inherited. From which parent, I was never quite sure, but my bet was secretly Mom.

"Are you enjoying your time in Skolvik?" my dad asked Veigar. I decided to focus on their conversation and not the other one further down that table discussing the different types of fish in Norway.

"I am. It's a magical place and my daughter just moved here. She recommended a few shops to visit, so I spent my day looking for souvenirs to take home."

"Ah yes!" My dad straightened. "We spent some time at the gift shop earlier today and the jewelers on Friday. Deb found some beautiful silverware."

"Were you able to find anything nice to take home to Iceland?" I chimed in.

Veigar turned to me with an overly congenial smile. "Not yet. But there's still time."

"You plan on staying for a while?"

"Ever since my wife passed, I've tried to spend as much time with my daughters as possible. So, we shall see what the family wants. At this time, my trip has an indeterminate end."

"Oh, our Lennie knows how that goes." Dad chuckled. "One second you're missing your ship, the next you're moving in."

A strained laugh left me and I brought my beer to my mouth and gulped down half of it.

The waiter returned and took our orders—plenty of stew, fish, and reindeer meatballs—and the rest of our dinner remained cordial and uneventful. Mom and Dad carried on conversation with me, Øyvin, and Veigar, while the other end of the table was in a riotous debate about sports—Andrew, ever the quarterback, steadfast in his belief that American Football was better than football.

Mom finished her stew and reached her hand across the table. "Lennie, you seem a bit quiet this evening? You doing okay?"

My final bite of meatball slid down my throat and I set aside my knife and fork. I had been quieter than usual. Mostly because I was listening to

Dad and Veigar's conversation. My guys had been less verbose too, likely doing the same thing.

"You know, it's okay to be sad we're leaving. It means you've had a good time," Mom said, her tone full of warmth and love I wanted to wrap myself in.

I was a bit sad. While I usually handled my mom best in small doses, and this trip had been no different, having everyone gathered together, smiling and laughing, was a joy I didn't want to end.

"It's been great having you all here."

She smiled back. "I'm so glad we could be here for you. We're so happy for you."

My heart swelled and threatened to burst with the outpouring of love I'd experienced this weekend. "Thanks, Mom."

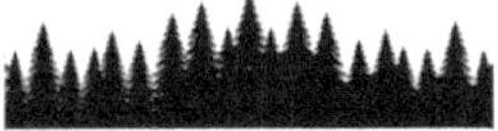

The cool night air brushed across the back of my neck as we stepped outside of the restaurant and started saying our goodbyes.

Mom took my hands in hers. "Now, I know we've just had a trip to see each other, but I want to know your holiday travel plans as soon as possible."

My stomach nosedived and pulled back up again, threatening to return my meatballs with it. I couldn't leave Skolvik. Couldn't leave the mountain. The last time I'd done that, the fjell had experienced cave ins and cracks. Damage that had taken weeks to repair.

I had a responsibility with this new magic, and to my new home, but I loved my family with every fiber of my being.

This was too hard. Pitting my two worlds against each other.

But at the end of the day, I couldn't hurt a society of fae just because I wanted to go to Ohio for turkey and Christmas morning.

"Well, Mom." I cleared my throat. "Since we were back for Thanksgiving last year, we'd been thinking we would spend the holiday here in Norway and share it with our Norwegian family."

Was it an American holiday? Sure. Had we discussed such plans? No, but we could. What was most important here was keeping the fae secret safe and the mountain protected. Especially considering a recent tourist's arrival in town.

Mom's shoulders deflated before she donned her hostess smile and squeezed my hands once more. "I'm sure you'll have a great time."

"We can set up a video call and maybe even a computer board game night too."

"Your brothers would love that."

Hugs, well wishes, and promises of phone calls filled the air as both sides of our family said their goodbyes. The young girls sobbed, tears streaming down little Amelia's sun-kissed cheeks as she clung to Andrew. I squeezed Ingrid and Knut-Arne and promised Kristoffer we'd call him in a few weeks for a catch up. Finally, I hugged my parents goodbye.

Dad sighed as he let go of me. "Well, Lennie, you survived the weekend."

"That I did, Dad," I said with a smile. "Are you ever going to tell me who was responsible for the Ohio State Fight Song being played as I walked back down the aisle?"

"Only the guy in charge of the speakers knows the truth."

I tilted my head to one side, giving him a look that said I wasn't buying a word of that.

Dad checked his empty wrist. "Oh, would you look at the time? Bye, pumpkin."

With a snort, I let them go. I'd bet good money he was behind the little stunt.

Half the group walked back to their hotel, the other climbed into waiting cars. We waved them all off and my heart cracked in one corner. It'd been so nice to have everyone in one location, to see tables filled with our loved ones. I swallowed the lump in my throat and wiped the corners of my eyes. My fingertips came back damp. *Don't cry, don't cry, don't cry.*

As I fought against the welling emotions, Espen wrapped me into a hug and Øyvin pressed his hand against my lower back.

"Your mother was right, you know," Espen said. "Sadness means you had a good time."

Øyvin grumbled in agreement.

I sniffled. "However much I hate you saying my mother is right, she does have a good point."

Snickering, Espen brushed his hand across my head where it rested against his chest.

They were right. I'd had a wonderful time. And all wasn't lost. I had a family here in Skolvik too. My guys, my friends, the villagers that seemed to have taken a reluctant liking to me and welcomed me into the fold. This was my home, and while I didn't have my immediate family with me, it was still brimming with love and care.

"Family is so important," a somber male voice said from behind us, and we spun to find Veigar near the doorway to Fisken. "Don't you agree?"

Emotionally spent and tired, I pulled out of Espen's hold. "What do you want, Veigar?"

A slick grin crossed his lips. "What's best for *us*: unity and regional stability."

"Yeah, yeah, yeah, you're Mr. Peace and Love. We get it." But I sure as hell didn't believe it, not with all the rumors and stories I'd heard about the guy.

"Believe what you want, Mrs. Solbakke Martin." He straightened his cuff links and turned down the road into the main part of town. "But I think you'll come round to my way of thinking quite swiftly."

"Doubt it."

My guys huffed in agreement, both stood with their arms crossed over their chests.

"You will."

"And if we don't?"

A wisp of a flame curled around the man's hand and disappeared. My stomach flip-flopped. "Family is such a precious thing to lose." Veigar's eyebrows rose above the top edge of his sunglasses, and he strolled around the corner, out of sight.

All three of us deflated, and I bent over, resting my hands on my knees. My heart beat so hard it threatened to jump through my ribs.

"Did he just threaten our families?" I asked.

"Mm-hmm," Øyvin replied as Espen nodded, his eyes locked on where Veigar had disappeared.

"What the hell do we do? Can he reach my side of the family? Would he go all the way to Ohio to do... whatever that threat just was?"

"I don't think so," Espen said. "But we should warn those *like us* in Norway to keep an eye out for anything suspicious, and we should prepare."

"Prepare for things to escalate? For a fight?" That's what Halvar had been saying at the Council meeting this morning. *I wonder if Espen and Øyvin had similar conversations with their factions?*

Espen hummed in the affirmative as I straightened.

"Exactly," Øyvin said. "He wants something. I'd guess more power, more control of the fae."

Espen slid his hand into mine as if he needed to reassure himself that I was still by his side. "I agree, but until we know for sure, we have to remain vigilant. He's already powerful and I don't think Skolvik would survive any further surprises from him."

I stared back at the place where Veigar had vanished. "Fuck."

11

LENNIE

The next evening, magical lights flickered against the barren, gray cavern walls and Halvar, dressed in all black, paced at the back of the youngster's training room. I hadn't seen any others training in here before, but that might have more to do with Halvar and the prior uncertainty about my powers.

"You summoned me." I raised my arms in the air like I was in a Miss America pageant. Luckily, I wore leggings and a light sweater, not some slinky little gown. Training in heels and a dress sounded like cruel and unusual punishment—then, again, this was Halvar.

"Thank you for coming." Halvar's silver hair caught in the beams of light. "As Torsten's text said, we need to increase your training immediately." An ominous tone laced his words and my gut twisted in on itself.

I set my water bottle down by the entrance and looked over at him. "Does this have to do with the town's latest visitor?"

He nodded once.

"Pretty sure he threatened my family last night." Maybe I shouldn't have been so feisty with him after dinner with the family.

"He is *the* threat."

I took an involuntary step back. I knew Halvar was worried. Hell, he'd been practically shrouded in concern at the emergency council meeting.

But hearing those words from him sent an uneasy wave of fear through every inch of my body. I definitely shouldn't have been testy with Veigar.

"What kind of training are we talking about?" I asked, pivoting back to his previous comment.

"Crack sealing, weapon forming, strength training, and making sure you *fully* understand your royal magic. What it can achieve for you on the field of battle."

"Hold up, big guy." I raised my hand and popped my hip to the side. "Did you just say, field of battle? You want *me* on a battlefield? Like the one on top of the mountain where you fought Balder?"

He nodded again.

Fuck me sideways. A woman really couldn't get a moment of uninterrupted peace around here. I rubbed my fingers across my forehead. With these powers and my new role, I didn't have a choice. I had to step up. I needed to do everything I could to protect my new home and not screw it up. "Where do we start?"

Halvar's lips twitched in what might have been the blossoming of a smile but quickly sank back into a firm line. "Seal the crack." He waved his arm over his head and brought it back down in the blink of an eye. An explosive snapping noise echoed around the room and a sharp divide formed to my left where the ceiling and wall curved together. "Stop the wall from caving in."

I gasped and bolted for the rugged gash, adrenaline shooting through me. The wall groaned and threatened to fall. Instinctively, my arms shot above my head and I pressed my hands into the highest point of the cave I could reach, right beside the yawning crack.

My magic swirled within me, desperate to be released and help. I listened to it and pulled forward that swell of warmth, pushing it down my arms and into the rock. An invisible wave of power burst from my palms and rippled toward the fissure.

The break stopped growing.

I was doing it.

Just like Halvar had done during our first training session where he'd pushed the ceiling above his head and shifted the stone, now the magic ebbing from me put the stone back into place. It wove over the crevice and stitched it together like I wielded a thread and needle—the jagged edges clicking back into place.

When the grating noise stopped, I remained in my outstretched position and slowly willed my magic to return to me. It did so gladly, like a puppy that'd been a good boy.

"Nicely done," a male voice said, and I spun around.

Torsten leaned against the back wall of the training cave. His hair was swept up into his signature man bun and the cape of his gray uniform draped over one shoulder. I shouldn't have been surprised to see him. The busy, teddy bear of a man with a wicked sense of humor and delightful life partner, was a staple by Halvar's side.

"How long have you been there?"

"Long enough to applaud your natural instincts."

"Awww, thanks," I said, and did my best not to preen. "I thought you were with Leif this evening. He said you were having a movie night when he stopped by the café this morning."

"He's been called in for emergency training with the local Forest archers." He twisted to Halvar. "Here to help with her other training as requested."

Halvar gave him a nod in thanks and turned his eyes back to me. "I have one more thing I want to test before we move to your royal and light magic."

I quirked a single eyebrow. "What's that?"

"Shield." Halvar waved his hands. A blast of light flared toward me and crashed against my chest, sending me onto my ass with a thud.

"What the fuck was that?" I yelled and rubbed my fist against the spot where I'd taken the hit.

"I rescind my comments about natural instincts," Torsten said.

An agreeing rumble sounded from Halvar's chest. "You have more to learn."

I pushed off the ground, rose to my feet, and brushed off my leggings. "Warn a woman next time—"

"Veigar will not give you a warning," Halvar interjected.

"Fair enough." He had a good point. Any man who threw around threats against someone's family wasn't the kind of guy to announce his actions. "So, you gonna teach me how to shield?"

He grunted and our training began in earnest.

We started with shielding for both Fjell and royal powers. The former consisted of creating a piece of stone as flat as slate that I could bury in the ground like a surfboard in sand or fasten to my wrist. The royal magic was a bit more complicated, but Torsten took his time explaining the movement and the intentions—a waving motion and *shield*. It took me several tries to get both to work even half decently, but by the fifth attempt of both, I was getting the hang of it and shielding faster.

Next, we moved on to forms of stunning magic with my royal powers. Balls of light zipped across the room as I practiced the easiest part, before we pivoted to equipping it to a sword.

"I've done this before," I muttered, feeling the stone sword hum with power in my hand as royal magic crackled at the end like lightning.

Torsten nodded. "In the throne room earlier this year. But did you know what you were doing?"

I shook my head. When the wolf barged into the throne room, I'd acted on instinct—a need to protect flaring within me. Drawing the sword had been second nature in that moment, but I would always remember how it felt. It was as if the mountain and my heart beat as one.

"We didn't think so," Torsten continued. "Being able to use both concurrently is imperative for you to protect yourself and utilize the magic to its full potential."

Halvar grunted in agreement where he leaned against the wall, his arms crossed over his chest.

My training continued with Torsten giving me orders on how to push and pull the royal magic in and out of me, guiding it down the sword. That was followed by basic sword handling and jousting from Halvar.

The way he moved with a blade was like an artist knowing exactly what brush strokes were needed for the perfect composition. But one thing was certain, Halvar wasn't used to painting with oils or watercolors. No, the beast from the mountain, with his assured actions and immense strength, had a history of painting with blood.

I mimicked his movements, and my arms slowly started to ache in protest. We'd been at this for hours, and in true Halvar fashion, he'd saved the most difficult task for last. While holding the sword wasn't hard, the repetitive motions and unrelenting orders from the sidelines turned me into a panting mess.

After what felt like another painful hour, we finally had a break. I took a gulp of water from the bottle I'd set by the entrance and relished the feeling of cool liquid sluicing down my throat. Sweat ran down the side of my face and pooled beneath my boobs, gluing my sports bra to my chest.

"You are a weakness." Halvar swept around the front of the room, his hands balled into white-knuckled fists as I set down my water bottle.

"That's kind of rude, don't you think?"

He narrowed his eyes at me. "You're a target. One Veigar will take advantage of at the first hint of an opportunity."

I let out a sigh. *That* kind of weakness.

"You mean he'll use me as bait? Try to kidnap me and make the boys heel like dogs?" *Been there, done that already.* Although getting kidnapped by Aurora and her merry band of wolf-shifters hadn't been a calamitous plight. They'd ultimately just wanted to question me and use me to get Espen's attention. They'd even fed me while I was holed up in their garden shed.

I doubted Veigar would be so kind.

No, that fae would probably dangle me over a ravine of fire. Maybe even a volcano.

Halvar strode straight at me. I took two steps back before stopping, forcing him to crash into me or halt. He brought us toe-to-toe and hit the brakes.

"He will hold your life over a precipice and force everyone's hand."

While I didn't like the thought of dying, especially at the hands of a Fire Fae, I was surprised that I was somehow The Chosen One in this scenario.

"He'll force Espen to bow to him or use his destructor powers," I started, breaking down the problem that Halvar was struggling to verbalize. The big guy had never been very verbose. "Which we all know Espen only whips out as a last resort. Veigar, through his son-in-law, Reuven, now King of the Fjord, will force Øyvin to submit. Hell, maybe even try to use him to get to me. Which won't work unless I've pissed him off that morning."

Halvar snorted and Torsten stifled a chuckle with his hand.

"But you." I pointed to Halvar. "You're the one I'm like, magically. And my magic is tied to the mountain. I'm the Fjell's Deputy Head Guard. A leader and council member. But only a demi-fae. I don't have full fae powers."

Halvar and Torsten's eyes met for a brief second and I stilled.

The air in the room felt like it had evaporated.

"What aren't you telling me?" I tilted my chin down and glared at them. My heart rate picked up speed, galloping faster and faster, as neither of them met my gaze. They'd been keeping secrets. "What other target do I have on my back?"

"Not informing her makes her weaker," Torsten said, pointedly not telling Halvar what to do. Smart, all things considered.

Halvar rolled his shoulders and straightened, looking every bit the role of Head Guard and protector of the mountain. "Our theory is that Freija had more magic than we realized when she died. A gift we believe was bestowed from the ancestors."

I tilted my head to one side like that was supposed to make sense.

"We think you got *all* the extra magic. It appears to have passed through me."

My eyebrows hit my glistening hairline. "You mean to tell me, I'm like the Energizer Bunny of the Fjell but with a whole extra battery?"

Lines formed on Halvar's forehead as his eyebrows pinched together.

"I'm..." I continued, hoping to clarify. "I have extra power that you don't have?"

"That is our working theory, but I do not know for certain as Freija never confirmed nor denied what powers, if any, were given to her."

Air whooshed out of my lungs. *Holy shit.* "But even with extra powers, I'm still partially human, right? Still classified as demi-fae?"

Halvar nodded. "Trygve doesn't believe you will have the full life span of a fae, but thinks it may be longer than your average human."

Well, that was a positive.

"When did you realize I'd been given more powers?"

"Earlier this year when you killed Wilhelm by slamming a light ball into his back," Torsten replied.

"And when you apparently stunned Aurora," Halvar said.

I winced. "She told you about that?"

He grunted.

"That killing light isn't normal, then?" I asked, looking to Torsten.

He shook his head. "I can't do it."

"Only monarchs are known to have that power," Halvar said.

"Do you have it?" I asked. "Or was it just me that got that bit during the transfer?"

Halvar's shoulders relaxed minutely, and he let out a long breath. "I haven't been successful, no."

Shit on a stick. I stared at the slate-colored wall and took in the ramifications of that. I had power that only fae monarchs had. Power that could kill—*had* killed someone on the spot. It'd hurt to use, burning and searing down my arms and arching my back, but was that because I didn't know what I was doing? Or was that a burden of using and inflicting that power on someone else?

"We aren't a hundred percent certain how that power is used or if it can be channeled into anything else," Torsten said, drawing my focus from my spiraling thoughts. "But our guess is the intention, just like the stunning magic."

I brushed stray baby-hairs off my forehead with both hands. An unwelcome shudder ran through me as the memories of that day resurfaced. The gaping maw of the wolf. The agony as he ripped through my leg. And the anger and desperation that settled into my bones when he moved on Aurora. "I was thinking about death and stopping Wilhelm when he launched toward Aurora. It would have to be that thought and a burning desire to protect someone."

Torsten murmured like that made sense to him, while Halvar didn't move a muscle, quietly taking everything in.

Silence settled over the room once more as the weight of that fact washed over us. I, a demi-fae, who was human only a year ago, had the power of a monarch. Enough power that I could kill someone on the spot. Magic that had once belonged to the Queen of the Fjell Fae.

"Why do you think Freija got extra powers from the ancestors?" I asked. "What did she need it for?"

The two men looked at each other once more before they turned back to me with thoughtful gazes. Torsten clapped Halvar on the shoulder.

"I'll leave this one to you," he said and meandered out of the room, tossing a "well done, today, baby fae" over his shoulder.

I returned my gaze to Halvar. Curiosity bubbling within me. "What else have you been keeping from me?"

He cleared his throat. "There's something you need to see."

12

LENNIE

"Where exactly are you taking me?" I asked as Halvar and I wound through tunnel after tunnel, deeper into the mountain.

His long strides ate up the rocky corridors, steps neither slowing nor faltering. "A location you must swear to protect."

"What do you mean by that?" Scurrying beside him, I did my best not to trip over my own feet. "I'll always protect the mountain."

He ground to a stop and narrowed his eyes at me. "Will you? Without question?"

The weight of his words settled across my shoulders, but I'd already agreed to it this past winter when I took up the role as Deputy Head Guard. I'd proven myself worthy of the title and sworn to take care of the Fjell. If I set my mind to doing something, I was damn well doing it. I'd also grown to know and like the fae of the fjell, and the village below the mountain was my home, my new family. "I'd do anything to protect those I care about, including this mountain. Except, perhaps, anything that would hurt Espen or Øyvin."

Halvar straightened and an emotion I could only describe as pride filled his gaze. He nodded once and set off down the tunnel again.

I shrugged. "I'll take that as an *okay great,* then."

We continued our downward trek, and I pushed away the memories of the last time I'd been this deep in the mountain's tunnels and the canine that had tried to kill me there. My lungs tightened, my breaths came faster, and I pinched my nails into the fleshy part of my hands.

I'm safe. Wilhelm is dead and gone.

I took a deep breath through my nose and pivoted to happier memories.

I'm safe. Wilhelm is dead and gone.

Øyvin baking me cookies and plying me with tea when I had a head cold this spring.

I'm safe. Wilhelm is dead.

Espen playing dress up with his nieces and nephew in Alvdalen this winter.

I'm safe.

The look on my guys' faces when I walked down the aisle to them.

The thoughts and mantra eventually drifted away as we stopped in front of a stone wall protected by two Fjell Fae guards.

Halvar gave them a nod and passed through the stone wall.

I snorted. "Those mirage walls will never cease to surprise me." Honest to hell, who knew where they were? How did anyone find them? There was probably some sign that I'd yet to learn about, and if I went testing walls, I'd probably end up bruised and with a gnarly concussion.

Following Halvar through the mirage, the magic washed over me like walking into an air-conditioned building on a hot summer's day. What I found on the other side, though, drew me to a stop and my eyes bulged to the size of camera lenses.

Rows of stone caskets with prone statues spread across the large room and rocky pillars the size of redwoods held the vaulted ceiling.

"You want me to protect the dead as well as the living?" My day was taking some seriously interesting turns. First training and the magic revelations, now a visit to the tombs. What was next? Were they secretly harboring the Norse Gods in the basement of this place?

Halvar huffed. "Herein lies a place only those with royal magic and Head Guards have access to. You shall be included in those numbers."

"You mean one of these"—I motioned to the tombs around me—"is a secret passage to a sacred place? Like in an Indiana Jones movie? Should I have brought a hat and whip?"

Halvar's throat bobbed. "This is the royal tomb."

Emotions barbed his words and scraped over my buoyant bubble of humor, bursting it. My smile dropped.

Freija was in here. One of these stone statues was the image of her representing the place where she'd been laid to rest. I peered around the room, but didn't see her likeness in my immediate vicinity.

While I'd been to her funeral, I didn't know exactly where they'd buried her. I assumed there was a royal tomb. I just never expected to find myself *in* it.

"I'm sorry." I cleared my throat and straightened up. "You said there was somewhere I needed to see?"

Halvar spun on the spot and strode to the back of the room.

I followed, my footsteps echoing off the walls of the silent chamber.

We reached the end of the walkway through the sarcophagi and stopped in front of a mural etched into the stone surface. The image encompassed the entire facade.

A pointy mountain sat in the middle of the wall with two large trees on either side. Their branches stretched onto the adjoining walls as if wrapping the room in a hug and the tiny leaves looked like flames. Swirls of water lapped at the base of the picture and in the bottom right corner was a wolf, baying to the sky.

"It's beautiful," I muttered. Photographs would never do it justice.

"This is a sacred space for the Fae," Halvar said. He placed his hand in the middle of the mountain, his chest rising and falling as he took a deep breath and pressed his magic into the stone. Silvery light flowed into the lines of the image, slowly filling every nook and crevice, until the entire mural shone. The back of the room illuminated with a soft glow and a gentle breath passed my lips in awe.

"Wow."

Halvar pushed against the center of the mountain once more. A grinding noise, like that of a large mortar and pestle, echoed through the chamber as the mountain swung inward on a set of hinges.

"Follow me," he said.

I picked my jaw off the floor and followed him through the triangular opening.

Inside was a small room, no bigger than a classroom, with walls made of the same light-blue quartz as the Fjell Fae throne. In the center of the space, atop the slate-gray floor, sat what could only be described as a pedestal or place of offering. From the rugged base to the cylindrical leg that held up a square-shaped platter, the small table-like structure looked like it belonged in a church.

As Halvar shut the door behind us and paced around to the other side of the room, I took a closer look at the sole object in the chamber.

On second thought, the top wasn't a complete square. Three corners were missing—shorn off as if someone had hacked them off with a pickaxe.

Straightening, I shoved my hands behind my back, stopping myself from reaching out and brushing my fingers across the glassy surface. My gaze drifted to my surroundings once more. There were no light sconces in here. Only a blue glow, as if the walls themselves were the light source.

Magic.

Definitely, magic.

"What is this place?"

Halvar stopped on the other side of the pedestal, his eyes locked on me. "This is the Temple of the Fae. The birthplace of our kind."

Air stilled in my lungs and my eyebrows hit my sweat-covered hairline. "What?"

"I do not know what your partners have told you regarding the history of the fae, but Skolvik has always been rumored to be where we first came from. That rumor is true."

"Well, shit," I muttered.

"The Fjord Fae protect the waters and creatures from threats like pollution. The Forest Fae protect and care for the flora and fauna. Fire Fae protect volcanoes and tectonic plate movement. And we, the Fae of the Fjell, are sworn to protect the mountain. That protection also extends to the Temple of the Fae."

My mind whirled with the new information and the existence of a sacred place for the fae—hidden away within the mountain. It was beautiful. Magical. A glittering shrine of history. "Why are you showing me this?"

"Because as Deputy Head Guard and holder of royal power, you have a right to know."

"Do all the Fjell Fae know about this place?"

He shook his head. "Only those on the Council and the few select soldiers charged with guarding the tomb entry."

"And they can get in here too?"

"No, only those with royal magic and a monarch's Head Guard have access." He raised his arm and tapped a spot on his wrist. A small white dot, a little larger than the one I had from Nora's hearing juju, marred his skin. A royal must've used their magic and granted him entry.

"And I have both title and power."

Halvar made a noise in agreement.

I looked around once more. It was a stunning place. The walls were like facets of a diamond, bouncing blue-toned light across the room as if it was twilight. No objects adorned the sides of the room, no carvings marred their flanks. The only other *thing* in here aside from me and Halvar was the fractured pedestal fit for a museum display.

I tilted my chin toward it. "What's that for?"

"This is why we are here," Halvar replied. "This is how Fae monarchs communicate with the ancestors."

It did look like a place of worship. A chamber where offerings could be made to gods and deities, or where prayers might be heard. The absolute silence in the room would allude to such a sacred space, too.

"How'd it break?" I motioned to the pedestal again.

Halvar eyed the broken corners. "I don't know for certain. But we believe that each of the other factions have a corner of the plinth and use it for their ceremonies."

"Oh. Is this where the new queen or king comes after their coronation to receive the recycled magic?"

Halvar squinted like he was surprised I knew about that process.

"Nora mentioned something about it."

Halvar's features relaxed. "Yes, this is where the Fjell heir comes and receives all the magic their predecessor had, plus anything that might be required at the time."

"Does that apply to monarchs of the other factions?"

"I'm not sure. I assume there is a similar process with their own shards from the Temple, unless they've been withholding information—"

"Which is plausible, all things considered." Like Balder being an ass and Veigar being a dick.

"Exactly."

My fingers itched to touch the pedestal and brush across the smooth blue walls, but I kept them clenched together behind my back.

"What we do know," Halvar continued, "is this cave has been a place monarchs have turned to for greater assistance from the ancestors."

If this was where King Olaf of the Forest Fae had come all those years ago and had his soldiers changed into wolf shifters, then the other royal lines must know of this place. No doubt told their trusted advisers too. "So, the other kings probably know of its existence?"

"Considering Veigar's arrival in Skolvik, I would believe so. I also think one of Freija's last visits here may have been to request additional power, but she never confirmed. Never got the chance."

"Hence your suspicion that I have more power than I know what to do with."

Halvar nodded and crossed his arms.

"Is this why Veigar is in town? You think he wants access?"

"We can only make assumptions at this time. Which is why I asked everyone at the emergency council meeting to find out as much as they could regarding Veigar's presence in the village."

"Yeah, I don't buy his 'unity and regional stability' bullshit either. I get the feeling he wants something more." He'd also crashed my wedding and threatened my family last night. I wasn't a fan.

"Agreed. Now, place your hand on it." Halvar motioned to the pedestal.

I reared back. "Erm… come again? You *want* me to touch it?"

"Put your palm on the pedestal."

The podium's glossy facets winked back at me.

"Will it kill me?"

"Probably not."

"That's not reassuring, big guy."

"I'll bury you with the kings and queens if it does."

I cocked my head to one side. "Really?"

"No."

"Are you making jokes again?"

"Also no."

He totally was. This was Halvar humor. He delighted in confusing me. One day I'd get the man to admit to making a joke. Or, at the very least, laughing at one of my own.

"What do I do?"

"Just put your hand on it."

"No incantation? No spell? No, *hear ye hear ye oh great and wonderful being from the beyond*?"

His jaw muscles tightened. "Put. Your. Hand. On. The. Pedestal."

"Have *you* ever tried it? Maybe it would respond to your royal—"

"Do it now," he grumbled and lurched toward me, malice shining in his eyes.

Fear shot through my body and I slapped my hand atop the pedestal. Lights swirled in the walls around us, lightning zipped down my arm, and my vision blurred before the world faded to black.

13

LENNIE

Someone had turned the lights back on... But why were they blue?

Why were they flashing?

Had I been teleported to a rave? That would be fun, but kind of inconvenient. The Norwegians knew how to party, but now probably wasn't the best time.

Or was it?

I peeled open my eyes and pulled my hand off the glowing pedestal beside me.

Definitely not a rave, but...

Magic twinkled in the walls as if someone had set an entire Christmas display of dancing white lights within the shiny blue stone. I looked around and my breath hitched.

Halvar had disappeared.

Fuck.

Where'd he go?

Did he get left behind?

Or had he teleported somewhere else? If this even was a teleport... which wouldn't surprise me at this point. With magic being real and me turning into a demi-fae, why wouldn't teleportation be real too?

I shook away the thoughts and refocused.

Halvar had mentioned the Temple being the place where monarchs spoke with the ancestors. But the room was empty. There was only me, the pedestal, and an eerie silence.

A strange sensation rippled across my shoulders and down my spine. My fight or flight instinct kicked in, raising the hairs on my arms.

I was being watched.

Not just by one person, but hundreds, maybe *thousands*.

It was as if I stood in the middle of a football stadium, the only player on the field, with a packed crowd watching my every move.

"Anybody there?" I asked, my voice echoing around the chamber.

The silence cheered back at me.

"Did I die?"

My body tingled and I pinched my arm. A sharp sting burst where I'd marked my own skin. "Okay, probably alive."

I tapped my palm against my clenched fist and brought it to my mouth like a microphone. "Testing, testing. One, two. One, two. Do we have any sexy trolls in the house tonight?"

The little light dots within the wall swished from the right side of the room to the left.

I stilled and cocked my head. No *body* responded, but the magic in the walls certainly had.

Weird.

Maybe the ancestors were these tiny blobs of light magic?

"Halvar didn't tell me what to do or what would happen. So... um... Hi, I'm Lennie Solbakke Martin. Wife of Espen Solbakke Martin and partner of Øyvin Håland. Some may call me a pain in the ass, but I'd argue I have a *great* personality. No, really. Ten out of ten, would recommend. I can party with the best of them, make you look fantastic in photos, and, as of this spring, make the second-best cappuccino in Skolvik."

Was I rambling? Sure. But what the fuck else was I supposed to do? Ask for guidance? Pray for my soul? If you asked my brothers, that ship sailed decades ago.

The walls shimmered, saying nothing.

I let out a huff and wiped my hands across my leggings. This whole experiment was proving fruitless, and I didn't want to get stuck wherever this was.

"While I appreciate the quiet types, this date isn't going great. It's not me, it's you. And with that said, I think it's my time to leave."

The lights in the wall zipped from left to right, congregating like a pack of fireflies on one side of the room.

"Glad you agree. Next time, maybe we can have some face-to-face action."

The lights brightened momentarily before dimming and spreading out again.

"Bye to you too." I placed my hand on the pedestal once more and pushed an ounce of my royal magic into it. "Take me home, please."

A tingling sensation started tickling my skin and grew into zapping, lightning crackling up my arm. Darkness clouded my vision again and when the world faded back into view, Halvar appeared in my periphery. He stood right where I'd left him, arms crossed and features as stoic as usual. Relief and joy swelled between my ribs. I'd never been so happy to see the guy.

"Where'd I go?" I asked.

"You didn't leave."

"What?"

He tilted his chin toward my feet. "You've stood there for a couple of minutes staring at the wall without blinking."

That would explain why my eyes felt dry. I rubbed at them with the backs of my thumb knuckles. "So, you didn't hear or see anything?"

Halvar shook his head.

"The lights didn't flash in the walls?"

"They did when you put your hand on the pedestal but stopped shortly after."

"And I didn't move at all? Didn't touch myself?"

His eyebrows furrowed. "Touch yourself?"

Ugh, on second thought, that sounded inappropriate. "I mean pinch myself. Did I pinch my own arm?"

"No."

I let out a harumph and set my hands on my hips. So, I hadn't been here. I'd been on, what? Some ancestral plane? Was that who had been watching me? The dead fae? Or maybe I was in my own head? "Did Freija ever tell you what happened when she spoke to the ancestors?"

"Not in detail," he replied. "Just that they responded."

"Well, they don't seem to be a talkative bunch. At least not to me."

He narrowed his eyes, brows pinching. "Care to explain?"

"The lights were on, but no one was home. It felt like I was being watched, though, but no one"—I waved my hands in front of me—"appeared."

Halvar let out a quizzical noise.

"Maybe they just weren't in the mood for a chat."

"Maybe," he mumbled.

"Or maybe they were offended that you sent a demi-fae?"

"Unlikely."

"Why?"

"Because in our entire history, and as far as I am aware, there has never been a fae like you."

"Say that again." I stifled a yawn with the back of my hand. "My ego liked it."

He rolled his eyes. "Go home. Rest. You train with my soldiers tomorrow night."

"More training?"

"Every night." Halvar's gaze cut to me. "There are two groups of people in this world: those who always prepare for battle and those who don't worry about it until it's too late. Only one of those groups survives when war comes calling."

Fuck. He had a point, and I wanted to be on the right side of history and not in that second group. I raised my hands and backed away. "I'll see you tomorrow after work, boss."

14

LENNIE

"Sleepy Lennie?" Someone shook my shoulder, and I groaned into my pillow. My thighs burned, my arms felt like spaghetti, and my eyes refused to open.

"Lennie." The soft voice brushed over my cheek again and someone swept my curtain of hair behind my ear. Sunlight beat against my eyelids.

Morning.

It was morning.

Yet, I felt like I'd flopped into bed an hour ago. "Five more minutes," I mumbled.

"You need to eat breakfast," Espen said. "Then get your cute behind to work."

Why did he have to be right? Why did I have to go to work? Did no one understand that training with Halvar all evening meant I needed a vacation day?

A palm smacked against my ass, and I flinched. "Wake up, Trouble!"

There's the other one.

I rolled over and peeled open my eyes. My two handsome men stared down at me. Espen perched on the edge of the mattress beaming like a happy puppy while Øyvin stood beside the bed, his muscled arms crossed, and an impatient frown plastered on his face.

"Øyvin made you bread rolls for breakfast."

I perked up. "Fresh bread?"

Øyvin grunted in the affirmative.

"What are you stress baking? Is it bread week? Is Paul Hollywood downstairs waiting to taste test your bake?"

"She's awake," Øyvin grumbled and strolled out of the room.

Espen snickered and pressed a kiss to my forehead. My eyes fluttered at the loving touch. We'd been so busy the past few days, I'd barely had a moment with them. Even last night, I'd come home from training after midnight and face-planted between the two of them in bed where they laid, fast asleep. My limbs could do nothing but flop on top of the covers and pass out. How I'd made it underneath the thin, summer duvet overnight was anyone's guess.

I reached out and grabbed my husband's shoulders, bringing him down to me. Pressing my lips to his, I swept my hands into his unruly hair and relished in the pleasure that settled through my body. He traced his tongue across my bottom lip, and I opened my mouth to him. He deepened the kiss further and warmth unfurled low in my abdomen.

I didn't want him to stop.

The things he did with that mouth of his could bring a smile to my face or a moan to my lips. One such low moan slipped from me, and he pulled back, panting, his eyes brimming with desire.

He brushed his thumb across my cheek. "You have no idea how much I want you right now, but you really do need to eat and get to work." He cleared his throat and adjusted his pants with his free hand. "We both do."

However much I disliked it, he was right. We both had duties to fulfill—me at the coffee shop and him at the police station. Thankfully, business was slowing with the impending departure of the final cruise ship of the season, but until then, our days would remain busy.

Once Espen left, I hauled myself out of bed, ran through the shower, and threw on a clean black T-shirt and jean shorts. Downstairs Espen sat at the circular dining table, sipping on a mug of coffee while Øyvin stood at the kitchen sink washing dishes. Golden light streamed through the windows, casting a warm glow over the spotless room—from the leather sofa to the light-wood table. It was like someone had set up professional-grade softboxes around the place, diffusing the light and making the space worthy of a magazine cover.

A plate with a stuffed bread roll waited for me at my spot. I plopped into my chair and settled on the checkered cushion. Lifting the top piece of the bun, I found cucumber, butter, and orange-pinkish goodness perched between the two lumps of golden bread.

"Who brought smoked salmon into the house?"

"Øyvin let me add it to the shopping list." Espen raised his coffee mug. "Saves you eating it only at Oddvar's during lunch."

My heart grew two sizes. I'd been obsessed with the smoky delicacy ever since I started working at the café, but never brought it into the house—Øyvin didn't eat fish and I didn't want to make him uncomfortable. Not that I thought he'd mind, but still.

"Thank you," I said and looked between the two of them.

Øyvin waved a hand over his shoulder, dismissing it like it was nothing.

I took a bite and choked down a moan at the salty, smoky, and soft morsel. Swallowing, I extended my hand to Øyvin and cleared my throat. He turned to face me, suds-covered hands braced over the edge of the sink. "This definitely deserves a handshake."

His brow furrowed. "What do you mean?"

My eyes rolled as hard as Halvar's did when I made a joke. "You really need to stop falling asleep on Sunday nights while I'm watching the *Great British Baking Show*."

"I listen," he replied and spun back to his washing up.

Espen chuckled, watching the entire exchange with a subtle grin.

It felt good to have a moment of normalcy amid the chaos that had invaded our lives. Not just the arrival of the Fire Fae King, but the wedding had been a lot. Then there were the threats flying around, the training session with Halvar, and the big guy revealing the Fjell Fae's secret temple deep within the mountain. Fuck, after this week alone, I needed a year-long vacation.

I took another bite of my breakfast as I thought back over last night. "Have either of you heard about the Temple of the Fae?"

Espen choked and spluttered on his coffee as Øyvin dropped a bowl into the kitchen sink, porcelain clattering against stainless steel.

Setting my roll back on its plate, I looked between the two men. "Don't lie to me guys. Tell me what you know, and I'll tell you what I know. Sharing is caring, remember?"

Øyvin peered over his shoulder and squinted at me—the depths of those blue eyes deepening. "What have you learned, Trouble?"

"You two go first. I'm pretty sure I'm not supposed—"

"Then you shouldn't," Øyvin said.

"But, this is important. I know it is."

Espen rubbed his fist against his sternum and cleared his throat. "I'm aware the Temple exists."

My head spun to him. "You are?"

"I am." He nodded. "It's the rumored birthplace of our kind. A sacred space somewhere in the mountain."

"Who told you about it?" I asked.

"Queen Ragnhild. Back when I first became her head guard. It's usually information only shared with royals and their inner circles for security reasons."

"But you've never been?"

He shook his head and brushed his hair off his forehead. "How do *you* know about it?"

"Halvar showed me where it is. Since I'm Deputy Head Guard and have some royal powers, he took me inside too."

Espen's eyes widened. "He did?"

"Stop!" Øyvin interjected, spinning to face us. He grabbed a dish towel and wrung his hands in it. "We shouldn't be discussing this."

I narrowed my eyes at his fidgeting. He rarely fidgeted, and when something was upsetting him, he took it out on the piano keys. "Why? What's wrong?" I asked.

"What happened, Øyvin?" Espen added.

Øyvin's throat bobbed and he set aside the towel, noticeably *not* folding it or hanging it up on the rail in front of the oven. Something really was bugging him.

He shoved his hands into his jean pockets and glanced between the two of us. His brows drew together, and my pulse kicked up at the sight.

"Reuven asked me to report on Fjell and Forest movements."

I froze, yet the house bobbed as if it had been set adrift down the fjord. "What?" I said, my voice shaking.

"Those were his words?" The chair creaked as Espen leaned back. "He wanted you to spy on us?"

Øyvin let out a breath and nodded.

He wouldn't do that. I couldn't believe for a single second that Øyvin would do anything to hurt us or the delicate alliances he'd fought so hard to forge. I trusted this man. I loved him. He wouldn't betray our secrets. Sure, he would challenge me any chance he got, but actively deceive and report on our movements to others? Not a fucking chance.

"What did you say?" I asked.

"I said I would. But it was a lie."

I knew it.

Øyvin would always be loyal to the Fjord Fae and the waters he'd sworn to protect, but I'd seen him pick me earlier this year. When Wilhelm and his hoard of wayward wolves descended upon the mountain,

Øyvin had chosen to stay behind and protect me instead of going back to the fjord with his king. A king, it now appeared, who was trying to use our relationship to get information on the other factions' movements and thoughts.

With my elbows braced on the table and my hands clasped at my chin, a sigh slipped through my lips. "We can't trust Reuven, can we?"

Øyvin shook his head.

"It would appear not," Espen replied. "When did this happen? When did he ask you?"

"Day after the wedding."

So only a few days ago. We'd barely seen each other in that time, so it made sense that he was telling us now. That would also explain why he'd appeared on edge and the stress baking.

I shoved the last bit of my breakfast into my mouth, scurried across the kitchen, and wrapped my arms around Øyvin's torso. His heart thundered against my ear where I pressed my head to his chest.

"I love you," I said.

He cradled my head in his hand and pressed his lips against my hair. "I love you too, Trouble," he whispered. "Now, tomorrow, and forever. You can trust me."

"I know," I replied, my voice barely audible.

He squeezed me tighter against him like he heard the weight of that truth.

I trusted him. Both of them. End of story.

A jazzy song sounded from Espen's pocket, the noise breaking the silence that hung in the room. It was the ringtone he'd assigned to the front desk of the police station. He pulled the device to his ear. "Good morning!"

I spun in Øyvin's hold. He refused to let go, looping his arms around my waist and pressing my curves against his body. The warmth radiating off him locked me in place. Forget work, I wanted to stay right here all day. Please and thank you.

Espen's brow furrowed and he gulped down the rest of his coffee. "I'll be there in a minute," he said and hung up.

"What's going on?" I asked.

"One of the security cameras outside the jewelry store *and* the webcam filming the town square were burned."

"Burned?" Øyvin and I exclaimed simultaneously.

Espen shoved his coffee mug into the tiny dishwasher and sprinted to the entry area. As he pulled on his work boots, I asked, "Did they see who did it?"

"No." He clipped on his utility belt. "No suspect. No witnesses. Just torched cameras."

"I bet Veigar is behind it."

Øyvin's chest rumbled against my back in agreement.

"We won't know for sure until we get this investigation underway," Espen said. "But I think you might be right."

15

LENNIE

Spending the day peering out the window between coffee orders, I looked for any sign of what had happened to the village security cameras. Nothing stood out to me, and there were no sightings of Veigar down main street, but that didn't lessen the worry that had taken hold.

After filling the last of the seasonal tourists' orders, I ate a quick dinner alone at home, before I bolted up to the mountain in my workout gear and ponytail for an evening training session with some of Halvar's soldiers.

I sauntered into the training cavern and was met by the clattering of swords, the crashing of stones, and grunts worthy of a college football gym. Fjell Fae soldiers in gray and black attire filled the gymnasium-sized hall, as far as the eye could see. A stone platform rose from the floor at the end of the space like a boxing ring without ropes, while a throng of people to my left worked on hand-to-hand combat, their fists raised in protective stances. To my right were strength trainers using rocks the size of microwaves and ovens as weights. It was like a prehistoric caveman had created his own gym in the mountain.

A pair of sparring soldiers charged past me, and I leaped out of the way before I could meet the pointy end of their swords.

That was too close.

"Evening," Torsten said as he stepped up beside me. "Ready for another night of training?"

"I don't really have a choice," I replied with a chuckle. Halvar had ordered the daily training sessions, and since he'd already threatened my life once this year, I wasn't in the mood to test his patience.

Torsten snorted and crossed his arms. "Don't you want to continue practicing how to protect yourself and the mountain?"

I did. Fear of Halvar aside, it was what had ultimately dragged me up the hillside the past few evenings. Learning how to use my powers to their fullest had taken on a new sense of urgency. One Halvar had been adamant about. And, while my muscles screamed in disagreement, he was right. I needed to be at full strength and competency if I was going to have a chance at protecting the mountain and my home.

"Where do we start today?"

Torsten motioned toward the sparring mats. "Over here."

I followed him across the room, and people parted before loitering around us in a large circle.

"You've mastered all the basics." Torsten removed his uniform cape and chucked it aside, letting it fall in a heap at the feet of the surrounding soldiers. "So, tonight, we're focusing on your death magic."

Air caught in my chest and my heartbeat tripped over itself. "Death magic? Did I miss something? Is there more you haven't told me about my demi-fae-ness?"

A trill of gentle snickers sounded around me.

"The killing light you used against Wilhelm."

My shoulders slumped. "Oh. *That* magic."

I wasn't a huge fan of that power. It still haunted me from time to time when I trekked through the mountain's tunnels. The burning and searing magic had wrapped around Wilhelm and killed him before he got a chance to rip out Aurora's throat, but it had left a mark on me too. It was going to take time to mentally recover from killing someone, but as Øyvin and Espen had reminded me: I'd done the right thing.

Wilhelm wouldn't have stopped.

He would have gone on seeking revenge, leaving a trail of bodies in his wake.

"Are you ready?" Torsten asked, drawing me from my thoughts.

I shook my head and arms, ridding myself of the strained emotions within me. "Yeah. How do you want to do this without me accidentally hurting someone?"

"We'll stop you."

"Who's *we*?"

He pointed to the watchful eyes around us.

I raised my hands. "Okay, if you think you can stop it."

"Everyone here is aware of the dangers."

"Are you, really?" I made a slow turn, catching the resolute faces of the men and women standing at the edge of the sparring zone. "You know I could accidentally kill you?"

Nods and murmurs of agreement sounded from the soldiers.

"Fine," I said. "Tell me how this is going to work, Torsten."

The stout man stepped forward with a soldier by his side. "Pretend this is Øyvin."

I tilted my chin at the guy. "He has brown hair. Let's call him Fake-Espen." The man looked nothing like my husband aside from the hair color. He had slim shoulders, gangly limbs, and a lack of facial hair that alluded to youth, *not* a clean shave.

"Okay, then. Espen it is," Torsten conceded. "Pretend this Espen is your husband and when one of the soldiers tries to attack him, you kill them."

My eyes widened. "That's your big plan? Seriously? And what if—"

Torsten stepped back just as another soldier lunged from my left toward Fake-Espen. I instinctively drew on my Fjell power and extended a stone sword toward the woman's abdomen. She dodged and sucked in her stomach, narrowly avoiding the shiny double-edged blade. Ragged breaths left my lungs, and I swallowed hard.

Okay, so, they weren't going to go easy on me. This was a proper fight.

Cool.

Great.

Awesome.

I could do this.

The woman circled me like a lioness corralling her prey. Keeping Fake-Espen at my back, I matched her movements and monitored her gaze for any tells. She fluttered her fingers and a stone sword extended from her grasp as a wicked smile crept across her lips.

Smithing magic like me and Halvar. Nice.

I tightened my grasp on the hilt of my blade. She launched, but I parried away her advances until we circled each other again. Her eyes flicked to my right. I didn't fall for it. A second later a roar sounded from that direction, and I spun, yanking Fake-Espen by the wrist and shoving him back. A broad male soldier lumbered across the space where I'd been standing.

Stun. I raised my sword and arced it from where the female soldier loomed and toward the incoming threat. Tingles ran down my arm, and sparks crackled across the blade. Forks of lightning shot from the top, zapping toward both assailants, and—

The ring of soldiers shifted, and a barrier of stone fell from the ceiling, caging me and my magic. My assault bounced off the stone and dissipated.

My sword arm dropped along with my shoulders. "What the fuck?"

Chest heaving, my blood raced through my veins. Fake-Espen was still behind me, but the guy seemed to be under orders not to help himself. This entire exercise was down to me.

The stone barriers rose, revealing the soldiers and Torsten.

"That wasn't the death magic, was it?" he asked, his eyes narrowed.

I shook my head.

"Let's try again, then."

"Fine." I had to do better, but that instinctive response had still been effective. Now, I just needed to focus on calling on more of the magic—going a level above the stunning magic to the power that could only be wielded by monarchs... and me.

Another soldier launched toward me, and I crossed my sword, meeting his blow with a grunt. He withdrew and slashed toward me once more. I lifted my blade in front of me and the two weapons met with a mighty crash. The energy behind the blow rattled my teeth and ignited that tell-tale burning sensation in my sternum. This guy, with muscles the size of boulders, was far stronger than the woman had been, but he was slower than her. I could use that to my advantage.

I took hit after hit, but my steps swept across the stone floor like that of a hummingbird—light and always moving, never yielding.

Don't let him near Espen.

Hit number eight cracked against my sword, and I pushed him back with all my strength, throwing my weight behind it too. The man stumbled back, giving me enough time for the roiling power in my sternum to sear through me. It was either him dying at my hand or Fake-Espen dying at his. There was only one option I'd accept. *Kill him.*

I thrust out my left arm and the lightning power seared down my scar. A crackling orb of blinding light flew from my palm—

A single panel of stone descended from the ceiling and pierced the floor. My magic burst against the wall like a firework, and I raised an arm over my face to shield from the sparks.

I did it.

With uneven breaths, I dropped my arm and found the surrounding soldiers' eyes as wide as telescope lenses—like they hadn't believed the rumors they'd been told. Torsten popped his face around the troll-sized stone surfboard in the middle of the circle. His man bun wobbled and a smile split his lips. "Much better."

My shoulders slumped and the adrenaline that had taken up residence in my limbs melted. I brushed the back of my hand across my forehead, bringing away beads of sweat. "Thanks, Professor."

"How about a quick water break after all that, hmmm?"

"Gosh, yes." My throat was as dry as the sands of the Sahara.

Fake-Espen gave me a quick nod and "well done" as he strode back to the group of dispersing soldiers.

Torsten and I wandered across the room, back near the entrance, where a fancy water-fountain with paper cups perched within a nook in the wall. The water station looked like something out of ancient Rome, although far more rugged. An arched shelf had been carved out of the slate wall, and a stream of water flowed from the top into a sink-like basin with a drain at the bottom. It was as if they'd installed their own self-watering dog bowl in the mountain's gym.

I grabbed a paper cup, stuck it under the water, and brought it to my lips.

The ice-cold liquid sluiced down my throat, and I bit my lip to hold back a moan.

"That feeling you just felt." Torsten grabbed a drink of his own. "That raw magic. How would you describe it? How is it different from normal light magic or Fjell magic?"

"A burning desire to protect. Then searing pain as it shoots out of me." It was the best way I could describe the sensation. It filled every pore of my being and begged to be let loose, to protect what was most important to me and kill the threat.

"Draw from that. That is where the death magic sits. That is what will help you, should you find yourself in a situation where you need it."

I nodded and took another sip of my drink, enjoying the momentary training reprieve.

Torsten turned his attention to the room, and my thoughts drifted to pressing information that the Council needed to be aware of. While I had him here...

"By the way, the big gossip at the police station and among the café customers is that someone's burning security cameras around the village. My first guess is Veigar, but why do you think he'd do that?" The town had been buzzing with the news of a potential arsonist in our midst. I had zero doubt that the lead purveyors of said information were three little octogenarian ladies who enjoyed their morning coffees by the window at Oddvar's. But how they'd found out about it so quickly was anyone's guess.

Torsten shuffled on the spot. "All the cameras?"

I shrugged. "Quite a lot, apparently. They got the ones on the jewelry store, the toy store, town webcam, even the library if Jorunn is to be believed."

"Hmmm. I don't see what he would stand to gain from that, but I wouldn't put it past him to stir up trouble."

"Can you let the Council know?"

He nodded as a voice rumbled, "Let them know what?"

I flinched. Twisting and peering around Torsten, my gaze met a pair of sky-blue eyes and black fatigues, a bundle of gray material clutched in one hand. Halvar cocked his head to one side, awaiting a response.

"Tell them what, Lennie?"

"Veigar's been burning security cameras around town. Maybe. Possibly. Probably."

His silver brows furrowed, and that mountain of a chest rumbled.

"Any idea what he'd stand to gain from that?" I asked. "Torsten and I can't think of anything."

Lines marred Halvar's forehead and his lips pinched together, that mind of his appearing to sprint through options and viable answers. He let out a long sigh. "Whatever it is, I would wager he's setting the stage for something or pushing up timelines. I have never known him to be patient."

"So, bad news bears, then?"

Halvar grunted and Torsten let out a minuscule groan, like he too wasn't a fan of the Fire Fae King's antics.

"Training successful?" Halvar asked, turning to Torsten.

"She did it. Called on the killing magic."

"Nobody hurt?" Halvar continued.

"No Fjell Fae were harmed during the demi-fae's training session," I deadpanned.

"Good." Halvar huffed. "Follow me."

I tossed my cup in the recycling bin beside the water station and hurried after the tall brute, Torsten right on my tail.

Halvar aimed for the back of the room and hopped onto the stone-slab-come-boxing ring at the back of the cavernous training gym.

"Everyone gather!" Halvar's voice boomed through the room, his words echoing against the rough-hewn walls. Men and women scurried across the space and assembled in front of the platform. I stood in their midst, arms aching but mind curious as to what Halvar had to say to the group.

A calm silence settled over the crowd. Halvar's eyes scanned the masses like a general inspecting his troops.

"It has been some time since we have altered our leadership within our forces, but things *have* changed." His gaze cut to me.

Shit.

"Lennie, our new Deputy Head Guard, please join me up here."

Double shit.

I'd always hated being called on in meetings, and now Halvar was dragging me in front of a host of soldiers. Fan-fucking-tastic.

I hoisted myself onto the platform. "You know, if you wanted to remove me from my post, you could do so without an audience." I straightened and brushed my hands across my thighs. "Or is this a public execution for something I've done wrong? Something I've said? Bad leadership potential?"

He grumbled and shoved the bundle of gray material into my hands. "Lennie Solbakke Martin, welcome to the Fjell Fae Army. Here is your official uniform."

My jaw crashed to the stone floor as a round of applause wrapped around us and I accepted the clothing. What the fuck was happening? What had my life become? Me... in uniform?

Finely woven wool with tiny silver threads at the seams stared back at me. I unfolded the material, and a pair of pants fell to the floor. "Sorry," I muttered, my eyes locked on the other two items, one in each of my hands. A jacket, like the ones I'd seen soldiers wearing around the mountain, and a waist-length cape that would fasten at the shoulder with the help of a black leather strap.

"How'd you know my size?" I said in a daze, unable to tear my eyes from the gift.

"I asked Øyvin and Espen," Halvar replied.

I chuckled. Yeah, Øyvin was, in his own words, "well acquainted with my curves" and had already bought me winter gear in the correct size.

But that wasn't what shocked me the most. Yes, I'd been bestowed with the title of Deputy Head Guard when I became a demi-fae with royal magic and successfully proved my worth to the Fjell Fae by retrieving their heir last winter. This, the uniform, was different, though. More meaningful. This was them welcoming me into the fold as one of their own.

A lump formed in my throat, and I swallowed it. "Thank you," I mumbled, unable to conjure up any other words to express the well of emotion bubbling up inside me.

"You're welcome."

Brushing my hand across the soft wool, a smirk tilted my lips. I glanced up at Halvar. "Still no hat, though?"

He crossed his arms and rolled his eyes.

"One day." I pointed the cape at him. "One day I'll get that hat from you."

"Only when you earn it."

I smiled. "Oh, I'll earn it."

"Good. Now, fight me."

My smile vanished. "You can't be serious."

"Very," he said, his voice unwavering. "Torsten, can you take her uniform for her?"

"Of course," my friend replied. He tugged the clothing from my grip and retrieved the pants from the floor before disappearing from the periphery of my vision and blending with the crowd.

"Here?" I squeaked. "You want to spar with me up here?"

Halvar nodded, his features unyielding.

I peered around the space. Wide, excited eyes stared up at me as if seeing Halvar spar with someone was a rarity and popcorn-worthy entertainment. So much for being welcomed into the Fjell Fae army family. The other major problem was a lack of sparring mats. There were none up here. If Halvar pulled my feet out from underneath me, I'd crack my skull open on the slab of rock.

Shifting my weight from one foot to the other, I wrung my hands together. "Are you sure about this?"

"Yes."

Halvar rolled up his sleeves, revealing thickly corded muscles that looked like they could choke a man in a headlock.

I swept my palm down the column of my throat and swallowed hard. Fingers crossed that wouldn't be how I met my demise. In fact, now would be a great time for Odin to shepherd me to Valhalla. Save me from the pain of death by the hands of one Fjell Fae Head Guard. I may not be a warrior or amazing leader, but if the Allfather could open the gates, that would be appreciated.

Then again, if I snuck out now...

While Halvar conjured a sword worthy of a beheading, I turned and slunk toward the edge of the platform.

"Lennie." His voice rumbled through the room.

"I, uh... Forgot something back at the water fountain. Won't take a moment."

Something whistled past my ear and air thundered against my eardrum. The people in front of me ducked as Halvar's sword sailed over their heads and smashed against the far wall.

My breath caught and my eyes threatened to pop out of their sockets. "What the fuck!"

I pressed my hand against the side of my head and pulled it away. No blood, but damn did that pressure hurt. I spun, my ponytail whipping through the air. "What was that for?"

"Fight me."

"Counter to a lot of my actions, I don't actually have a death wish."

Halvar crossed his arms and quirked a single brow. "You have had plenty of training, and, as the only other fae with both royal and Fjell Fae magic, let us see what you can do with a matched opponent."

He pointedly excluded Nora who resided in the dungeon. But she was a bitch who'd killed her sister and the love of his life. I couldn't fault him for leaving her out of the equation. "So, this is a science experiment?"

He shrugged.

"Fine." I set my hands on my hips. "But when I die, I promise to come back as a ghost and haunt these tunnels, wreaking more havoc than I did while alive."

Halvar ignored my threats and motioned with his hand for me to step further into the center of the platform.

I shuffled forward and sent a silent message down to the devil, warning him of my impending arrival.

"We duel with whatever weaponry we can conjure." He said. "Do you agree to the terms?"

"Terms? What is this ancient warfare? A Renaissance joust? Is this where you tell me you're actually Thor and have a *really* big hammer that can zap me with all kinds of lightning—"

"Lennie..."

I huffed. There was no getting out of this. I had to spar with Halvar. Be his science experiment and try not to land myself in a stony casket. "Sure," I muttered.

"Don't hold back," he said as a stone broadsword slowly emerged in his hand.

I shuddered at the sight and summoned my own blade—a warm flow of energy pouring from my sternum as I called on the Fjell Fae magic. "If you say so."

His reply came in the form of him settling into a fighting stance: legs bent slightly, elbows angled just-so, and his gaze locked on me.

I felt like an actual deer in the headlights of an oncoming truck. A really, really, big semi-truck that would barrel right through me.

Bending gently at the hips, I set one foot out in front of the other into what Espen would liken to a high-lunge position. My grip tightened around my stone sword, and I steeled myself for the onslaught of a fight, my mind flying as fast as a camera stuck on sport-mode shutter speed.

What would Espen say about this? Would he be angry? Would he cheer me on from the sidelines like he did during our winter training sessions?

And what would Øyvin say? *No*, I shook my head. I knew exactly what Øyvin would say. He'd remind me it was a challenge—something I could either win or lose.

The mere thought of winning kicked that Martin Family competitive gene into the *on* position. There wasn't a chance I was losing. Even if it was to the beast of the mountain. Martin Family Rules: Wins Only.

I narrowed my eyes and glared back at Halvar.

Challenge accepted.

He swung, and I met his attack with my own blade. The force of the blow reverberated through my body, threating to dislodge the sword and take my arm. I pulled back and struck again, careful to avoid the pointy bit.

Halvar was certainly stronger and faster than the other two I'd dueled with today, but I still got the feeling he was holding back. His steps lacked an urgency that the others had.

I thrust the tip toward his stomach. He knocked aside my advance. I twisted and spun, only giving him my back for a split second before we started circling each other again.

The push and pull continued. Both of us launched volleys of royal magic at each other, too. The audience watched on with rapt attention—their eyes wide, focus locked on us as we danced across the proverbial mat. My muscles screamed, begging me to sit on the edge of the stone platform and take a break. But I knew what Halvar was like. Knew from whispered tales and rumors that he was a battle-hardened warrior. If I showed any sign of weakness, he'd exploit it.

I had to keep moving.

Yet, the blows didn't stop coming.

"Are... you trying... to kill me?" I asked.

"No." Halvar launched again, gripping his sword with two hands, the blade slashing through the air toward me. I pushed out a volley of stunning magic. He teetered and twisted out of the way, narrowly avoiding the balls of light.

Rounding back, he prowled and studied me, his chest as still as if he were meditating along sandy shores.

Meanwhile, my breaths came in short bursts, matching the staccato clashes of our swords.

With blade in one hand and magic in the other, I charged.

"Have you."

Block, push, zap.

"Ever."

I twisted and countered another strike.

"Wanted to?"

Our swords crossed, and we stared into each other's eyes.

"Yes."

"What!" I pushed off him and hobbled back to my side of the boxing ring, letting my sword arm droop. "When?"

"Arm up!"

I did as I was ordered, my shoulder muscles screaming in reply.

"After our first meeting in the throne room," he answered.

The first day we'd ever met. When Espen had brought me to a meeting with him and Øyvin at Queen Freija's request. About a year ago. I narrowed my eyes at Halvar. "What stopped you? My charm and sharp wit?"

Silence responded as Halvar bowed his head and turned away slightly. My stomach dropped to my toes and my shoulders sagged.

Fuck. No, it wasn't me who'd stopped my own untimely death at his hands. It was Freija.

Apparently, I had a lot to thank the late Queen for.

Unable to do so in person, perhaps the best way to honor her protection and power was to protect the one thing she cared for the most: the mountain.

That certainly had been my intention with everything that had happened this year, but now that knowledge offered me even greater motivation to do just that. Protect the mountain. Protect these people. Use this magic I'd been given for good.

A muscle feathered in Halvar's jaw as he straightened. The light magic in his palm evaporated and was slowly replaced by an axe that looked like something out of a Viking movie. Two sharp stone blades protruded from a thick gray handle. He peered down at the runic design on the cheeks of the weapon. Untold pain flooded his gaze, and my stomach flip-flopped at the thought of causing him such emotional turmoil.

I needed to pull an Espen. I needed to pivot.

"Hypothetically speaking. If a Fjell Fae wanted to make the world's largest rock, how big would that rock have to be?"

Halvar rolled his eyes, and the crowd chuckled at my remarks.

Bingo.

"Hey, some people around here finally found my jokes funny."

Halvar didn't give me time to bask in the joy from my audience. He barreled forward once more, aiming both weapons at my sword.

He crossed his weapons, and my sword struck at the apex. Pulling upward, he started to dislodge it from my hands. I jerked a hand free and blasted a plain ball of light at his face. With a grunt of alarm, he threw his head back and narrowly avoided the royal magic before scurrying to his side of the platform. The light flew across the room and evaporated over the crowd.

Magic! I needed to keep using my magic. It would keep me on my feet longer, especially considering he'd put his away and gone back to what I could only assume were old habits. Magic would help me win this thing. And if there was one thing I really wanted right now, aside from a long-ass bath and foot massage, it was to win this sparring match.

We lunged toward each other once again.

Stun. His axe descended, and I shot my stunning magic at his arm. It wrapped around his wrist, and he splayed his hand dropping the medieval weapon. His eyes widened, leaving me an opening. My blade sparked with power, and I swung it at his with all my strength, throwing my weight behind it. The stone edges crashed against each other, and my magic zipped down the opposing weapon.

Halvar grunted, and his sword flew across the ring, clattering to the floor.

Silence so quiet I could hear my own pounding heartbeat settled across the room.

"Holy shit," I mumbled.

Gasps and murmurs swelled and echoed off the rugged ceiling and walls. Magical sconces flickered, casting random shadows across Halvar's body.

Holy fuck. I'd just disarmed Halvar. My arms burned, my stomach was in knots, and it felt as if I stood on the edge of death's abyss where Satan himself waited for me with open arms. But I'd fucking *disarmed* the beast of the mountain. I'd won!

Halvar turned to me slowly. Light and shadow danced across his features. "Well done," he said, with a nod of approval and his lips tipped into a smile.

16

LENNIE

I ran through the village, dodging locals on their morning walks, zipping past stores, and narrowly avoiding the goddamn summer skier in his skintight suit. He really needed to get a cup. I'd have stopped to tell him, but... I was late.

Beyond late.

Sparring with Halvar a few nights ago and daily evening training sessions with the Fjell Fae this week were taking a toll on my mental and physical resolve. My strength and skill were improving, but damn was it exhausting. So much so that I'd slept through my alarm.

I scurried through the front door of Oddvar's Café wearing Espen's black T-shirt and a random pair of jeans, my ponytail flailing behind me, and ran straight into someone.

"Ope!" Hot coffee sloshed over my forearms as I reached out to steady myself. I hissed at the scalding liquid on my skin. Today really wasn't my day. "I'm so sorry," I said and stared up into a pair of mirrored-sunglasses.

Shit.

With her wavy black hair, porcelain skin, and coffee dripping from her hands, Salka, was *almost* the last person I wanted to run into. I'd seen her from a distance, wandering around town every so often, but I'd never spoken to her since she moved to Skolvik this past winter.

"Here, let me get that." I took the half-empty cup of coffee from her hands and shuffled over to the counter. Oddvar narrowed his eyes at me but continued serving another customer. Setting aside the mug, I rinsed and dried my hands and turned to find Salka waiting by the counter. I grabbed some paper napkins from our stash and passed them to her. "Again, I'm so sorry. Are you hurt?"

"I'm fine," she replied, taking the napkins and wiping down her hands. I gave her a quick once over to check for coffee on her clothes but her rust-colored linen dress that cinched into a bow on one side of her waist was stain-free.

There wasn't even any on the floor where we'd collided, thank goodness. We couldn't have people slipping and falling.

"I'll make you a new cup. On the house. Again, I'm so sorry."

"It's all right. No one was hurt." She gave me a gentle smile. She was right, thank fuck. Although my wrists had turned red from the hot liquid, hers appeared unmarred.

"What was your order?" I threw on my apron.

"Macchiato, please. To go."

Interesting. Someone around here who liked having some milk or foam in their coffee. It was a rarity here—most Norwegian's liked their coffee dark with minimal accoutrement. The tourists were always different, though.

I set to work creating the drink, noting that she'd changed her order from a café mug to a to-go cup. Oddvar always wanted customers to stay in the café as the chances of them ordering a second drink or food increased. I'd just brought those chances with Salka crashing down. This Friday really was turning into a sucky Monday.

"So, are you enjoying living in Skolvik?" I asked, hoping to break the tension between us and assuage any ill will thanks to my clumsiness.

"It's a nice town. Not too much different than Iceland, but a lot more trees."

"You don't have trees?" I'd never been myself, but most places had trees, didn't they?

She chuckled, the sound warm and inviting. "We have some trees, but not nearly as many as Norway. Our terrain is more… arctic tundra. Brush, basalt, and even some glaciers."

I nodded, having seen photos online. My heart longed to photograph Iceland's black sandy beaches, the crystalline glaciers, and the other-worldly waterfalls. Not to mention…

I returned to the counter with her drink, gently setting it down. "And volcanoes."

She bit her bottom lip. "Yes, we have those too."

The air heated, and my palms started to sweat as I stared at her sunglasses. My own wide eyes stared back at me in the mirrored glass, and I shook my head, breaking away. I grabbed a rag and wiped down the clean counter as she picked up her cup.

"Thank you for the new drink."

I tucked the useless cleaning towel into my apron, and rocked back and forth on my feet. "Of course. Again, I'm sorry."

She gave me a closed-lip smile and headed for the door with her Macchiato.

"Well, that was awkward," Oddvar said, his arms crossed and lips pinching at one corner. "Thank you for making her another coffee."

I wiped the back of my hand across my forehead. "Uh-huh." I knew next to nothing about the woman other than she was Reuven's wife, Veigar's daughter, and liked to go on long walks around the village. Aside from that, she was an anomaly and a question mark. I didn't want to assume the worst and perceive her as a threat to the fae here in Skolvik, but part of me couldn't help but panic at her presence. A Fire Fae near this many trees? It couldn't be safe. Unless she was super kind and had absolute control over her fiery powers. Satan help us, I hoped she did.

I took a deep breath and spun around, setting to work on some sandwiches and getting on with my workday. Customers came and went, brown goat cheese was sliced, and drinks were brewed to perfection. Local gossip about burned cameras drifted around the room, and when the crowds thinned in the late afternoon, I sent a slowing Oddvar home. I could wipe down tables and close up shop. He obliged with a weary nod, hanging up his apron and buttoning his cardigan to the top button. His departure left me in the stillness of the café. Just me, the machines, the lingering smell of coffee grinds, and a caddy of cleaning supplies.

I reached for the spray bottle as the bell above the door rang.

"Did you forget something?" I turned and all the breath inside my lungs evaporated.

The person I most definitely *did not* want to run into walked through the door.

Yeah, today was not my day.

I set aside the caddy and assessed the man for weapons and threats. His hair was perfectly coiffed, his linen shirt tastefully rumpled, and his pants looked like they'd been hand sewn in Italy. Not a single weapon graced his hands or his hips. But that didn't mean he wasn't a threat. He'd already made that known. Plus, based on the Fjell Fae Council's tales, Veigar didn't need weapons—he *was* the weapon.

"We're about to close." I swallowed the lump in my throat. "Can I get you something to-go?"

Veigar peered around the space, his sunglasses shielding his dark eyes. "I'm here to see if you might deliver a message for me."

My eyebrows met my hairline. "You want me to pass something along?"

"Yes, please."

"Look, if you have something to say, you should—"

"You're the Deputy Head Guard, are you not?"

Who the hell told him that?

I nodded.

"Then you are a leader among your people and a sufficient point of contact."

I crossed my arms over my chest and popped my hip. Hearing someone of his standing call me a leader was some serious whiplash, but he wasn't wrong. This was my new role. I had the uniform now too. So, I needed to own it, especially when other powerful beings crossed my path.

"I'm the Deputy Head Guard, but I believe you may want to talk to Halvar, my boss." Wasn't delegating part of being a leader? Couldn't I toss this to the big guy and avoid being in the same room as this walking, talking bomb?

"Diplomacy isn't the man's strong suit."

I pinched my lips together to refrain from snorting or laughing.

Veigar sighed, his shoulders dropping. "Perhaps I should find someone else." He bowed his head and turned to the door.

Halvar's comments about getting information from Veigar rang through my mind as my opportunity to find out exactly what the man wanted sauntered out of the building. If I wanted to know, I had to act. Fuck it, I had to be brave. Not just for me, but for the mountain, for my new home.

I ran across the café and threw open the door. "Wait!" This was stupid. Beyond stupid. It was signing my own fucking death record. "Let's hear it then."

Veigar's lips tilted up at one corner. I strode back behind the counter with my heart in my throat and made the King of the Fire Fae a cup of coffee.

17

LENNIE

Coffee sloshed over the rims of the mugs as I set them on the table by the window where *His Majesty* had taken up residence. Ironically, it was the same table I'd sat at the day I'd missed the cruise ship. Though, this time, *I* was the one asking the out-of-towner questions and wishing them on their merry way.

"So." My voice wavered, but hopefully not enough that he'd notice. "Tell me a bit about yourself, and why you're *really* here."

Veigar slowly reached up to his face and removed his sunglasses. *Damn.* I swallowed hard under the assessment of his pitch-black eyes as he folded the glasses and tucked them into the front of his button-down shirt.

Silence hung heavy in the café, sweat beading at the nape of my neck as I waited for his reply.

"I'm here to help."

My eyes narrowed at him. "With what?"

"Stability and the endurance of the fae. We've been around for a long time. I want that to continue without internal or external threats."

External threats? Was that a dig at me being brought into the fold? Or were there other things besides human knowledge of our existence that could cause harm to the fae? Or maybe he was just trying to throw me off?

His smile twisted at one corner like he could hear my anxious thoughts.

If this was his attempt at trying to unnerve me, it wasn't working... entirely. "What do you want in Skolvik, Veigar?"

"My hope is, with your connections to each fae faction, you might pass along a message for me. Specifically, the fae need unity and new leadership, and I'm here to offer my services."

It was just as we suspected. "They're doing fine without a hegemonic douche-canoe in charge."

"Says the woman who killed an Alpha wolf."

My eyebrows betrayed me and drifted toward my hairline. "How do you know about that?"

"A king has his ways."

Or a daughter who'd found out and passed along information.

I let out a long sigh. "Okay, so you're the Fire Fae equivalent of Miss America and you want world peace. Tell me why *you* should get the crown."

Veigar furrowed his brow like he had no idea what I was talking about. "I'm the leader of an entire faction of fae that lives harmoniously on an isle in the North Atlantic where life flourishes, secrets remain secret, and our way of being is not under threat from ill-equipped leaders, like promoted Head Guards after the failure of keeping royal lines alive."

Well, that definitely felt like a dig at both Espen and Halvar, all in one sentence. *What a dick.*

I took a sip of my coffee and set the warm mug back on the table to one side. "And why do you think that qualifies you to lead the other three factions?" There better only be four types of Fae or I'd skewer my husband and partner for not giving me the full Fae-101.

"All three remain leaderless."

"I doubt King Reuven sees it that way."

"My son-in-law is brand new to the throne. He's already committed to defer to my advice and leadership."

Fuck. Øyvin's suspicions were right. We couldn't trust Reuven. My first impression of Reuven wasn't of a man who buckled to others, and, based on the stories from the Council meeting, it sounded like Veigar's temper was fiery in every sense of the word. But then again, what did I know about being a ruler? I clasped my hands together and rested them on the table. "So, you want to be everyone's leader."

"I think I'm the most qualified candidate for the position."

"I'm not sure Halvar would agree with that."

A suave grin swept across Veigar's face. "Halvar and I have never quite seen eye-to-eye."

"I sensed that at my wedding reception."

"A lovely occasion."

"One I don't recall inviting you to."

He smiled, and a bead of sweat ran down the underside of my arm. Either I was nervous or someone had turned on the heating in here.

Veigar tilted his head to one side. "Haven't you noticed all the problems the local factions have with their leaders and how the natural world has suffered from it? Polluted waters, rock falls, I'm sure the forest has had some struggles too."

I pinched my lips between my teeth. Hot weather and drought conditions aside, there had been a lot of issues across the board this past year.

"You know I'm right."

He was. No matter how much I disliked the guy for his history of violence and threats to my family, he was correct in his assessment.

"You are." I sighed.

"And balance and harmony would benefit us all. With me at the front, leading, we could mitigate the troubles we currently face and prepare for future eventualities... together."

This entire conversation felt well outside my area of expertise, but I had to get as much information out of him as possible. Especially considering his chatty mood. "What happens if we don't agree to your terms?"

"I *escalate* matters."

There he went again with the lack of clarity and threats.

"How?" I asked. "How would you 'escalate matters?'"

His lips twisted into a sly smile, onyx eyes twinkling with mad delight. "Have you ever seen a village on fire?"

Fuck. This guy was a wild card.

Tapping my foot on the floor, I narrowed my eyes at the man. "I think we can both agree that I'm not your biggest fan. You crashed my wedding, threatened my family, and appear to be threatening my home. Not to mention burning down security cameras all over the village. Quit the bullshit, Your Majesty, and tell me what you really want."

"I don't know what this accusation is regarding security cameras—"

"Bull-mother-fucking-shit."

He let out a low hum of annoyance and cocked his head to one side. "You do have a way with words."

"I'm a walking, talking dictionary of profanity."

"It would appear so." He reached for something in his pocket, and panic flared within me. I pulled on my magic. It whooshed down my arm, and I crafted a sharp stone knife. The tip glinted in the light from the window.

Veigar's eyes widened, but he didn't stop moving. "Now, now. No need for violence."

There was a missing *yet* at the end of his sentence that I felt in my bones. "I'll be the one to decide that."

"Will you now?"

"Yes."

"All right," he said and plopped a triangular lump of sky-blue stone onto the table between us.

My breath hitched, and I cleared my throat to cover my own shock. If that was what I thought it was...

My shoulders slumped and I slid my hands back into my lap but gripped the knife just in case Fire Grandpa decided to go ten rounds.

He leaned back in his chair, arms crossed. "Do you know what this is?"

I shrugged. "A rock."

"More specifically?"

"A blue one."

He shook his head and bit his bottom lip. "You have quite the sense of humor, too, Deputy Guard."

"You should come to one of my stand-up shows."

"Perhaps I shall."

"I'll leave tickets for you at will-call under the name, Dolly Parton."

He let out a huff. "Enough of this coy behavior."

Here we go. I'd finally got under his skin and irked the man into truth. A dangerous game, but hopefully it would give us more information and have him play his cards right into my open and waiting hands.

"Pretend all you like that you don't know what this stone is, Lennie. I know, you know. You didn't school your features fast enough to hide your shock."

Okay, the fucker had me there. Unless he was lying to me, this was a piece from the Temple's pedestal. A piece that likely granted him some sort of access to the ancestors who could bestow powers. I swallowed hard and straightened in my seat. "Let's say I know what that is. What meaning does it have regarding your purposes here in Skolvik and request to be leader of all the fae?"

"We must find the missing pieces of the Temple and bring them back together, as they once were. For only then can we be truly united, truly one fae with the power we need to succeed."

What a load of—

"Over a thousand years ago," he started, "back when the fae factions started wandering further afield from this region, a Fjord Fae king grew restless and more powerful than the other three monarchs. After much arguing, the four factions decided to split the Temple plinth, sharing a piece with each group and leaving the Fjell Fae to protect the Temple."

Holy shit! Did Halvar even know this? I didn't dare move, not even to take another sip of coffee, and let Veigar keep talking.

"With a shard, each monarch may commune with the ancestors and ask for help in the form of greater power or skills that match their element."

Yeah, Halvar had not been this descriptive in the Temple the other day.

"It is believed," Veigar continued, "that if you can combine all the pieces in the Temple, the ancestors can grant even more magic—power previously unseen that could help our natural world and resources avoid devastation from pollution, destruction, et cetera."

Hmmm. Øyvin had once said that if monarchs died the region would fall into ruin, with animals and plants dying, rockslides becoming the norm, and pollution tainting the waters. That had certainly proven to be the case when Freija and Balder died. We'd seen an uptick in cave-ins and from what Øyvin had said, the wall beneath the fjord's surface hadn't been as strong until Reuven returned and took up the mantle as King of the Fjord.

Maybe Veigar was on to something.

I wiggled in my seat. "Why are you telling me this?"

"Because you asked, and I'm tired of your games."

Fair enough, but one thing still nagged at me. "If we brought together the pieces and you had a little chat with the ancestors, would the enhanced dosage of power help *you* in any way personally?"

He shrugged.

Nevermind. Fuck this guy. He's just another power-hungry man.

A low chuckle escaped from my chest. "Let's get your words right, shall we?" I stabbed my knife into the wooden table and the blade twanged in reply. Veigar didn't flinch. "You want to unite the fae under your rule and bring all the missing pieces of the Temple back together so *you* can obtain more power?"

He sneered. "So *we* can all gain more power to protect our natural world, protect the Nordic Fae."

"Bullshit." Smelled like it. Sounded like it. Didn't believe it for a second.

"You may not believe me—"

"You've yet to give me reason to, Your Majesty." Sweat dripped down my spine and an eerie smile crept across his lips. "What exactly would you do to make the lives of the Fjord, Forest, and Fjell Fae better? How would you lead? Would you sit on your throne of lava and command from your island in the Atlantic? Threaten people and their families if they stepped out of line?"

The muscles in his jaw clenched, but the rest of his body relaxed—that cool and calm veneer remaining firmly intact.

"Would you use the power you get from that rock and the place it may or may not belong to—"

"You know exactly where this is from," he interjected, pointing at the shard.

"I'm not done talking. Wait your turn." Heat flushed through my body like the hot Midwest winds in the middle of August. "Will you use the newfound power to help the factions in Norway and Scandinavia? Or will the only recipients be those in Iceland?"

He took a deep breath and crossed his arms. "I will help all fae. Protect us from harm. Ensure our duties to nature are upheld."

My gut twisted and bells went off in my mind. That sounded like a lot of pretty words. Partially truthful words. And yet, my gut screamed at me that we wouldn't like the consequences of this bologna sandwich. The ancient fae had split up the temple pedestal for a reason.

Maybe it was because of everything that happened over the past year to the fae in Skolvik, or maybe it was my royal magic warning me not to trust him. Either way, I didn't believe a single word.

"By doing what exactly?" I asked. "How will you uphold your responsibilities to nature?"

"By uniting the factions to help one another. Work together."

"They already do."

"We could add the Fire Fae to that mix," he replied. "Use the fire powers to assist."

"I don't know how safe that would be. Aren't you in Iceland to work with the tectonic plates and volcanoes? Won't those be a hazard out here in Norway?"

I could picture it perfectly: volcanoes erupting from the snow-capped peaks of central Norway, lava flowing down hillsides into the fjord, and forests set ablaze.

"It will be perfectly safe," Veigar said, his tone firm and confident. "I'll make sure of it."

"What about these nasty little eruptions I keep hearing tales about?" There was nothing *little* about them at all. Eyjafjallajökull erupted years ago and stopped all air travel over northern Europe for days. And that apparently wasn't the first time this man's temper or actions had caused such an explosive reaction.

Veigar brushed his finger across the table and then rubbed it against his thumb as if inspecting for dust. "Minor disruption; that won't happen here."

"They didn't sound like *minor disruptions* to me."

"Do you always believe everything you hear?"

"No, but over the past year I learned that this thing called magic is real. So, I've decided to continue doing life with more of an open mindset."

"And that doesn't apply in this situation?"

I shrugged one shoulder. "I've always questioned leaders. Hard habit to kick."

"Wise woman."

"Thank you. Now, let's get back to the main point here." I leaned forward, putting my hands on the table. "What happens when I deliver this *unifying* message and Halvar tells you to get fucked? What then?"

He mimicked my previous movement, shrugging a single shoulder. "Like I said earlier, I'll resort to other methods of persuasion that you and yours won't be able to counter."

Another day, another threat. What had my life become? One second, I was a human tourist who had missed her cruise ship, the next I was a demi-fae promoted to Deputy Head Guard within a secret society of fae in the fjords of Norway.

"Oh, I wouldn't underestimate us, Your Majesty." I slowly pressed my palm down over the hilt of my blade, magically crushing it and pulling the power back inside me.

Veigar's soulless eyes watched closely, and a single salty eyebrow quirked toward his hairline. "Such violence."

My palm slammed against the wooden table. "Judge me and move on."

He chuckled, pocketed the shard, and rose from his seat, the chair scraping against the floorboards. "That I have. And yet, I don't think I'll be going anywhere." He returned his sunglasses to his face, pushing them up the bridge of his nose.

I stood from my own seat, my shirt glued to my back. "Shame."

"Please share my offer of becoming the fae leader and requesting the stones be united with your counterparts. And keep me informed of how the Fjell Fae and others wish to proceed." He sauntered to the door and rested his fingers on the knob. "I hope to hear back from you within twenty-four hours."

I swallowed hard. "Will do." I plastered on my most bitchy smile. "And before they close for the day, I'd recommend stopping by the town's gift store. They have a miniature troll that looks just like you."

A low rumble sounded from his chest.

"Too far?" I asked, my tone chipper and hiding my own worry. That might have actually been too far. I'd never been good with lines. Always felt a need to cross them. Even to my own detriment. Definitely something I could work on. "I thought you said you liked my jokes?"

Veigar yanked open the door, the bell chiming above him. "Twenty-four hours."

With that, he strode outside and clicked the door shut behind him.

As he sauntered down the street and out of view from the window, all my bravado vanished like a balloon fart-exhaling air. I crumpled to the table, resting my forehead on my arms.

"What the fuck just happened?" I yelled to the café's empty chairs.

I may have put a big ol' target on my back, but at least I now knew for certain what Veigar wanted: To unite the fae factions and pull together all the pieces of the Temple.

With all those parts in place, and no doubt a fiery army that looked like a legion from hell itself, the Fire Fae King would be unstoppable. A shudder ran through my bones. I couldn't let that happen. Even if I got myself hurt in the process, I wouldn't let him take over.

18

LENNIE

I put away my cleaning supplies and apron, locked the café from the inside, and barreled through the streets of Skolvik. I needed to get home. I needed to tell the guys what had just happened. I needed to tell the mountain too.

Yanking my phone out of my pocket, I dialed Torsten and brought the device to my ear. The dial tone beeped twice before he picked up.

"Hello? Lennie?"

"Get me Halvar."

"What happened?"

My chest heaved, my words coming out in a jumbled, panted mess. "Veigar... Stopped by... Café."

"Hang on. Here he is."

"Speak," Halvar's gruff voice thrummed down the phone.

"I spoke to Skolvik's latest wayward tourist. He doesn't want world peace."

"Obviously."

Through erratic breaths and *ope, sorry*s as I dodged villagers out enjoying an evening stroll, I told them everything the Fire Fae King had just said, plus the fae history he'd slipped into our impromptu story time.

"Thank you for letting us know," Halvar said when I finally finished. "We will take this to the Council immediately. Can you inform Espen and Øyvin?"

I skidded to a stop outside the boat house. "About to do so."

"Good," he replied and hung up.

I tucked my phone away in my pocket and pushed open the front door.

A trill of somber music drifted past me and the smell of chocolate chip cookies and something syrupy filled the air. I cast my gaze around the room and found Øyvin at his piano and Espen on the couch reading.

"Where are the shards?" I asked, breaking the peaceful ambiance.

Both men stilled at my question, the music cutting off with a clank.

I slammed the front door behind me. "Where are the Forest and Fjord shards?"

Øyvin turned back to the piano and continued playing. "I don't know what you're talking about."

"We had this discussion the other day. I know there's a Temple of the Fae. I also now know that each fae faction has a piece from the temple that their monarchs probably use at their anointing ceremonies and to *commune* with the ancestors." Not that I'd had much success with that endeavor myself.

The music stopped again, and Øyvin's shoulders rose and fell like a marionette given slack.

Espen set aside his book, resting it on the coffee table as he took a deep breath and turned his gaze to me. "What happened, Lennie?"

"Veigar just showed me his own shard, stone, thingy. We had a chat about his five-year plan for the region."

"He did what?" Espen's voice was the lowest I'd ever heard it.

"The King of the Fire Fae decided he wanted to chat, and I took my new leadership role to heart and had a *tête-à-tête,* as the French say. He proceeded to inform me why he's in town and threw down a mother-fucking gauntlet!"

Øyvin turned on the piano bench, his eyes locked on me. "What *exactly* did he say?"

"That we could bow to him as our new leader or face his almighty wrath."

"And about the shards?"

"That he wants all of them and access to the Temple. *For only then can we all be truly united, truly one fae,*" I mimicked. "Oh, and that we have twenty-four hours to get back to him."

The temperature in the room dropped, the bubble of domestic bliss bursting. I leaned back against the door and took a deep breath, willing my heart rate to stop running wild.

"The Forest Fae shard is hidden and safe," Espen said. "No one aside from the Council of Elders knows where it is."

I tilted my chin at Øyvin. "What about the Fjord piece?"

He squared his shoulders. "The Fjord shard cannot be accessed by any non-Fjord Fae without assistance from someone with the correct credentials and ability to breathe under water."

Well that certainly protected it from outsiders. But what of the threat beneath the water and within the Fjord Fae palace?

"And what about King Reuven?" I asked. "Would he offer it up to Veigar? Would his wife? Because Veigar just told me Reuven is, and I quote, 'committed to defer to my advice and leadership.'"

Øyvin stilled and a muscle in his jaw feathered.

I pressed on. "You've already aired your concerns about Reuven and his loyalties. Do you think he's going to give it to Veigar?"

Øyvin sighed. "He might."

Yeah, we were well and truly fucked.

I told them everything else Veigar had told me, then slunk across the room and plopped onto the sofa beside Espen. "Please tell me the Forest Fae shard is a thousand miles from here."

Espen pursed his lips and blinked twice. My stomach dropped to my toes.

"It's in Skolvik, isn't it?"

He shook his head.

"Within driving distance?"

He looked to the floor and his brow furrowed as if trying to decide how much information to reveal. He brushed his hair off his forehead and sighed. "It's thirty minutes away."

"So, close but not easy to find."

That was great. Perfect even. If there was an emergency, we could probably go get it and if not, it was hidden away—

"You've kind of already seen it," Espen added.

My shoulders fell. "What?"

"You've already seen it."

Ice washed through my veins, and I slumped further into the couch cushions. Grabbing a throw pillow, I pressed it against my stomach like some squishy shield that might protect me from the direction of this conversation. "I don't remember you ever showing me a piece of blue stone."

"In the graveyard." Espen's eyes met mine and a serious tone laced his words. "At the old stave church. Where Queen Ragnhild is buried alongside Mads."

"Holy shit." I had seen it. Earlier this year when we stopped at the ancient church on our way to Alvdalen. It had been right in front of me, embedded in Ragnhild's gravestone. Above her name and beneath the engraved crown was a sky-blue stone that matched the one Veigar had just shown me. The same type of crystalline structure of the plinth in the Temple. But instead of protected within a mountain, the Forest Fae shard was out in the open for anyone, myself included, to see.

I covered my mouth with my hand. The Forest Fae stone was hidden, but also wholly unguarded. "Are you positive no one else knows its whereabouts?"

"People may have guessed, but the truth remains with the Council." He twisted to Øyvin. "You will say nothing of this."

Øyvin bowed his head. "You have my word."

Espen reached out and held my hands in his. "I ask that you don't tell Halvar either, Lennie."

"I promise." I squeezed his fingers, then swiveled and peered over my shoulder to the piano. "What about the Fjord shard, Øyvin?"

He took a deep breath and let it out through his nose.

Would he relinquish the details, or would he keep this secret, even though neither Espen nor I would ever be able to descend into the depths of the fjord like he could?

"You promise this information doesn't leave this room?" Øyvin asked, pursing his lips and giving us a serious look.

"You have my word," Espen replied.

"Me too."

He nodded like our promises would suffice. "The eye of Jörmungandr beholds the monarch's key," he said, sounding like he was extolling a prophecy not a hiding spot.

I scrunched my nose. "The what now?"

"The sea serpent, the monarch's pet, is carved into the Fjord Council chamber walls. His eye contains the stone."

Damn.

I brushed my hair behind my ears and stared at the ceiling. "So, they're basically all in Skolvik."

I didn't need to look at them to know what they were thinking, the fear that ran through their minds. I could feel it in the silence. The well-being of the fjord region and the fae in it rested in a precarious position. We were teetering on the brink of battle—one that could have devastating consequences for everything I'd grown to love and call mine over the past year.

Espen's phone beeped and he pulled it out of his pocket, swiping a finger across the screen. "Fuck."

My stomach twisted in on itself again, bile churning like a tornado. "What happened?"

"Ylva just texted. Apparently, there is a new wildfire in the skiing town, Geilo, about halfway between here and Alvdalen."

"Any fatalities?" Øyvin asked.

"Unknown. But this seems like too much of a coincidence."

"How come?" I asked.

He typed out a quick reply before setting aside his phone and refocusing on me. "Because the town is very similar to Skolvik as far as its position. It's nestled in a valley, surrounded by forested slopes, and has limited road access."

Øyvin grumbled.

"So you think, what, that Veigar is doing a test run before moving on Skolvik?" He wouldn't do that right? After we'd just chatted. Or maybe our conversation was a distraction while someone else ran tests for him further inland?

"Maybe. I've instructed Ylva and some other soldiers to scour the region and keep watch over different zones. They will alert us of any suspicious movements or fires nearby."

"What information does Ylva have on Geilo?" Øyvin leaned forward and resting his elbows on his knees.

"Authorities aren't certain of starting location nor cause, but the ground is almost as dry as it is out here."

Fuck. I'd never witnessed a wildfire in person, but based on the photos I'd seen online and the dehydrated woods, it was little wonder fear had engulfed the room.

"Okay, so we have wildfires in Norway that might be started by a Fire Fae and Temple shards to deal with in addition to a walking volcano living among us," I said, hating each and every word as they came out.

Øyvin grumbled again, his gaze locked on something on the floor.

Espen straightened, a determined look washing over his features. "Veigar can't get hold of the shards." He turned to me. "He can't get access to the Temple."

"I doubt he's going anywhere near the Fjell considering him and Halvar aren't exactly besties."

"Halvar is in danger." Øyvin's ominous words settled over me like a joke.

I scoffed. "No one is a threat to Halvar."

The guys looked at one another, and my heart skipped a beat.

"That may be true," Espen replied. "But if there ever was anyone to truly match him in battle..."

My stomach twisted itself into a knot and I squeezed the pillow in my lap a little tighter. "I thought you were the almighty *Destroyer*? In fact, I've heard words from Halvar's own mouth, that you would always be a threat."

Espen straightened up like I'd just given him a second-hand compliment, his eyes wide with excitement, floppy hair bouncing. "Really?"

"Yes, really. Back when you were poisoned, he warned me that you might be behind the shit going down with the fjell, the landslides, etcetera."

Øyvin's lips turned down at the corners. "He had a point."

"You don't believe that, do you?" Espen's voice notched higher, his eyes widening. "You both know I would never purposefully cause harm with those powers. Not here. Never here. Not unless it was my last option."

"I do know," I said and took his hands in mine. "Very well. Which is why I defended you. Told Halvar he was full of shit."

"Did you use those exact words?" Øyvin's voice rumbled.

"I... Erm... He got the gist." I highly doubted I'd ever tell the big guy he was full of shit, at least not to his face. I didn't have a death wish. "Either way. You're all mighty and powerful."

Espen beamed and brushed his thumbs over my knuckles. "I am. But both Veigar and Halvar have more experience, more life led than I do."

Note to self, find out exactly how old Halvar is.

"So, that's why they're a threat to each other?"

Espen half-nodded, half-shook his head. "Yes and no. They have battlefield experience and are both immensely powerful beings. They can raze swaths of soldiers in a single attack, pierce through attackers with fire or stone, and sever heads with their bare hands."

A shiver ran through me as the echo of Balder's head being ripped off by Halvar flashed through my mind.

Øyvin cleared his throat. "They are god-like tacticians that should not be underestimated under any circumstances."

"Ruthless," Espen added.

I wiped my hands across my face. We couldn't have them starting an all-out brawl in the streets of Skolvik. The picturesque wooden buildings wouldn't withstand Halvar's wrath, let alone Veigar's fire.

"What can we do?" I looked between the two men, hoping they might have an answer that didn't include a deadly dance between the fae factions.

Their eyes narrowed, both of them mired in thought.

A moment later Espen rolled his shoulders and puffed his chest. "We prepare as best we can and do our best to keep Veigar away from the other shards and Temple."

"Agreed," Øyvin said. "And we find ways to remove him from Skolvik."

It wasn't ideal, but it wasn't nothing. Perhaps fluid plans were best in these kinds of situations? Maybe we needed to be willing and able to pivot at a moment's notice? I certainly had enough experience of shit hitting the fan—even in the last year alone—that I knew how to triage a problem. Whatever happened, we'd face it together.

"What a fucking mess," I muttered and stifled a yawn. "And what a day."

Espen's hooded gaze flicked to mine and he tilted his chin up. "Come here, wife."

A wave of warmth washed over me, prickling against my skin. The things that man said and did could melt me into a puddle of love in seconds—and I never wanted that feeling to end. I set aside the throw pillow and scooted across the couch. Espen opened his arms, and I snuggled into his embrace with a sigh. Adrenaline ebbed from my system like a draining battery.

This.

This right here was what life was meant for.

The little moments of love and peace that punctuated the wild and crazy days.

And I loved this life. The village I'd been abandoned in, the secret magical world I'd stumbled across, and the men I now called mine. No matter the damage it did to my body, my mind, or my precious sleep schedule, I'd defend it until my last breath. Protect them at all costs.

I peered over at Øyvin, whose eyes snapped to mine like he could hear my thoughts as loud and clear as his own. The look alone sent goosebumps across my arms. "Get over here," I whispered.

Without saying a word, nor breaking eye contact, he strode over to the sofa and settled beside us. He traced a finger up the side of my thigh, and I squirmed in Espen's arms. Øyvin's hand skirted up my side and swept between my breasts before coming up to cup my cheek. A tiny smile curved the corner of his lips, and I melted all over again.

"Arms up, Trouble."

I leaned away from Espen, lifted my arms over head, and let out another yawn. Øyvin gently gripped the hem of my shirt and, in one fluid move, had it off me. Folding it into a neat square, he set the material on the coffee table.

I nestled back into Espen's hold, and he kissed the top of my head. The warmth of his body pressed against my curves, and I inhaled the scent that always lingered on him, the leather and moss smell that I now associated with home. It was like the forest he'd sworn to protect clung to him no matter where he went.

A clicking noise sounded, and my breasts dropped down. Espen peeled my bra off with a moan of a hungry man.

Øyvin palmed one boob and nuzzled into my neck, inhaling like he needed my air to live. Espen cupped my other breast, and heat welled between my thighs at the sensation of them worshiping and caressing my curves. The way they pleasured my body was like musicians composing a symphony. They knew which strings to pluck, which parts of my body would elicit notes of pure satisfaction.

Øyvin's fingers slipped from my breast down under my jeans and between my thighs, finding my center ready and wanting. He stroked that mound of need and tender sparks hummed through my body. Eyes fluttering shut, a moan slipped from me and Espen caught it with his lips.

This was the perfect Friday night. The best way to end a chaotic week. And there was one way to make it even better. "Come upstairs with me," I mumbled.

Both men rose to their feet, and Espen pulled me up off the sofa.

His smile reached the corners of his eyes. "Gladly."

19

LENNIE

My eyes peeled open, goop filling the corners as late-summer rays streamed through the gap in the curtains. Lying on my side, I stretched and arched my back, brushing my fingers and stomach against two other bodies. "What happened?" I asked, my voice raspy.

The last thing I remembered from the night before was snuggling up with my guys and kissing them. Had I fallen asleep during sex? Would they actually continue without me? No, that couldn't be right. Espen would never. Øyvin on the other hand... No, he wouldn't either. He'd spout something about ethics too. And, honestly, if they had sex with me while I was asleep it'd be both weird and rude.

I peered over my shoulder and found the Fjord Fae watching me, his blue eyes twinkling like the tops of water ripples in morning light. "Good morning, Trouble."

Turning beneath the soft duvet, I faced Øyvin and brushed my hands across his bare chest. A low rumble hummed against my palms.

"What happened last night?" I asked again.

"You fell asleep," he replied.

"Really?"

"As soon as your head hit the pillow."

I groaned. Fuck Halvar and his coitus interrupting workouts. I needed to give the man a new nickname. No longer would he be *Big Guy*. Oh no no. He was now *Cockblocker*.

A palm brushed over my ass, and I let out a sigh.

"You did seem rather tired during our chat yesterday," Espen said and nuzzled into my neck while wrapping his arm around my stomach.

"Yeah, but who falls asleep with two guys pawing at them?"

"You," Øyvin deadpanned.

I groaned again. "Can we make up for lost time?"

Espen's lips spread into a smile and trailed up the side of my neck. Øyvin brought his palm against my chest again, kneading one of my boobs. My nipple rose to attention, and he rewarded it by circling his thumb around it. A moan slipped from me and morphed into a yawn. I did my best to swallow and hide it.

"Don't fall asleep again," Øyvin said and stopped his ministrations.

"We can't have sex if you're going to doze off," Espen added.

Fuck. They were right. I couldn't fall asleep on them. Not again.

I shimmied free of their grasps and shuffled to the end of the bed before falling off with a thump. Scrambling to my feet, I set my hands on my hips and flipped my hair over my shoulder.

"Let me go make us coffee. That'll for sure keep me awake," I said. "It's been like a week since we've done the deed, and I don't want to miss another *yoga* session because I'm either drunk or asleep."

Two restrained grins peered over the white duvets.

"I'll take that as a yes, then."

Espen nodded vigorously.

Without further preamble, I yanked on a pair of leggings and a random T-shirt from the dresser, which from the clean linen smell and white color, was probably Øyvin's. The wooden steps creaked beneath my feet as I loped downstairs, the smell of brine and a cool morning dew brushing across my exposed skin. Water lapped against the underside of the house and golden light seeped through the windows of the main living space.

I aimed for the kitchen and set to work on making some coffees. Two black and one with plenty of sugar and creamer. If I was going to stay awake all day, I needed the caffeine and sugar-high.

As the sugar landed in my mug with a plop, sending a drop of coffee over the rim, the doorbell rang.

I stilled.

Who the hell would be visiting us at this time of day? And on a Saturday? All our friends were usually fast asleep or, in Ylva's case, patrolling the forest to get over the self-inflicted hangover from a heavy Friday night at Fisken.

The peeling ring of the doorbell echoed through the house again, and I tossed the tablespoon I'd been using into the sink. Metal on metal clattered, matching the incessant ringing.

"All right, all right. I'm coming."

I padded across the room and yanked open the front door.

A shock of spiky white hair, a wrinkled face free of makeup, and a pressed button-down uniform greeted me.

"Bente," I choked out.

What the hell was Espen's boss doing here? "Espen is upstairs. Let me go get him."

She cleared her throat. "Evelyn Solbakke Martin"—my eyes widened and my heart stopped beating—"you're under arrest for arson. Please come with me."

20

LENNIE

Well, I'd done it. I'd officially landed myself at the police station. After a year of avoiding Espen's place of employment, I'd been perp-walked here sans-bra by an official summons from the Chief of Police herself. The consequences of my actions were biting my ass and not in the pleasurable way I'd prefer.

I glanced around the interrogation room I'd been bundled into. It was cozier than expected. The white-washed walls were bland, but there was a slight yellow tint to them that made the room feel sun-drenched, even without any windows. A two-way mirror adorned the wall behind Bente and a clock ticked away over the door to the hallway. It wasn't as austere and intimidating as the one's I'd seen in movies and on TV shows. But happily basic would be a good description.

Bente settled into the wooden chair across from me and set down a pile of folders on the table. Her collar cinched around her throat, pressing against her neck, while the silver threads of the town's police department emblem on her breast-pocket sparkled at me in greeting. "Mrs. Solbakke Martin—"

"Call me Lennie, please."

"Lennie. Can you please explain what you did last year on the night of December 23rd?"

Well, fuck. I sucked in a breath. I was challenged by my now partners to raise my own ear magic and walk across the village while holding the ear-mirage in place. That went to shit when I accidentally magicked myself naked. Fuck out of luck, I decided to bolt. Miraculously my night ended with me getting plowed by the aforementioned gentlemen. It'd been a lose-win situation, but that was almost a year ago.

"Well..." Bente prodded, her brows raised toward her gel-infused hairline.

I clasped my hands together on the table. "I lost a bet."

"Really? That's how you want to explain what happened?" She nudged a manila folder across the table with my name on it.

I didn't need to open it to know what was inside. Images and screenshots of my naked ass barreling through town, hoping I wouldn't get picked up by anyone's security cameras. Unluckily for me, the town had been riddled with them, including a goddamn webcam that live broadcast the harbor to the town's website. By New Year's Eve I was the proud owner of a new nickname: The Streaking American.

"Look, I made a grave mistake. Had my cheeks caught on camera and have to live with the embarrassment of that for the rest of my life." Which was probably a damn sight longer than her own now that I was a demi-fae. "The footage captured of me is unfortunate, but I did not burn those cameras."

"So, you *do* know where my questions are heading?"

I nodded. The burned cameras had been the main topic of discussion at the café this week. Who knew how long it had actually been going on for. But I had my suspicions.

"As the woman at the center of our investigation, I have some questions for you. Please answer them honestly and we will get this over with."

Would I need a lawyer present for this? Did Skolvik have any lawyers? I didn't recall ever seeing a legal office, but maybe there were some who worked remotely and might be able to stop me putting my foot in my mouth. I pinched my lips together and motioned for Bente to proceed.

"Where were you yesterday morning?" she asked.

"Working at the…" Oh, wait a second. "I was running a bit late, but working at Oddvar's Café."

"Why were you late?"

Exhausted from relentless training with Halvar and Fjell Fae soldiers. "Overslept. Accidentally turned off my alarm instead of hitting snooze."

"Can anyone vouch for your time of departure from home? Did anyone see when you left the house?"

Fuck. No, nobody could. Espen and Øyvin had both left for work by the time I scrambled out of bed in a panic.

I wrung my hands in my lap and shifted in my seat, the chair squeaking beneath me.

"Where were you three nights ago? Around eleven o'clock?"

With Halvar. I'd been training with Halvar, but she couldn't know that. I swallowed hard. "In bed."

Her eyes narrowed. "Can anyone vouch for that who doesn't live in your household?"

"No."

"I see. What about four nights ago around midnight?"

Same. Training.

At my lack of reply, Bente pulled her phone out of her pocket and tapped on the screen before turning it to me. A video clip from the town's webcam, pointed toward town square and the harbor. A blonde figure lumbered across the frame, stopped in the middle to catch their breath, then kept going.

I winced. "Evening stroll?" Even I didn't buy the wavered answer.

Bente shook her head then picked up another folder and scooted my cheery Christmas moon-shots to the other edge of the table. Opening the new folder, she pulled out some large photos and positioned them in front of me.

"Do you recognize these buildings?"

The top left of the jewelry store stared back at me. The white swirly lettering marked the front windows and in the center of the frame was a singed spot, blackening the white wood siding. I turned my focus to the other photo. The red-painted library was well cared for, window boxes blooming with multi-colored flowers, a signboard outside promoting the children's reading hour on Saturday mornings, and windows filled with drawings by local school kids of their favorite characters. All that joy was marred by a charred patch, the black mark spreading like an explosion had hit the right corner of the building.

"Those are the *Gullsmed* and *Biblioteket*," I said. Hopefully my use of the local tongue would buy me some favor in this situation. Because right now, things weren't looking good for me.

"Can you tell me how those cameras were burned?"

I leaned back and furrowed my eyebrows. "Umm, no. But I could make some guesses."

"What would those guesses be?"

I couldn't tell her the truth. Studying the photos again and keeping my eyes firmly on the images, I started spitballing ideas. "Blow torch. Lighter. One of those fire stick thingys you guys handed out on Christmas Eve at the caroling event—"

"A *fakkel*?"

I snapped my fingers and pointed at her. "Yeah, that."

Her head shook like she didn't believe me.

"A firework," I continued, grasping at invisible straws of hope. "A flare. Matches? Oh no wait, what about a flamethrower? That could reach the eaves of the buildings where the cameras are."

"Have you ever seen a flamethrower here in Skolvik?"

My knees bounced and I pressed my clammy hands together. "No, I haven't."

"Where would you consider buying one?"

"Well, first of all, Chief— Can I call you Chief?" She shrugged like she didn't really give a damn. "Well, Chief, I'd consider purchasing any of the aforementioned items from the camping and hiking store."

"Really?" Her brow's pinched together. "Why there?"

I shrugged. "Because I've seen a lot of random stuff in that store that doesn't exactly fit the bill for hiking or camping. Like, who needs a four-burner grill on their hiking trip? Or a unicorn shower curtain? Or allergy-friendly laundry detergent?"

"I wouldn't take that large of a grill on a hiking trip, but one of the small charcoal ones are wonderful for day hikes."

"Really?"

She nodded and then tapped the photo of the library. "Did you burn down the cameras, Lennie? Was it to erase the photographs? To seek revenge for—"

"Revenge for what?"

Bente brought back the Little Christmas Eve Lunar Event folder and pushed it toward me. I flipped it open and found picture after picture of my buns and boobs sprinting through the village. I knew it had been bad—the locals were still laughing at it months later—but seeing them all spread out like this... It was little wonder that Bente thought I was on a revenge spree.

Shutting the incriminating folder, I shoved it back across the table. "It wasn't me, and you have no proof."

"We have very strong motive and unaligned accounts of your whereabouts during the arsons."

I wiped my hands across my face. Was this happening or was I still asleep? Please, Satan and whatever deities were watching, let this be a nightmare I could wake up from and laugh about later.

Bente stared at me, eyes narrowed, surveying me like my silence might hold the answers to her questions.

"Look, it wasn't me." My mouth went dry, and my legs wouldn't stop bouncing of their own accord. It was like my own muscles were nervous of the woman, wanting to abandon me in my time of need. "Where is Espen?"

She hadn't let him talk to me on our walk over here. But if Espen could chat with Bente, he could tell her I was innocent. If anyone could vouch for me being a somewhat-kind-of-good-slash-improving citizen of Skolvik, it was my husband.

"He and Øyvin are in the hallway waiting," she replied.

"Can I see them? Just for a second?"

"No. Did you burn all of the cameras in the village?"

Nausea roiled through my stomach. Maybe I did need a lawyer?

21

ESPEN

A buzz of energy ran through the entire station, from the glossy front desk to the white-washed hallway outside our two interrogation rooms. My shoes squeaked against the floor as I paced back and forth in front of the three gray chairs that sat opposite the rooms, dodging Øyvin's outstretched legs as he pretended to nap in one of the rigid armchairs.

"You knew this would happen eventually," he mumbled, not bothering to open his eyes.

I huffed. He wasn't wrong, but I thought I could protect her from her own antics. Stop this inevitability from happening.

Pranks and jokes? Sure.

But arson? She would never.

She cared about the village and her neighbors. That wasn't the Lennie I knew and loved. She didn't have some secret vendetta against anyone here in Skolvik.

"It wasn't her and you know it."

A low grumble emanated from the Fjord Fae.

"She wouldn't. She must've been framed."

"Yes, but those security camera photos of her aren't great, and the fact that she hasn't already been charged with public indecency for her actions on Little Christmas Eve is a miracle."

I pushed my hands through my hair, pulling it off my forehead. "This is really bad."

"Uh-huh."

"But they don't have any evidence for this, though. For the burned cameras. We didn't find any link or footage of the culprit earlier this week."

"No images of a perpetrator at all?" Øyvin sat up properly in the chair and rested his elbows on his knees.

"None. The footage cuts out as flames wrap around the device. It's as if someone is standing behind the camera or at a distance, purposefully avoiding the field of view."

Øyvin grumbled. "I think that tells us all we need to know."

"It does, but it can't be proved to the... erm... locals." No, the humans couldn't know that a Fire Fae walked among them, torching their precious security devices. They had to find a culprit, and the only viable option right now appeared to be my wife, even if the evidence was circumstantial and reaching.

"They shouldn't be arresting her," I muttered. Sure, they could bring her in for questioning as she was guilty of public indecency, but still... I plopped into the chair beside Øyvin and raked my hands through my hair again sending the already messy strands into a bird's nest of disarray. "I just want them to let me in."

"You're her husband. You know that's a conflict of interest."

I was, and I did. But that didn't stop the swell of emotions growing within me like uncontrollable weeds. I wanted to rip them out and replace them with the bubble of happiness I'd woken up to: the feel of Lennie next to me, the warm duvet cocooning us as the morning sunlight doused us in a gentle glow. She was always beautiful, but there was something ethereal about her in the morning, however grouchy she may be. It was as if the sun radiated from *her*, illuminating her in a halo worthy of an angel.

Øyvin cleared his throat, drawing me from my thoughts, and peered over at me. "We also don't know *exactly* what evidence they have or don't have. They might have kept something from you."

He was right...

But that didn't mean I couldn't find out. I jumped from the chair and strode down the hallway to the front desk. Jens, the station manager, perched in a tall office chair behind the high white-and-gray desk, his glasses sliding down his nose as he peered at his computer screen.

"Jens!"

The man startled.

"Sorry to disturb you." I rested my forearm against the tabletop and gave him a smile. "Was there any new evidence brought in on the camera investigation?"

The lump in his throat bobbed. "Um... I... Erm... I really can't say, Officer Solbakke Martin."

"Don't worry. I'm one of the investigators on the case."

He dropped his chin to his chest and stared at his hands, wringing them in his lap. "Y-you were removed."

I reared back but kept my tone calm and friendly. "When?"

"T-this morning. The Chief made the request before bringing in your wife."

My smile fell, and I took a deep breath to steady my thoughts. This would be fine. We could still handle this. It was protocol to remove an officer from a case if one of their family members was involved, and I didn't want to break the Station's rules. However much I didn't like them right now, they were in place for good reason. We couldn't have conflicts of interest.

Lennie would be fine. I had to trust her. She may have had an uncanny ability to land herself in trouble, but she was kind, determined, and smart—traits I truly admired in her. She would explain the mix up to

Bente and set the record as straight as possible without revealing the Fae secret.

A colossal boom sounded outside, and I gripped the edge of the desk as the walls and floor trembled. Dust rained from the ceiling, showering us all in a thin layer of debris. The plant pots flanking the front door crashed to the floor, cracking and spilling soil over the polished tiles.

What was that?

"Earthquake?" Jen muttered from where he'd half-ducked beneath the desk.

I shook my head and peered around the space, assessing for any damage. Smooth walls sans cracks stared back at me, the floors equally unmarred.

Jens sneezed, his eyes watering.

"Bless you," I muttered.

No, it wasn't an earthquake. Something, or *someone*, had happened outside. And I'd wager it was the start of another grueling chapter in my life.

Adrenaline flooded my system, and my thoughts calmed, focusing on the most important things.

I rushed down the hallway toward my wife and friend.

The door to the interrogation room flew open, and Bente popped her head out into the hallway. "Everybody all right?"

I skidded to a stop and nodded, but my brow remained furrowed. Whatever just happened outside was bad. Part of me wanted to run and check, see exactly what had caused the explosion. The other part didn't want to leave Lennie. Either way, I took the opportunity presented to me and strode for the open door. "Lennie! Are you okay?"

Bente's arm shot out, bracing against the frame and blocking my path.

"It wasn't me. The arson or that boom!" Lennie yelled back, probably hoping people would start to catch on that not all calamities in the village stemmed from her. And, for the most part, that was true.

A low rumble emanated from behind me, and I peered over my shoulder. Øyvin stood a few feet away, glaring at Bente. She pursed her lips and didn't waver in her stance.

The sound of ringing phones and yelling echoed down the hallway, matching the harried rhythm of my heartbeats.

"Bente, let me in to check on Lennie, please."

She opened her mouth to speak, but smacking footsteps drew our attention away.

Jens came running down the corridor, eyes wide, panic engraved in the lines on his face. "We have a massive problem," he said between panted breaths.

"What was it?" Bente and I asked at the same time.

"The oil plant down the fjord exploded."

Øyvin stepped into the man's path, towering over him. "What!"

Poor Jens looked like he was about to wet his trousers but nodded.

"Okay," Bente said and exited the interrogation room. "We need to gather all officers. Jens, put out the call including members off duty. I also want a direct line open to the village fire station in case we need to contact them. Our response will follow the protocol laid out in the disaster plan. Jens, please have that PDF sent to all officers as a reminder too."

"Yes, ma'am." The man spun on the spot, sprinting down the hallway.

"Now, you three."

I turned to Bente, awaiting orders, and found Lennie had snuck into the open doorway. She wiggled her brows at me, and I bit my lip to hide my growing smile.

"I'm going to let the questioning go for now, Mrs. Solbakke Martin," Bente said, facing Lennie. "You're not *off-the-hook* as you Americans say, but I may ask you to return to the station at a later date for more information."

"Yes, ma'am," Lennie replied with a salute.

Bente pivoted on her heels and looked up at Øyvin. "As we have you here. I'll have the police boat take a few officers down fjord, but might we borrow your boat to assess the situation too?"

"Of course. I was planning a trip down the fjord to check on the waters myself." Though knowing what I did about him, the Fjord Fae probably hadn't planned on taking his boat. Swimming over there was likely faster, but... We needed to keep up appearances. However annoying that might be under current circumstances.

"Excellent. Thank you." Bente strode down the hallway and we all followed after her. "I want as many eyes on this as possible."

I couldn't agree more.

22

ØYVIN

After a quick stop at the boathouse for Lennie to put on a bra and "I Heart Skolvik" sweater, all four of us climbed aboard my boat and set off down the fjord. Wind lashed at our faces as the shiny, white vessel skipped across the water at full speed, keeping pace with the silver-and-black police boat, its blue light whirring above the skipper's alcove.

I stood behind the wheel with Espen between me and Bente, while Lennie bounced up and down on the uncushioned seat on the prow. My stomach twisted in on itself, adrenaline coursing through my veins.

Who did this?

How bad was it?

How many creatures had already been impacted beneath the water-line?

Bente had her phone to her ear, talking to someone about the cause behind the explosion. Unfortunately, I could only hear what she said and not the other person on the line.

"No casualties?" she asked, and I held my breath. "Good."

I let out a sigh of relief and caught Espen doing the same as he peered ahead at the scenery, his face marred with lines. Emerald pines shot into the sky along the fjord's flanks while water sloshed against the rugged shoreline. Jagged peaks and cliffs loomed above, casting shadows over parts of the water. Spray splashed my face as we hurtled along, and I was glad I'd put on my long-sleeved shirt this morning. It may have been late Summer, but the wind was unforgiving as it raked across my cheeks and promised cooler days to come.

As we rounded the bend in the fjord, chaos unfolded before us, and I slowed the purring engines.

My fingers clenched around the wheel as I sucked in a smoky breath.

On the fjord's left embankment sat the oil refinery. Copper and gray silos the size of three-story buildings and thick pipes sprawled along the water's edge. Flames licked every inch of the property, and a tower of black smoke billowed into the clear blue sky, blocking out the sun. Wailing sirens and the smell of burned metal and fuel filled the air like an invisible, toxic cloud. Firetrucks dotted the scene, with specialized tanks and foam aimed at the main part of the blaze. Even a fireboat floated along nearby, its water jet set on the foliage surrounding the massive inferno.

I cut the engines and let us drift, as the intense swell of heat buffeted our faces. "Shit."

Bente hung up with a clipped goodbye, shoved her phone into her jacket's breast pocket, and sighed.

"Cause?" I asked.

"They suspect a pipe leak, but won't know more until the flames are out and the site can be safely accessed. All employees have been evacuated and accounted for, though."

That was good. But my thoughts swam back to Reuven's request. He'd asked to monitor the waters around the oil refinery only a few days ago. Had he known something was about to happen? He wouldn't have been behind this, would he? Or was he warning me about his wife? His father-in-law?

My gaze landed on Lennie, and she mouthed, "Why?"

I shrugged. Until I could get closer, get into the water, I couldn't be sure. I scanned the fjord, searching for oil and pollutants in the waterway.

Bente cleared her throat. "They're concerned about the chemicals used to put out the fire spilling back into the fjord."

"As they should," I mumbled. Tension gripped my shoulders. If Bente weren't here, I'd jump in and start cleaning up.

Fuck, I had to do something.

I glanced to Espen and found his gaze locked on the terrifying scene. He brushed his hand across his beard, his chest rising and falling in jagged motions like he was trying to contain an outburst or a panic attack.

"You all right, Espen?" Lennie asked, having also noticed the unusual behavior.

He flicked his attention to her, those amber eyes filled with fear and something I couldn't quite name, but reminded me of when he'd shied away from discussing the southern war that happened twenty years ago. He quivered minutely and straightened up. "I'm glad no one is hurt."

"Me too," Lennie muttered.

Bente waved over the police boat and ordered them to move toward shore and take a closer look. The officers did as requested, cruising closer to the scene.

"You stay here," Bente said with a nod to me.

"Yes, ma'am."

I looked back out across the water. This was all too suspicious. An explosion at the local oil refinery in the weeks following the Fire Fae King's arrival and coffee shop proclamations? There was a good chance this wasn't just an errant pipe failure. My money was on the Fire Fae King or his daughter. We couldn't trust either of them, or anyone affiliated with them. Who knew how long it would take for someone to come forward and claim responsibility or for us to investigate?

For now, though, I needed to do my job.

"Lennie? Trouble?" I whispered and Lennie twisted in her seat to face me. I cocked my head toward Bente behind her back and mouthed, "Distract her for ten seconds."

I needed to assess the water. Feel it. Check it.

Lennie rose from her seat and wobbled slightly as the boat bobbed. Shifting closer to Espen, she bumped into him as the vessel swayed. He wrapped an arm around her, steadying and pressing her against his chest. Those big brown eyes peered up at him taking on a doe-like look that some would confuse for innocence, but I knew better. That was a tell-tale sign she was up to no good.

She pointed to the blackest part of the refinery. "That looks like it might be where the fire started."

Bente's gaze followed her finger, while Espen furrowed his eyebrows and peered at me, searching for clarity. I leaned over the edge of the boat, one hand centimeters above the waterline. I tilted my head and widened my eyes.

Distract her. Now.

He nodded to my non-verbal request, and spun, giving me his back and blocking me from view.

I dipped my hand into the water and pushed some of my magic into it. A trill of warmth skittered down my arm and burst into the water. It sung back to me, but not its usual harmonious tune. No, this felt grim, darker, like something had cut the strings to the keys. I raised my hand, dragging some of the liquid upward for a closer look. Rainbow swirls slid over the curve of water. I inhaled sharply and pursed my lips.

Fuck.

Slicks of oil had made it into the fjord.

I needed to get down there fast. Send soldiers out to clean up before it could spread and start killing the local wildlife. And it wasn't just creatures that lived within the water that would be threatened by this. Birds that used this waterway for nourishment could mar their feathers with this mess, and humans could get it on their skin if they weren't careful.

I plopped the crest of water back where it belonged and caught Lennie watching out of the corner of her eye, her brows rising in question.

"There's already oil in the water."

She spun, Espen's arm still wrapped around her middle like he was worried she might fall in even though she was nowhere near the railing.

"What can you see?" she asked.

"Can you see a slick?" Bente chimed in, peering around Espen. "I can't see any signs."

"It's just beneath the surface." I returned to my spot behind the driver's console. "I wouldn't be surprised if it gets worse within the next few minutes."

Espen let out a frustrated hum and Lennie sagged in his hold.

This was bad. Really, really, bad. Not only was there a massive fire emitting who knew what kind of pollutants into the air, but oil had seeped into my fjord. If the Fjord Fae didn't clear it up quickly and inconspicuously, lives dependent on it would be harmed.

"We should go back to town," Bente said. "We've got work to do at the station."

Lennie turned to face her again. "And you're sure you don't need me to come back in for questioning?"

The evidence didn't look good, but they couldn't hold her unless they had something concrete.

Bente scanned Lennie once from toe to head. "Not today."

Thank fuck.

Lennie slumped against Espen. "Thank you."

"I agree, let's head inland," I announced, starting the engines again. "I'd like to see how far this oil might stretch."

"Agreed," Bente replied.

"Start her up, Captain," Lennie said and wobbled back to her perch at the front of the boat.

The engines roared to life, matching the fear igniting inside me. Whoever was behind the explosion, it felt like they'd just set off a cannon marking the start of a war.

23

LENNIE

We wound our way back down the fjord at a significantly slower pace. While the others focused on the water, looking for rainbow-colored sheens and lumps of black detritus, I focused on our surroundings. I'd never been this far down the fjord, at least not from this vantage point. The first and last time I'd been down here had been with Øyvin *beneath* the water.

The mountain peaks were harsher here, more dramatic, like they were cast in a production and doing their damnedest to live up to the expectation set for them. Skolvik harbor was a dot down the way, surrounded by trees and steep hills. My gaze drifted to the left mountainside, and a reminder of something the Fjell Fae Council had said danced through my thoughts. "Do you think there may have been any other impacts from the explosion?"

"There is a crack up there." Bente pointed to where I'd just been looking.

"Yeah, would that be impacted? Could the blast have widened it?" And what would the culprits stand to gain from that? My money was on Veigar or Salka being behind this. Or perhaps it was whoever had been starting wildfires in other parts of the country.

Bente narrowed her eyes. "You know about the fissure?"

"Ummm." I swallowed hard and pulled my hair into a ponytail. "Yeah, I saw it on a hike. Some folks have been talking about it in the café too."

Bente nodded like that made sense—it had been a common discussion topic in Skolvik since before I'd arrived. "It's a significant concern for the village. If that part of the mountain fully dislodges and falls into the fjord, not only will it take all that forest with it, it'll cause a massive tsunami-style wave that would wash out the entire town."

Blood rushed from my head, and I clenched my fists at the horrific image Bente painted with her words.

"Is there anything you can do?" I asked.

"We have an evacuation protocol in place." Bente sighed. "I don't ever want to use it. But if that piece weakens, I'll have to ask villagers to leave their homes." She stared back down the fjord. The refinery was gone from view, hidden by the bends in the waterway, yet the black plume of smoke in the sky marked the problem. "But we may already have one such issue on our hands."

My eyebrows pinched together. "What do you mean?"

Øyvin cleared his throat. "She means, the water may be severely polluted by that explosion. Many people rely on these waters for their livelihood."

Shit. I hadn't thought about that. Of course, it would impact the people who relied on the fjord for a living and not just the wildlife and fae that called it home.

"But that crack," Bente said, drawing my attention back to her. "That crack is our biggest threat. These waters are known to be almost self-healing. The pollutants evaporate like magic. So, with help from our crews and some government resources, we can have the oil slick cleared in no time."

I refrained from looking at Øyvin, lest my face reveal any of my thoughts surrounding *why* exactly the fjord had a reputation among the locals. Instead, I peered back up at the mountain in question. The one I was all too aware of thanks to my connection to the Fjell Fae within it.

An idea sprung to mind.

"Bente," I started, my tone cautious and calm. "Why don't Espen and I hike up to the fissure and make sure the explosion didn't cause any further ruptures? I can bring my camera and take some photos for you."

My beautiful camera hadn't had an outing in a while, and this would be a useful way to get it outdoors while also helping the town.

"That would be wonderful," she said. "Thank you, Lennie. We have laser systems up there to warn of any shifts, but I'd like updated images. I can share them with the geologists in Oslo too."

I smiled. "Happy to help."

A few minutes later we docked the boat alongside the boathouse and climbed ashore.

"I'll head back to the station, please report your findings to me as soon as you return from your hike."

"Of course, boss," Espen said, and I nodded in agreement, glad to lend a hand.

We rounded the corner to the front of the building, our footfalls tapping against the wood planks before muffling against the asphalt of the road.

As we said our goodbyes, Bente tilted her chin toward the house. "There's a note on your door."

The three of us spun on the spot.

A small, white envelope was taped to the front door with *Lennie* scrawled across it.

Who's handwriting was that?

24

LENNIE

We said goodbye to Bente and watched her disappear down the road before scrambling to the front door. I yanked the envelope off and ripped it open. Inside was a *Greetings from Skolvik* postcard with an aerial shot of the village and fjord. I turned it over and my stomach flipped into my throat.

I grow weary of waiting. Your deliberation time has concluded.
I gave you ample warning.
- V

"Fuck, he really did mean twenty-four hours," I muttered and handed the card to the guys who'd been reading over my shoulders. "And I haven't heard shit from Halvar. Not that I was expecting to. This non-reply is probably the big guy's way of saying 'go fuck yourself.'"

"Well, I think it's safe to assume the explosion was Veigar's calling card too," Espen said.

"Yes, to both." Øyvin grunted and peered at the water lapping along the dock. "I'm going to head below. Start clearing up his mess."

I rose to my tiptoes and pressed a kiss to Øyvin's lips, drawing his attention to me. He cupped my head with his hand and deepened the kiss like he needed to reassure himself of my well-being. If I could, I'd stay here with both of my guys, kissing and cuddling—finally having sex with them—as the world collapsed around us. But I wouldn't. Couldn't. I had a responsibility to them, the mountain, and my home. With a whimper, I extracted myself from Øyvin's hold. "Stay safe."

"Whatever you do, stay out of the water until I say so," he said.

Espen and I both nodded.

A moment later we entered the house as a gentle splash sounded from outside.

After I quickly changed into hiking gear and Espen slipped into his police uniform, we trudged up the slope on the north side of the fjord and headed for the fissure in the mountain. My camera dangled against my chest while sweat beaded beneath my T-shirt and behind my ears. The cool breeze was a balm as it washed over my heated skin and wound through the forest. Thick trees rose all around us, their needles and leaves weaving a dense tapestry that let through peeks of blue sky.

I peered to my right and found a gentle grin on Espen's lips. The sight warmed my heart and reminded me of the first time we'd hiked together on the trails up here. That day he'd told me all about the Forest Fae and shown me his healing magic by coaxing a sapling into growth. Now look how far we'd come.

I slid my hand into his. His amber eyes found mine, those damn luscious lashes of his framing the warm gaze like it was in a museum.

"What?" he asked.

A sigh drifted from my chest as my shoulders rose and fell. "Just thinking about how much has happened in the past year."

"I was thinking the same."

"Really?"

"Mm-hmm. How we went from you punching me to going on a dinner date. Then hiking around here to marrying you. We may have faced a lot of challenges in that time, but it's been the best year of my life." His thumb brushed across the back of my hand. "I'm so glad you stayed."

Every nerve ending in my body tingled in reply and I squeezed his hand. "I'm glad I stayed too."

I really was. These men and their secret magical society had changed my life for the better. I'd once been searching for a place to call home, a place where I belonged that filled me with excitement. Skolvik, the fae, and my partners were exactly that. I'd found love in the most unexpected of places and wouldn't change it for the world.

From days at the coffee shop, to the hikes through the forest, to *yoga* sessions with my partners, my life was full and complete. However...

"I'll admit, though, this isn't how I wanted to spend my Saturday afternoon and evening. But, explosion and interrogation aside, I don't mind the turn of events."

"What were your plans for tonight?" Espen asked, swinging our joined hands back and forth between us as the sun dappled across our faces.

"Honest to hell, I just wanted to get laid by my husband and partner."

Espen chuckled and tugged me against his chest, bringing us to a stop. With his thumb and finger, he tilted my chin up. "I'll never tire of hearing you saying that."

"That I want sex?"

"No, that I'm your husband."

A smile swept across my lips and those conga-line dancing butterflies returned to my stomach. Everything about this man made me happy. His gregarious personality, general excitement for life, and the way he cared for the world around him. He loved his people, loved his family, loved me. I leaned in to kiss—

"Well, isn't this sweet," a male voice drawled up ahead and my attention snapped toward the terrifying sound. Veigar emerged on the trail in all-black hiking attire, his sunglasses perched on his nose. "Husband and wife out for an evening hike. Do enjoy the view."

My stomach fell so far out of my body it prepared to tumble down the hillside and into the fjord.

Espen's hold on my hand tightened. "Veigar."

"Espen," the Fire Fae king replied as Salka came up behind him in her hiking gear. They sauntered past us, heat radiating off them like a furnace in winter. With a knowing grin, Veigar looked like a barn cat that had made a kill and proudly lain it on the front steps of the house. Salka meanwhile didn't move her face at all. It was as if she was giving a blank sheet of paper a run for its money, keeping her secrets to herself.

"What are you doing out here?" Espen's voice was clipped and firm.

"The forests in Norway truly are spectacular," Veigar replied. "So lush and full of... life."

Espen tightened his jaw, and his left foot slid forward, putting himself between me and them.

"We got your note," I said, hoping I could diffuse the tension swarming around us.

Veigar tilted his head like a man doffing his top hat. "Wonderful, and yet, I've had no reply from the mountain."

"I don't think you're going to get what you want."

"What a shame."

"Leave us," Espen bit out. "Leave Norway."

Veigar's lips twisted into yet another stomach-churning smile. "I don't think I will."

"He has decided to stay a little longer," Salka added, and my shoulders tensed.

"Do enjoy the view," Veigar said. "The mountain is so... majestic."

What did he do?

I didn't say a word, didn't need to. I spun and my legs moved of their own accord, needing to run, needing to get to the site as swiftly as possible. Espen did the same, sprinting along behind me. Letting me take the lead and leaving the two Fire Fae in our dust.

I bolted through the trees, leaped over logs, and carved up the rugged trail beneath my feet. My lungs heaved, sweat spreading across my back, as I pressed on.

The flora along the path appeared unharmed as I hurried past it, but up ahead... What would I find? What could they have done with their fire powers? What had he done to my mountain?

Øyvin was correct. We couldn't trust Reuven and I really didn't trust Salka. Especially right now.

Sunlight shone through the thinning trees as the two of us rushed out into the opening, wild heather and rock-filled brush spreading before us.

I sucked in a lungful of air and set my hands on my hips, scanning the scene.

The hillside appeared free from harm—bees flitted from clusters of pink heather and purple blooms peeking through rocky outcroppings. A gentle breeze danced through the plants making them wave at us in greeting and swept through the loosened strands of my hair that had fallen from my ponytail. I looked to my right, toward the pointy mountain top. The jagged gray edge carved a line through the darkening blue sky, remnants of sunlight bouncing off specks of quartz embedded in the stone.

Espen wandered further up the clearing while I got out my camera. Pulling off the lens cap and securing it in my legging's pocket, I turned on the device and aimed at the darkest spot of the craggy mountain.

The stone edge opened like a monster's maw, the serrated edges looking more like teeth than pieces of rock. The gap between the top and the bottom edge of the fissure was large enough to fit a man length wise.

Shit. Even from this vantage point and without the camera's zoom, the fissure had shifted since I'd been here this spring with Torsten. Widened like it'd been pried apart by Thor himself.

I snapped a few pictures for Bente. While her handy laser contraption had probably noted the movement of the mountain, seeing it was another thing. Hopefully, these pictures would help her and the other decision makers in the village.

With pictures taken at all zoom levels, I returned the lens cap to its rightful home and turned off the camera.

Espen still surveyed the edges of the clearing, sticking close to the tree line, searching for any clues of malpractice. What exactly had Veigar done here? Was he the one who'd widened the crack or was that a result of the explosion down the fjord? Or maybe Salka was behind it? There was no doubt in my mind that he'd touched something he wasn't supposed to. We'd angered him enough and he didn't seem like the kind of man that was told *no*. Nor took kindly to hearing the words when they were thrown at him. But what could he have done?

I knelt on the ground and pressed my hand into the soil, pushing some of my magic out, acting on natural instinct and need to check on the rocky facade beneath. A warm flow of energy washed down my right arm and spread into the dry yet hardy vegetation.

An oscillating sensation ebbed back to me, like a heart beating beneath my palm. My eyes fluttered shut, and I focused on that pulsing.

Thump.

Thump.

Thump.

It was like I'd reached into the mountain's chest and asked permission to see what had hurt it. Threads of power wove across the entire mountain, and I could... I sucked in a breath.

I could *feel* them.

All of them.

Each thread had its own distinct pattern. A clear and beautiful picture, in its own right.

I swallowed the lump in my throat. These were the Fjell Fae residents. The people of the mountain. I'd heard mutterings of the royals being tied to the mountain itself. Hell, since I'd inherited some of Freija's magic there had been cave-ins when I went to Ohio and Alvdalen. Halvar himself said those were caused by my absence and that his presence alone wasn't enough to stop them.

But this was more than that. This was an undeniable connection to the fjell and its residents.

I'd felt this before, but only briefly, when the wolf had stormed into the throne room this past winter. I'd slid in front of Halvar and Aurora, drawing a sword that had sparked with royal magic. In that same moment, the lights within the room had beat in tandem with my own heart. It was like the mountain and I had been one and the same. A part of a greater whole.

Placing my other hand to the ground, I pushed more of my power into the earth and let it flow up the hillside toward the fissure. It glided and danced up the stone beneath the soil, reaching and reaching and—

Black.

My shoulders curved inward, and a shudder ran down my spine.

Where the fissure lay was a pit of darkness. A gaping wound with fractured strands of magic around its edges where countless soldiers and Halvar... Halvar had tried to heal this too. But he'd failed. The massive, splintered piece of rock hung off its rightful home, threatening to fall at a moment's notice. And there, among the other pieces of Fjell Fae magic, was a glob that didn't belong. The magic was dark, hot, and angry as it clawed its way into the rock, shearing it further. Melting the fragile bindings that kept it in place.

My eyes flew open.

This was going to come down. This hundred-yard-wide piece of land was going to fall into the fjord and wash out any and all life in its path before the ensuing tsunami throttled the town.

"Fuck," Espen muttered, drawing my attention.

My gaze found his—fear filling his eyes—and my gut lurched again.

I ran up the hillside to where he stood beside a copse of birch trees. "What's wrong?"

He pointed to a lump of ash by his feet.

"That's odd," I said. "Why would Veigar light a fire up here? We didn't see any smoke and there are no smoldering embers, so it can't be fresh. Maybe some other idiot started a bonfire up here even though the Station and you rangers put a ban on them for the summer?"

Espen lips downturned and he shook his head. "How many soldiers did the Fjell Fae send up here to monitor the fissure?"

"What?"

He pointed around us. "How many soldiers did Halvar send up here?"

Three lumps of ash dotted the landscape. Scorch marks in the terrain beneath them. My lungs contracted, my hand flying to my mouth. "Fuck."

They'd burned the soldiers alive!

They'd killed them and messed with my mountain.

My lips trembled. How dare they!

A groaning noise sounded from the top of the hillside and our gazes snapped to the source. Tiny pebbles of soil and stone skittered down the mountainside, but the land, mercifully, didn't move. That didn't mean it wouldn't in the near future, though.

Bile churned in my stomach, images of terror and devastation flashing through my mind. Veigar was meddling with the town and putting everyone—fae and human alike—in his crosshairs.

"That part of the mountain is unstable." I sucked in a breath to hold back the rage and tears. "I felt what I can only describe as Fire Fae magic in there, weakening it."

"How long do you think we have before it falls?"

This was way above my pay grade, but I had to trust my gut. "Days, if we're lucky."

"We need to warn the village."

"And the fjord," I added. "We have to warn those living underneath the water before this comes down on top of their heads and crushes their homes."

"I'll text Øyvin," Espen replied and pulled out his phone.

While he focused on that, I took a moment for myself and the lives we'd just lost. I plucked three wildflowers from a nearby mound of rock. The delicate purple blooms fluttered in the breeze as I set each atop the three lumps of ash. "Thank you for your service," I whispered to each. I may not have known those soldiers by name, but they deserved better than this ending.

They deserved to live long lives with their loved ones. They deserved to be honored for their sacrifice. They deserved so much more than what had no doubt been a horrific and painful death.

I swallowed hard.

"Lennie," Espen yelled from the trailhead. "Let's go!"

I nodded and bolted after him. We needed to get back to town. We needed to warn everyone. If Veigar wasn't going to get what he wanted, then no one would have it or their lives.

We careened down the hillside, moving as fast as we could without tumbling over our own feet or fallen trees. I yanked my phone out of my pocket, miraculously not falling on my face in the process. Scrolling through my contact list, I found the name I needed and clicked call. The line rang twice before the recipient picked up.

"Torsten." I didn't give him a chance to say hi. We didn't have time for that. "Get Halvar on the phone, now."

Whatever the man heard in my voice, spurred him into action. His breaths panted down the line and muffled footfalls sounded as if he were running through the tunnels to get to the big guy. A few seconds later I got who I wanted.

"What's wrong?" Halvar's rumbling voice echoed through the call.

"Veigar has fucked with the crack. Left behind three piles of ash too."

My words were met with silence, then, "I'll prepare the soldiers. Clear the town."

"On it."

I hung up just as Espen brought his own phone to his ear. A second later he said, "Bente, evacuate the village."

25

ESPEN

I bolted into the station and aimed for my office near the back of the building. Passing Jens at the front desk and the abandoned interrogation rooms, I hurtled down the hallway and barreled through the door to my room. I didn't spend much time here and had left the place in disarray. My hiking pack was thrown in the corner, boxes of papers sat untouched beside the metal desk, and several pointy snake plants perched on the windowsill. But the one thing I was looking for waited for me on top of my dusty filing cabinet.

Grabbing my rolled-up copy of the town map, I strode back down the hall to the main conference room. Voices grew louder the closer I got.

"We need to canvas each street."

"Boat owners need to be alerted too."

"Do we have extra vans for the elderly? Those unable to drive themselves?"

The cacophony continued as I stepped into the brightly lit room. The entire Police force had squeezed into the space, some sitting around the sleek conference table, others standing against the wall, taking everything in. Bente stood in front of the white board at the head of the room.

Her wizened gaze shot to me and the voices died down. "Do you have the map I asked for?"

I held it aloft, then unfurled the large map of Skolvik across the table. Colleagues further down the table set their coasters and mugs on the corners to stop the paper from curling in on itself. Stepping back, I settled in an open spot against the wall between two fellow officers who also happened to be Forest Fae.

"Now, then," Bente started, her voice filling the room. "I agree we go road by road as outlined in the emergency plan. I want teams of two attacking each street, one person on the left side, the other on the right."

Quiet murmurs of understanding flitted around the table.

"As for the boats." She braced her fists on the table and leaned forward. "Espen, can you talk to Øyvin? He's the de facto harbor master around here. Have him alert the other boat owners."

"Of course." I held back a wince. Øyvin had enough on his to-do list beneath the fjord; adding this could slow down the Fjord Fae evacuation efforts. But we had to keep up appearances. "I will let him know. I'm sure he has everyone's phone numbers and one word to the local fishermen will have them all coordinating among themselves to get their boats out of here."

Bente gave me a single nod. "Good. They'll need to get the vessels all the way out to the Atlantic to keep them safe, should a tsunami happen."

Rumbles of agreement sounded, and I couldn't have agreed more. A tidal wave would be devastating in the narrow passages of Skolvik Fjord. The water would likely ricochet from one side to the other, sloshing back and forth until the ferocious force eventually dissipated.

I listened in as discussions continued, all while mulling through what I'd need to do for the Forest Fae. Ylva was already working on alerting residents in the region that could be impacted, while a text to Turi had informed the Council of Elders what was happening. I hadn't had time to respond to her expletive laden text in my rush to get here.

"Now, the disaster plan includes a few officers remaining to watch over the village and a few to block the roads in and out of town. I'm okay keeping the blockades but I've decided I won't have any officers remaining in the village. Your lives—"

"I volunteer." The words were out of my mouth in an instant.

"No," Bente said. "I can't allow it."

"You can. You will."

"Espen."

I pointed to the map. "Boss, my cabin sits high up on the hillside. Probably out of reach of any tsunami that might crash through town."

"That *potential* is what I'm concerned about."

"I appreciate that, but someone needs to stay behind. It was in the plan for a reason. The cameras are gone. We need eyes on the town to protect it from theft and stop individuals from entering."

"You're newly married. I won't—"

"My wife agrees with me."

We hadn't talked about it, but I knew she would. If she were here, Lennie would have interrupted Bente and volunteered long before I piped up.

Bente let out a long-winded sigh. "I'm not going to win this argument, am I?"

I shook my head. While I couldn't elaborate further on *why* I was the best person to stay behind, I had to make her agree. I had to protect the forest and the village.

"Your bravery is commendable... and stupid."

I smiled. "Is that your way of saying you love me like a son?"

She snorted and waved her hand with a smile. Chuckles and chortles rose from the other officers.

She really did treat all her officers as an extension of her own family. It was one of the many reasons why I respected and liked her.

I found her gaze again. "I'll be fine. I will call you every few hours or if there are any updates or concerns."

The room fell silent again, everyone looking between me and Bente as the Chief considered my stance and proposal. She shuffled her feet and clicked the cap on her whiteboard pen on and off as her eyes turned glossy with thought. With a shake of her head she said, "You'll obey any order I give you from afar?"

"Always."

Another sigh left her, and she deflated a bit. "Fine. But only you and Lennie stay."

"Only me and Lennie," I repeated with a nod.

With her spiky head bobbing and a determined look plastered across her face, Bente turned her attention to the rest of the room and the map spread out before her.

"All right! Split into pairs. I want the village cleared of all people by tomorrow night at eight o'clock." She clapped her hands together. "Let's get to work!"

I wiped the sweat from my forehead, another street canvassed and cleared, a full evening of work almost complete. As the sun neared the jagged horizon, something moved out of the corner of my eye.

Ylva waved from where she leaned against the last house on the street, the eaves of the white-wood building casting her in shadow. "Get over here."

Scurrying toward her, I asked, "What have you got for me?"

She crossed her arms as I stopped in front of her. "Bad news, I'm afraid."

"Shit. We have enough going on already."

"You wanted to know if there were any changes or unusual events."

"What happened?"

She peered around, making sure none of the other officers or villagers were close enough to hear us. "Another wildfire started up about an hour east of here."

Fuck. I pulled my fingers through my hair, pushing it off my forehead. "Do they have a cause yet?"

She shook her head. "The locals think it might be summer tourists not putting out a camping fire correctly, but most of the tourists are gone for the season. So..."

Yeah, it was well past peak camping season. Only expert adventurers traversed the mountain woods at this time of year, and they all knew the rules, especially after another hot summer had left the country looking more like tinder than a verdant oasis.

Ylva's phone beeped, and she pulled it out of her pocket. "Ah, I don't want to say this is perfect timing, but I had those incoming archers check out the scene—without getting too close to alert suspicion among the humans—and they suspect Fire Fae based on the burn pattern. It's not natural and they think they've found multiple starting points."

That sounded like classic Fire Fae techniques. "Did they find any of Veigar's soldiers?"

"No."

"Are our archers still in the area?"

"They're awaiting next orders."

I tapped my foot against the asphalt. Veigar really was done waiting and seemed to be spreading us out. Or, at the very least, flexing his strength elsewhere in the hopes we would relent our opposition. Which we Forest Fae, and our friends, did *not* plan on doing any time soon.

"What do you want me to do?" Ylva asked, pulling me out of my head.

I had enough going on right now trying to clear the village. Until that was done, I needed to keep my focus locally. "Let me get the humans out of town while you focus on our people. I trust you to do what's best."

She nodded, gave me a tiny salute, and strode away with her phone pressed to her ear.

I turned back to the street I'd just cleared and found several families loading up their cars with their most prized possessions. The sight was like a punch to the gut. I texted Lennie and Øyvin, letting them know the news and got expletives in response.

As I stared down the street, families locking up their homes wondering if they would ever be able to return, I couldn't have agreed with my partners more.

"Fuck."

26

LENNIE

Øyvin didn't come home that night, neither did Espen. Both were busy with their respective jobs—alerting residents of the impending danger—and I'd been tasked with packing go-bags to take to Espen's cabin. I spent the next morning shoving spare clothes into our duffel bags and Øyvin's fancy-schmancy silver suitcase, and hauled them up the southern hill to the cabin before running back into town.

I sprinted past people loading up their cars and store owners boxing up window displays—saving as many of their precious wares as possible. Flower pots sat abandoned, curtains had been drawn, and keys clinked in locks as residents said goodbye to their homes and businesses.

I stumbled into Oddvar's Café, my chest heaving as sweat beaded along my hairline and beneath my white T-shirt. Chairs were stacked on tables, their wooden legs pointing toward the ceiling, the bread case sat empty, and rootling behind the counter was Oddvar.

The octogenarian's wispy eyebrows saluted me as I shut the front door.

"You heard the news?" Oddvar grumbled.

I nodded and crossed the room. "I was the one who reported it to the Station."

Oddvar's nose twitched, and he shrugged before motioning wildly around himself. "Help me with all this stuff, will you?"

"Of course." That's why I'd come here. I knew the man would need help packing up the café and loading his car. I wouldn't let him do that by himself. "Where should I start?"

He waved at the commercial-grade coffee pots and Robertina, my favorite espresso machine. "These will be covered by insurance."

"They cover potential tsunamis out here?"

"They cover landslides," he said with a nod to the back of the building. "This way."

He retreated into the storeroom, and I followed in the wake of his flapping, emerald cardigan. The storage room, that was barely larger than a pantry but could somehow fit a few people inside it, smelled like coffee and cleaning supplies. A smell I'd affectionately come to associate with Oddvar and his café.

Basic wooden shelves lined two of the three walls, with the final one housing the little kitchen set up with a fridge and freezer for our sandwich making. He turned his attention to the shelves, stacked with mugs, bags of beans, and boxes of teabags, among a whole host of other things.

Crouching down and eliciting several creaking noises, Oddvar pushed aside three large bags of sugar and retrieved a wooden box I'd never seen before. The size of a bread-bin, it reminded me of the one Gunvor had kept her cousin Vigdis's things in. However, this one was dark blue with traditional hand-painted white and yellow flowers.

I crossed my arms. "What have you got in there?"

Oddvar peered up at me, the lines around his eyes tightening as if he wasn't sure he should tell me.

"Have you been pilfering cash from the store, Oddvar?" I asked, a joking note in my tone.

He scoffed. "Never. Take this for me."

I reached out and took the box from his grasp, shocked by the surprising weight. As he rose, I assessed the box. "No really? What have you stashed in here? Gold? Your favorite mug? A mug made of gold?"

He tapped the box and motioned for me to exit.

I spun and sauntered back out into the bright light of the café, setting the lidded container on the counter beside a cardboard box that had been labeled *café*.

"Can I look inside? Or is it a secret?"

Oddvar tugged on the sleeves of his cardigan. "It's coffee."

My shoulders dropped. "What? Seriously? That's it?"

"They're special beans."

"You have a secret stash of beans?"

He pulled the box from the counter and gingerly set it in a cardboard one. "They're mine."

"You mean to tell me you've been making your own coffee with these beans and not the ones you sell to patrons?"

He nodded once.

"And you never thought to offer any to me?" I set my hands on my hips. "I thought you loved me, Oddvar."

He scoffed again and wagged a finger at me. "If you tell anyone, I will fire you when they deem it safe to return."

A laugh ripped from me. "Deal."

We set to work packing up his box and filling another with bits and pieces he deemed necessary for survival or worth taking with him. From a portable coffee pot and recyclable cups to napkins and teaspoons. Wherever he was staying, he could run his own rustic coffee shop from these items alone. As long as the patrons only wanted black bean juice.

"Lennie?" he said, breaking the companionable silence between us.

"What's up?"

"You'll take care of my café while I'm gone?" Oddvar asked, his thick accent adding another emotional layer to his words.

I swallowed a lump in my throat and my heart clenched like someone had wrapped their fist around it. "Of course. I won't let anything happen to the café nor our precious Robertina." I stroked a finger across the top of the fancy espresso machine as Oddvar failed to hide his eye roll. "Embrace the name, Oddvar."

He grumbled and stacked his pour-over container into the box in front of him.

"Thank you," he muttered, and a tiny smile tilted his lips before vanishing like it would be offensive to be caught.

"No, Oddvar. Thank *you*. I don't think I've ever said it properly. Thanks for taking a chance on me. For hiring me."

I'd needed a job when I moved here and wanted one I'd be good at and passionate about—which was hard in this economy. Sometimes you needed to find a job that would put bread and butter on the table. And I had with this one, but it had also become a place I enjoyed working and had taught me so much. Working here had fully entrenched me in the community. And Oddvar, along with my own plucky courage, was to thank for that.

His mouth twitched and he waved his hand at me. "No crying. Back to work."

I smiled. "Yes, boss."

We continued packing things up, wrapping favored mugs in towels and discussing where Oddvar would be seeking shelter. Apparently, he'd be staying with his youngest son in Bergen on the coast. They'd already made plans to visit a few good restaurants together and go on a fishing trip. Just the thought of Oddvar out on a boat with his family brought another smile to my face.

As I taped up the box I'd been working on, the bells above the door chimed. In walked Solveig, Dagny, and Jorunn in a wild assortment of T-shirts and unshapely pants, their silver and white hairdos in more disarray than I'd ever seen before.

I shuffled past Oddvar and around the counter to see the trio.

"We came to say goodbye," Solveig said and swept me into her arms. I hugged her tightly, before bracing my hands on her shoulders and holding her at arm's length.

"Where are you going for shelter?" I asked, my tone firm.

She patted my hand with her own. "Over the mountain to Vanheim. There are several hotels over there that have opened their doors to us."

"That's good to hear." I squeezed her shoulders and turned to the others. "What about you two?"

"Trondheim." Jorunn leaned against the counter and wiped the back of her hand across her forehead. "To see my daughter and grandchildren. The youngest just started walking."

"That'll be nice. And what about you Dagny?"

She doffed her hair in an attempt to tame the wayward curls. "My niece is coming to pick me up and take me to Oslo."

"Sounds like you're all going to have a nice time with family. It'll be a good distraction from everything happening here."

Solveig's eyebrows pinched together. "Where are you going, Lennie?"

Hadn't she already heard? Or was this part of their gossip-slash-factfinding mission?

"Espen and I are staying to watch over the village. Chief of Police approved it."

Gasps sprung from each of them while Oddvar grumbled behind the counter.

"You're staying?" Solveig exclaimed.

Jorunn shook her head. "You shouldn't be staying."

"Agreed, what a horrific honeymoon," Dagny added.

I choked out a laugh. "Would it surprise you to know that we never had any honeymoon plans?"

All three gasped in unison again while Oddvar grumbled something else inaudible.

"Unacceptable!"

"Foolish!"

"Do we need to have a word with you husbands?"

"Now, now, Ladies," a male voice said and I turned to find Espen in the doorway. "Who says I won't take my wife on a honeymoon at a later date?"

The elder trio swooned, but my eyes worked their way from his boots to the ends of his floppy strands, scanning for anything amiss. His black cargo pants and matching police T-shirt clung to his muscles. His utility belt hitched around his hips. The only sign that anything was wrong was the exhaustion weighing his movements and the bags under his eyes.

Like a lost puppy, I drifted toward him, wanting to be in his orbit and as close as possible.

A warmth filled his gaze as he took me in and smiled.

"Where would you take her?" Solveig asked.

I turned in Espen's hold and he wrapped his arms around my middle. His thumb tucked beneath my shirt, and he brushed tiny circles on my skin, sending a trill of tingles across my entire body.

"Yes, where *would* you take her, Espen?" Jorunn added.

"Spain?"

"Croatia?"

"Greece?"

"Bali?"

"Wales?"

"Wales? Why on earth would he take her to Wales?"

"It's where they filmed a lot of *Game of Thrones*."

"No," Jorunn said. "They filmed in Northern Ireland."

"Are you sure?"

My head shot back and forth. When the three of them got going, it was like watching Olympic-level table tennis.

"Besides, Wales is damp and wet!"

"Fine. Scotland, then."

"That's not much better."

"They have castles." Dagny turned to me. "Do you like castles?"

"Ummm, sure," I replied. "I guess castles are—"

"See," Dagny interjected and flapped her hands. "She likes castles. They should go to Scotland."

Espen set his chin on my shoulder, his beard brushing against the sensitive skin of my neck. "Should we stop them?" he whispered.

I shook my head. "They'll run out of steam soon."

"Would you die for her? Take a sword for her? Protect her life with your own?" Dagny asked.

Or not.

"Don't listen to her, Espen." Solveig waved her hand at her friend. "She's been watching *Game of Thrones* again and wants to marry Jon Snow."

Dagny harumphed, dipped around Solveig's hand, and shoved her finger toward Espen. "Answer the questions."

The band of Espen's arms around my stomach tightened. "Always."

His answer hooked on something in my chest and tugged. How had I gotten so lucky to find him? I twisted, rose on my tiptoes, and leaned in for—

"No kissing!" A gruff voice said.

I bit my bottom lip and stared into the merriment in Espen's eyes. "There aren't any customers here, Oddvar. And he's not behind the line."

"Rules are rules," he replied. "Now, help me with these boxes. I'm ready to go."

Espen winked at me, and I brushed the tip of my nose against his, promising that kiss later.

Espen and I each grabbed a box, letting Oddvar lead us to his gray sedan parked outside the café. It was odd seeing cars on the pedestrian-only walkway, like a final sign this town was in a panicked frenzy. The ladies offered moral support before saying a final goodbye and scurrying down the road out of sight.

Oddvar locked up the café and turned to me. He shoved a big ring of keys toward my chest, a troll keyring dangling off them. "Take these."

"You're trusting me with your keys?" I asked, accepting the bulky collection he'd amassed over the years.

"Take care of the café and the village."

"I will." I nodded and shoved the wad of metal into my leggings pocket. The keys poked against my upper thigh.

"Good." He climbed into his car. Rolling down the window, he added, "Don't die."

Espen and I chuckled as my boss drove down the street.

I leaned into Espen's embrace, enveloping myself in that welcoming smell of leather and moss. Letting out a sigh, I relaxed in his hold. So much had happened in the past few weeks. My parents had been in town, I got *married*, and then had been interrogated for arson. Who the fuck got married and dragged down to the local police station in the space of a week?

Movement down the street drew my attention. Veigar sauntered around the corner, his sunglasses trained on us. His lips curled up slowly at one corner, and a ball of dread settled in my stomach. What the fuck was he up to now? Hadn't he done enough?

He continued walking across the street, slowly clapping his palms together, and disappeared behind another building. My gut twisted at the sight and fear took hold.

"Where's Øyvin?" I whispered.

Espen squeezed me tighter. "Still in the fjord."

27

ØYVIN

We started on the north side of the fjord, escorting eighty-nine fae from their homes and sending them toward the coast or into the depths of the palace. Standing on the silty fjordbed, I stretched my arms above my head and then behind my back, watching fae and creatures coming and going. Soldiers zipped by, swimming through the murkiest depths of the watery inlet. I let out an extended breath as another family swept past me, their bags hitched over their shoulders, heading toward the fjord's southern slope.

This was just the start of our evacuation efforts. We still needed to put in magical buffers around the palace and clear more of the cave homes down fjord, not to mention help anyone above water who might need the extra assistance.

An elderly fae in a long, green dress and gray cloak drifted past, her large military-style duffel bag swamping her fragile frame and slowing her movements. She looked ready to collapse in a few meters.

"Let me carry that." I lifted the bag from her back, the air pockets around us allowing communication underwater.

"I'm doing quite well. Thank you," her voice croaked.

I grumbled and hoisted the oversized, canvas bag over my shoulder as she squeaked in a minor protest. The uneven weight settled against my back, bending my knees slightly. She shouldn't have been carrying this. It must've been twice her weight.

"Did no soldier offer help?" I asked.

"Several did," she replied through heaved breaths. "But I refused."

Lennie should meet this woman; they'd get along well. Perhaps *too* well. I shook off the thought of my partner corrupting more little, old ladies with her wry sense of humor and chaotic personality and refocused on the task ahead of me.

"Are you heading to the palace or down fjord, ma'am?"

"The palace, please," the woman said and gently set her hand at the crook of my free arm. The touch was so delicate, her body so frail. *Should I carry her too?*

Her long gray hair waved around her in her air pocket and a determined look hardened her fragile features.

A minute smile tugged at my mouth, but I locked it away before she could see. No, I wouldn't be carrying her. But I'd be making sure this resolute elder got to safety under her own steam.

"Are you prepared to swim, ma'am?"

She nodded and set her shoulders.

I pushed off the fjordbed and used the lightest amount of my power to propel us forward. Her air pocket brushed against my own as her jaw tightened and her brow furrowed. She was fully committed to making it, a trait that reminded me of Lennie and sent a wave of warmth through my heart.

We took our time swimming through the chilled waters of the deepest part of the fjord, moving through the darkness and aiming for the lights of the palace that glowed in the distance. Thank the ancestors I'd requested additional light magic be used around the entrance and Valdemar had granted my wish without question. He understood we needed to do everything in our power to make sure people got to safety without trouble.

I swam at a pace she seemed comfortable with, and it wasn't long before we arrived at the palace entry, the aquatic creatures carved around the arched passage shrouded in beaming light.

Sweeping into the entry, we removed our air pockets and she released her hold on my arm. Her body slumped to the floor with a thump.

"Shit."

I dropped her bag and hoisted her back onto her feet. "You did it. You made it."

"I did," she whispered.

A bubble of pride built within me as I scanned her for injuries.

Pale skin.

Heaving chest.

Spindly fingers.

Nothing appeared amiss, her cloak concealing and protecting her body well, but the way she swayed in my hold alluded to exhaustion.

Her feet wobbled beneath her, and I tightened my grip on her elbows as another soldier shot over to us.

"Take her bag," I ordered.

The soldier nodded and lifted the canvas sack over his own shoulder.

"You've made it this far," I said to my charge. "But let me carry you the rest of the way."

A low rumble sounded from her and her jaw tightened.

I bit back a smile. "Ma'am."

"Oh, fine."

It wasn't like she had much choice. If she tried to take another step, she'd probably hit the floor again. I hooked my arms under her knees and against her back and hoisted her up. She was as light as a seashell tumbling across the shoreline. Her body trembled in my hold as we continued our journey, but she refrained from any more grumbles or obstinate commentary.

I strode through the shiny, gray hallways and turned into the palace's ballroom. The grand space had been turned into a makeshift shelter, with dividers separating gathering spaces and cots with wool blankets neatly folded at the ends. It looked like something out of a war scene; something that hadn't happened here in a long time, and certainly not in the century I'd been Head Guard.

The vaulted, polished ceilings glimmered, their fish scale pattern appearing to ripple thanks to the magical balls of light that dotted the space. Beneath them, Fjord Fae milled, children playing in the back corner with dolls and cars, while adults watched over their young, chatting animatedly with each other.

I found a free cot in a quiet corner and set down the woman.

She shimmied onto the bed and pulled the thick blanket across her legs, her dress peeking out from beneath the wiry weave.

I motioned to the soldier with her things to set her stuff beside the cot. He gingerly rested it on the floor before returning to his post.

"You'll be safe here," I said with a curt nod to the woman. "What is your name, ma'am?"

The lines around her eyes creased. "Ingeborg."

"Well, Ingeborg, the soldiers here will be available should you need any assistance."

She waved me down and I bent at my waist, bringing my face closer to hers. Frail fingers pressed against my stubbled cheek. "Thank you, Øyvin."

I tilted my head to the side. "You know my name?"

"I know who you are, Head Guard." Her lips pulled into a slim smile. "I also knew your mother."

A bolt of pain shot through my chest, ripping it apart. I straightened and took a step back. Ingeborg's hand fell back into her lap.

"She'd be proud of you."

A lump settled in my throat, and I swallowed it down. "You knew my mother?"

"Unni was a dear friend. Helped me when my husband passed, and I moved beneath the surface permanently."

That sounded like something my mother would do, but must've happened a long time ago as I couldn't remember ever having met the woman in front of me. "How long have you lived in the fjord?"

A dreamy look crossed Ingeborg's face, her eyes glossing over as if lost to a memory. "The day I moved, a man rode into the village heralding the mysterious creation that had arrived on Norwegian shores. It was a carriage that didn't need a horse."

She was talking about cars. The first car in Norway had arrived in the 1890's. I wiped my chin and tried to avoid widening my eyes. She'd been beneath the water for over a hundred years. That would explain her pale complexion and frail figure. We Fjord Fae may have been capable of living and breathing underwater, but that didn't mean there weren't adverse effects to long term submersion.

"That was a while ago," I said. "Haven't you been above at all since then?"

She shook her head and fussed with the edge of the blanket. "Time passes and we move along. I belong down here."

I gave her a nod. I understood that draw to the water. It was why I lived right above it.

"Let any of the soldiers know if you need help," I said and moved to step away.

"I am grateful for your assistance." She smiled. "Please do stop by for conversation when you have a moment to spare. The company would be appreciated."

My chest spasmed again. This woman, that I couldn't recall meeting before, cared about me. "I will."

With that, I moved back to the entrance of the ballroom and took stock of the scene. The space had been completely transformed from the last event here. Reuven and Salka's coronation celebrations and ball had been full of fancy food, traditional trinkets, and magical displays of light and power. Silvery fish made of light had swum around the ceiling, tables along the room's flank had been laden with delicacies from chocolate to fruits from far off places, and in the center of it all was a crowd of dancers, twirling around in their finery and uniforms. Today, though, all that remained was a beautiful room filled with austere furnishings and people who feared they might never return to their homes.

But, there were no injuries.

No casualties.

No harm had been done to our residents... yet.

"They seem to be doing well," a male voice said, and my second-in-command, Sigurd, stepped up beside me. His black hair was held back by a piece of leather, the sleeves of his uniform rolled up to his elbows, like he was ready for an impromptu sparring match or cleaning session. Either wouldn't have been a surprise.

"Have you seen the King?" I asked.

He turned his gaze to the room. "Uh, no I have not."

He's probably in his office.

"I'll go find him," I said. I needed to give him a brief update and see if he wanted us to expand our shelter into the soldier training rooms or open up empty barracks. "You'll stay and guard the guests?"

Sigurd nodded. "Yes, sir."

Winding through the hallways, I gave short nods to the soldiers I passed and made my way to the royal quarters. If there were anywhere in the palace that I'd surely find King Reuven, it was in his office. I strode through the hallways and past artwork of the creatures we'd sworn to protect, until I reached the thick wooden door to Reuven's office. I lifted my hand to knock and—

Muffled voices sounded from the nearby Council chamber.

My hand fell back down.

More voices. Different voices.

Odd. Very odd.

There wasn't a meeting scheduled until tonight. I was supposed to give an update on the evacuation efforts to the full Council at eight o'clock. Who was in there?

I crossed the hall, strode into the Council chambers, and was met by ten sets of eyes. I ground to a halt and my breath caught in my throat. "What's going on?"

All the chairs around the Council's meeting table were filled, except mine. Reuven sat in his larger chair, peering at me sidelong, his hands clasped in front of him and resting on the table. Tension flooded the room as an awkward silence unfolded.

"Has something happened?" I asked.

"We could ask the same of you. This is an emergency meeting," Reuven said. "Aren't you supposed to be evacuating residences?"

Had they been meeting without me? How long had this been going on for?

"I was looking for you. The residences on the northern fjordbed have been evacuated. Your Majesty," I said, careful to make sure my voice didn't waver. "Is there something we need to discuss?"

"Is there enough space for everyone in the ballroom?" he asked, his gaze locked on the table.

"We may need to open up other rooms depending on the number of people who evacuate their homes further down the fjord."

"Any places in mind?"

"The empty barracks."

His head snapped to the side. "You mean the rooms that sit empty because you didn't notice that soldiers were derelict in their duties and supporting my wayward father? The soldiers he corrupted on your watch and put up for slaughter?"

I tightened my jaw and clenched my fists. "Yes. Those." I'd never forgive myself for not noticing the soldiers acting oddly sooner. But now wasn't the time to wallow in that shame. We had greater worries on our doorstep. "Do you have other concerns I should be aware of?"

Council members' eyes drifted toward the table, heads hanging low as they all shifted in their seats.

"I have revoked our alliance with the Fjell Fae. We are moving forward with a new Fire Fae alliance."

I knew it. I knew this was coming. My chest rumbled. "Why?"

"Because it is what's best for the Fjord."

"That's a fucking lie and you know it." The words were out of my mouth before I could stop them. "We are stronger when allied with the Fjell and Forest."

Reuven's seat scraped across the stone floor as he rose to his feet. Straightening to his full height, his gaze locked with my own. "Øyvin Håland, as your loyalties no longer remain with the Fjord, you're hereby relieved of your duties. Effective immediately. You'll be stripped of all titles and rank, but not banished from the palace. However, please remove your belongings from your office."

My heart stopped beating.

28

LENNIE

The sun was setting across the fjord, the curtains drawn for the night as I curled up on the sofa. My limbs ached and waves of worry washed through my mind like someone had turned on the spin cycle in the laundry machine. But even with the chaos and threats hanging over my little family and the town, I was proud of the work I'd done today. We'd successfully evacuated Skolvik. And now, me, Espen, and Øyvin were the only ones who remained.

The back door to the boat garage swung open and Øyvin stepped into the house. His hair was disheveled and his T-shirt and jeans clung to him as a puddle trailed in his wake. If the sight of Øyvin soaking wet wasn't enough of a warning, those tantalizing lips of his sat in a firm grimace that had alarm bells ringing.

I kneeled on the couch. "What's wrong?"

Eyes distant oceans of shock and anguish, he swayed on the spot.

My heart skipped several beats, and I gripped the arm of the sofa. "Øyvin, say something."

He shook his head.

Launching from the couch, I crossed the room in three swift strides and pressed my hands to his wet chest. Heat radiated from him, yet the water droplets remained cold as ice.

"Øyvin."

His gaze drifted to mine and he ran his hand up my arm. "I was fired."

My breath stilled in my throat and my eyes widened. "What?"

He nodded slowly.

That wasn't possible. I couldn't believe it. He was the Head Guard of the Fjord Fae. End of story.

"You're perfect at your job, though," I said, and his mouth tilted up at one corner before dropping back down. "They can't fire you."

"He can and he did."

This was wrong on so many levels. Øyvin had done nothing wrong. He'd always protected the Fjord Fae, unlike Reuven and his ass of a father-in-law. What a piece of shit. I pulled out of Øyvin's hold and moved to step around him. "Fuck Reuven."

Øyvin's hand shot out and he grabbed my wrist. His eyes met mine, his expression marred with shock. "Don't. You'll get yourself killed."

"Not the first time I've gone toe-to-toe with a monarch in the last few weeks—"

"I won't have it be your last," he said, and his unyielding tone sent a shiver down my spine.

"Last what?" A male voice said behind me, and I spun to find Espen closing the front door, done with his shift at the police station. His gaze raked over us, as if looking for injuries or problems, before pivoting to the puddle on the floor beneath the Fjord Fae. "Tell me what happened."

Øyvin pulled me into his side like he needed a life ring to keep him afloat. "Reuven fired me."

Espen pushed both hands through his hair, his eyes as wide as camera lenses. "He can't have."

"He did."

"What about this?" I brushed my hand over his wet T-shirt. "Did your magic disappear?"

"I broke my air bubble halfway home and swam normally the rest of the way."

My breath caught again, calculating just how far that was. Half distance from here to the Fjord palace was over a mile. "You swam all that way?"

He nodded.

My heart broke in two and I pulled him in for a hug. He grunted as my arms squeezed his torso. What was happening? Why the hell would anyone fire someone as dedicated to the fjord as Øyvin? They'd have to be insane to do so... Then again, maybe Reuven was crazy like his father?

Heat radiated across my back and Espen's hand settled on Øyvin's shoulder. "I'm sorry, my friend."

Øyvin's head bobbed once, his eyes narrowing with warmth and appreciation.

While I didn't like the circumstances, it was always nice to see my two guys supporting each other.

"You get in here too," I said over my shoulder to Espen.

He chuckled and pressed his front to my back, wrapping his long arms around both of us. I settled the side of my face against Øyvin's chest, listening to the steady thrumming of his heartbeat. Here, between the two of them, was my happy place. My body relaxed into their holds, and I relished the feel of being sandwiched between them. This right here was my home, my everything, and fuck did I hate that it had been hurt today.

I stepped back from Øyvin, pushing Espen with my butt. Motioning to Øyvin's state of dress, I said, "Dry off."

Staying in those wet clothes wouldn't help his mental state.

His grimace had disappeared, replaced by a gentle line, but his eyes shone with more ease. Like our group hug had temporarily settled the storm that'd been raging there.

He moved his hands to his sides and splayed his fingers. The puddle on the floor slowly receded and evaporated before he lifted his magic to his clothes. His jeans and shirt lightened as the powers swept up his body. The Fjord Fae magic ended at his hair, sending it into a tangled disarray that reminded me of wheat fields on a windy summer's day.

"Better?" he asked as his magic washed over my dampened front too.

"Much better," I replied. "Now, do you want to tell us *why* Reuven fired you?"

Øyvin inhaled and motioned to the sofa.

I followed his request and Espen did too. He kicked off his work boots and threw his police utility belt over the back of the couch. The little radio and gadgets landed with a thud against the supple brown leather. The two of us curled up next to each other and focused our attention on our partner.

Øyvin dropped onto the piano bench and wiped his palm across his face. "Reuven said my loyalties no longer remained with the fjord."

I scoffed. "Has he not met you?"

Øyvin's eyebrows flicked upward once. "I was worried about *his* loyalty to the fjord. But when he asked me recently if I would keep information from the two of you... I hesitated."

My heartbeats collided with each other and I clutched one of the throw pillows to my stomach.

"Why?" The words slipped from my lips, but I already knew the answer.

Øyvin's intense gaze met mine and heat washed through my body. "You know why."

Ever since I'd met him, Øyvin had prioritized the fjord and the fae that lived there. From clearing it of pollution, to leading the soldiers, he'd dedicated his life to the well-being of the waters. He loved the fjord. However, on several recent occasions, he'd put his love for *me* above the Fjord Fae.

"He sees you as a weak link that can't be trusted anymore."

"Mm-hmm."

"He doesn't want you reporting back to us," I muttered.

The air in the room thickened, filling with unspoken truths that we knew in our bones and our hearts.

We were a unit.

A family.

A powerful trio formed of three different factions and forged by love.

While I would always uphold my duty to protect the Fjell Fae, I wouldn't let anything come between me and these two men. They were the loves of my life and I'd protect them at all costs.

My magic swirled within my sternum as if it understood my allegiance and accepted it.

Espen took a deep breath behind me. "On that note, the village has been cleared, and the remaining officers have driven over the mountain to Vanheim."

I raked my fingers against my scalp. "They shouldn't have been forced from their homes."

Øyvin grit his teeth and Espen muttered, "Agreed."

Nobody should ever be forced from the place they called home. Asked to pack up their most cherished belongings and flee from a foe. In this case, it wasn't just an environmental disaster that loomed above them like an anvil; it was a living, breathing menace that could scorch the earth beneath their feet in a single heartbeat.

The tension in the room reached boiling point, and frustration whistled in my ears like a screeching kettle. "I hate how everything is falling apart around us."

"It may get worse before it gets better," Espen said.

"Don't say that."

"He's right, Trouble."

Rising from my spot, I threw the pillow back onto the couch and started waving my hands about as I stomped back and forth in front of the sofa. "First Balder steals magic and Nora kills Freija, resulting in the battle on the mountain top. Then the wolves attack us, and Wilhelm uses my leg as a chew toy. Now this?"

It was too much.

"Our lives may be facing a challenging chapter right now," Espen said, "but we'll get through this. Together."

We could. No, we *would*. But that thought didn't quell the frustrated energy trying to burst out of me.

"I hate this bullshit! I hate that there's a threat to this town and its people. I hate this feeling like I can't do anything about it. And I hate that I haven't fucked my partners in over a week! We haven't even consummated the marriage!"

I set my hands on my hips and panted. That last bit may have been too far, but dammit, it was true.

The room stilled and dust motes danced in the light from the kitchen.

My pulse beat in my ears and water lapped against the boat hull in the garage. The sound always seeped through the walls and cast the entire house under its lulling spell.

Espen stood and extended his hand to me. "Come along then, wife."

My toes curled at the title and my body flushed, cheeks probably pink from the emotions humming through me and the heated look in Espen's eyes. I placed my fingers in his and let him lead me to bed.

Once upstairs, Øyvin splintered off to one side of the bedroom while Espen corralled me toward the mattress.

Warmth swept around me, swaddling me in a loving haze. "Everything will be fine in the end," Espen whispered. He brushed his hand across my cheek and tucked my hair behind my ear.

My heart thrummed in my chest, and I hoped he was right as I leaned into his touch.

A low rumble sounded from Øyvin, and Espen bit his bottom lip as he swept to my side, his hands gliding over my hips.

Espen had always been more touchy-feely with me than Øyvin. Always needing to be physically connected to me in some way. Øyvin, on the other hand, always needed to have me in eyesight, where he could watch my movements and protect me from trouble. I didn't mind either, really. They were the same in the bedroom too.

Øyvin leaned against the dresser and crossed his ankles. A heady look of lust washed across his face. His gaze rose lazily from my toes to the top of my head, visually caressing every inch of my curves like he was seeing them for the first time.

My breaths faltered.

He shook his head.

"Are you seriously going to deny me sex after more than a week of celibacy?"

His lips quirked at one corner, and he cast a look at Espen. His voice was thick with passion as he said, "Undress her."

Espen smiled. "Gladly."

The Forest Fae stepped between me and Øyvin, blocking him from view. Espen's long lashes skimmed the tops of his cheeks as a satisfied grin settled across his face. With deft, yet slow movements, Espen skimmed his hands down my torso before flipping underneath the hem of my tank top. He gently pulled the material up and over my head, tossing it aside. Where it landed, I didn't know. Nor did I care. All I could focus on was the swelling warmth within my body and the molten look in Espen's eyes.

He grasped my shoulders and spun me around so Øyvin could see what he was doing to me. Then he slid his hands across my stomach, and I sucked in a breath as he popped open the button on my denim shorts.

Øyvin's eyes flared.

A whimper slipped through my lips.

Espen hitched his thumbs beneath the waistband of my shorts and pulled them down, dragging my lacy black thong with them. They pooled at my feet, and, without breaking eye-contact with Øyvin, I stepped out of them. Espen kicked them away as those blue oceans watched me from across the room. It was like he could drown me, and I would love every second of it.

Nuzzling against my neck and eliciting a shudder from me, Espen unfastened the clasp on my bra and removed it, throwing it between us and Øyvin. Before I could say a word, he pressed his body against my back and palmed my breasts, taking one firmly in each hand.

I groaned at the attention, and my eyes fluttered shut from the bliss that seeped through my body. As he toyed with one nipple, he smoothed his hand down my stomach once more and pressed two fingers against my clit.

A satisfied moan slipped from my lips. It'd been too long since I'd been touched like this. Sparks zipped in the most desirable places as Espen circled that tender bundle of nerves while gently kneading my breast. That pleasurable sensation swelled within my core, begging for more attention, and my legs wobbled. Espen moved his ministrations to my other breast and my nipple peaked against his rough palm.

An unintelligible sound emanated from me.

"Come for us, Lennie," Øyvin said.

I stared him down, wanting to be defiant, but my body wouldn't let me. Stars twinkled at the corners of my vision and my core pulsed.

Espen increased his pressure and pulled on my nipple so hard I saw galaxies. The two of them, working me into my undoing, was enough to drive me straight toward that precipice that promised release. I ground my ass against Espen's thighs as he nipped the hollow behind my ear.

"Now, Trouble."

Øyvin's words sent me careening over the edge and I let out a strangled moan as my body convulsed with bliss in Espen's arms. He tightened his hold on me, not letting me fall to the floor.

"Fuck," I whimpered.

Espen tilted my head to his and pressed his lips to mine. The kiss promised more passion and was laced with a love so consuming, it couldn't be defined, nor captured.

Øyvin growled. "Get on the bed. Now."

I did as requested, too dazed to counter.

The cool cotton duvets brushed against my hot skin as I climbed onto the bed. I turned and faced my guys, both of whom watched me like hawks waiting to dive onto their prey. Those looks were enough to have me panting again—my soaking core already needing more from both of them.

I stared directly into Øyvin's eyes. "How do you want me, partner?"

His tongue swept across his bottom lip. "Get on your back."

Fuck, yes. I did, relishing in the sensation of having them watch my every move.

Being worshiped like this by the two of them was a high I never wanted to come down from.

Øyvin reached over his shoulder and pulled off his shirt in one swift move, the fabric sweeping across his muscular form. In what felt like slow motion, he removed his pants, neatly setting them atop the dresser behind him. Without even touching me, it was as if he was all over my body.

Another shiver of pleasure ran through me. Fuck, I wanted them both so much.

Reaching the edge of the bed, Øyvin climbed up and pulled me by the ankles, hitching me closer to him.

He traced his fingers up my thighs and avoided the place where I wanted him the most. My core fluttered with need. I wriggled and he clamped his hands over my thighs, holding me in place.

"Øyvin, please," I said, my voice barely a whisper.

He hooked my legs over his arms, letting them hang in the crook of his elbow, and baring me for him.

A low rumble sounded from his chest. "I will never tire of this view."

He slowly pushed his cock inside me, gliding through the wetness that pooled between my thighs, and wringing a moan from me. The fullness was everything all at once. Based on the quirk of his eyebrow, he knew it too. Øyvin pressed his hand right above my clit and moved his thumb to the bundle of nerves while holding the top of my thigh with his other hand.

I fisted the duvet beneath me.

Having removed his clothes, Espen joined us on the bed and leaned over me. He pressed his mouth to mine with a desperate passion, kissing me like I was the air he needed to breathe, the only thing that might keep him alive. Our lips brushed against each other, tongues lapping, souls intertwining. He bit down on my lip, and I responded in kind by sucking on the tip of his tongue. He groaned and pressed himself against my side. His cock rubbed against me, and I wrapped my free hand around it, pumping once.

"Lennie," he ground out.

Øyvin continued slowly pushing in and out of me.

I swirled my thumb across Espen's tip.

"Fuck." His head fell back.

If I had enough oxygen in my lungs I would've agreed. These men knew how to handle me. Knew how to wring every last drop of tension and passion from my cells and weave them together into a photograph of pure ecstasy.

Øyvin picked up the pace, slamming against me. Each hit sent a zap through my core, building up that precious release once more.

The air in the room sizzled with need. I wanted to run my fingers through Øyvin's hair, wanted to hear Espen's stuttered breath as he finished, wanted both of them—

Øyvin pumped into me again and I unraveled alongside him with a loud moan.

My hand around Espen's cock stopped as I rode out my release. It was a promise, an undoing, a possession. It was everything and then some.

Espen pulled my hand off him frantically. "Let me..." he panted. "Let me finish inside you."

I nodded. Unable to form words.

As Øyvin shifted and pulled out, I sighed at the empty feeling he left behind.

He flopped onto the bed beside me and brushed his knuckles across my heated cheek. "Beautiful."

My entire body flushed at the word.

Espen nudged me onto my side and curled against my back. Sweeping his hands over my curves, he worshiped them like a delicate masterpiece. The feel of skin against skin was an irresistible vice, and I arched against him as he pressed his cock against my ass.

I'd gladly take a lifetime or three of lying between the two of them, letting them touch me wherever they wanted.

"I love you," I whispered. "Both of you."

"We love you too," Espen breathed against my neck.

"Forever and always, Trouble."

Our breaths intertwined and I pressed my lips to Øyvin's. He pushed his fingers into my hair and squeezed, tangling himself in the locks. Espen splayed a hand across my thigh, guiding my leg to rest over Øyvin's hip. The movement opened me up for him, which he took full advantage of—brushing his fingers slowly around my thigh and back through my soaking core. A low grumble emitted from both men, their chests vibrating against my front and back.

My body numbed, tingling in the best way. Heat wrapped around us like a hedonistic vice, unrelenting in its hold.

"Espen." The name was a prayer and a plea.

He murmured against my neck, and the sound sent a shiver down my spine. Without further preamble, he slid inside me from behind. A groan escaped me and Øyvin caught it with his mouth. Together the three of us morphed into a tangle of moans, gentle thrusts, and loving touches. Our hands were all over each other. Sliding and holding. Feeling and kneading. Gripping and kissing, as we ebbed toward that precipice once more.

My orgasm pulsed through me in a heady haze I could only describe with one word: love.

29

LENNIE

I awoke to gentle caresses, sandwiched between the loves of my life with the duvet covers draped over our lower bodies. Øyvin cradled my head against his chest, while Espen lightly pressed my fingertips to his lips. Early morning sunlight seeped between the curtains, the only sounds gracing the dawn were delicate breezes from our breaths and the steady hum of Øyvin's heart.

It was one of the most peaceful moments I'd had since moving to Norway. Like a perfect photograph, where the light hit just right, the depth of the scenery was luscious and layered, and the entire composition evoked a sense of calm.

I could lay here for days. Listening to the gentle rhythms of the two men at my sides. Cocooned in a safe blanket of warmth. Their arms wrapped around me like impenetrable walls of a fort or castle.

The thought of forts drew my mind to the threat facing the village and fae.

"What do we do?" My voice was barely a whisper, yet broke the silence like an axe cleaving a log. The question was meant to be rhetorical, a slip from my mind, but I must not have been the only one thinking it as the sun rose.

"We're going to need help," Espen said. "And we'll need each other."

He meant the factions. The alliances we'd forged. But what good could the Fjell and Forest do against the Fjord and Fire Fae? We needed more than each other. We'd need a fucking miracle. It wasn't like they had secret forces or weapons that could save them... Or did they?

I looked to Espen. He was a weapon of sorts. His destructive powers balanced with healing magic. Yet, what could he do against Veigar? Against the Fjord?

"Where do the fae go for help?" I asked.

Espen pulled my hand against his chest. "The ancestors."

My eyebrows furrowed. "Like Forest Fae King Olaf did with the wolves?"

He nodded.

"But we don't have any monarchs. At least none that are on our side."

A low rumble escaped Øyvin.

"But we have access to the Forest Fae shard," Espen said.

"What could we do with it? Ask for help? Would the ancestors even listen to you?" The questions spilled from me as my groggy mind slowly woke up. I needed coffee if we were going to talk strategy at this hour.

Espen's shoulder rose and fell.

"Only those with royal blood or royal magic have been known to successfully commune with the ancestors," Øyvin supplied.

My mind flew to one such royal heir in Alvdalen. Maybe Aurora could help us out? Though, with what we'd put her through earlier this year, I highly doubted she'd be charitable. In fact, the more I thought about it, she'd probably cackle down the phone and hang up on me if I asked. We'd need to find another. I hadn't exactly been successful reaching out to the ancestors when Halvar had me slap my hand on the pedestal in the temple. Maybe Torsten would have better luck?

"We could get Torsten," I said. "Or maybe even Halvar?"

Espen released his hand from my grasp and brushed a stray hair behind my ear. "We also have you..."

Øyvin clutched me tighter to his chest, his broad palm pressing against my back.

"Yeah, because that went so well last time I was in the Temple," I said with a scoff. "I'd grade that first date a solid 5.5. Awkward, but not awful considering they weren't exactly a talkative bunch."

"Doesn't mean you can't try again," Espen countered, ever the bubbly ray of optimistic sunshine.

I guessed I could try. Maybe without Halvar in the room... Or... Wait a second...

The most stupid, hypocritical and bat-shit idea drifted through my mind, but I latched onto it with both hands like it was a life-raft in the middle of the tumultuous North Atlantic: what if I went to the Temple and brought the Forest Fae shard with me and asked for help?

Would the ancestors talk to me then? What was the worst thing that could happen? I'd get smoted for trying? Sent to hell a little earlier than expected? I'm sure the devil would welcome me with open arms after all the chaos I'd been responsible for over the past year alone.

I bit my lower lip. "I have an idea."

Espen bolted to a sitting position, and Øyvin tilted my head to meet his.

"What are you thinking?" Øyvin asked.

"It's crazy. Would make me the shittiest leader in Fjell Fae history. Halvar would probably decapitate me, slice and dice me into a million pieces and distribute them to the fae as a warning of his—"

"Lennie, focus," Espen said.

I swallowed hard. "What if we unite the Forest Fae piece with the pedestal in the Temple of the Fae? What would happen? Would that increase our odds of favor with the ancestors? Or would I just be doing the same exact thing Veigar is trying to do?"

Looking between the two of them, I found their eyes wide, their expressions stuck in a state of shock and thought.

It was *exactly* what Veigar wanted to do. But maybe, if we did it... If *we* were the ones to unite the Forest Fae shard with the pedestal, we might be able to gain more powers to defeat Veigar and whatever army he had. It was pure lunacy, but I'd never been one to shy away from crazy ideas.

I wriggled from Øyvin's hold and sat in the middle of the bed, my legs crossed. Draping one of the white duvets over my shoulders like a shawl, I took a deep breath.

"It's not the worst idea," Espen said. "For starters, you wouldn't do what Veigar wants with those stone, would you?"

I shook my head. "I don't want to be an almighty ruler of all."

"Which is why that stone is safer in your hands than they are in his. Didn't he mention that a Fjord King was once getting corrupted by power? Getting too powerful?"

"He did."

"History has a tendency to repeat itself if we don't pay attention to it. Giving you the stone to use for good *is* a good thing compared to what Veigar would do."

Tension rolled from my shoulders as I sagged on the spot. All I wanted was to do good by the mountain, my home, and my guys. I wouldn't use whatever powers those stones might bestow for my own gains.

"Do it." Øyvin's gaze shot to mine. "We should do it."

"Are you sure?"

"We don't stand a chance against Veigar without help. Especially with Reuven and my— *his* forces standing against us."

If there was anyone who knew how the Fjord fought, it was Øyvin. And with his mind for military matters, he'd also have a good handle on what the gameboard looked like.

"What are we facing?" I asked. "What does each faction have in their arsenal that we need to account for?"

"The Fjord has several hundred fae soldiers beneath the surface that can muster at a moment's notice. The Fjell probably the same."

True. I'd seen a lot of them during my training sessions.

"The Fire Fae legion is small but mighty. I wouldn't be surprised if Veigar had brought across fifty to a hundred soldiers even if only half that could emaciate a regiment."

Images of black-eyed Fire Fae burning down human corpses flooded my mind and a shudder ran through me.

"As for the Forest,"—Øyvin looked to Espen—"their greatest weakness is fire."

Espen shifted and propped himself against the pillows. He dragged both hands through his hair, tangling the tendrils. "He's right. Veigar's forces, no matter how large or small, are hard for us to combat. They only have me as their biggest weapon. And I'm not sure I can save us. Reuniting the shards and asking for aid could help us monumentally."

I'd long suspected Espen was the Forest's fail-safe. A dangerous gift bestowed by the ancestors to *literally* level the playing field. But even Halvar feared Veigar. And, if I was completely honest, that scared me.

"Would you consider getting the Forest shard for us?" I asked.

Espen looked to me, his gaze filled with emotion. He nodded. "We'll take the police car and drive to Queen Ragnhild's grave."

"Thank you." That was going to be hard for him. But the more I thought about it, the more I believed in this insane idea. There was only one thing that might upend it. "We get the Forest Fae shard, bring it to the Temple of the Fae, and ask the ancestors for help with Veigar. Do we tell Halvar?"

"You've always just asked for forgiveness." Øyvin arched an eyebrow. "Why stop now?"

I snapped my fingers and pointed to him. "Very true, but I'm trying to be a good leader here."

So far, as Deputy Head Guard, I'd give myself a solid C grade. Not the worst, not the best, could do with refining and a better understanding of what it meant to be a leader. But if there was one thing I was sure of, it was that I'd do whatever it took to protect my family and new home. Fae and humans alike.

Espen's gaze flicked to Øyvin. "You're not going to like my response."

Øyvin's eyebrow inched higher.

"We don't tell Halvar until after we've accessed the Temple," Espen said.

Yup, this was as bonkers as my dad wearing University of Michigan colors.

"So, I sneak into the mountain with the Forest shard, slap my hand on the pedestal, and beg the ancestors for help."

"It seems like our only option," Espen said with a sigh.

"It's not," Øyvin piped up.

I squinted at him. "What do you mean?"

He swallowed hard. "I'll get the other one."

What?

"Come again for the demi-fae?" I stared at the blond-haired man leaning against the headboard. "What do you mean, you'll 'get the other one?'"

"I'll steal the Fjord Fae shard for us too."

30

LENNIE

"You can't be serious." My voice rose as I jumped off the bed and dropped the duvet on the floor.

Øyvin's gaze followed the material like it was a greater sin to let it fall to the ground than steal something from the Fjord Fae King who had fired him yesterday.

"Are you sick?" I rushed over, bare tits jostling, and placed my wrist against Øyvin's forehead. Not clammy, just his usual warm self. "Did the sex last night mess with your head?"

It had been a pretty epic love-making session. Not just carnal, but an emotional joining of... Yeah, I had it bad.

Øyvin nudged aside my arm. Brushing his fingers down it, he took my hand in his. "We might have access to both stones. And I won't let it get into Veigar's hands."

Espen cleared his throat. "Not that I condone theft, because I don't. But how do you propose stealing it?" He scooted off the bed and headed toward the new dresser that housed his clothes. The light-colored wood scraped as he opened the top left drawer and pulled out a clean pair of boxer briefs.

"I'll need Lennie's help," Øyvin said.

I flinched.

Espen shook out his underwear with a *flap*. "I don't want her anywhere near—"

"Don't worry," Øyvin cut him off. "I'm going below alone. But I need her help first."

Espen bobbed his head like he could work with that, while I crossed my arms and narrowed my eyes at the Fjord Fae.

"Don't look like that," Øyvin said.

"Like what?"

"Like you aren't powerful enough to help me."

"I mean, tell me what you want, Asshole, and I'll see what I can do."

He smirked at the pointed moniker.

"You are powerful," Espen said as he settled on the bed, wearing a black police T-shirt and cargo-pants, both of which clung to his toned muscles. I did a double-take. How had he gotten dressed so fast?

"Sure," I conceded and looked back at Øyvin. "But what exactly can I do to help you steal a shard from the Fjord Fae? If I remember correctly, you said it was in the Council chambers in the Palace."

Øyvin nodded.

"So?"

"I need you to make me a blade or weapon that can cleave through the ancient granite bedrock that houses the shard."

Arms falling to my sides, a chortle bubbled out of me. "A rock sword that can hack at other rock? Without breaking the pretty piece of rock we want? How hard could that possibly be?"

Øyvin's gaze didn't break from mine. "You tell me, Trouble."

I wiped the back of my hand across my forehead. I *could* make stone swords, decently sharp ones. But what Øyvin wanted sounded more like a chisel than a blade. I'd never made one of those. Fuck, I didn't even think I'd actually seen one in person. Only ever in movies. But... I did have Halvar's smithing powers. So, in theory, I should be able to smith a bunch of different weapons out of stone.

Setting my hands on my hips, I let out a sigh. "I'll give it a try."

After a quick shower and some breakfast, we reconvened our planning session in the living room. Øyvin perched on his usual spot on the piano bench while Espen sat on the sofa, his arms spread across the back. I pushed aside the coffee table and stood in the middle of the room, sunlight angling through the windows and casting the entire space in a strong orange glow. At this time of year, even nine o'clock in the morning was as bright as midday—the land of the midnight sun living up to its name with over sixteen hours of daylight in late summer.

I took a deep breath and focused on my magic. I'd grown accustomed to its swirling presence. It wasn't an extension of me, it was part of the mountain that lived in me, connected me to the fae world. Or at least, that's what it felt like.

A swell of warmth built in my sternum and the memory of a short sword filled my mind. I drew my hands over each other and pushed the magic out of me. A slate-gray dagger took shape, the point shimmering in the morning light, the weighty hilt and grip cooling in my palm.

"What's that for?" Øyvin asked, his voice still rumbly and husky.

"Practice sword," I replied. "Got to get the juices flowing before I start on your piece."

Øyvin huffed.

"You're doing great," Espen said from his spot on the sofa with a beaming smile.

He was right. I was doing great. Crafting swords came naturally to me now—like an instinctual reaction. Within seconds I could draw on my magic and give it form.

I set the smooth, stone blade on the coffee table. "We can use that as decor. Maybe a paperweight."

Both men snorted a laugh.

I turned to Øyvin. "What kind of pick or axe do you need?"

He pulled out his phone and tapped the screen a few times before typing something in. A moment later he turned the device to face me. "Something like this."

Leaning in, I took a few steps closer to get a better look.

A short, thick chisel stared back at me—the butt rounded for impact from a hammer, the blade section sharpened to a wide point. That shouldn't be too difficult to make. I'd need to pay particular attention to the blade section, but it was small and would be easily concealed underneath Øyvin's clothes.

"I'll try," I said and retook my spot in the middle of the living room.

Closing my eyes, I focused on the image Øyvin had just shown me and placed my palms over one another while leaving a small gap between them. I pushed my magic out of me, willing it to take the desired shape. An effortless swell of warm energy pulsed between my palms. Opening my eyes, I found the chisel forming with near invisible ripples flowing around it. The mottled black-and-gray piece of stone dropped into my hand as it finished up—the tendrils of magic vanishing.

"Well done," Espen said.

I let out a breath and rolled my shoulders. I'd done it. But would it be strong enough to hack through rock?

Something in my gut twisted. A sensation I felt the need to listen to.

I quickly called forward a plain rock into my palm and knelt beside the coffee table. Placing the chisel at an angle against the blade, I raised the stone above my head and aimed.

"What are—"

"Not on the ta—"

I slammed the rock down on the chisel. The pointy tool crumbled. The stone in my hand smashed against the dagger, clattering together and sending reverberations up through my arm. My teeth juddered against each other, and my body quivered. I lifted the stone and assessed the underside. Tiny hairline fractures webbed from the point of impact, but the two pieces remained intact.

Frustration rumbled through my chest as I stared down at the broken chisel and plopped the stone onto the table beside the blade. "It's not strong enough."

There wasn't a chance in hell that thing was going to cleave through rock successfully. We needed something weightier, something sharper, something that wouldn't potentially crumble in Øyvin's hands.

We needed...

A smile tilted my lips. "I have another idea."

"You seem to be full of those today," Øyvin said with a pointed look at his dust-covered coffee table.

"Quit the sass." I snickered. "This one will help you too."

He smirked and raised his hands as if to say *fine, go on.*

I turned to Espen. "You know how you said you don't condone theft."

Espen's eyes went as wide as the satellite domes on the cruise ships that visited the village. "What are you about to do?"

Ten minutes later we stood outside the camping and hiking store staring at the floor to ceiling window of my cheesing face holding up a pair of hiking boots.

"I mean, at least it's kind of classy," I muttered even though the only thing *classy* about it was my nice Norwegian jumper and traditionally patterned red hat.

"Really?" Espen's voice cracked. "I mean... It's something."

"And you." I turned to Øyvin. "What do you think of this artwork before us?"

He glanced down at me with hooded eyes, those luscious lips pressed together in a firm line, and shoulders set back. "I want to know why you did it," Øyvin said. "Why did you agree to do an advert with the store?"

"I wanted to make sure I was earning my keep and they approached me about the opportunity, saying I'd be the perfect fit as I was a former tourist." I tilted my head to the ad with *Lost in the woods? Get your gear here!* arched over my head. "This is how I'm paying for your Christmas presents this year."

Espen squeezed my shoulder. "You didn't have to do that."

"We take care of you now," Øyvin said.

My vocal cords failed me as those conga-line dancing butterflies were back in my chest, jiving to the rhythm of my partners' words. If we hadn't been out on the streets of Skolvik on a mission, I'd have started kissing them right here. But, we had a robbery to complete. One where the livelihood and safety of countless humans and fae rested on our shoulders. And, somewhere around here, a Fire Fae king lurked. So, we needed to keep moving.

I looked back at the store and rubbed my hands together.

"How do you plan on sneaking in?" Espen asked.

"Oh, we're not sneaking." There was nothing sneaky about my plan. "We're robbing the place in broad daylight."

Espen squeaked.

"We're going to smash this window, storm inside, and grab what we need."

Espen let out a strangled whimper and started pacing in a circle. "That's not just stealing. That's vandalism. Breaking and entering. Theft. Destruction of property. We can't do that."

I bit my lip and stifled a smile.

"Trouble…"

"Ugh, okay we're not breaking in." I pulled Oddvar's overflowing keyring from my pants pocket and jingled it. "We've got the key."

Espen pressed his hand to his chest. "Now is not the time for joking. I don't think I can handle it."

"Oh, you handle me quite fine, husband."

His eyes lit up before he pulled on his collar and cleared his throat. "So, the keys."

"Explain," Øyvin added.

"Oddvar's has been around for eons, and over the years other businesses have come to trust the man. Many of them have given him back up keys to their stores in case of emergencies."

"And he gave them to you?" Øyvin asked.

"Apparently, now is an emergency." I'd been surprised by it myself. But Oddvar had trusted me enough to hire me and was now entrusting me to watch over his business while he fled to safety.

I stepped forward and started testing keys on the lock. While he may have had a whole bunch of them, none were labeled. The eleventh key slid home and allowed me to turn it. The front door clicked, and I pressed down on the handle. Hinges squawked as the door swung open.

Turning to the guys, I motioned for them to go first. "Lost in the woods?" I said, mimicking the slogan on the window. "Get your gear here!"

Espen chuckled and swept inside while Øyvin rolled his eyes and followed.

The store's interior looked like something out of a horror movie. Shadows blanketed the racks and shelves, the only light coming from the windows at our backs. The wood beams holding the ceiling aloft seemed more like gnarled trees looming over us, while the shelves felt like they were concealing haunted corn-maze actors, ready to leap out and scare you with their chainsaws and gory makeup.

A shiver ran down my spine as I followed the guys past the cash register and into the depths of the store.

Espen came to a stop in front of an aisle of yoga gear and exercise equipment. "What exactly are we looking for, Lennie?"

I pulled up beside him and Øyvin. "Ice picks."

"Clever girl," Øyvin said, and a bubble of pride swelled inside me.

If we couldn't make our own chisel, then finding any sort of climbing gear or ice hacking equipment was our best bet. Bonus points for tools that were made of steel.

"And if they don't have any?" Espen asked, his amber gaze filled with light and his cheeks flushed.

I shrugged. "Then we head over to the hardware store and *break in* there too. But I'd prefer something that is more portable. Swimming into the palace with a chisel and hammer, or even a sledge hammer, isn't exactly inconspicuous."

Øyvin grunted.

"You raise a good point," Espen said, peering through the store. "Let's split up and take an aisle each."

We divided the store into sections. Espen would tackle the middle while I took the left and Øyvin took the right. I doubted ice climbing equipment would be near the swimming and hiking section, but I couldn't be sure. This place had a wild array of items. Where the middle part was pretty normal with clothes, the rest of the space was littered with objects that couldn't possibly be considered nor needed for camping or hiking.

They really needed to re-brand themselves as a general store.

I set off to the left and scanned the head-height shelves for anything that looked remotely pokey.

An orange rubber ducky glared at me from beside a display of hiking boots. Five boxes of unicorn floaties begged for new homes, while the heavy bags of intricately folded tents weighed down the shelves below them. Nothing along here looked helpful.

I spun to the wall at my back. Covered in backpacks of all shapes and sizes, the display was a colorful rainbow of variety that outclassed Øyvin's vast collection of spices. From cute little pink ones that my nieces would love, to monstrous green ones that could only be wielded by someone Halvar's size. The store had every backpack one could ever need. But none of them had axes attached to them.

I peered up at the top shelves. Maybe they'd stashed the winter stuff away for the season like we'd done with our heaviest wool sweaters?

Labeled boxes lined the uppermost shelves. *Jul, påske, halloween.* Those must've been seasonal decorations. *Båt, truger, is.*

Is.

"Bingo," I said.

But how the hell was I going to get the ice-labeled box down from up there? I needed to find a ladder. Scurrying around the store, I eventually found what I needed and dragged the a-frame ladder to the left-side wall.

I set it beneath the shelf, clambered up, and grabbed the box.

"Let me get that," Espen said, appearing beneath me. He reached up and I heaved the large cardboard box into his waiting hands.

"Thank you," I said as I climbed back down.

He set the box on the floor, and I opened the flaps. Inside was a mound of carabiners, rope, two helmets, and half a dozen pick axes for scaling ice and glaciers.

I gave myself a round of applause, the claps echoing around the silent store. "Double bingo."

"Well done." Espen picked up something from beside the other shelving unit. "All I found was this."

My eyes widened as I rose and took in the long stick in his hand. "What the hell is that?"

He beamed. "Fishing spear."

"You Norwegians and your outdoor activities will never cease to amaze me. Do they teach you how to spear-fish in school too?"

"No," Øyvin grumbled as he stepped into the aisle. "But most of them know how to fish by the time they're five."

Figures.

"Well, I got lucky." I plucked an axe from the box and gently waved it for him to see. "But did you find anything that might be useful?"

"Unless Espen wants a new shower curtain for the cabin, I found nothing."

I chuckled.

"That won't be necessary," Espen said and stashed the spear on the shelf beside him.

Movement by the front window caught my eye. A sliver of silver glinting in the light. "Get down."

Both men dropped into perfect push-ups while I splooted on my stomach like a puppy. My heart hammered against the floor, my breaths coming out in short pants.

Out on the road, Veigar wandered past with his hands behind his back, like he was out for a stroll along the French Riviera. I could just make out his profile, his mouth opening and closing. Was he talking to someone? He paused and peered at my advertisement. Tilting his head to one side, he mumbled something else.

Shit.

Had he seen us? Would he attack us in here? My initial instinct to hide would say yes. He'd killed those soldiers on the mountain without any other warning than his note. And, while unconfirmed, he'd been the one to set fire to the oil refinery down fjord. Halvar and the Fjell Fae Council were right. Veigar was ruthless when he didn't get what he wanted.

The Fire Fae King shook his head and continued his walk down the street, vanishing from my view on the floor.

A shiver ran down my spine and I pulled my knees underneath me—Espen pressed his hand against my back. "Wait. He might circle back."

Staying on my stomach, adrenaline coursed through me like a live wire begging to be tripped. Espen brushed his hand in circles against my lower back, while Øyvin peered over his shoulder.

After another few minutes on the floor that felt more like a lifetime, Espen said, "Okay. We should be all right, now."

Both men flipped onto their haunches and slowly rose, their gazes locked on the large windows at the front of the building.

I scrambled to my feet with as much grace as an antelope on ice. I grabbed the ice pick that was a little longer than my forearm and featured a jagged axe point. Øyvin plucked it from my grasp and tested its weight before measuring it against different parts of his body. The handle was a bit long, but against his torso, it should work.

"Yes?" I said, my voice sounding more hopeful than I felt.

He nodded and grabbed one of the ropes from the box. As quickly as a sailor, he fashioned a few knots and tied the neon-pink string around his middle, holding the thin, metal axe against his T-shirt-covered stomach. "I may need to use a layer of magic, pretend to be in my uniform, to help conceal it."

A whoosh of air left my chest, and I braced my hands on my knees. One of my crazy plans had worked... but we still had more plans to see through.

"Let's get this tidied up and get out of here," I said. "The quicker we get the two you-know-whats, the quicker we might get rid of Veigar."

We strode back through the village, peering around corners before continuing in case the Fire Fae King was still on his midday stroll.

The red, wooden walls of the boathouse waved in welcome as we approached home. What had once been a place I'd stomped toward with anger, was now a place I'd run toward if in danger. I peered up at Øyvin as our footsteps tapped against the dock by the front door. "When are you heading below?"

"Now," Øyvin replied.

"Already?" I squeaked. "We haven't discussed exactly what happens next. We need more time."

"I have everything I need."

Espen brushed his hand down my arm, offering an ounce of reassurance.

"I've already been planning," Øyvin continued. "You've done your part. I just need you to wait here and have your phones on in case something goes wrong or if I need to abort."

That competitive gene kicked on and I straightened. "Nothing will go wrong."

Øyvin pressed in on me, and my head tilted back to look at him. Those blue eyes shone with a determination that could power through defensive lines on a football field. A sense of need and pride tugged low in my belly at the sight.

"If something does go wrong"—he swallowed hard—"promise me you'll get the Forest shard and run to the mountain with it anyway."

I shook my head. Nothing was going to go wrong. We'd get that damn rock and the one at the graveyard and kick Veigar out of town. Together.

"Lennie..." Øyvin said my name like an order and a promise.

"If something goes wrong, I'm coming after you."

"Don't."

"I will."

Øyvin let out a long-winded sigh and backed us toward the edge of the dock, the water lapping at the pylons beneath us. "I love you. Your courage. Your dedication to the people you call family. But I won't let you get yourself killed for me."

I narrowed my eyes at him while my heart fluttered like a million fireflies had taken up residence. "Fine," I conceded. "But since when do you decide who I can and cannot die for?"

"Since you married us."

My limbs felt as if they would melt into the fjord and I spread my hands against his broad chest.

He smirked and tipped my chin up with his finger and thumb. "Would you cry for me, Trouble?"

I chuckled. "Don't get your hopes up, Asshole."

Yeah, I probably would.

A wicked grin swept across his face, and he pressed his lips to mine in an all-consuming kiss before spinning and diving into the fjord without me.

31

ØYVIN

As soon as my head submerged, I pulled on my magic and created a bubble of air around me. I pressed my hand to my shoulder and pictured my Fjord Fae uniform. The magical illusion rippled into place. Hopefully, this would help conceal the weapon tied to my stomach and people wouldn't take a closer look at a soldier walking through the palace in their uniform. The only problem would be if word had spread of my termination... I'd deal with that problem if it arose.

I pushed forward through the cool, dark waters, aiming for the Fjord Fae palace. Schools of fish flitted past, their beady eyes watching me with equal amounts of uncertainty and curiosity. The colors of their scales shifted beneath the diffused rays of light, reminding me of how I'd changed in the past year and what I was setting out to do.

In Reuven and Veigar's hands, the Fjord Fae shard was a weapon—something they could use against other fae and against my partners. I couldn't let that happen. It would destroy the peace among the fae and my new family. I didn't like stealing from my people, but I had to. Had no other choice.

The betrayal burned a hole in my chest, but I ignored the singe.

My heart thumped heavily against my ribs as I approached the palace entry that loomed ahead like the maw of a whale. Two soldiers swam around the entrance—the same number I'd usually station there. Inside, two more stood sentry with fishing spears in their grasps. I removed my bubble and kept my head down.

Keeping my breaths and steps even, I continued on as if nothing were different. I was Øyvin Håland, come to work for the Fjord Fae. Not to steal their most prized possession.

The soldiers gave me brief glances, but didn't question my presence.

I let out a quiet sigh of relief.

Assessing the scene as I strode through the pristine corridors, I took an indirect route to the Council chambers that wove through the living quarters and not the busier tunnels.

Muffled sounds of daily life crept out of vestibules and apartments.

Lights flickered against the polished stone.

Fjord Fae went about their business.

Life in the Palace continued as if nothing was amiss.

Exactly as I needed it to be.

As I approached the long hall that led to the King's quarters and Council chambers, a door opened up ahead and I spun back around the corner. Sigurd stepped out of my old office.

I bit back a grumble.

It had been less than twenty-four fucking hours and they'd already reassigned my office space.

So much for loyalty.

At least, by the looks of the silver-threaded cape that hung from Sigurd's shoulders, they'd picked a decent successor. Sigurd was a good man. A bit of a sycophant it would seem, but good nonetheless. I'd trained him myself. If only I'd trained him to stand up against shit leadership. Then again, how good had I been at standing up against Balder and his authoritarian ways?

I shook off the thought and turned my back as Sigurd and a small group of soldiers headed past me down the main hallway.

Don't move and they won't have reason to look at you twice.

Taking five steady breaths, I waited until the sound of their steps abated, then peered back into the main thoroughfare.

Soft sconces and marble-smooth walls shimmered back at me.

Empty.

Perfect.

I strode down the hallway as fast as possible, listening for any signs of movement or life. Everything was quiet, and I sent a quick thank you to the ancestors I was about to betray. I had good reasons for doing this, but I wasn't sure the ancestors would agree.

They can yell at me when I'm dead.

Pressing my shoulder against the thick Council chamber door, I nudged it open and held my breath.

Unlike yesterday, the chairs sat vacant, the table free of forearms and tales of tyranny. At the back of the room, its sky-blue eye blinking at me in the low light, was Jörmungandr.

I shut the door behind me with a gentle thud and crossed the room to the sea serpent carved into the back wall. The carving itself was a marvel—stretching the length of the room and wrapping toward the monarch's seat at the head of the table. Only the Monarch, Head Guard, and select council members knew what the stone really was. Everyone else was led to believe it was decor. Whenever anyone walked through the—

My breath caught again.

The door.

I'd almost forgotten.

It wouldn't lock. Never had.

But I needed to slow anyone who might enter and dampen any sound that might flow through its slats.

Focusing on the warm well of magic in my chest, I pulled on a thread of it and crafted a wall of water. The thick, aqueous barrier would muffle any noise and buy me a little time. I settled the boiling translucent rectangle over the door where it sloshed around in its confines like a liquid bandage.

Pressing my hand to my shoulder again, I dropped my miraged uniform and turned back to the stone wall. The rope around my middle came undone with two easy tugs, and the ice pick Lennie had so cleverly suggested I use, fell into my waiting hand.

I planted my feet, grasped the axe with both hands, and focused on a point beside the shard.

Ancestors forgive me.

I swung.

The axe chipped at the rock, reverberations skittering up my forearms. A tiny fracture sprang from the serpent's socket like the lines around an old sailor's eyes. I could press some water into the crack, forcing the stone to separate from the shard, but it likely wasn't deep enough. Not yet.

According to Lennie, that shard was most likely a triangle. Like the icebergs that floated past the island of Svalbard, there was more beneath the surface. Only one corner of blue sprung from the snake's eye—there was more underneath that I had to be careful of.

I aimed at the other side of the eyeball and swung again.

The pick impaled the rock with a sharp crack. Bits of stone splintered and sprinkled across my feet.

Prying at a loose piece, I popped it off the wall and let it thump to the floor. A larger chunk of the shard stared back at me. How long had it been ensconced here? Hundreds of years, at least.

I set down the axe and pushed a bubble of water into the cracks around the stone. Drawing on more magic, I willed the bubble to swell and push against the stone around it. Creaking filled the empty chamber, and the cracks splintered further, more dust falling across my shoes. I brushed aside rock with my hands and water magic until a large enough hole formed over the shard.

Putting my hand into the gap, I pulled out the shard.

The bright stone shone in my hand. Cool against my palm, it reminded me of a lump of ice. Almost translucent, yet filled with a blue that was similar to both the sky and the floating cathedrals that passed the northernmost shores of Norway. "Fuck."

A piece of Jörmungandr's cheek fell from the wall and crashed against the floor, drawing me from my stupor.

Whipping around, I faced the door. The water barrier remained intact, no movement of the door handle either. But that didn't mean there wouldn't be.

I needed to get back home. Get back to Lennie.

I grabbed the rope and tied the shard against my stomach.

Setting the now dilapidated axe on the table, I put my hand to my shoulder and pulled another illusion over my clothes. This time, instead of my uniform, I settled for a long-sleeved white shirt and dark jeans. Plain and unassuming. If anyone asked what I was doing down here, I'd tell them I'd forgotten something in my office but hadn't been able to find it.

Waving my hand, the protective wall of water disintegrated.

With adrenaline humming through my veins, I gently opened the door and peered out into the hall. No movement. No noise. Reuven must've been in the living quarters and Sigurd headed for the wall. It was about time for daily checks—at least this was when I'd always gone to the wall.

Feeling confident there was no one lurking, I swept into the hallway and strode for the exit like I belonged here and the Fjord Fae shard wasn't strapped to my front.

A wave of guilt washed through me as I passed doorways, Fjord Fae going about their day, and the turn toward the ballroom where displaced fae were sheltering.

I'm doing the right thing. Stealing the shard would help all three factions, including Fjord Fae. This was protecting them from someone who didn't have their best interest at heart. Someone who had aligned with a being who would rule us like a dictator, bringing fire and brimstone to our precious waters.

There was zero doubt in my mind that Veigar would harm the creatures in the fjord. He'd already lit the oil refinery on fire for merely ignoring his wishes and not considering falling in line. Men like that were volatile and unworthy of trust.

"Øyvin," a frail, feminine voice croaked, and I ground to a stop as Ingeborg stepped out of a nook in front of me.

Small eyes peered up at me from her hunched form.

I cleared my throat and gave her a toothless grin. "Ingeborg. Are you well?"

"I'm quite well," she replied. "Thank you for asking."

"Good."

She touched her hand to my elbow. "But I'm concerned about you. I heard a rumor that you'd been dismissed?"

Fuck.

"I... Yes. I was."

"That's such a shame. They'd better have a good reason other than this ridiculous notion that you could no longer be trusted with our fae secret."

So that's what they'd been telling people. Not that I couldn't be trusted by Reuven, but that the Fae in general couldn't trust me to not keep our society's existence a secret from humans.

"The King and I no longer see eye-to-eye," I said. "You must excuse me, I need to head home. My partner is waiting for me."

She let me pass with a hum I couldn't place. Did she not believe me? Even if it was taken as a lie, I didn't have time to wait. If I hung around, I could get caught.

I twisted and looked over my shoulder. "Have a good day, Ingeborg."

She raised her hand in goodbye.

I spun and ran directly into someone. Heat washed over me like a bonfire and I steadied the person who tumbled into my arms, holding them away from my body.

Black eyes stared up at me and all the oxygen in my lungs evaporated.

"Your Majesty," I coughed out. "I didn't see you there."

Salka's brows furrowed as she regained her footing and brushed her hands over her plain black dress.

"What are you doing down here?" she asked, her voice tinged with suspicion. The sound reminded me of smoke drifting off a fire, of flames curling around logs and making the moisture in them pop.

"Forgot something in my office."

I kept my gaze locked with hers, holding my ground.

"Did you find it?"

I shook my head. "Must've already been thrown away."

"Shame."

"Indeed."

Her tongue swept across her top teeth, and I took a step back, bowing my head. "Apologies for crashing into you. Have a good day."

I didn't wait for her reply. I strode as fast as I could for the next turn in the hallway before sprinting for the exit.

If she went to Reuven and told him she'd seen me, he'd send soldiers after me for questioning. I didn't have much time. I needed to get back home, to Lennie, above the water where the two of them could defend me if needed. Not that I wanted them to have to, but I knew, deep down, that they'd do whatever it took to protect me. Lennie had said as much before I dove into the fjord today. And Espen... the man had become a close friend and partner. Did I love him like I did Lennie? No. That was impossible. But another bond had formed between the two of us over the past year. One built on camaraderie and care, and sealed by the love we shared for the same woman.

The main entrance to the palace came into view and I ran for it, ignoring the confused looks on the guards' faces. I dove through the large hole in the wall and into the cold waters of the fjord.

The weight of the fjord pressed down on me as I built an air pocket around myself. Using every ounce of magic within me, I propelled myself through the water.

Fish darted out of my way.

Ripples and bubbles crashed together in my wake.

Up.

Up.

Up.

The murky waters grew lighter and clearer the closer I got to the surface.

Something large moved beneath me, rippling through the depths and disturbing the currents. I clenched my jaw and swiftly scanned the darkness. Inky water and a distant, rocky fjordbed stared back at me. Nothing was down there. But that didn't mean I wasn't being followed.

I swam.

Harder.

Faster.

Using more magic than I ever had.

A jet of water blasted past on my left and I flinched.

Rip current. Dangerous. Lethal even.

A quick glance behind me didn't calm my fears. Three figures gave chase.

I turned back and pushed my magic to its limit.

Move.

Move.

Move.

A moment later the pylons of our house came into view, ripples of the red-and-white building painted across the surface.

Two shapes moved up there. One blonde, the other dark.

My chest ached and my arms trembled as I untied the shard from my stomach.

"Put it down, Håland!" A firm, male voice echoed through the water. Pressure wrapped around my ankles pulling me back. I opened my free palm and aimed it backward, shooting a pulse of power and freeing myself.

"Stop!"

I didn't listen.

A tickle ran down my spine and the water around me rippled. *Shit.* I dodged to the right, narrowly avoiding another jet that could haul me back into their arms.

Too close. They were too close.

With a final push of magic, I breached the surface and burst my air pocket.

Cool air whipped across my cheeks and through my hair.

I slammed the stone onto the dock, peered into Lennie's beautiful wide brown eyes, and said, "Run."

32

LENNIE

Øyvin was yanked beneath the surface.

"No!" I clawed my way to the edge of the dock and leaned out over the water, stretching my hand toward the circular ripples where he'd just been.

"Lennie, no!" Espen hauled me back and pulled me across the weather-worn planks.

My body trembled and my breaths caught in my chest, screaming for release. "What just happened? What the fuck just happened?"

Espen held the Fjord shard in one hand and his free arm banded around my torso.

"We have to go after him. We have to save him." I scrambled against Espen's ironclad hold, my shoes scraping and screeching across the dock. "We have to help him!"

This couldn't be happening. Nothing was supposed to go wrong. I needed to get him out of the water. *Now.*

My breaths grew ragged as I fought against Espen, scratching at his police jacket.

Water rippled out on the fjord, not far from the boathouse, and an arc of translucent scales breached the surface like the Loch Ness Monster.

Every ounce of oxygen inside me disappeared and my limbs went limp.

"Run!" Espen yelled against my ear and spun me toward the road.

I didn't have to be told twice. Sprinting across the dock and onto the street, I ran as fast as I could toward the village.

"Police station," Espen said, coming up beside me.

I nodded. My breaths sawing in and out of my lungs. "Wh-what the fuck w-was that?"

"I don't want to stick around to find out."

Agreed.

Tears streaked across my cheeks as we bolted for Espen's workplace. My legs pistoned as I pumped my arms at my sides, pushing my body to move faster.

The austere walls of the station came into view, the lights in the windows turned off, save for the one above the front door. Parked against the right side of the building sat a lone police cruiser, blue lights above white-and-neon-yellow lines. Espen pointed toward it and we both aimed that direction, slowing as we reached it.

I came to a stop and bent over, pressing my palms against my thighs as I sucked in lungfuls of air. "What do we do? What do we do? What do we do?"

"There's nothing we can do. We made a promise to him." Espen corralled me against the side of the station and gripped my chin, forcing me to look at him. "There is nothing we can do to save him, Lennie. Neither of us are strong enough, can't breathe under water like they can. We'd be signing our own death certificates by diving into those waters right now."

"We could try."

He shook his head. "While I love your strength and resolve, you know I'm right."

My chest rose and fell like an animal caught in battle—fight or flight instinct kicking in. I loved Øyvin. Would do anything for him. Even take on yet another monarch whose powers probably far outweighed my own. My rational mind recognized the stupidity of that insurmountable task, but my heart felt differently.

"We'd die trying to get to wherever he's been taken," Espen said.

"So, you think he's been captured?"

"I think it's a distinct possibility. But I can't be sure."

There it was. The *what if*. What if they hadn't spared him, hadn't sent him to a watery prison, and instead just killed him on the spot. My shoulders slumped as the thought ran through me, my muscles giving up on me as the grief settled in. Espen caught me and pulled me into his embrace.

"We need to leave now," he whispered into my hair.

"We can't..." My throat tightened. "We can't just abandon Øyvin."

"There is nothing we can do."

"I can't just leave him to die," I said, my words soft and without force. Like they recognized the reality of our situation. "It's my fault."

"Lennie." Espen brushed his free hand through my hair, tucking it behind one ear and pulling my focus back to his grief-stricken gaze. His voice dipped into a stern tone. "We promised him to get the job done even if something bad happened. We're in that scenario, so we need to get to the stave church. I need you to focus."

He dropped the sky-blue stone into my palm. It was triangular and rounded at one corner with a jagged main edge. But it looked just like the material the Temple was made of.

"It's my fault," I muttered again, staring down at the lump of rock.

"None of this is your fault."

"This was my idea. My plan. And it fucking failed. Some kind of leader I am."

He tilted my chin to face him. "You haven't failed."

"Not yet."

"Leaders make plans. Sometimes they work. Sometimes they don't. And while it's admirable that you're trying to take responsibility—which is a valuable trait in a leader—Øyvin volunteered to do this. In fact, Øyvin was the one who suggested stealing the Fjord Fae shard."

"He wouldn't have thought of it had I not suggested—"

"You don't know that."

He was right. I didn't. But guilt and fear still sat on my chest like a boulder, pressing down and cracking my ribs.

"We haven't failed yet." Espen moved his hands and held my head in his palms. "We follow through with what we need to do, and we trust that Øyvin is far stronger than you're giving him credit for. We get the other shard. We stop Veigar. We save the fae. Can you do that with me, Lennie?"

However much Espen's words rang true, it didn't feel like it. Not right now. This whole thing had been my crazy plan and, like most of my ideas, it had jettisoned off the rollercoaster rails and plummeted to the ground with an almighty crash.

"Yes," I replied with a gentle nod.

"Good." He pressed his lips against my forehead and my eyes fluttered shut for a brief moment.

He was right. I'd made a promise, and we had a mission to complete.

We peeled out of the police station parking lot, blue lights swirling above the car as Espen zipped out of town. I clutched the Fjord shard in my hand, letting the rough edge bite into my palm while rubbing my other hand across my thigh. Focusing on the contrast in the material—cool stone versus soft denim—helped me lower my heart rate and drew my attention away from my tumultuous thoughts.

Ten minutes outside of town, we slowed. A police barricade—several wooden barriers and another cruiser—blocked our path.

"Don't worry," Espen said. "He's with us."

"By *with us*, you mean Fae?"

Espen nodded. "Forest Fae."

"How many of your soldiers do you have on the roster down at the police station?"

"Only a couple."

"Handy."

One of his shoulders lifted. "They're part of the volunteer force of rangers. So, yes, it's convenient. But they don't report to the office that often. They primarily work in the field and report to me."

It was like they'd thought this all through. Then again, most of the fae I'd met were several hundred years old, so I guessed they'd had time to plan for all eventualities.

Espen shut off the car and opened the door. "Stay here."

With the shock and adrenaline draining from my system and emotions welling inside me, I wasn't going anywhere.

He strode over to the other cruiser and exchanged a few words with someone through the car's window. A moment later he removed the blue-and-white wooden barrier from in front of our car, opening the road for us.

As Espen got back in and started the engine, I said, "Bente really did mean *nobody in or out*."

"Can't be too careful. Every entry into town is blocked. And a ten-mile minimum radius has been cleared of all residents."

I stared ahead once more and hoped the roads would stay barricaded. We couldn't have any innocent humans stumbling into town. Not with Veigar on the loose and a mountain threatening to crumble. Hopefully, the severity of the potential natural disaster would have folks thinking twice before heading for Skolvik.

The thought of innocents being hurt or killed opened the floodgates to my emotions. I swallowed a hard lump in my throat and tilted my head back against the headrest. What if someone like Solveig or Dagny came back to get something and got caught by Veigar before we could get to her? What if Veigar burned down the village? What if Øyvin never resurfaced?

A tear welled at the inner corner of my eye, and I wiped it away with a finger.

Espen flicked his gaze to me. "He'll be all right."

I fidgeted in my seat and turned the shard in my hand as another tear slipped down my face. "You can't know that for sure."

Silence responded.

We all understood the risks. We all understood what might happen. But like a fool, I'd let hope swell inside me, let it unpack the throw pillows, set its toothbrush in the jar beside the sink, and flop onto the couch.

Another tear streaked down my cheek, and I closed my eyes. Grief settled over me. That unwelcome beast gnawing at my insides. I couldn't calculate the odds of Øyvin's survival. Fuck, I didn't even know what had been strong enough to pull him under like that. But Reuven was a king and must've had more power than Øyvin. He'd have some royal power like me and Halvar too. But how much and how he would use it was anyone's guess.

A hand rested on my thigh, and I opened my eyes. Another tear fell into my lap.

"We keep moving," Espen said, his voice thick with emotion. "We keep moving and do what we need to do to save the Fae from Veigar and protect Skolvik."

I sniffled and set my hand atop his.

He moved his fingers and squeezed my hand. That melancholy monster inside me backed down slightly, bowing away from the brightness that was my husband.

With a glance over at Espen, I nodded.

It was all we could do. I wouldn't let the villagers down, nor the Fjell Fae, and most of all, Øyvin's sacrifice.

I sucked in a lungful of air, held it for four seconds, before controlling its exit. I just hoped it hadn't actually been a sacrifice, that he was still alive, still with us and hadn't been sent to the ancestors he constantly begged for patience from.

Twenty minutes later, Espen pulled down a narrow road, gravel crunching beneath the tires. The last time we'd been down here the entire place had been covered in a thick layer of snow. Now, luscious green leaves waved as we passed, moss crawled over boulders within the forest, and the dense canopy opened into a clearing where the stave church loomed like a gargoyle.

The building looked as if it had been hammered together with nails and planks from a Viking ship. Thick wood beams stacked on top of each other formed the walls, while black, weather-worn shingles covered the different tiers of the roof. At the top of each high point of the roof were dragons whose long snouts aimed toward the sky, projecting their doom and gloom on all those who dared come close.

The car came to a stop in front of the stone fence, and Espen shut off the engine.

Silence filled the vehicle as a mournful aura seemed to float off the building and through the ancient graveyard.

"Are you ready to do this?" I asked.

Espen lifted my hand to his lips and kissed my knuckles, then sighed and nodded.

33

ESPEN

I climbed out of the police car, my heart in my throat, but my world at my side. If this went wrong, not only would her life potentially be at risk, but the Council of Elders would never forgive me. The Forest Fae shard had been with us for centuries and used to transfer magic from the ancestors to the monarch. But, when Queen Ragnhild died with neither heir nor successor, we'd chosen to hide the sky-blue stone with her and her Head Guard. Never to be used again.

Until now.

The time had come. I knew it in my bones. In my soul. We needed the power in this stone to stop Veigar. His igniting of the oil refinery and murdering Fjell soldiers was tame, child's play for him. Whatever he planned to do next would be much, much worse. And we had to do whatever we could to counter that. Including stealing the Forest Fae shard.

Lennie and I strode across the parking lot, gravel grinding together beneath our shoes. The ancient dark-wood stave church rose out of the grassy clearing, its tall steeples defying gravity. Dragon heads from Viking ships glared at us from the roof beams, and the Christian cross on the top spire pointed toward the clear sky. The surrounding forest was as still as the occupants of the graveyard, and the wind barely rustled the verdant foliage.

Passing lines of gravestones, we made our way toward the site's newer additions.

I brushed my hand over Mads' gravestone first, letting the stone scrape across the pads of my fingers. If he were here, if he were put in this situation, would he do the same? I'd like to think so. He'd always advised me not to fear my destroyer powers and let them find balance with my healer side. But I had never given in to that. Didn't dare to. Not until that day twenty-one years ago when I'd unleashed terror upon the battlefield that had claimed his life and Queen Ragnhild's.

My gaze shifted to her marker, and I took two steps back.

Something pressed against my lower back, and I glanced over my shoulder. Lennie stared up at me, and my muscles relaxed properly for the first time since leaving Skolvik.

She'd seen my powers unleashed too—just not quite to the same extent. I'd still been weak thanks to the poison last autumn, but had buried a large swath of Balder's forces on that mountaintop. Whether those soldiers had deserved such a burial or not was another matter. The most important thing that day had been the need to protect the Forest Fae, and her. Always her.

Reaching out, I nudged us in front of Mads' grave and positioned Lennie behind me. "Stay here."

Her brow furrowed and she glanced between the two graves. She pointed to the blue stone peeking out of the front of Ragnhild's gravestone. "Isn't that it?"

I shook my head. "Decoy."

"Smart."

"Now, stay behind me, please." I lifted my hands in front of me and pulled on the mass of dark energy that sat like a knot in my sternum ready to unleash hell at a moment's notice. Like it could hear my thoughts and feel my intent on using it, the power sat up and begged to be set free. I rolled my shoulders, let a sliver of it past the gates, and down my arms. Pushing it outward, I aimed my hands at the top of the gravestone and launched the magic.

Power crashed against stone and a sharp crack shot through the air.

Lennie flinched and sucked in a breath.

Shit. No.

I clenched my hands into fists and spun. I shouldn't be doing this with her so close. "You shouldn't be here. You should be in the car. Out of harm's way."

She tilted her head to one side, and her gaze flicked to my balled-up hands.

Fear lanced up my spine. I should have been more careful. Should have known better.

Lennie took my right hand in hers and peeled open my fingers. "Stop your worrying right this second, husband."

My heart stilled at the title.

She entwined her fingers with mine and stared up at me. Those large brown eyes held me ensnared—they always did. The sight of them, the sneaky smile perpetually crinkling the corners, the light shining out of her. Everything that she was—it was intoxicating in the best way.

And something that needed protecting from the destructive force that resided within me.

"You won't harm me," she said, drawing me from my thoughts.

"You don't know that."

That signature smirk appeared, though, far less joyful than usual. "Yes. I. Do."

And there was that challenging nature that Øyvin loved so much.

I let out an extended sigh, and she pressed her free palm to my chest.

"I trust that the power in here"—she tapped against my sternum—"won't dare hurt me."

"And how can you be sure of that?"

"Because you love me too much to ever cause me harm."

I freed my hands and cradled her head. "I do—"

"See?"

"—but we can't trust that destroyer part of me."

"Yes, we can."

There was her obstinate side. The part that always got her into trouble, but I loved it, nonetheless.

"Espen Solbakke Martin, you know, deep down, that you'd never hurt me. Your power knows that too. Try."

I shook my head.

"Try it. Quickly."

I could barely handle this woman, and I wouldn't have it any other way. She was an unyielding storm that swept in and crushed any other thoughts of continuing this life without her in it. And she did have a valid point. It didn't feel like my power wanted to hurt her. Quite the opposite. I closed my eyes and reached inside myself, focusing on that churning constant of magic. I gingerly willed the tiniest amount toward her and... the power bristled and retracted.

Fascinating.

I tried again. This time the power pushed back, begging to go in the other direction.

Very fascinating.

The dark mass wanted to be unleashed but pointed away from her. Like it wanted to defend and protect *her.*

She was right.

Opening my eyes, I found my world staring back at me. That awe-filled and righteous look was enough to shake the fears from my mind.

I was using these destructive powers for good. For the good of my people and the rest of the fae in our region. I glanced over my shoulder at the two graves—one now slightly cracked, the other unharmed. What *would* they think about this?

I scoffed at myself. Mads would've told me to trust the powers and find that balance. While Queen Ragnhild would've told me to do whatever I could to protect our people. *No fear, no relenting, no remorse.* Those words rang through my mind like an echo from the past, and a shiver ran down my spine. Lennie was right, and so was Queen Ragnhild's old motto.

"Aaaaaand?"

I turned back to Lennie and sucked in a breath. "I don't think these powers want to hurt you."

"See. Told you." She gave me a wobbly smile and pointed to the gravestone behind me. "Now, let's get that magical little rock out of the grave and get back home."

Brushing my hand across her cheek, I said, "Thank you."

"I love you too."

"And yet, you couldn't possibly love me more than I love you."

"Oh, that we can debate at length another time."

And there was that unrelenting competitive side her entire family had.

"I look forward to it."

"Now…" She grabbed my shoulders, turned me around, and smacked my bottom. "Let 'er rip."

"You really do know how to break the moment."

"Oh, I learned how to pivot a conversation from my darling husband. You should meet him sometime. Great guy, stellar ass."

I snorted. "He must do yoga."

"So much yoga."

As a warm breeze drifted across the graveyard and our words settled, I focused on the cracked stone in front of me. A sharp fissure cleaved vertically from the top of the grave and down toward Mads' name. I raised my hands once more and pulled on my magic. It flowed down my arms and shot out toward the grave. With another *crack*, more fissures appeared. I blasted it again, and splinters cut through *Mads Robertson*.

Another shot of power. *I'm sorry.*

Another crack. *I'm sorry.*

A final push to knock the lumps aside. *I'm so sorry.*

A blue shard tumbled onto the grassy mound with a thump.

It was done.

Stepping forward, I retrieved the stone. The sky-blue lump of rock shone in the sunlight, its glassy surface smooth and cool to the touch.

Lennie wrapped her arms around my torso. "Well done."

I pulled her tighter to me, brushing my hand over her back as I pressed a kiss to the top of her head. "Thank you for believing in me."

"Always," she whispered.

"Here." I handed her the shard. She took it and watched as I knelt and picked up the pieces of Mads' gravestone. I precariously rearranged the lumps, doing my best to set them back where they belonged. But... I let out a frustrated sigh. The pieces were too many, and the grooves too damaged—

"Let me." Lennie dropped to her knees beside me and shoved the Forest Fae shard back into my hands.

With deft movements, she twisted and adjusted the stones like large puzzle pieces. Then, with a deep breath, she closed her eyes and pressed her palms against the gravestone.

My eyes widened and my heart sputtered as the fissures on the rocky facade healed and the broken chunks melded back together once more. I'd never witnessed her use this form of Fjell Fae magic before. Those training sessions at the mountain were working. She was learning and... she was good.

With another deep exhale, Lennie pulled back her hands and opened her eyes, studying her work. The cracks were gone, the gravestone had reformed, the only sign that anything had changed were the faint scars where the fissures had been.

"You're incredible." The words tumbled from my lips on a whisper.

Lennie turned and looked up at me, her eyes full of pride and sadness. "Make sure Øyvin hears you say that when we get him back."

An invisible knife twisted through my heart. Denial. Pain. The oncoming onslaught of grief. I hoped to the ancestors he hadn't been killed in the fjord. But we had no way of knowing. If he'd been taken, they'd have confiscated his phone. And if he'd been killed...

I swallowed hard and Lennie's eyes locked on the movement.

Damn.

I had to stay strong. Had to maintain composure, because if Lennie saw how worried I really was, she'd fall apart.

"I'll tell him," I said. "Loud and proud."

A wistful smile twisted her lips. "Good."

We rose to our feet and wandered out of the graveyard, the stave church looming behind us as we went. I slipped my hand into Lennie's and gently squeezed as a tangle of emotions settled onto my shoulders. Worry, sadness, and fear retook their seats, but a bubble of joy settled in beside them.

We'd done it. We had two of the shards in our possession. Now all we needed to do was return to Skolvik and rush them to the Temple in the mountain without getting caught by Veigar... or anyone else for that matter.

As we reached the car, a warm gust of air washed across the parking lot, and I stilled. "Did you feel that?"

Lennie spun and faced me, her brow furrowed. "Feel what?"

Where had that wind come from? Hadn't it been still since we got here? An unseasonably warm gust didn't just come out of nowhere... unless a storm was rolling in. I shrugged. "Probably nothing."

"Come on," she said, her voice breathy and laced with weariness and grief. "We've got a world to save."

34

LENNIE

Holding a shard in each hand, I examined the pieces in a daze as we sped back toward town. Each lump of quartz-like stone was unique but shared the same triangular shape with one jagged edge. If anyone else found them they might think they were two halves of a whole, but I knew exactly where they belonged. They were a perfect match for the pedestal that sat in the middle of the Temple of the Fae.

I stared out the window, brush and leafy birch trees whizzing past as Espen drove what I could only assume was *exactly* the speed limit. Øyvin would probably grumble and roll his eyes at that.

My heart fractured further.

Øyvin.

Memories of him playing the piano flooded my mind. The smell of him baking chocolate chip cookies for me feeling as real as if we had a batch stashed in the car.

I didn't want to believe he was gone. Couldn't stomach the idea. He had to be alive. He had to come back to me. Because if he wasn't and he didn't—

A lump clogged my throat, and I swallowed it down.

I couldn't think like that.

And yet... It felt like this was just the beginning. This was the first quarter, and we were down fourteen points already with three whole quarters to go. Football games may be won in the fourth and final quarter, but, even with both the Forest and Fjord shards in our possession, we were already down a man. Our team was missing a key player, and an awful feeling took up residence in my stomach.

"People are going to die, aren't they?" I said, breaking the silence in the car.

Espen nodded. "It's inevitable."

I sighed.

"We will win this, Lennie. We're going to be all right."

I glanced over at the ray of sunshine behind the wheel. "I really admire your optimism."

"I know you can be optimistic too."

"I don't feel it right now."

"Then get that frown upturned or however the saying goes, because we're going to do this," he said, his voice filling with urgency like a rally cry. "We're already doing this. We're getting those stones to the Temple, asking the ancestors for help, and kicking Veigar's ass right out of town." A gentle smile played on his lips. "I believe in us, Lennie."

The way his gaze warmed as he briefly glanced across the center console had me melting into a puddle of hope. Hope that we would do this. Hope that we could save the fae from a dick-tator. Together. The three—

My brain stalled on the number, and I faced the window again.

There wasn't three of us right now.

Espen cleared his throat. "Are you really going to let some ancient asshole take the mountain away from you? Let him tell *you* what to do?"

I rolled my neck and breathed through my nose. He was right. If I could barely take orders from Halvar, there wasn't a chance in hell I'd be kneeling to a man as volatile as Veigar. A man who didn't have the best interest of the fae at heart.

The only men I'd be getting on my knees for were my partners.

Martin Family Competitiveness: Activated.

"You really do know how to get me going, don't you?"

He snickered and a flush pinked his cheeks. "In more ways than one."

My responding chuckle was drowned out by a whooshing roar from behind us.

"What kind of backfire was that? This thing have turbo boosters or something?" I twisted in my seat, peering over my shoulder at the road behind us. My eyes widened and my entire body flooded with adrenaline.

Flames shot up on one side of the road, quickly jumping the asphalt and igniting the trees on the other side—a wall of orange and red chasing us.

"Espen, we have a problem."

He peered into the rearview mirror. "Shit!"

The fire swelled behind us, licking its way up the trees and devouring them whole. They were like kindling, oversized matches that ignited in the blink of an eye. A burst of flames shot toward us, and I clutched my seatbelt. "Drive, drive, drive!"

Espen slammed his foot against the pedal and the car shot forward, pushing me back against my seat. I swallowed hard as he gripped the steering wheel, his knuckles turning white.

The flames barreled around the bends—the roads up here twisting back and forth along the mountains that shielded the fjord on both the north and south sides. I clung to the "oh shit" handle as we sped down the hillside, the blaze barely twenty yards behind.

"What the hell is happening? Is that a forest fire?"

"Yes..."

"But? I sense a but."

"He brought his best backup." Espen slammed his palm against the top of the steering wheel. "Fuck."

We'd already surmised that Veigar wasn't alone—those wildfires further inland were way too suspicious—but, we hadn't exactly had time to discuss his forces in extreme detail. "What else does he have in his arsenal?"

"Herja."

"And that is?"

"She's Veigar's Head Guard."

My eyebrows hit my hairline, and I swallowed hard. Of course he had his own Head Guard. Why wouldn't he? And one whose name sounded like she ate Norse Gods for breakfast to bulk up. "Omen of death and devastation by chance?"

Espen nodded.

"Fuck."

"This must be her handy work. She must've snuck past our scouting parties."

I peered over my shoulder again. Flames swept across the road, chasing us like a lion desperate for food. Was Herja standing in those flames? Or was she behind them, pushing them toward us?

"You've fought her before?" I asked as the car veered around another precarious switchback, my shoulder bumping against the window.

"No, I don't remember a time when she's been back on the mainland. But if there's anyone as volatile as Veigar, it's her."

"Can we just set Halvar on her? Watch the big guy slice and dice her into bite-size pieces?"

"We can ask, but if Herja is here and not at the mountain then I'd imagine Halvar might have his hands full with Veigar himself."

I blanched. "They're dividing us. Spreading us out."

Espen sighed, and I didn't like the sound. Not one bit. It sent my stomach plummeting.

"We're going to have to split up," he said.

"Nope, don't want to do that." I shook my head. "I've already lost one of you today, I'm not losing both."

Espen sighed again, this time sounding like he agreed. "The stones, remember."

I looked down in my lap to the two Temple shards and swore. He was right. Dammit, we *did* have to split up.

"I have to get out down here and stop it," Espen said between gritted teeth.

"What are you going to do, bury the fire?"

"No." Espen pulled the steering wheel to the right, drifting us around another sharp bend. "Can't do that."

"Huh?"

"There's still oxygen in the soil. The roots will catch. It won't put out the fire."

"Then how the hell are you going to take on that?" I pointed over my shoulder.

"Magic."

"And a helluva lot of luck."

"Yes, that too."

"Espen!"

"Lennie!"

I huffed.

"I can bend it away from the town, tear down parts of the woods and create fire corridors," he explained. "It's not easy but it can be done."

"Like trenches and barriers to funnel the fire in a different direction? Stop it from encroaching further?"

"Exactly." Espen yanked on the wheel and pulled to a hard stop beside the other police car, still parked where we'd passed him earlier.

He shut off the vehicle and rushed out. I unbuckled my seatbelt, dropped the shards onto my seat, and followed him to the other officer. The poor guy's eyes blew wide as the raging inferno curved around the bend behind us—a decent distance away thanks to Espen's rally-style driving.

Espen gave orders of what they were going to do and what calls needed to be made to Ylva and the fire station.

Before I had a chance to absorb what was being said, Espen spun to me and held me by my shoulders. His features were locked in Head Guard, leader-mode: brows drawn, eyes alert, lips pursed.

"You're going to have to drive back to Skolvik yourself," he said.

"You want me to drive the police car? Government property?"

"You have to get those shards back to the Temple."

"Doesn't mean I like leaving you by yourself out here to take on *that*."

I didn't like it at all. But I also had a duty to the Fjell and a responsibility to get those shards to the Temple. I'd made that promise to Øyvin too. And no matter what had happened to him, I needed to follow through.

"I know," Espen said, his voice thick with raw emotions. "I don't want to let you out of my sight, but we have to split up." He shoved the keys into my hands. "Take the car and drive as fast as you can."

The fire loomed and crackled, felling trees with cacophonous thuds. We didn't have time for lengthy farewells.

I lunged at him, wrapping my arms around his neck and pressing my lips against his. He tasted of peppermint and coffee, his signature smell of leather and moss washing over me. I pulled back and whispered, "Don't die. I can't lose you too."

"You won't." He brushed my hair off my forehead, fingers trailing down my jaw before letting go. "I promise. Now drive."

I nodded and spun before I could let the emotions bubbling to the surface boil over onto the road. There was a mission to complete.

Sprinting to the police cruiser, I climbed into the driver's seat and pulled the chair forward so I could reach the pedals.

Three. Why are there...

I glanced at the footwell and then at the center console, the gearshift pointing toward the roof. "Oh my fuck, it's a manual!"

We were doomed. There wasn't a chance I was getting this thing back to Skolvik. This hatchback would be my coffin. Of all the places for me to die, of course it would be in a police cruiser on fire. I could picture my brothers' reactions perfectly: once they got over their grief, they'd cackle themselves to death.

"For fuck's sake." I stomped my feet on the clutch and brake pedal, put the car into neutral, and turned the ignition. "Trust me not to notice the type of transmission until now."

The car sputtered to life, and I cautiously released the handbrake. Easing pressure off the pedals, I squeezed my foot on the gas. The car juddered and groaned, and I let out a wince. Hopefully Espen was too busy with the fire to notice that I was about to break his boss's car.

With another flustered attempt at getting the car moving, I crunched it into first gear and got it rolling forward. "Thank Odin and all his sons this is mostly downhill."

The fact that the rest of the journey into town was a winding ribbon of asphalt that snaked back-and-forth down the mountain was a saving grace for both me and the car's gearbox.

I let it remain in first gear, which, based on the shudders and scratchy noises, it didn't like. But dammit, I wasn't going to ruin my chances of getting back to town, nor accidentally jettison myself of the road's steep embankments—most of which terminated at the fjord's shoreline, hundreds of yards below.

After five minutes of rolling and picking up some speed, I peered into the rearview mirror and found it empty of flames, but filling with smoke. Gray tendrils reached between the trees, curling around branches and pulling their way through the brush.

"Don't you dare die on me, Espen," I whispered.

I'd lose my mind if I lost them both. Even as I rolled toward town, I wasn't sure if I hadn't already lost a piece of myself to the darkest depths of the fjord.

As I finally entered the village, I blew through stop signs and barreled around corners. The car careened into the vacant lot beside the police station, tires screeching. Through some quick trial and error, I shut off the vehicle and breathed a sigh of relief, resting my head against the steering wheel. I'd made it. The car's gears and transmission may be in worse condition than this morning, but I'd done it.

An eerie quiet hung over the town as I grabbed the two stones from the passenger seat and clambered out of the car. The stillness sent a shiver down my spine. Lights were off in all the buildings, streets sat completely empty, and a smoky haze inched down the southern mountainside. It was like the place was waiting for something awful to happen, like it knew what lurked on its streets.

Shaking off the thought of Veigar sneaking around town, I popped open the trunk and searched for something to hide the stones in. Collapsable traffic cones, clear evidence bags, and a first aid kit stared back at me. Opting for the aid kit, I dumped its contents into the trunk and shoved the two shards inside, zipping it up tight. It was the most conspicuous of my choices—a first aid kit on the eve of battle might even be smart.

Slamming the trunk shut, I turned my attention to the village. It was time to get these back to their original home.

35

ESPEN

Watching Lennie drive away had terror seeping into my bones. But it wasn't nearly as terrifying as the scene behind me.

The fire was otherworldly. An inferno as tall as the pines that blanketed our hillsides.

In quick movements, I made a meter-wide trench near the bend, then watched it jump the barrier like it was nothing. Flames wrapped around branches and ate the forest floor as the asphalt cracked and leaked oil. Heat blasted against my face like I'd opened an oven, and I narrowed my eyes against the intensity, sprinting back to the police barrier before it could catch me.

"Stand back," I said to Morten Olsen, the police officer and Forest Fae who'd been stationed here.

"Yes, sir!"

Once we reached a safe distance back from the fire, I pulled on that ball of power lurking within me, waiting to be unleashed. With a deep breath, I stretched my arms out and curled my hands into fists. The trees in the flames' path folded over one another, snapping noises joining the popping fire as their roots strained and broke. I pushed the power away from me and moved the fallen trees back from the fire line, setting them closer to the cruiser where we stood. We didn't need to add fuel to the fire, but I needed these trees out of the way.

Embracing the overwhelming roar through my muscles, I pulled on all my strength, ignoring that need to be careful, and let loose again. Magic flowed from me and widened the trench before the flames, throwing the upended soil and ash back into the oncoming disaster.

Seeing the forest in so much pain boiled the blood in my veins.

I grit my teeth and eyed the destroyed road. No one would be entering town now. Hopefully, the firebreak would slow the advancing flames, but if it didn't... "Ancestors help us."

Siren noises pierced the echoing cacophony, and I turned to find the fire truck pulling up beside the police car.

Thank goodness. We needed water up here.

Ylva hopped out with a wild light in her eyes, her blond braids bouncing over her shoulders, and a fireman's jacket wrapped around her frame.

I smiled. Glad to see our long-held emergency plans among the Forest Fae had been successfully put into motion. Infiltrate local ranks. Take ownership of leading the efforts. Use our powers to help the humans when we could.

"I think Fire Chief suits me, don't you?" Ylva said with a cocky grin as she modeled the oversized jacket.

"Take that thing off before you break it."

"Buzzkill."

"Buzzkill?" That was a Lennie word if I'd ever heard one. "You've been spending too much time with my wife."

Ylva shrugged out of the jacket and threw it back into the truck's cab. "You were invited to Tequila Tuesdays at Fisken. Not my fault you can't *hang with the kids these days.*"

I wiped my hand across my forehead, about to launch into my plans, when a wall of skirts descended from the back of the truck's cabin. Narrowing my eyes, I tilted my head to one side as Heidi hopped out and landed beside Ylva. The other truck door swung open and out jumped Anders Langholm.

What on earth?

I schooled my features, hoping he hadn't seen my reaction. He shouldn't have been here. Neither should Heidi, but she was Forest Fae and he was human.

A few others piled out of the firetruck, all of whom I recognized as members of Ylva's elite cadre, the most powerful soldiers in our regiment. They went about getting the hoses off the truck and my attention flicked to Ylva as she strode up beside me, her own gaze locked on the stalled inferno.

"Ylva," I said, keeping my lips as still as possible. "Care to explain why Anders Langholm is here?"

She waved her hand, not taking her eyes of the fire. "Minor inconvenience. Apparently, he decided to shelter in the fire station's attic. Said someone should be here in case of emergency."

Good grief.

"So, you brought him with you?"

"He wasn't exactly amenable to staying put when he saw the fire break out."

"And he didn't call in for back up?"

"No, I stopped him." She set her hands on her hips as the man in question started unfurling a hose off the truck. "Told him I'd already done it."

I brushed my hand over my beard. "What are we going to do with him?"

"Like I said, minor inconvenience."

Heidi jabbed something against the man's throat. His eyes went wide, and he dropped to the road like a puppet with broken strings. The other Forest Fae caught him before he could hit his head and then picked him up and loaded him back into the truck.

Today was getting worse by the second.

I strode over to Heidi. "What did you just give him?"

"A delicate little concoction that packs quite the punch. Personal favorite." She snickered as she adjusted her hair into a bun on the back of her head.

"What does it do? Will he remember seeing us?"

"No, it'll render him unconscious for roughly forty-eight hours and scramble his thoughts. He won't know dream from reality."

A sigh slipped from my lips. I knew Heidi's potions and tinctures were effective and potent, but... Ah, I shouldn't be complaining. It had come in handy.

"You're welcome, by the way," Heidi said as if reading my mind. "You know my work is effective. Didn't your wife enjoy that tea I gave her for Christmas?"

I shook my head. Yes, Lennie had very much enjoyed that brew. So had Øyvin and I. It had left Lennie a hyper-sensitive, moaning and writhing mess. And we'd wrung seven orgasms from her that night. It was a very merry Christmas.

"Okay, let's focus," I said, an order for them and myself. I couldn't be thinking about Lennie right now. If I did, I'd end up sprinting to the mountain on the other side of the fjord and whisking her somewhere safe.

The group that arrived in the truck and Officer Olsen gathered around, their gazes falling to me.

"While some of you shoot water at that, I need to keep building these trenches." I motioned to the ones currently holding back some of the blaze. "But we need to work up and down the mountainside, clearing any debris and trees along this line." I continued giving orders. The fae nodded, accepting their tasks.

Ylva motioned between her and Heidi. "We will stay here."

"Good." I didn't want the healer walking the woods alone. We might need her, and keeping her here at our makeshift base was best.

"All right, everyone! You have your tasks!"

"Yes, sir!"

As one of the Forest Fae finished preparing the firetruck hose, Ylva pulled a large sack out of the vehicle's back seat and gingerly set it on the road. Heidi scurried over, hitched her skirts, rolled up her sleeves and bent down, opening the bag. She extracted what looked like a poultice at this distance—a ball of gauze-like material held shut with twine. The two women conferred and mumbled, heads nodding as they assessed more of the little bundles.

"Ladies, what are those?"

Ylva set aside one of the balls and smiled. "A side project I've had Heidi working on."

I didn't like the sound of that. With a quick look over my shoulder to make sure the fire hadn't jumped the line—*it hadn't*—I set my hands on my hips and asked, "What exactly does this little *project* entail?"

Heidi's eyes went wide. "Kaboom!"

"Bombs?" My voice peaked and cracked. "Heidi!"

"I'm highly adept at potion-making, young man."

"Yeah." Ylva smiled, the overly gleeful look filling every corner of her face. "Let the woman work."

I rolled my eyes and checked on the fire again. The hose, and the Forest Fae manning it, started launching water at the flames behind the ditch. At least someone was following orders.

Heavy metal music sounded from my pocket and my stomach sank. I pulled my phone out and didn't bother looking at the caller ID. The plume of gray and black above me had probably been spotted over the mountains and set off alarms.

"Bente," I said, answering the call while Ylva and Heidi whispered about their *project*.

"Where's the fire?"

My boss didn't even hesitate. She never did.

"Forest south of the Fjord. Ten minutes outside the village center."

"Contained?"

"Almost—"

"I'll call in the Coast Guard plane and the authorities in Oslo for—"

"No need." My stomach twisted in on itself. I hated lying to Bente. But I had to protect our secret, the fae, and the humans. "I've already reached out. We have support coming in on the other side and the Meteorological Institute says rain is on the way."

Bente cleared her throat. "Good. And you're following protocol with the local firefighters?"

"Yes, ma'am."

Both the human plan and the fae plan. The only hitch was the Fire Fae King and his Head Guard roaming around that I couldn't account for.

"Good. Call me if you need anything or if the weather report shifts."

"Will do." I hung up before the conversation could take a turn.

Leaving the two women to their explosives, I rolled up the sleeves on my police jacket and set to work clearing the forest behind the trench. Branches creaked, needles and pine cones fell to the ground, and roots snapped like pops of ancient gunpowder. Ripping apart the woodland cut at something inside me. These trees had stood for hundreds of years and could've weathered hundreds more. They were home to fae and countless creatures.

Rabbits, deer, and birds fled past me, seeking shelter. A massive elk with a scorch mark on its hindquarters rumbled down the hill toward the water, trampling over the plants in its path.

These innocent flora and fauna were the true victims here. But ripping the roots up and clearing the landscape would prevent an equal fate for the rest of the forest behind us.

With sweat clinging to my brow and heat battering me, I continued my work, grateful for the efforts of Ylva's cadre doing what they could. Heidi stepped in too, desperately attempting to heal some of the plants I'd ripped up.

"Any luck?" I asked her over my shoulder.

Her hands waved over a scorched sapling. "Yes, but it will take time."

A whistling noise that didn't belong drew my attention back to the fire line, and a shiver ran down my sweat-soaked spine. A figure emerged from the inferno, long hair blending with the oranges and reds, broad shoulders draped in leather, palms filled with flames.

Herja.

Lennie was right calling her an omen of death and destruction. The woman was as tall as Halvar and somehow twice as menacing. Those black eyes darker than the clothes she wore and the coals burning at her feet. Herja was a powerful Head Guard who protected the island of Iceland like a hawk protecting its nest. Rumor had it, even without the royal magic, she was almost as powerful as Veigar's daughters. It was little wonder Veigar had appointed her as his General.

I rolled my shoulders and stepped closer, careful of the imposing heat that could incinerate me in seconds.

"I don't think we've had the fortune of an introduction," I yelled across the expanse as she stopped on the other side of the road trench. "My name is Espen Solbakke Martin."

"Oh, I know who you are, little destroyer," she said, her voice a rumbling bellow. "The legend of you and your power has crossed the North Atlantic."

"Then you know what'll happen to you if you don't turn back and leave Skolvik."

Her mouth lifted into a lopsided grin. "We look forward to the challenge, Forest Fae."

We?

Shit.

I took a quick step back. "Heidi, grab your special project!"

A second later more figures appeared among the flames. This time, humanoid creatures made of fire. Four in total.

"What the hell are those?" Ylva yelled over the roaring wildfire.

I lifted my hands and settled into a defensive position, ready to unleash my power.

Words didn't exist for the creatures that prowled on the other side of the wide ditch between us and the flames. Their entire body, from head to toe, was formed of fire. Where a face should be was orange, white, and yellow—no eyes, mouth, or any other discernible features. They were fire incarnate, walking from tree to tree and setting them ablaze.

I shot my power toward the closest one, churning the soil beneath its feet. As Herja scrambled away, her minion stumbled into the ravine. If I buried it, would it keep living? Flames could smolder under the ground if they had the material to continue burning, and the soil here beneath the road didn't have as much life or roots calling it home. The being clawed against the edge of the trench, and I didn't wait another second, sending a mound of dirt and asphalt down upon it.

One down. Three remaining.

My focus turned back to where Ylva launched a bomb at Herja and one of the creatures. The Fire Fae neatly dodged the blow and explosion, but the humanoid wasn't quick enough. A green plume engulfed it.

"Cover your mouth!" Ylva yelled, and I shoved my face into the crook of my elbow and held my breath. The updraft from the fire swept the ominous cloud over and up, stinging the corner of my eyes.

A split second later it dissipated, and I inhaled a smoky breath. "Any chance that was poison?"

"Of course." Heidi handed Ylva another bomb, then scuttled back toward the fire truck.

The impacted creature disappeared among the flames at Herja's back. She twisted her fingers, and her lips curved into a gut-wrenching grin. A fire-being stepped out of the flames like a phoenix reborn and another materialized at its side. Hair rose off my arms and my scalp prickled as if it were being poked by hundreds of tiny needles.

"She's been toying with us," Ylva yelled.

I grit my teeth together and nodded in agreement. While I now led a simpler life, I was far from useless, and Queen Ragnhild had hired me for a reason. I had the skill and experience to lead an army, and the power to end a war. Herja, a warrior in her own right, was tempting us to play our hands, lose our ammunition in a game of folly, but I had every intention of outlasting this game of cat and mouse.

"Hold fire!" I roared. "Regroup!"

The nearby cadre ran to join us, and Ylva backed up with me, assembling at the firetruck, its flashing lights still on, blue beams bouncing against the smoky air.

Herja launched a ball of flame over our heads and my gut lurched. Time was up and I hadn't even been able to hand out new orders.

Another fireball arced over our heads and crashed against brush further down the road, igniting the kindling and sending a wave of heat against our backs.

Shit.

We didn't have time to spare.

"All-out assault on them all, especially Herja." I looked between the group and my commander, Heidi watching on with the blank stoicism of a nurse in an emergency room. "Arrows to the head. Bombs. Throw everything at them."

"Yes, sir."

I cast a quick glance back at our enemy and squinted through the smoke. Herja watched her creatures closely but didn't let them stray too far. As if they were only allowed as far as her arms could reach.

Realization dawned, and I let out a panted breath.

"They're tied to her. She has to maintain control to keep them sustained." Which meant we had to kill her to kill them.

My gaze met Ylva's, and she nodded in understanding.

"All-out assault," I repeated. "Attack her."

"Yes, sir!"

The group dispersed, Heidi wisely staying back behind the truck and out of harm's way.

Our soldiers called forward their powers, crafting sharp bows and arrows, notching them and letting them sail. Herja dodged one and launched a wisp of fire at the other, letting it crumble to ash in the air.

I launched another volley of destruction, aiming at her feet.

She tumbled and scrambled back toward the flame. Regrouping with her own team.

Pulling on another string of destructive power, I threw even more soil and debris at them.

"Everything we've got," Ylva yelled, clutching something to her chest.

I turned my face to her.

She gave me a single nod.

The next second she was running. She launched into the air over the trench and threw the bomb in her hand at Herja.

The green explosion clouded everything. The biggest bomb we'd thrown yet.

And Ylva flew straight into it.

My heart stopped, and I stilled.

As the cloud of poison cleared, a figure with blonde braids and a wild grin appeared... alone.

She did it!

I raised my hands above my head in victory. "You brilliant woman! I knew I chose well when I picked you as my second!"

She stuck out her tongue and winked.

Flames moved behind her, and a smoky breath lodged in my throat.

Herja lunged from the inferno and wrapped her arms around Ylva's torso and throat. My friend's eyes blew wide, a silent scream ripping from her lips as Herja squeezed. The next second Ylva went up in flames.

36

ESPEN

"NO!"

I crashed to my knees. Smoke coated my lungs and the heat from the fire stung my eyes as I stared at the pile of ash that had been my best friend two seconds ago.

Herja's lips split into a crazed grin, and she laughed. The nauseating sound echoed through the crackling flames and that black swirling mass of power in my chest unraveled and broke free.

I was death.

I was pain.

I was destruction.

Rising to my feet, I pulled tree after fiery tree from the ground and launched them toward the Fire Fae. She ducked and dodged but wasn't fast enough to escape scrapes from branches before they too turned to ash.

The soldiers on my side all retreated.

The flame creatures vanished.

It was just me and Herja.

Locked in a battle of death.

I roared and raised the road before me into the air, launching the ribbon of asphalt at her. She scurried out of the way, but not without getting hit by small chunks of tarmac. A volley of fire balls responded, and I sidestepped them.

That destructive, invisible power flowed from me, widening the trench, tearing apart the soil, and throwing trees out of its way. The opening ground chased her like a wolf hunting its prey, snapping at her heels. Another snap and she tripped. Crashing to her knees, she scrambled for purchase, before falling into the pit with a scream. A whip of fire lashed against the tall sides of the ravine.

But it was useless.

Useless against me.

Useless against the destruction that I'd become.

I slid down the muddy side and faced her.

"How dare you take my friend," I growled. "*How dare you threaten my home!*"

As she tried to regain her footing, blood seeped from her split lip and her eyes lacked any remorse. "Veigar always gets his way in the end."

"Not this time."

Power erupted from me like a shaken bottle exploding after being capped for over twenty years. Green, sinewy power crept from my hands and wrapped around her like a vice, twisting and contorting, pulling at her very being and soul.

Death filled my thoughts, my vision, the commands for my magic.

She didn't stand a chance. One second she was standing, the next she was in the dry dirt at my feet, writhing in pain.

"You're undeserving of final words." I twisted my hands, ordering my magic to kill, to destroy.

Herja jerked then curled in on herself like the worm she was. Her eyes widened, lids extending so far it looked like they were pushing the balls out of their sockets. With a cough and shudder, the skin around her throat tightened, and she took her final breath. A second later her body bloated, her skin pushing outward before it started to dry and disintegrate. The pungent odor of decay mixed with the smoke in the air, but I ignored it and continued pushing my darkest magic into her. Her body blended with the bloody dirt beneath her, and a moment later all that remained was her skeleton.

The sight drew some sick satisfaction through my chest as my heartbeats collided with each other. She deserved worse. Deserved torture. But my patience had blown away with the ashes of my best friend.

Ylva was gone.

Her smile was gone. Her laugh was gone.

She would never command an army again.

Would never tease me.

Would never smile and laugh and make crude jokes with my wife, the two of them forming a blossoming bond of friendship and camaraderie.

The one who tried to beat me at everything like a younger sibling. The friend who had been my valued confidant for centuries. The one person I trusted as my second-in-command. She made me laugh, called me out on my teasing, and bolstered my confidence whenever I worried about using too much power.

She's gone.

With an agonized roar, I pulled on another dreg of my power and ripped Herja's bones apart. They flew in all directions. Some into the flames she'd been born of, some into the woods she'd yet to harm. Let her rotten form feed and rejuvenate the forest she'd destroyed.

As my ears rang, a single tear ran down my cheek. My chest rose and fell rapidly, my panted breaths dancing with particles of ash.

The demon was destroyed, but the wildfire still raged.

I fell to my knees again and tilted my head back. Smoke blanketed the sky, turning the sun red, while flames continued eating away at the remaining tree tops. There was too much kindling around. Too much food for the fire. We needed more water.

We needed a Fjord Fae. I needed my partner. I needed Øyvin.

37

LENNIE

Racing through town and up the hillside toward the main fjell entrance, my hair whipped around my face as my legs propelled me forward. Gripping the first aid kit containing the shards, I didn't dare look over my shoulder at the fire crackling on the southern side of the fjord. Didn't dare stop in case Veigar decided I was an easy target. Didn't dare think about the threats looming over my home.

We had to... No, we *would* survive this.

At least the two of us that remained.

My stomach twisted at the thought of Øyvin and the shocked look that crossed his face milliseconds before he was sucked into the fjord and taken from me.

Shaking off those encroaching thoughts, I plowed through the rocky mirage concealing the mountain's main entrance and raced through the rugged hallways. Down and down and down I went. Deeper and deeper within the tunnels I now recognized and called home. Light sconces lit my path every six feet, the magic within them flickering as I passed. The rocky walls bounced and absorbed light in its cracks and bumps and uneven facades. The temperature remained steady, neither hot nor cold, and kept me comfortable, even in a T-shirt and jeans. It was as if the mountain could self-regulate its body temperature and protect its denizens from inclement weather or hazards.

A stone door ground shut somewhere behind me, pebbles skittered at my feet, and an image of a large black wolf flooded my mind.

Vicious teeth.

Gut-wrenching howls.

Pain searing through my leg.

Power wrapping around Wilhelm and killing him on the spot.

My breath caught in my throat and my steps faltered. Coming to a stop, I leaned against the cool rock wall and clenched my eyes shut, hoping to rid myself of the unwanted flashback.

I did the right thing. I did the right thing. I did the right thing. If I hadn't killed Wilhelm, he would've killed Aurora and then turned back to finish me off. Yet, killing him still didn't fully sit right with me. I'd never wanted to be a killer. Never thought I was capable of it.

My lungs constricted. *I did the right thing.* "I'm safe. Wilhelm is gone," I muttered and slowly reopened my eyes.

Wilhelm had been on a warpath, intent on hurting me to hurt Espen. Members of his pack had injured and killed Fjell Fae. The former Alpha had been out for blood, and I'd stopped more of it from flowing. I needed to keep reminding myself that.

I took a deep breath and tapped the toe of my shoe against the hard ground.

No, it would never feel right, but I'd protected my home, and I was going to do so now too.

With another long inhale, I straightened and hurried through the tunnels, aiming for the Royal Tombs.

Nobody look too close.

Scuttling past a confused fae, I gave them a broad grin as if nothing were amiss.

Don't look at me.

I bolted around another corner before slowing to a walk.

Nothing to see here.

My grip on the first aid kit tightened as I passed a couple groups of soldiers. Several bowed their heads or muttered a polite "ma'am" as they went by. I returned the nods, feeling a little out of place and unworthy of the deference, especially considering the cargo I carried and my intentions with it.

Hoping none of them noticed my sense of urgency, I kept moving until I reached the miraged entrance to the royal tombs. The rocky facade was a strong illusion, and anyone would walk right past it if two uniformed soldiers with sharp looking swords weren't guarding the entrance.

They stood with their feet braced, hands resting on the weapons hitched to their belts.

I slowed to a stop and swallowed hard, pulling forward as much courage as I could muster considering the anxiety riding my every move, hoping my crazy scheme wasn't about to fall apart. With a nod and a tiny salute, I said, "At ease, soldiers."

The two men furrowed their brows, but bowed their heads and twisted out of the way, granting me passage into the tomb.

Holy shit, that worked! Even without a badge or a hat, they knew who I was.

Sucking in a tiny breath, I strode past them with purpose, like I was meant to be there. I didn't dare breathe again until I was three rows deep into the lifeless chamber, the mirage hiding me from view.

Stillness wrapped around me, the smell of dust and granite lingering in the air. Heart racing, I rushed past the prone statues staring blankly upward, and headed for the back wall.

My magic pulsed as I closed in on the dormant mural. The jagged mountain loomed beside two large trees with flaming leaves, swirls of water curved at its base, and a wolf bayed in the bottom corner. A starry sky glittered above the entire scene.

"Let's do this," I muttered and pressed my hand to the middle of the stone mountain.

Open. Silvery light spread through the carving, rousing it from its slumber. The light filled every nook, crack, and crevice, until the whole thing cast a glow over me and the kings and queens of centuries past.

"Okay, I'll concede." I huffed, staring at the illuminated stone. "Magic is cool."

I pushed my shoulder against the mountain and the rocky door groaned open, granting me entry into the Temple.

Glossy sky-blue walls and plinth stared back at me as I stepped inside. "Yeah, this will never get old."

Using my butt and my fists, I leaned against the door and pressed it shut—just in case someone who wasn't allowed to be in here decided to show up.

I set down the first aid kit and retrieved the stones, then moved over to the center of the room where the pedestal sat waiting to be repaired. Setting one shard on the floor, I focused on attaching one at a time.

Distinct jagged lines and grooves graced three corners of the pedestal. I brushed my fingers across the southeast corner, the cool stone and sharp edges grazed my fingertips. It reminded me of the harsh peaks that dotted Norway.

I adjusted the shard in my hand, trying to get it to fit like a puzzle piece—turning and re-angling. When it didn't work on the first corner, I moved to the southwest. The shard slid into place like the final piece of a puzzle. All that was missing was that perfect click that sounded like my camera's shutter button.

"I wonder..." Could my magic fasten this back on? Would it be the royal magic or the Fjell magic at work?

Fasten. Pressing my magic into the corner, I willed the piece back into its spot, asking it to reattach to its home. A grating noise was followed by a drawn out click, and I opened my eyes. The shard had reconnected itself to the pedestal, sharp lines fused back together. The blue chamber light glowed brighter, washing across my face as I stared around in awe.

"One down. One to go. Call me Bob the Builder because I'm fixing this thing!"

Grabbing the second shard, I ran my hand across its jagged edge, feeling the bumps and ridges. I tried it against the left most corner before shifting back to the front right. It slotted in perfectly on the second try. A match.

"Your turn. *Fasten.*"

I pushed my magic outward once more and fused the second shard to the plinth. It shifted into place, a faint silvery line forming between the addition and its base. Lights in the wall swirled and my hair lifted on a phantom breeze. I took a step back. "Woah, there."

My heart hammered against my ribs, my lungs tightened, and my eyes widened.

"What's happening?"

No one replied, but the wind shifted direction, coming at me from the left.

I turned toward it, looking for a gap in the cave, but found none. I was completely sealed in. No other beings, no other objects. It was just me, the pedestal, and the empty first aid kit, abandoned on the floor.

I scanned the plinth-like structure like it might jump and attack me. Halvar hadn't mentioned exactly how it worked, other than to put one's hand on it. And the last time I had, I'd been on the world's most one-sided date, with only twinkly blue lights to laugh at my jokes. What would happen with the shards returned to their spots? Would it zap me harder when I touched it? Would it kill me?

I shook my head. I'd come this far. There was only one thing left to do.

"Fuck it."

I stepped up to the pedestal, took a deep breath, and slapped my hand onto the top.

Lightning shot through my right hand and up my arm, ripping a scream from my lips. The magical lights in the cave walls swirled wildly, flashing on and off, as the errant wind kicked up and spun my hair around me. It was like being caught in a mini tornado I couldn't escape.

Warm voices echoed against my mind in a language I couldn't understand. *Striith. Steinabarn. Timi.* It was all a jumbled mess. But someone, or many somethings, tried to talk to me.

"We need help," I ground out, my teeth clenched so tight they might crumble to dust. "We need your help... Please."

A welcome yet stern intent settled through my bones, like they agreed or accepted something.

The pain subsided for a split second, and I sucked in a breath. My lungs heaved, my body spent and raw—

Power shot through my arm again and curved my back. Knees buckling, I pressed my free hand to the edge of the pedestal only to be assaulted by more power and pain. My vision blurred, my legs trembled, sending me crashing to the floor, and then everything went black.

38

LENNIE

Death had finally found me. Pain thundered through my mind, and I groaned, pulling my burning hands to my chest as I slumped against the pedestal. Blue light glowed against my clenched eyelids. Who knew you carried your dying agony with you to hell? Maybe that was my penance for all the bullshit and stunts I'd pulled in my time.

Something heavy, yet soft, brushed against the floor behind me, and I stilled.

"Satan, is that you?"

A soft laugh trilled past.

Satan was a woman? No... Wait...That laugh...

Air caught in my throat as I blinked open my eyes. That laugh wasn't possible. Couldn't be here. Had died in a throne room almost a year ago.

I stared ahead at the wall of the Temple cave, too scared to move a muscle.

"I'm definitely dead."

"Far from it, Lennie Martin."

"What the fuck?"

Forget the fear. I needed to see this.

I shifted onto my hands and knees, peering around the pedestal. My eyes widened and I swayed on the spot as I took in a ghost-like Queen

Freija. Her thick, navy velvet dress brushed against the floor, her hands clasped in front of her like a respectable monarch, and her copper hair was in a perfect up-do. If it weren't for the hazy appearance and the light glow around her entire body, plus the fact that I'd watched her die, I'd have thought she was in hell with me.

"I imagine it would take something quite miraculous to kill you, dear."

"Is that a joke about my unending run-ins with bad luck? Or are you the ghost of Christmas past? Because if it's the latter, I'd like to go back to Christmas last year. Heidi gave me this ah-mazing tea and my partners rocked my world… seven and a half times. Though, I never told them about the half—it would be a whole thing about who started it and who would be the one to finish me off."

Freija stifled a laugh with her delicate fingers, a faint blush brushing across the tops of her cheeks.

"You shouldn't be able to blush if you're a ghost, right?"

"Rise and let us talk."

I pushed to my feet, swaying like a drunkard as I did. "Am I dead and in hell? Or was there something in the Temple's air that has me tripping out?"

She shook her head.

My eyes bulged once more. "Holy shit, you're actually—" For the first time in my life, words failed me.

She was here. An ancestor. I was communing with an ancestor. In the Temple of the Fae. *Fuck me sideways, I did it!*

I gave myself a high-five and bumped into the pedestal. The thing didn't move, but I took two steps away, eying it warily as if it might zap me into unconsciousness again.

Straightening and pulling on my confidence, I continued my crazy plan. "We need the ancestors' help."

"We heard." She tilted her head to one side. "And saw."

"What do you mean, 'saw?'"

She waved her hand through the air. "We keep an eye on things from our side."

"Like *beyond the veil*?" I said, giving her a haunted edition of my jazz hands.

She nodded.

"Are there others watching over?"

"They all do."

I crossed my arms over my chest. "And they sent you as a messenger?"

"We agreed that I might be the best person to converse with you, seeing as we had a prior acquaintance, and my magic now resides in you."

"Partially." I raised a single finger. "You gave some to your baby daddy too."

She inclined her head briefly, but not fast enough for me to miss yet another flush of pink dancing across her cheeks.

"Anyway," I started, not interested in discussing her love life. "You're here to give me a boost? Level me up? Grant me some ancient power that could knock out Veigar with a single flick of the wand—I mean wrist?"

"No need."

"What? Have you not seen what's happening outside? Did my fusing those two shards to the pedestal do nothing?"

She gave me a calm and diplomatic look. "Adding those shards helped you reach us, and can be of benefit if needed."

"Then charge me up, because the need has arisen."

"You have everything you need." She pointed to my chest. "In there."

I snorted. "I mean, Espen will be the first to tell you that my left boob is amazing, but—"

The Queen rolled her eyes, a gentle smile tugging at her lips. "Your heart."

"Oh, okay." I nodded like that totally made sense. *It didn't.* "Care to further explain? There's a history in this town of people and fae not giving me all the details and lessons I need. I think it's time we rectify that."

Another soft laugh trilled from her, and she started pacing, her long skirts brushing against the stone floor. "Last year I requested more power from the ancestors. I feared that forces were out to undermine my reign and harm my mountain. Little did I know that said forces had corrupted members of my own household."

Nora. *Fuck that bitch.*

"The ancestors granted my request, but it was too late." She let out a breathy sigh. "However, that power appears to now reside in you and Halvar... Well, mostly you, it would seem."

"So, you knew shit was hitting the fan?"

"I'd use alternate terms, but yes. The mountain's magic was unstable, the fissure down the fjord expanded at a far more exponential rate than years past, and I grew weaker. I needed power that would hold my mountain together and shield my people from harm."

"You rebelled, though. You illegally transferred that magic to Halvar and, by extension, to me."

A sly yet playful look crossed her features, reminding me that she had been monarch for a very long time and held centuries of wisdom too. She crossed her arms and straightened, those, now ghostly, gray-and-brown eyes staring at me with the force of a sledgehammer. "I did what I needed to do to protect the Fjell Fae."

"Arming a god-like Head Guard and crafting a demi-fae to be his sidekick," I mumbled.

"The latter was certainly a surprise, but one I'm grateful for."

"Really?"

She nodded. "You have a great capacity for love and care. Protective instincts that run deep. I saw those traits during our meetings and have seen them flourish since joining the ancestors."

My chest warmed and I shuffled on the spot, avoiding her gaze. No one aside from my parents and my guys had ever been so bluntly honest with what they saw in me. What I valued so much. Most people saw a tendency for chaos or heard my loud mouth first. But Freija hadn't. She'd seen past that to the core of who I was as a person.

I took a deep breath and looked back up. She smiled, radiating warmth and something I could only classify as regal-ness.

"Thank you," I said. "So, you didn't turn me into a demi-fae on purpose?"

Not a hair moved out of place as she shook her head. "I don't know how it happened, but I have a theory."

"And that is?"

That sly look returned, like she wanted to withhold the information and watch me squirm. "Something you yourself have found in Skolvik."

I refrained from rolling my eyes. Of course, talking to an ancestor would include cryptic messages and lore. That's how it always went in movies. Apparently, the Nordic Fae were no different. But what exactly did the two events have in common? Something I'd found and something she'd given—

"Love." I sighed. "It's love, isn't it?"

"There is no greater power than that."

I had to agree with her there. Although the killing magic I'd used on Wilhelm earlier this year had packed a punch too. Thinking of enemies, we needed to get back to business. I needed to know how exactly we could overpower Veigar before he and his minions decimated my new home.

"Well, I'm sorry for what happened to you and promise to take care of your magic."

She tilted her head in thanks.

"Now, how exactly are we supposed to use this extra power"—I waved at my tits and sternum—"to take out Veigar?"

"Halvar will know. But I'd wager a cunning plan to isolate him, then using the stunning and killing powers, will be your best recourse."

"Oh, I'm familiar with that power."

"Just remember, Veigar has that ability too."

Of course he did.

I pushed my hair away from my face and let out a shuddered breath. Nothing was ever simple. "Any advice on how to deal with Veigar? Any insider monarchy-information?"

She swayed on the spot, dress brushing the floor, and raised her chin. "Men with great power and confidence will brave this world alone. A man with no power and only confidence will surround himself with followers to boost his appearance of power."

"Sage advice. Tracks with Balder." But which one was Veigar?

Freija's image flickered, and she peered over her shoulder before turning back to me. "I cannot help you further. But whatever you do, however you do it, protect the mountain and your people," she said, her voice trembling.

"I have a lot of people in my life I want to protect."

She smiled like she knew and understood that feeling. The need to care for, nurture, and protect that which you cherished most. It was something that had always been part of me, part of who I was. But my community of loved ones had grown to encompass a lot more than my family in Ohio. It now consisted of two—one—handsome fae that would put his life on the line for me, and a village that laughed at my antics while quietly welcoming me into its fold. Not to mention an entire mountain that looked to me as one of their leaders.

"I promise to protect your mountain too," I said.

"Thank you."

She flickered once more, and the hem of her dress faded. We were running out of time. Whichever ancestor controlled this magic allowing her to talk to me, was about to hang up. I wished I knew more about the ancestors.

"You said they... you... watch over us?"

"Mm-hmm."

Hope sprung to life in my chest, and I clenched my hands into fists.

"Did you see if Øyvin was killed? Can you see beneath the water?"

Freija peered over her shoulder as if someone was talking to her from the great beyond. Her gaze turned back to me, her eyes crinkling slightly at the corners. "I cannot say."

My heart beat an unusual rhythm, hope and despair competing against one another. "Please? You must know something?"

Her lips pursed into a firm line, and my stomach sank.

The sad heartbeat won.

Freija flickered a third time, and she glanced over her shoulder before looking back to me, her eyes widening. The air around us took on an urgency as if the line between me and the ancestors was thinning. Time was up.

"One final question before you go?" I asked.

While I had her here, there was one question that had been nagging me for almost a year. And if anyone knew the answer, it would be Freija.

"Proceed."

"How old is Halvar?"

She laughed and a knowing smirk swept across her face. "Now that is something I dare you to ask him some day."

"You want me to die, don't you?"

She chuckled again. "No. But I'd find it entertaining to watch you ask him."

Like mother, like daughter. Aurora had also enjoyed watching me struggle.

"Is he a Norse God?"

"Ask him that too. Goodbye and good luck, Lennie."

She waved her hand and pain washed through me once more. I crumpled to the ground as the world around me turned black.

39

LENNIE

Something hard and cool pressed against my cheek and my bones ached as if they'd been training with Halvar for a week straight without pause. I stretched one leg out from where I was curled up in a ball. A fiery spasm shot through my calf and a whimper slipped past my lips.

"What. Have. You. Done?" Halvar's voice ground out, and I blinked open my eyes. The beast of the mountain leaned against the closed temple door, his arms crossed, eyebrows furrowing so hard they might jump off his face in fear.

Shit.

"Erm... What brings you here on this fine day, good sir?"

The muscles around his left eye twitched as a grimace settled across his features.

I winced. "Please don't kill me. I come in peace."

"Get up."

I rose to my feet and groaned as my body shouted at me. Whatever magic lived in the pedestal had left my limbs feeling flayed. Taking a deep breath, I straightened and faced Halvar head-on with my hands on my hips. "How did you find out I was in here?"

"The guards informed me."

Ah, should have guessed they would report back to him of any visitors to the royal tomb.

"You never said I was banned from entering."

Halvar clenched his jaw. "No. I didn't. You are allowed to be in here. Now, tell me what you did."

"I took initiative. Returned some pieces of stone that belonged there and asked the ancestors for some assistance." I pointed over my shoulder to the pedestal that was now only missing one corner instead of three.

A single silvery brow rose toward Halvar's hairline and the tension in his muscles dissipated as he inspected the temple's centerpiece from where he stood. "I see you've been busy getting help from your partners."

"I did. But Øyvin is missing after the... erm... theft of the Fjord Fae shard."

A line formed between Halvar's eyebrows, and he peered around the room. "Dead?"

My throat tightened. "The ancestor wouldn't tell me what happened to him, but he was sucked into the fjord, and we haven't seen him since."

"So, the ancestors responded this time?"

"She did."

His gaze cut back to me, his eyes betraying a hint of emotion.

"Queen Freija confirmed your suspicions. That I have more royal magic than you." *Don't let it go to your head. Don't let it go to your head. Don't let it go to your head.* "Said she'd visited the ancestors and asked for help last year. They granted her some extra power to deal with the stuff that was happening at the time."

A low rumble sounded from Halvar's chest.

"Did she offer any help?" he asked, avoiding the cloud of emotion choking the room and focusing instead on the battle at our doorstep.

"She recommended a *cunning plan* and the lethal stunning magic I used on Wilhelm. But warned of Veigar's ability to use that power too."

Halvar nodded, his features pinching as his mind turned to thought.

"I'm going to leave the cunning planning part to you. My recent plans *have* worked, but not without an absolute shit storm of chaos."

"That, I can agree on."

I snorted. At least I was self-aware and honest about my modus operandi.

"Come." He stepped aside and motioned to the door. "Let us head to the main entrance. There is something you need to see."

Halvar pulled open the door. I grabbed the abandoned first aid kit, folded it up, and shoved the material into my back pocket before following him through the royal tomb and into the winding tunnels.

The big guy moved like a graceful lump of rock, striding swiftly through the hallways, his broad frame leading the way. We wound up and up until we reached the main entrance where two soldiers stood guard, both bowing their heads to us as we breached the exit point.

I stepped out of the mountain and an orange glow swept across my face. The descending sun had turned red, blocked by an ashy haze. My jaw dropped as I looked across the fjord and found the entire hillside ablaze.

"Oh my god."

Flames engulfed trees and jumped tens of feet into the air, black smoke flooding the sky.

I sucked in a smoky breath. My husband was somewhere in that. I longed to rush over there, to throw my arms around him and shield him from harm. But my rational brain knew better than to act on that. If I did, I'd put us all in danger and put his life even more at risk.

"He can handle it," Halvar said, his tone filled with certainty.

"I don't doubt it. But I'd be lying if I said I didn't want to stand beside him right now."

Halvar grumbled like he understood but wouldn't elaborate. He didn't need to. I knew his feelings toward Queen Freija were the same.

He'd loved the woman and would do anything for her. Just like I would for my guys—guy.

My gaze shifted to the fjord and another wave of longing washed over me. *Please don't be dead.*

"How quickly can you call on the killing powers?" Halvar asked, mercifully drawing me from my simmering grief.

Death. I unleashed sparking and searing tendrils down my arms and opened my palms at my sides. Orbs of lightning crackled and popped, promising agony and a swift demise. I glanced up at Halvar. "You tell me."

Halvar let out a low hum of appreciation and turned his attention back to the wildfire. "Good. Very good."

"You're not worried about me being overly juiced up by Freija's magic?"

He peered at me out of the corner of his eye. "Do you intend on harming the mountain?"

"No."

"Then I have no fear."

"What *do* you fear?" I asked, hoping he wouldn't mind me asking.

Another low rumble rocked through the big guy's chest. He pointed to the village where a speck of salt-and-pepper hair in a blue suit sat on a bench looking out over the harbor. "That."

"You have any specific plans on how to handle *that*?"

He crossed his arms. "I do."

"Let's hear it then."

"Veigar's powers are near incalculable."

"But let me guess, you majored in Calculus and minored in Trigonometry?"

He looked at me like I'd spoken a different language then shook his head. "He can muster creatures of fire, shift the earth's crust, summon lava—"

"Lava?" There was me thinking huge balls of fire were our biggest threat from the Fire Fae King. But creatures? Lava?

"We must stay alert and spread our forces to protect the region," Halvar continued. "With our combined Fjell and Royal powers, we are entities he has never fought before. Something he cannot entirely account for in whatever plans he has."

"What plans do you think those are?"

He pinched his lips together. "Divide the most powerful."

I looked out across the fjord and valley again. Espen was dealing with the fire. Øyvin had been dragged beneath the water. The Fjell was without a monarch for the first time in what I'd heard was well over a thousand years. Halvar was right. Veigar had spread us out to pick us off, one by one.

The man in question rose from the bench at the end of the dock and sauntered back into the village, disappearing from sight.

"He will start his attack tomorrow," Halvar said, a solemn tone in his voice.

"How do you know?"

"A long time ago, when battles were fought more frequently, he would always send in Herja first. Like a calling card and a warning."

Anger swept through my veins. "What do we do?"

"You protect the village, Lennie. I'll protect the mountain."

40

LENNIE

I ambled down the mountainside, aiming for the place I now called home. Forest gave way to asphalt, and an eerie calm seeped along the quiet streets. In twenty-four hours, the town of Skolvik had gone from a beautiful and vibrant village filled with laughter and life to a ghost town. All thanks to one man and his need for power and standing among a community the humans didn't even know existed.

Turning off the main drag, I strolled down the side street lined with gray cobbles and passed Fisken. The sun had set, a faint glow still peeking above the horizon and the cooler air brushed across my cheeks.

I didn't trust for one second that Veigar wouldn't attack the town in the middle of the night. But dammit, I needed sleep. Talking with the ancestors had done a number on me and the weight of everything that had happened today bore down on me like a mountain. From Øyvin stealing the Fjord Fae shard and disappearing, to Espen and I driving to the stave church to retrieve the Forest Fae shard, and everything after and between.

It was too much for a single day.

And yet, here I was, on the precipice of a battle I felt unprepared for, against an opponent who could wield fire of all things. I dragged my palms across my face.

There was still work to do. There was still a village to watch over. But I couldn't do shit if I didn't lie down. I pushed myself onward, putting one foot in front of the other, and made my way home for a long night of likely restless sleep in an empty bed.

41

ØYVIN

No one was coming.

After over a century of service to the Fjord, not a single soldier, not a single member of my faction, rose from the depths to protect the village and the waters from an invader.

I swallowed the lump in my throat and gazed across the abandoned town, water dripping off my clothes onto the dock.

Stores were shuttered, plants wilted in their window boxes, and streets once rife with joy sat empty.

No one was coming.

I shook my head and straightened. I wanted to yell and scream and tear the fjord apart.

Beg for people to open their eyes and see what Veigar would do to us.

We needed to work with our allies for the freedom we desperately needed. We'd already experienced the losses that came with a power-hungry monarch—we did not need another hegemonic person to take his place.

Fuck. I'd hoped Reuven was different. I'd hoped he cared about the fjord and its well-being. But like so many others, he'd buckled and caved when the pressure mounted.

I wouldn't though. I refused. However much I wanted to dive into the fjord, swim for its furthest reaches and turn my back on everything—I wouldn't. If no others came, I'd stand by myself. I'd stand in the face of adversity. Challenges so insurmountable even a King had bowed to ease the impending blow.

No one was coming.

But I was here.

I'd sworn an oath to protect this fjord, and I intended to keep it. Reuven may have taken my title, but I'd never fall back on my word. Never stop protecting what I cared about.

And it wasn't just the Fjord anymore either. This was my heart's home. The place that brought a smile to her face, a teasing twinkle to her eyes, and made every day worth waking up for.

I took a deep breath and turned to face the village.

Smoke rose from all the forests around town, curling into the gray sky that hung over the scenery like an ominous wave ready to crash and destroy. White and red and blue painted homes sat in its path, bracing for their demise.

"So," a feral voice danced between buildings, echoing out to where I stood on the dock. Even the water beneath me stilled at the cutting tone. "Only one man wished to defy me?" Veigar stepped out from between two buildings and launched a ball of flame at my stomach—

I gasped for air and my eyes flew open. Gone was the barren town above the surface, only mottled gray walls stared back at me.

Chest heaving, I wiped my hand over my forehead, pushing back my limp and sweat-slicked hair.

It was a nightmare. Just a fucking nightmare.

I tilted my head back against the cold stone wall and took another deep breath, trying to stay in the present.

Water dripped to the polished floor somewhere deep within the hollowed caverns beneath the palace, lending an unwelcome percussion to my addled thoughts.

Hours, days. It must've been days since my capture.

No food, just water. Given at irregular intervals to keep me guessing about the time.

It was a good tactic. One I'd used myself when we'd interrogated prisoners with Balder after the battle twenty-one years ago.

But now, here I was, chained to the smooth stone walls of the palace dungeon. A prisoner myself.

Hopefully, stealing the Fjord Fae shard had been worth it. Worth whatever cruelty Reuven and Veigar planned to inflict on me for tampering with their plans. I knew, with every fiber of my being, Lennie and Espen would succeed with our own plans. They worked well together. They'd take care of each other.

Footsteps echoed down to my cell at the very end of the hallway—the darkest one we had, only a tiny sconce of magical light illuminating the desolate square space.

I straightened and moved my hands toward myself, tugging on the chains. The ice-cold metal manacles bit into my skin, cutting off my magic. The unnatural feeling of loss sat in the pit of my sternum felt like my powers had been ripped from my body.

The steps grew closer.

Black boots appeared first.

Navy pants.

Navy uniform jacket.

Cape with lavish silver embroidery.

Here we go again.

Reuven's face materialized from the darkness. His pale features and scar were so much more ominous in the dull light down here. He looked like one of the creatures from the humans' folktales that crept out of freshwater lakes and lured the innocent into their dens.

I sneered.

With a *snick*, he unlocked the iron bars and stepped through the magically enforced door—ripples of light magic and water magic wrapping around the metal beams. If anyone touched them, aside from the monarch, little would remain of their hands.

The door clanged shut behind him. He crossed his arms and tilted his head to one side. "So, Øyvin Håland. Ready to finally explain your actions?"

I stared at the King, my silence filling the space between us.

A smirk twisted Reuven's lips. "Really? Still no apologies for your betrayal? No remorse for what you've done to your people?"

My mouth remained shut, and I cast my gaze to his feet. Emotions I couldn't fully place swam through me on a torrent of anger and confusion. But I wouldn't let him see them.

"Your actions have put the safety of the Fjord Fae at risk."

I highly doubted that, considering *he* was the one who'd allied himself with Veigar. If anything, I'd given us a chance to survive whatever onslaught the Fire Fae King was about to launch at us.

"No?" Reuven said, his voice mocking and calculating. "Nothing?"

I turned away, staring blankly at my dreary confines.

"What if I told you I had your young American partner strapped to my throne and struggling for air?"

My anger ignited. I grit my teeth and faced him. "You'd already be dead if you laid a finger on her."

Reuven grinned like he'd won a game of chess.

"Do you have her?"

The snide grin didn't budge.

"Do you have her?" I growled again.

"Why did you steal the Fjord Fae shard?"

He had to be lying. Espen wouldn't let Lennie be captured... not again.

"Tell me why you thought stealing the Fjord Fae shard was a good idea?" Reuven crouched in front of me. "You defied your king. You defied your own kind. The people you swore to protect. All for what? Love?"

I grimaced. "You know nothing of love."

"I know everything there is to know about love and the sacrifices a man will make to protect it."

My chest rumbled, and I turned my head. I doubted that.

No one could possibly understand what I would do to protect Lennie. I'd sacrifice myself to make sure she lived the life she truly deserved. One that would bring about that unwavering smile of hers. A life where she could take all the photos she'd ever want to, make different types of coffee from the rarest of beans, and dance away to Christmas songs while making a mess of our home. I'd lived hundreds of years. She deserved just as many, if not more, for the troublesome joy she'd thrown into my life in the past year.

I shook my head, needing to quell the emotions ripping through me.

"Disagree with me all you like, Øyvin Håland." Reuven rose back up to his full height. "But the lengths I have gone to protect my own are near incalculable. I've stared into the flame and sworn an oath—"

"And fuck you for it!" I snapped.

Reuven stilled and his lips tilted up at one corner. "I swore an oath to Veigar that was also a *lie*."

Oxygen caught in my throat and my chest tightened. Had I heard that correctly or was I hallucinating after going without food? Or was this a lie? An attempt to get me to reveal our plans with the shard?

"Do you really think I'd stoop to the level of my father?" Reuven's brows furrowed as he squinted at me. "To madness, manipulation, and corruption?"

"I don't believe you," I ground out. I didn't believe in anything other than the love I felt for a woman above the surface who filled my days with smiles and challenges.

He sighed and readjusted his footing. "Let me rephrase then. I'm glad you stole the shard."

What? My shoulders slumped. I must have been delirious from the lack of food.

Reuven nodded like he could hear my thoughts. "You heard me."

This had to be a hallucination. "Explain."

Water dripped somewhere in the distance as Reuven strode back and forth in front of me, his hands clasped behind his back, his broad shoulders relaxed—a man at ease with his burdens. He stopped and faced me once more. "That stone must never get into Veigar's hands."

"Now I really am dreaming."

Reuven chuckled once and shook his head. "Do you really think I'd jeopardize the safety of the fjord? The last time those pieces of the Temple were all assembled, a Fjord Fae King took advantage and become more powerful than the other monarchs. Something we cannot allow Veigar to achieve. Not with his history."

"You're married to Salka," I said. "Isn't that an allegiance?"

"That alliance was forged between Veigar and my father. Not me. It was part of a plan they put into works decades ago in an attempt to rid our world of the female monarchs. A plan that Veigar was manipulating behind the scenes. A plan that my father fell for and foolishly died for."

Fuck. If that was true, Veigar had been playing a long game of chess with everyone, including Balder.

"Ever since I've returned," Reuven continued. "I've made one thing clear—that I would always protect the fjord and its residents."

"You've failed to show it."

Reuven reeled back and pursed his lips. "I've done what I needed to do to keep myself and my people safe."

My chest rumbled in disagreement.

"We may have different methods, Håland. But we're on the same side."

"Prove it."

"I am not an ally of my father-in-law."

"Does he know that?"

Reuven smiled. "Best we keep it that way until the most opportune moment to remove him."

"How does Salka feel about that?"

"Her relationship with her father has always been strained and tenuous. Didn't help when he arranged for her to marry me."

"Trouble in paradise?"

"Leave my marriage out of this, and I won't start asking questions about yours."

I grunted. Fair enough.

"Just know she is *not* allied with her father. Neither is her sister."

I raised my hands, the chains clinking against the stone. "Why should I believe you? You fired me, then dragged me down here and put me in chains."

"You *did* steal the shard. There had to be some kind of punishment to keep up appearances," he replied. "I can't have Veigar getting suspicious."

"I still don't believe you."

He sighed and crouched down, bringing us face to face again. His aquamarine eyes stared back at me, the scar that cleaved his right eyebrow and ended at his cheek shifting slightly. He reminded me of a weathered ship, worn rough around the edges but still afloat and capable of destroying others. Resting his elbows on his knees, he asked, "Did you ever wonder *who* was setting fire to security cameras around the village?"

"Veigar."

Reuven shook his head. "Salka."

I flinched. None of what he was saying made sense. "Why would she burn them? What stake does she have in this?"

"Veigar's orders."

I knew it. "So, you *are* aligned with him."

"No." He rose back to his full height, his cape fluttering around his waist. "We're pretending to be aligned with him until an opportunity to kill him presents itself. Someone has to stop him, and I'm in the best position to do so."

He had a point. If anyone could potentially undermine Veigar, it was the heir who'd been living under his own roof... biding his time. Fuck, he may have not been Balder, but Reuven was just as cunning as his father, if not more so. A man with the entire chessboard in front of him and ten moves ahead of his enemies. I tilted my chin up at him. "Explain."

"You've never been one for patience, have you?" Reuven chuckled.

I shrugged.

"Veigar is an intelligent and unstoppable force. One that anyone in their right mind should be wary of. However, since he lost his wife, he hasn't been the same."

"Depression?" I asked. If anything ever happened to Lennie, I knew I'd sink into absolute despair.

"Madness and delusion. It certainly started out as grief, but after using the Fire Fae shard and communing with the ancestors, he returned to his Small Council one evening and informed us that the ancestors had told him he was meant to return the shards to the Temple and lead all the fae."

Fuck.

"How long ago was that meeting?" I asked.

"Roughly twenty years."

I hung my head. That was just after Queen Ragnhild had been killed by Balder's forces. Veigar had been biding his time for decades, lying in wait until the board was in his favor. Taking the time to plan out his attack and maneuver everyone into position before stepping foot in town. We were fucked, but at least we had one thing helping us. One thing that I had to believe based on the evidence presented to me. We secretly had Reuven.

He pulled a thick metal key from his pocket and shifted closer. "Can I trust you to follow my orders moving forward?"

"Do you have my partner chained to your throne?"

He shook his head.

"Will you do everything you can to protect the fjord and its residents, including the humans?" I asked.

"I swear to you: I will."

"Swear it on your crown."

He swallowed and nodded. "I swear that I will relinquish my crown should I ever fail to protect the fjord and its denizens, both fae and human."

That would suffice.

I raised my hands, metal scraping against stone. "And you have my promise to stand by your side... if you give me back my job."

He smiled. "The position has always been yours."

"Then why did you fire me?"

"Veigar's orders," Reuven replied and shoved the key into my left restraint. "He had a plan for each of the Head Guards. Destabilize internal infrastructure."

"A scary prospect."

"Indeed," he said. "And one that's working. Herja has already set the southern hillside ablaze occupying Espen, and I have it on good authority that Veigar's already attempting to unsettle parts of the mountain."

That was two head guards, plus me, preoccupied and out of the way. But, there was one person that hadn't been accounted for in that calculation: Lennie. That troublesome piece of my heart that lived outside of my body would wreak havoc if something came between her and what she loved. If Veigar crossed her path, then her vocal gymnastics would be the least of his worries, especially since she'd been personally trained by Halvar.

My chains fell and clattered on the floor. I pressed myself onto my feet and rose slowly. My muscles screamed from lack of use, making me sway.

"And Veigar doesn't suspect anything?" I asked, resting my back against the frigid and damp wall.

"Not that I'm aware of. But that's about to change."

My gaze snapped to his. "How?"

His lips curved into a wicked smile. "Have you ever seen what Jörmungandr can do?"

42

LENNIE

The cabin wasn't an option to sleep in, not with the fire this close to town, so I slept at the boathouse, hoping the water wouldn't rise up, drag me into its murkiest depths, and drown me for taking what belonged to the fae of the fjord. Sleep found me in fleeting moments, but every creak and bump had my eyes flying open and sent my heart racing. When the sun finally crept over the mountainside, I clambered out of the lonely bed and texted Espen, Torsten, and Øyvin.

Espen was awake and alive. Watching over the diversions he and a team had created. His added, *I also have news to share when I see you in person,* had my stomach flip-flopping.

Lennie: Are you injured?

Espen: No, but we've sustained some casualties. Will talk in person when this is all over.

Fuck. My gut twisted in on itself, and I got the feeling today was only going to get worse.

Lennie: I'm sorry.

When he didn't reply, I checked in with Torsten. The mountain had suffered some cave-ins overnight and a guard had been killed near the main entrance during a skirmish with some Fire Fae.

Memories of ash mounds flooded my mind. Had the soldier been burned completely? Or had he sustained severe burns? Either way, the loss settled over my shoulders. Even though I didn't know the person's name, they were still one of us, one of mine, a member of my extended fae family.

I brushed aside the awful feeling of grief and sent one final text to Øyvin.

Lennie: Jeg elsker deg.

I didn't expect a reply, and my heart ached when none came.

With a sigh, I pulled on the thick wool pants of my uniform and slid the jacket over my T-shirt, fastening it at the base of my neck. It fit like it had been tailored to my body. Øyvin really had got my measurements right.

A lump settled in my throat at the thought, and I swallowed it down.

Grabbing the dark gray cape, I threw it over my shoulder and secured it with ease.

It may have been the end of summer, but the temperatures outside were cooling and... It felt right to wear the uniform. If I was going to die fighting for my new home today, I'd do so wearing its colors.

I hauled my butt downstairs, the creaky steps wishing me good morning as I descended. The living room sat empty, shadows creeping across the floorboards, trying to hide from the rays of light seeping through the curtains.

As I aimed for the coffee pot, a crack sounded from the hillside outside the boathouse, and I bolted out the door. Smoke drifted past on the breeze, casting a haze over the street in front of me.

I peered up at the hillside. Had another part of the valley fractured?

After pulling on my boots, grabbing my keys, and locking the front door, I ran across the street and fell to my knees in the brush-covered hill. Dried grass and twigs poked at the woven fibers of my uniform like kids begging for attention. I pressed my hands into the ground and pushed a thread of my magic into the soil, hoping my Fjell Fae powers could detect anything.

Warm power danced down my arm and into the ground. What returned was a calm sensation that washed over my skin as if the rock beneath the forest was reassuring me that everything was all right.

I let out a sigh of relief and retracted my hands into my lap.

My brows knit. "But if you're okay, where did the noise come from?"

Spinning and rising in one fluid motion, I turned and stared at the mountain across the fjord. Trees blanketed the slopes, peeks of gray slipped through the foliage, and the cliff where a tiny waterfall usually flew into the fjord lay dormant. Everything looked normal aside from the haze that hung in the valley.

Something flickered in the periphery of my gaze, and I whipped my head toward town.

A puff of smoke rose from the harbor.

"What the fuck is that?"

I clenched my fists and pressed my lips together. It had begun.

Throwing my hair into a ponytail, I ran for the village.

Having risen above the mountains, the red-tinged sun loomed over the smoke-filled valley, looking more like an omen of death than a contributor to life. My cape fluttered behind me, its woven strands catching the falling ash. Clumps of the gray stuff floated on top of the fjord, making the water look like a foamy coffee.

I slunk down main street, my senses on high alert, watching for any movement or signs of flame. That puff of smoke had come from somewhere, but here, in the middle of the village, the trail had blended with the rest of the haze in the air.

A Fire Fae soldier in a red uniform rounded the corner at the other end of the street with an orb of dancing flames in his palm. I stopped in my tracks, sucked in a breath, and coughed it out.

Shit.

His head whipped in my direction and he raised his arm, launching the ball of magic toward me. I tucked and rolled behind the store on my right, my shoulder and hip smarting from the asphalt's blow.

Scrambling to my feet, I leaned against the wooden wall. Was I the only one protecting the village? Halvar wouldn't do that to me, right? He'd send reinforcements.

Someone whistled in the street, and the eerie tune sent a tickle down my spine.

This was like something out of a horror movie. Hopefully I wasn't the ditsy blonde who got herself killed, but the idea that crossed my mind certainly wouldn't help. And yet, it was my best option.

I drew on my Fjell magic and crafted a sharp broadsword. The weight of the stone worked my muscles, perfect for causing injury.

Taking a deep breath, I yelled, "You don't have to do this. Peace is sexier!"

The whistling stopped.

I squatted and raised the sword with both hands, readying to swing.

A wave of heat brushed my right cheek, the one facing the street, and soft steps tapped against the road. *He was close.* And that warmth... That warmth was their calling card. It happened any time I was close to one of them. How hadn't I noticed that sooner?

I braced and flame licked around the corner, singing the building and drainpipe. I took two steps back, narrowly avoiding losing my eyebrows. The Fire Fae soldier stepped past the building, and I charged at him.

He fashioned a flaming sword, and our blades clashed above our heads.

I peered up. "How the fuck is that hard?"

He sneered and retracted. I pushed forward.

We clashed again and again as I pressed him back onto the main drag.

Sweat slid down my forehead and my breaths sawed in and out of my lungs. I readjusted my grip and parried another strike. A clattering noise sounded to my right, but I kept my focus on the man in front—

An arrow shot through his neck and caught fire. The soldier's eyes rolled, and he dropped to his knees. I swung my sword across his sternum and pulled when I felt resistance. The blade carved across his chest and blood oozed from the gaping wound. His body flopped to the ground.

I tilted my head to the sky and swallowed down bile. "That's gross."

The act of killing didn't sit well with me, but I didn't have a choice. Looking back down, a puddle of maroon pooled around him. "Better you than me, buddy," I muttered and wiped my blade across his back.

Cautiously stepping over him, I turned my focus back down the street, no longer empty. Forest Fae and Fjell Fae brawled with several Fire Fae. Magic swirled around them, soldiers dodged blows, and the two local factions worked together—not quite harmoniously, but even with missteps and bumping into each other, they were trying.

With practiced efficiency, the five Fire Fae soldiers backed away and started regrouping. My brows furrowed as they nodded to one another, some form of silent agreement flowing between them.

Four Fjell and two Forest Fae stood between me and the Fire Fae, but didn't block the view as our enemies lifted their chins.

Arms of flame emerged from each of the men, like something was crawling out—

My eyes went wide, and I waved my free hand over my head. "Regroup! Back here! Now!"

The alliance of soldiers spun and ran for me, and we sprinted behind a store.

"Would somebody care to tell me what the fuck those are?" I panted as we lined up against the building, our backs pressed to the wood.

"Fire monsters," a Forest Fae soldier said. Her dark hair was in braids like Ylva's and the sight had me hoping my friend was okay wherever she was. I owed her a beer for losing a bet recently. "They're like lava creatures."

I peered back around the building. There were at least fifteen of the flame aliens, each one sans face or features. Their gangly limbs crackled and sparked, stray embers flying off them like fleas. "I can see that."

"Only the strongest Fire Fae soldiers can summon them," someone else said as I watched the terrors creep down the street. "Rumor has it more than half of their army dies in training because they're too weak to control the monsters."

"So Veigar's forces might be thinner than ours?" I asked, not tearing my eyes from the horrors. Øyvin had suspected as much, but this seemed to confirm it.

"Yes."

Well, that was news I could've done with sooner. And yet, that wouldn't make much difference right now. There were twenty of them, and only seven of us.

"Anyone got any suggestions on how to kill them without becoming a scorched marshmallow?" I asked and looked back at the group.

"Behead them," a Fjell Fae I recognized from the training room said.

I smirked. "Someone went to the School of Halvar."

A brief smile swept across the man's face, and a Forest Fae I'd never met before held up her hand. "This morning's report mentioned the fire beings. You need to take out the Fire Fae, not the creatures. Their lives are tied to their master."

I peered back around the corner. The monsters were maybe ten yards away, but my gaze caught on the line of Fire Fae in the middle of the skirmish. They were protected by a ring of their own making—the monsters acting as a first line of attack and defense. Their focus was locked on the beings' movements. "Oh my god, they *are* controlling them!"

The reports were right, the Fire Fae's monsters were extension of themselves. We needed to take out the Fae.

"Work together, slice through the fire aliens, and get to the Fae." I looked around at the fear-filled yet determined faces around me. "And don't die."

"Yes, ma'am," they replied in unison, and I flinched, peering one last time around the corner. Since when—

A ball of flame shot past my face, and I reared back. There was no time to think about becoming an authority figure. I had a town to protect.

We launched back into the road and attacked the unwelcome beings. I swung my sword at the fire creatures, aiming for their heads. The battle swelled around me, clashing noises and yips of pain filling my ears as I focused on staying alive.

Movement on the far side of the street caught my attention as several more Fjell soldiers appeared behind the Fire Fae, boxing them between us. I breathed a momentary sigh of relief, thankful for the aid.

Windows shattered, flower pots exploded, and screams of pain filled the air. And the smell... I gagged. It smelled like someone had stuck their hand in a bonfire.

People on both sides fell, but only the monsters rose back to their feet, just like the Forest Fae had said they would.

Another fire alien got his gangly arms around one of my Fjell soldiers and the man screamed as his skin melted around his neck. A few seconds later, his head popped off. My stomach churned at the sight.

I beat back another creature and sliced through his arm. He clutched his stump and dropped to his knees, before flopping onto the ground.

"Another sword, please!" Someone in green yelled from beside me and I quickly fashioned another one.

"Here!" I tossed it to the Forest Fae, who plucked it out of the air and stabbed it through a lava creature, making forward progress toward the Fire Fae soldiers in the center. But not enough...

How the fuck did we get to them? We needed something that could strike them all at once. Something like a wave or a storm that could strike them down with a single bolt of lightning.

Lightning.

The monster at my feet started to rise, but I chopped through its chest. I stared at my free hand and a memory from a stony tunnel filled my mind. The faint echo of a wolf in pain sent a shiver down my spine but a smile across my face. I had lightning. Or, at least, some sort of bolt-esque power that Torsten called my death magic.

More yells ripped through the street, drawing me back to the battle.

Another Fjell Fae slammed onto the ground, burn marks flaring across his cheek.

We were losing people. There was no time to wait.

"Back behind me or off the street!" I yelled and pulled on the magic in my sternum. Time to *kill* a few more people out to hurt what was mine. The Fjell Fae at the other end of the street scurried down side roads, heeding my warning. As the last of our team swept behind me, power seared through my body, arcing my back as I screamed and let loose. Lightning shot from my palms with a crack, and I crashed to my knees.

The magical, deadly light shot down the street and wrapped around the remaining Fire Fae. Shouts of agony ripped through the air. Electricity crackled around their middles and contracted as if squeezing life from them. More sparks flew out of their throats as they dropped like puppets with their strings cut.

I lowered my hands to the road, holding myself on all fours as the magic, the power given to me from Freija, appeared to electrocute the men from the inside out.

The last of the soldiers fell, his eyes wide and locked on me, not blinking.

Silence descended alongside the ash.

43

LENNIE

The fire monsters fizzled into smoke and drifted into the haze like they'd never existed, while five red-clad figures lay among other fallen soldiers.

My arms ached like someone had taken a sharp rake and carved them into slices, and a throbbing sensation slowly subsided in my head. I rose to my feet, my vision blurring before refocusing on the carnage that filled the main street through town.

Green and gray capes lay in puddles of blood, a scarlet stream running through the gullies that normally carried rainwater to the fjord. Today they'd be spilling blood into the water.

Soldiers scrambled past me, heading for their fallen friends. I stumbled down the road with them, looking for the injured who might still survive if we got them help. Hair smoldered, blood pooled, and burn marks marred most of the bodies on the street. I pulled my cape over my nose and mouth trying not to inhale the smell of burned flesh.

Joining my fellow fae, I helped turn people over and checked for injuries while keeping an eye on our surroundings—there could be more enemies out there. Aiding in lifting a scarred but breathing Forest Fae, I brought him to his feet and gave him to another Fjell Fae. "I just need to double check," I said with a look over my shoulder to the Fire Fae.

The Fjell Fae nodded and took the full weight of the injured.

I stepped through the carnage and crouched beside one of the Fire Fae. His long black hair hung limp over his forehead, his eyes wide and glassy. Placing my hand in front of his nose, I checked for any breaths. None came.

I moved on to the others, double checking what my gut already knew. The royal magic, my magic, had killed them where they stood. I'd murdered five enemy soldiers with one colossal wave of power. Rising to my feet, I swallowed the growing knot in my throat and suppressed the shiver that threatened to run down my spine.

"I did what I needed to do," I muttered. "I did what I needed to do. I did what I needed to do."

"All dead?" someone yelled, and I nodded, turning back to the fae on my side.

Injured and intact faces stared back at me, and my gut lurched. We needed to get them to safety. We needed to get them out of harm's way before more Fire Fae soldiers showed up, or worse, Veigar. Because if *that* was what Fire Fae soldiers could do, what the fuck kind of magic did Veigar have? No wonder Halvar had been so worried.

I stepped over the dead, looking away from their distant gazes, and focused on the task at hand. Where could I shelter the injured? Where would welcome them—

A light bulb went off in my mind. I knew exactly where we could take them.

"Follow me," I said and hauled ass around the corner and down the street. Oddvar's Café sat up ahead, the white-painted corner-building a beacon of light in the smoke.

"Can someone call for a medic?" I asked. Hopefully the mountain had one to spare for the village as I didn't think Heidi had stuck around. If she had, I hadn't seen her lately.

"Already did," someone replied.

I pulled Oddvar's keys from my pocket and launched up the stone step to the front door. "Thank you! Now, get them inside." I unlocked the door and shoved it open. The bell trilled above me as soldiers streamed past, the injured hanging between them or over their shoulders. One man in particular looked like he was on death's door. Boils and burn marks marred his left side, his uniform singed in spots and melted onto him in others.

Soldiers cleared space and rested the injured on the floor, organizing them based on the severity of their injuries. I motioned to one of the women who'd carried one of the wounded. "Help me flip these tables and make more space."

"Yes, ma'am," she said, and we set to work. Wood scraped against industrial flooring as we flipped over the tables and used them as shields against the windows, chairs clattered as they were moved aside, and the smell of coffee lingered in the air, reminding me of the establishment's proprietor. Oddvar may have been a quiet and introverted man, but part of me knew he would have offered to help those in need. And right now, we had five soldiers in need, one of them seriously so.

"Where's the field medic?" I asked the woman helping me.

She wiped her forearm across her brow. "I was told the Fjell assigned three to the village. One of them is on the way."

The door chimed again, and I whipped my head around and pulled on my magic.

Trygve stepped inside wearing his signature white tunic, flowy pants, and brown apron, with his hands raised above his head. "It's only me," he squeaked.

Half the room lowered their weapons, myself included, collapsing the short blade I'd formed in what must've been less than a second.

"What the hell are you doing down here?" I yelled at Trygve. "You're not a field medic!"

"I volunteered." He wiped his hand underneath his bowl cut like he'd just run a marathon. "I wanted to help you."

"I do have a history with getting injured, but that's not on today's agenda."

"Let's certainly hope not." He smiled. "But I came, and I will help heal our soldiers."

I sighed. He had a right to go where he wanted, where he thought he would be most useful. "Well, you better have plenty of burn cream on hand."

He patted the pockets of his apron and nodded before setting to work. I peered out of the window, keeping one eye on the street and the other on Trygve. He flitted from one person to the other, spending most of his time darting back to the man on the other side of the café—the one with the most severe burns. Would he make it? Would any of us?

A flash of red appeared down the road. "Get down!" I yelled.

Everyone dropped to their haunches and knees.

I peered through a gap between tables. It was a red-uniformed soldier. Not Veigar. But, still.

"Everyone stay down," I muttered.

Nobody moved.

The man crept down the street, passing the café, searching high and low like we might be hiding inside stores or on the rooftops. Which wasn't a bad idea for the Forest Fae archers. If we still had one. They could pick off soldiers from above.

I shook my head.

Where the hell had I learned to think like that? Halvar? No, he didn't talk enough. Espen didn't talk strategy all that often, not unless Ylva goaded him into it. A painful smile twisted one corner of my mouth.

Øyvin.

Øyvin thought like that. Whenever he walked into a space, he checked our surroundings as if scoping out threats. He was a guardian through and through.

I took a deep breath, quelling the rising sadness. That's exactly what I had to be.

We'd taken out five enemies. Now, we had to remove the rest.

The Forest Fae woman beside me readjusted her legs and I grabbed her arm. "Are you the archer? The one who shot an arrow through the Fire Fae's throat?"

"Yes, ma'am."

"Good." I pointed at the Fire Fae disappearing down the street. "Do that again. Go."

She nodded, grabbed a Fjell Fae soldier by the crook of his elbow, and together they ran out of the café.

As they left, another Fire Fae appeared from the right and bolted after them.

Shit. Shit. Shit. Shit. Shit.

I jumped to my feet and dashed out the door. Someone needed to protect their backs.

Power surged through me, and I swept my hands over each other quickly, crafting a long sword that would put distance between me and the Fire Fae. Careening into the middle of the street, I added some stunning magic and raised the blade.

The Fire Fae soldier screeched to a stop, his eyes wide as they flicked over my weapon. His blond hair reminded me of Øyvin, but his eyes were pitch black.

"Wanna tango, hot shot?"

He cocked his head to one side and sneered.

"I'll take that as a no."

I swung my sword and pushed the magic out of it. A ball of stunning power zipped between us, and I raced after it. One thing I'd learned in training with Halvar and his soldiers was to keep the onslaught going. Keep them on their toes. So, I pushed my legs as fast as they would go and arced my blade through the air as I drew close. The soldier dodged the magic orb but stumbled and lifted his hand above him as he fell back. Fire flew from his palm. I heaved the sword down with as much force as I could and closed my eyes as I made contact. A wet sound met my ears, followed by a bump, then an almighty scream.

I opened my eyes and found blood pumping out of what remained of the man's arm. Falling onto his back, his features contorted in pain as he stared. I flipped my sword, pointing it downward, and gripped it with both hands before plunging it into the man's chest.

He flopped as blood spurted from his new wound.

My breaths came hard as I stared at the damage I'd done. "Holy shit."

I pulled my blade from his sternum and wiped the end across his thigh. A streak of red marred his ruby uniform and blood so dark it was almost black slipped down his sides.

I'd done that.

I'd killed yet another being.

But I'd also protected my own soldiers.

Slow claps sounded behind me.

I spun and sucked in a breath.

Veigar grinned from ear to ear, clapping as he took two more leisurely steps forward. He stopped five doors down. "Impressive."

"You should see what I can do with my tongue."

"I'd rather have it ripped out."

Well, fuck that was graphic.

"Leave Skolvik, Veigar." I raised my sword and pushed more stunning magic into it. The power prickled down my arms, flooding the blade as light glinted off the blood-stained tip.

He flicked open his hands and twin flames filled his palms. "No. This is where I'm meant to be. Where they said I should be."

What the fuck is he talking about. "No, this is not your home. Shoo shoo."

He narrowed his eyes at me, done with my jokes. The next second he threw the fire from his hands at me. I dodged underneath the first ball of flame and smashed my sword into the other. The orb exploded like a firework and small embers rained over my face. My skin stung in all the spots where it made contact.

I wiped my cheeks and pulled back my hand. No blood, but damn, that hurt.

Veigar smiled like he got a kick out of watching people in pain.

Sneering back at him, I collapsed my sword. I needed to keep my distance from him.

Calling on both my Fjell and royal magic, I quickly crafted a small rock in one hand and a ball of stunning magic in the other. Both were smaller than I'd have liked, but as another volley of fire flew my way, I didn't have time to dwell on size.

I launched the rock at Veigar's head, then the sparking orb of light.

Summoning another volley, I winced. They were smaller than the ones before. Was I running out? Had I used up everything on those five fae back in the street?

Two more flames shot toward me. Our brawl continued back and forth. One launching fire, the other rocks and light. My muscles ached, arms spasming and thighs yelling at me as I attacked Veigar with everything I had. His counters were perfectly timed and barely avoided. His hair sat perfectly atop his head, shirt unmarred compared to the debris and dirt on me.

This was easy for him. Too easy...

I furrowed my brow.

His attacks felt basic, limited, like he was holding back. Halvar had said he could wield fire creatures—which I now knew weren't a joke—and use lava. But Veigar hadn't used either with me...

He was toying with me.

I peered at him through wisps of hair that had broken free from my ponytail and growled.

Veigar's lips arched into a menacing grin. He lifted his hand and a ball of flame sprung to life between his fingers. He looked at the orb, then flicked his gaze to me.

I widened my arms, welcoming the fight. "Come on, Asshole! Give it your best shot!"

A low and evil laugh danced down the street from him. His eyes shifted to my right and he threw the fire ball—

"No!"

In horrifying slow motion, the flaming orb crashed against Oddvar's, igniting the wood paneling.

An anguished scream ripped from my throat, and I rushed toward the café. Trygve's wide-eyed gaze peered out the window.

I barreled through the front door as another explosion smashed against the building, shattering one of the windows.

"Get out! Get out, now!"

The fae inside scrambled around, gathering their comrades and stumbling out the front door.

I grabbed an injured soldier by the scruff and hauled him to his feet. The man winced, his green and brown uniform in smoldering tatters. "Move or die."

He whimpered, and I shoved him toward a Fjell Fae just as flames burst through another window and crashed against the counter. I ducked behind my cape and scurried over to the last remaining fae. He lay on his back, staring at the ceiling, boils and blackened tissue mottling his arm and one side of his face. His chest didn't move.

"He's gone." Trygve gently touched his hand to my shoulder. "Come. Out."

I nodded and charged through the smoke and into the only slightly fresher air.

The fae had gathered on one side of the building, out of Veigar's sight. Some scouted for threats, while others could barely stand. Shit. They needed a place to hide. A place where Trygve could work his magic.

I know.

"Get to the boathouse." I shoved my keys into Trygve's trembling hands. "Take care of the injured there."

The boathouse was a short walk from downtown, but far enough away that the maimed and injured shouldn't be harmed or caught in actual crossfire.

"Miss Lennie, we can't—"

"You can and you will, Doc. Go!" I spun to my team. "Take them. Get them to my place."

"Yes, ma'am!"

A moment later, the group of soldiers and patients ambled down the road, heading away from the danger that walked these streets.

I turned back to the carnage that crackled before me. Flames licked up the side of the white, wood building and a charred line of black crept up its cheery facade.

The final window shattered, and I raised my cape, shielding myself from the shards and smoke. The roof let out an ominous groan.

Shit. That was coming down.

I scrambled to the other side of the street, pressing myself against the store. Heat battered against my face as I stuttered a breath, watching the café burn.

I'd failed Oddvar. I'd promised him we'd watch over his precious café. And now look.

The smell of wood, metal, and coffee filled the air along with my failure. My shoulders slumped and I leaned back against the boutique behind me as a tear spilled down my cheek. I'd fucking failed. The one thing Oddvar had asked me to do, and I'd screwed up.

A roar of flame shot up from within the café and the roof crumbled in on itself.

I fucking failed.

But it wasn't my fault.

This was Veigar's doing. Yes, he'd found yet another weakness of mine, but I wasn't the one who set fire to the café. I wasn't the fucking arsonist. He was.

Gritting my teeth, I pulled on the rage that crashed within me, needing to be set free. I'd kill him for this.

I glanced around the corner, an orb of killing magic crackling in my hand.

But Veigar had vanished.

44

LENNIE

The anger within my chest popped along with the crackling of the burning business, and I dropped my hands to my sides with a whimper. I was losing everything I loved. From one of the happiest places I'd ever known to the heart-wrenching loss of my partner. All the pieces of my life were disappearing on me.

Swallowing hard, I crouched, letting the weight of my emotions fill every part of my body. Silent tears streamed down my face as the flames danced before me. The windows on the shop next-door to Oddvar's started turning black, flickers of auburn licking the sills. There was nothing to stop the fire eating its way through the row of buildings.

There was nothing I could do to help either.

No fire truck.

No hose.

No water.

No hope.

Shaking my head, I rose to my feet and stumbled toward the harbor, my mind lost to the darkness.

Mist caressed the streets of Skolvik and curled around buildings, mixing with the lingering smoke and stench of burned timber. Something else marred the air. Something I couldn't quite place. I peered down at my singed uniform and my stomach somersaulted. Wool and flesh. Not mine, thankfully. But the fallen soldiers. That's what I could smell.

My lips trembled, and I brought my fist to my mouth.

This village, these people, the fae, didn't deserve this. This desolation wasn't their fight, wasn't their fault. This was the action of a bored and entitled king whose volatility risked the Fae's exposure more than any other conflict I'd borne witness to in the past year.

This wasn't the stability he said he wanted.

This was utter chaos.

I pulled up beside the concrete planter I'd hidden behind last Little Christmas Eve and leaned my butt against it. Soot buried the delicate pansies in the container, while the tree within it swayed like my confidence as I stared out across the fjord.

The few boats that remained bobbed quietly within the harbor like innocent bath toys as warmth radiated through the village. A light gust of wind brushed through my hair, the flyaways and stray tendrils tickling my cheeks and sweaty neck, like the calm before a deadly tornado set to decimate the Midwest.

This battle would be no different. I could feel it in my gut. Knew it in some deep, hidden part of myself.

Those soldiers who'd just strolled through town weren't the only ones, they were a first wave. A line of fae sent to test us—see what the scenery looked like before focusing and taking the true shot.

I peered over my shoulder. A thick plume of black smoke rose from where Oddvar's lay, and my heart tore into pieces.

Fuck I was failing hard.

I wiped my hands over my face and took a deep breath. "I can't think like that. I can't let him win."

I couldn't. I wouldn't. But fuck did everything hurt right now.

And yet... I could sit by and watch the fire carve through the forests and cascade over the mountaintops. Or I could fight back. Like the rest of the Martin Family, I'd never back down from a challenge, and like my partners, I'd do everything I could to protect my home and my friends.

I looked around me, hoping to find something that might help. Fisken sat empty and locked up. Flecks of ash twirled around the town square and brushed up against the plant containers. Out on the fjord, nothing broke the surface. No one was coming to save us. My husband was caught in his own battle, my partner was missing—likely dead—and I was alone.

But I wouldn't let that stop me.

I couldn't let this village fall to Veigar. I'd promised to protect the mountain and with that came my home, my family. "Fuck it, I may not be a true leader, but I'm not going to let these people down."

Footsteps thrummed behind me, and I spun, drawing a sword—

Soldiers. *Fjell* soldiers. Half of them in uniform sans cape, the other half in black fatigues. A few Forest soldiers too. Their gazes locked on me as if seeking guidance, and I drew in a sharp breath.

The one closest tilted his head in my direction. "Orders, ma'am."

I let loose the oxygen from my lungs slowly as if it might somehow accidentally ignite the cinders around the village.

Anger and rage filled my veins, and my power thrashed within my chest, begging to be unleashed.

No more nice Lennie.

No more quippy little remarks.

I was no longer the innocent tourist who didn't know anything about the world of the fae.

"Ma'am?"

A feminine scream of pain sounded from somewhere in the middle of town, and my head whipped toward the noise. Someone was hurt. Someone—

A jet of orange lava shot toward the sky like the geysers in Yellowstone, and all the oxygen in my lungs evaporated.

Fuck this guy.

I pushed power down my arm and into my sword. Lightning arced at the tip, crackling through the eerie silence that hung heavy over the village.

"We find him," I said. "We find King Veigar and we rid this town of him and his minions. We remove him from the board entirely."

Fuck him for coming for my family. My home. These fae.

I stood among the ring of soldiers like a quarterback hyping up his teammates before the big game.

"We protect the Fae," I added. "Whatever it takes."

"Whatever it takes," the soldiers replied, and together we turned our attention to the battle.

45

LENNIE

Footsteps stomped against the street, the sound echoing off the abandoned buildings. The soldiers in front of me spread into a line, weapons forming from thin air. Blades as long as my arm, rocks so jagged they looked like porcupines, and shields as tall as surfboards filled the line-up. I stepped into the middle, drawing more power into my own sword.

A dense barrier of maroon-clad soldiers marched into the town-square from multiple side streets. I sucked in a breath and steeled my spine.

The fire in the soldiers' palms blazed like torches of a mob.

My men and women shuffled, but held strong, their gazes locked on the oncoming masses.

"Those pointy rocks good to launch?" I asked no one in particular.

"Ready, ma'am," a male voice a few fae down from me replied.

"Good." Adrenaline humming through me, I eyed the scene like one of my brother's football games. "Take out the right side first. Don't let them pincer and force us up the middle."

My order rippled down the line as the onslaught raised their hands and launched balls of fire at us.

I sidestepped an exploding orb and charged to the right. Our line of soldiers clashed against the Fire Fae. I swung my sword as shrieks of pain filled the air. The blade connected and drew blood, rocks flew past my head, and the heat from the Fire Fae battered against me. Sweat pooled around my hairline as I spun and swung, moving like my life depended on it.

Blazing heat encased my wrist. I winced and whirled. Fire Fae.

I swung again and pushed stunning magic down my arm. The fae whimpered, released his grip, and I buried my blade in his stomach.

A roar of anger sounded behind me. I yanked my sword from the fae eliciting a wet *thlum* and twisted. A fiery sword careened toward my face. I caught it in a bloody cross maneuver before pivoting and landing more stunning magic at the fae's face. He dropped like a fly meeting a zapper.

Sucking in a breath, I continued fighting.

Swing.

Zap.

Dodge.

Breathe.

Lunge.

Move. Move. Move.

Blood spattered across my uniform and face, and my hair clung to my cheeks as sweat slid down my temples.

Gray, green, and red blurred into a quagmire of death and destruction.

The line of soldiers that had come down the middle street past Fisken moved in on us, squeezing our left flank.

"Fuck!"

I launched over bodies and embers, splashing through puddles of blood. Numb to my own body and any injuries. I couldn't focus on that.

I had to keep moving.

Keep swinging.

Ducking, I narrowly avoided another ball of fire to the face. A scream sounded behind me, and I shook off the thought of someone else taking the hit.

The magic in my sternum swirled like a twister, ready to attack at a moment's notice.

A wave of fire rolled toward me, and I threw up a stone shield and crouched behind it. The flames licked around the stone, cooking it like a pizza. Pulling my hands off the heat, I pressed my shoulder against it. The smell of singed wool drifted past me.

Shit.

I didn't dare glance at my uniform. I knew what I'd find. Bare shoulder. Crumbling fibers.

The flames died out, and I readied a round of stunning magic. This would have to do. I couldn't chance using more killing magic right now, but we needed to turn the tides. I popped my head around my shield. Other Fjell soldiers prepared their next volleys as the Fire Fae crept closer, using their own flaming shields for protection.

They were going to overrun us if I didn't do something.

I collapsed my sword, rose to my feet, and flung aside the tall shield.

The line of Fire Fae stopped, their eyes trained on me.

Good.

I filled both palms with stunning magic and launched it at them.

One ball made it over the expanse and crashed against a fiery barrier, while the other sailed over the line and landed somewhere behind them. A scream ripped through the air echoing with another noise. Something piercing, wailing even. Was that a siren?

My brow furrowed as I prepared another volley.

Blaring sirens crashed through the town square and the fighting slowed as a firetruck followed by five motorcycles careened from the right and into the melee, sending a line of Fire Fae flying. Which felt a bit ironic. My soldiers and I fell back, using the vehicle's high sides as a shield for a momentary reprieve from fighting.

The firetruck came to a stop and Espen hopped out of the driver's seat. His hair was all over the place, his uniform almost black with some sort of debris, but his eyes found mine in a heartbeat.

My chest spasmed. He was all right. He was alive. He was here.

I stumbled toward him, vaguely aware of the soldiers around me. Yells of "Fall back!" sounded from the other side of the truck, but my focus remained locked on my husband.

He grabbed my hand, yanked me to him, and folded around me. The smell of smoke overwhelmed his usual scent, but I was home. He crushed his lips to mine and it felt like a lifeline. I pushed my fingers into his hair, pressed against the firmness of his body, and bathed in the sweep of his lips. He was here. In my arms.

"Are you hurt?" he asked as I burrowed into him.

"I'm fine."

He brushed his hand down my back. "Good."

"You? Are you injured?"

His chest rose and fell slowly, an extended exhale skimming over my head.

I tensed. "What happened? And where's Ylva?"

His body shuddered.

I pulled out of his arms and looked around. Soldiers on both sides were regrouping. Espen and the firetruck had been a helpful interruption, but we didn't have much time until the onslaught started again. I couldn't see Ylva anywhere and the truck's cabin looked empty, save for an archer who was setting up shop in the backseat with his bow and arrow pointing out the other window. "Where is she?"

"Lennie." The tone of his voice had my head whipping back to him and air catching in my throat.

He shook his head and his lips downturned.

My stomach sank. "No, no, no no nononono."

This… No, it couldn't be happening. She couldn't be gone. "Tell me she's injured and Heidi is stitching her up after giving her some magical tea she steeped this morning."

He swallowed hard like anger and sadness were on the brink of overwhelming him. "I can't."

My heart took another hit, fracturing. I wobbled, and Espen caught me as our breaths came sharp and heavy. She was gone. The tenacious and spirited woman was gone. Espen's best friend. My friend. A fierce woman with a magnificent mind for strategy. I couldn't believe it. It couldn't be true. And yet, based on the pained expression on Espen's face, it was.

I wrapped my arms around him and squeezed. He nuzzled into my neck and breathed in, his chest trembling. If we weren't in the middle of a battle right now, I'd cocoon him in blankets, bake him *sirupsnipper*, and ply him with all the snuggles in the world. It would never make up for the loss, but I'd do anything to soothe the blow a little bit and allow him the space to grieve. But, as it was…

Tears welled in the corner of my eyes, and I brushed them away before they could fall.

"Tell me who did it," I said, my voice unwavering. Whoever had taken my husband's best friend better have met an untimely end or I'd be delivering one.

"Herja."

"Is she dead?"

"Yes."

"Good. Do you need anything?"

Espen opened his mouth to reply as heat washed over the truck. We both peered at the sky. Three orbs of fire flew over our heads and landed on the main dock, singing the wood.

We were out of time.

Another small flurry of fire arched over us, like they were testing their range, and I shoved my sadness into a box. I'd grieve our friend when this was over. She'd want us to kick some ass on her behalf and then wash down the day with some throat shattering aquavit. And fuck it, that's exactly what we would do.

I steeled myself and looked up into my husband's equally tormented gaze. "Any chance there's another truck lying around town that we can use as a lineman against these assholes?"

He pointed to the rear of the truck. "No, but back-up arrived from Alvdalen."

Four large wolves and a figure in black with bright white hair stepped out from behind the vehicle. "Marius," I muttered, taking in the sight of the small pack with vicious teeth. They must've been the ones on the motorbikes behind the firetruck when it careened into town.

The young Alpha gave me a quick nod as if he could hear my thoughts. "Ylva sent for us. I'm just sorry we couldn't get here sooner."

"I'm glad you're here." Espen patted Marius's shoulder.

"Me too," I added. We needed all the help we could get.

"Aurora is here too," Marius said.

"What?" She was the last person I expected to visit Skolvik.

Espen nodded and looked toward the hillside where his cabin sat. "Her and a few other wolves are escorting Heidi back to my place and setting up a healer location."

Good. Surprising, but good. However, the wolves could probably still get hurt by the fire balls flying around.

"Are you and your crew going to be fast enough to avoid getting burned?" I motioned to the panting pack beside us.

Marius's mouth curled at one corner. "Don't worry about us." He moved a few steps back and shifted into his majestic gray-and-white wolf form. Joints and bones snapped and cracked as the furry creature took shape.

That will never not be weird.

The canine spun, silently communicated something with the pack, and a moment later they sprinted toward the north side of town where the village met the slopes of the mountain.

"They're heading around the perimeter," Espen said, drawing my attention back to him.

"Do you have any other Forest Fae beings to help us? Eagles? Bears? A really big moose perhaps?"

"No." He rolled his shoulders back. "But you've got me."

"Finally. You gonna let the beast out to play?" I'd seen what he could do, but I wanted to know *exactly* how devastating his powers could be, and I wanted them aimed at the Fire Fae King.

His lips tilted into a tiny smile, and he gave me a wink. "Whatever you do, stay behind me."

There was a sex joke in there, but now...

Quiet. It was too quiet.

We both stilled.

An eeriness settled over the town square and nobody spoke, nobody moved. It was like someone had hit the mute button on the TV. That feeling like a tornado was about to blow into town washed through me again, and my body involuntarily trembled.

Espen glanced around frantically, searching for the cause, then stopped. He peered over my head, the muscles in his jaw tensing.

"Espen?" I twisted and looked over my shoulder to see what had caused his eyes to narrow.

The fjord rippled like something was moving beneath the water.

"Stay here for a second," he said and stepped away, walking around the front of the truck. Magic swirled in his hands where he held them at his sides. It reminded me of the movement he'd done on the mountain last year, right before he ripped apart the ground and buried a few dozen Fjord Fae soldiers.

I peeked around the truck. The Fire Fae backed down the streets, hands braced, eyes locked on the water, giddy sneers crossing several of their faces.

My stomach lurched, and I ducked behind the truck again.

Whatever was about to breach the surface had them excited.

Espen bravely turned his back on the Fire Fae, stepped behind the truck, and started barking orders. He moved around the shielded space, the Forest Fae following his commands and getting into various strategic positions, while the Fjell Fae looked to me.

I shook off my anxiety and the crush of emotions the day was delivering. "Listen to him too," I yelled across the square. "That's an order!"

Responses of "Yes, ma'am" met my ears and they all began working with their Forest counterparts again. Several Fjell Fae started making shields for the different groupings, passing them around, while Forest Fae filled quivers with knotty branches they created from thin air.

Espen looked over his shoulder, pride beaming from him.

The water undulated again, and everyone stopped moving.

I stepped up beside Espen and called forward my stunning magic. I still wasn't sure how long I could last using only killing magic, so it was best to save that for later and not potentially run myself dry before I got the chance to kill Veigar.

Ripples grew and the water bubbled in spots on the fjord, small waves lapping against the dock pilons. A moment later a brown-haired head with pointy ears emerged and I sucked in a lungful of smoky air.

The Fjord Fae were here.

"Fuck we're screwed," I muttered and felt Espen deflate beside me as more breached the surface.

We had Fire Fae on one side and Fjord Fae on the other. It was a fae sandwich—the kind I wasn't interested in.

I slipped my hand into Espen's and squeezed. "Do you think you can take out all of them?"

He watched the Fjord Fae closely. "Depends how many there are."

Fjord Fae rose from the deep like monsters, creeping toward shore. Their heads materialized from the water, the group spanning across the entire width of the fjord. They moved as if they could walk on water, using it and the shoreline like stairs.

Their uniforms, all different shades of blue, gave the illusion of an oncoming wave. At the front was their King and Queen. Reuven and Salka moved like graceful statues, scanning the town's harbor front. His cape fluttered around his waist while her dress—the most majestic shade of purple I'd ever seen—flowed from her like a waterfall. Together, they led the masses toward the harbor like war generals.

"Is that too many?" I asked Espen.

"That's an astonishing amount of destruction and decay."

"What do you mean?"

"It's a lot of deaths. Doable. But a lot." His hand squeezed mine again, and I got the feeling he didn't like where this was heading. The ancestors must have enjoyed giving him those destructive powers, found some entertainment in it. Because Espen was not a destructive person. By nature, he wanted to heal and cause the least amount of harm. If given the chance to choose what powers he'd be granted, it would never in a million years be these. Death wasn't cavalier or frivolous. It meant something.

I looked around at the fae on our team. Some cowered at the sight of fae rising from the depths, others narrowed their eyes at them like they were considering how to tear them limb from limb. Most of the latter were Fjell Fae... Probably trained by Halvar. The only way we were surviving this was unleashing my husband and clawing our way out of the skirmish.

Reuven and Salka walked across the water's surface and stepped onto the closest dock.

My muscles tensed.

"Shields up!" Espen yelled and dropped my hand. Turning to me, he added, "Reuven will have stunning magic too. Don't know how long he's trained it or if Veigar may have given him pointers, but brace yourself."

"Don't get zapped. Got it."

He looked back out. "And watch for Salka."

The woman in question glided down the dock, her dress leaving no watery mark in its wake. More soldiers stepped onto the other docks that pierced the shore. Then they stopped, scanning the scene before them.

Espen touched his fingers to my elbow. "Don't die. I'm not done living life with you yet."

"Same." I gave him an emotion-filled smile. "I'm nowhere near done with you. Never will be."

He leaned in and placed a chaste kiss to my lips before breaking away and refocusing on the oncoming royals.

I took a deep breath and pivoted around the edge of the firetruck, watching our back and our front. The Fire Fae relaxed in the side streets. Some leaning against buildings, other crossing their arms and preparing for the shit-storm coming from the fjord. They looked like bored teenagers waiting for a fight to erupt. Especially compared to Reuven and his legion of men and women—their postures braced and ready for combat.

Reuven's gaze slid to the forest fire on the hillside. Blackened trees burned like torches in a picture of orange and smoke.

He wasn't paying attention to me. Salka was, but Reuven was focused on the flames. This was my chance. I pulled stunning magic down my arms, biting into my bottom lip as the magic tingled like pins and needles. Sparks swirled around my fingers, and Reuven's head snapped back to me.

He shook his head and twisted his hands in an ethereal motion in front of his chest.

A droplet of rain plopped on the tip of my nose. Another followed, splashing against my cheek before the skies opened and rain fell like a much-needed storm during a drought.

"What the hell?" I muttered.

Murmurs sprang up from our soldiers.

Espen drew his hands to his sides, readying himself and his powers. Ribbons of sickly-green magic curled between his fingers, and I fought against the urge to run—my inner fight or flight response screaming at me to stay away from the stuff.

Like me, the Fjord Fae didn't move either. Some still in the water, others on the docks.

I peered around the firetruck. Fire Fae looked at each other and back toward the fjord and up at the skies, confusion marring their movements.

"I think we can trust them," Espen said, his voice teeming with an emotion I couldn't quite place.

"Doubt that." I turned back toward the harbor. "They took..."

My words faltered as a navy-clad figure sans cape stepped out of the water and onto the dock beside Reuven.

"Øy... Øyvin."

He was alive. Thank his ancestors, he was alive. Rain dampened his blond hair and shoulders as he unclenched his fists. His eyes found mine, and a whimper left my lips as my knees threatened to buckle. He was there. Right there.

Bows grew taught and soldiers twitched out of the corner of my eye.

"Hold!" I yelled, keeping my gaze locked with Øyvin. "Why'd you keep him alive?"

"Reasons," Reuven replied.

Could they really be on our side? Was that what was happening?

Øyvin gave me a gentle nod and a tiny smile. That was all I needed to see before I started running.

I bolted down the dock and it was as if I'd fired a starting gun. Spouts of fire flew over my head, Reuven and Salka working together with the Fjord Fae to stop them. All hell broke loose, but I could only see one thing. One person.

I launched myself at Øyvin, wrapping my arms and legs around him like a koala, my momentum sending us over the edge of the dock and into the fjord.

The water swallowed us into its cool embrace, stinging parts of my arm, shoulder, and wrists. Øyvin righted us, ensconced me in an ironclad hold, and placed a hand against my lower back as I nuzzled into his neck. A moment later I was dry again and a thin bubble of air wrapped around us, shielding us from the water and providing enough oxygen to breathe.

I pulled back and stared at him. His eyes were so blue, so clear, and slightly hooded as he stared down at me. His skin was paler than normal, sallow, like he hadn't been eating or drinking enough. His gaze flicked to my lips and I surged forward, pressing our mouths together. He tasted like salt and hope. I threaded my hands into his hair and held him against me, needing to meld our bodies together. I never wanted us to be apart again. It had only been days, but it felt like a lifetime.

He touched his lips to the tip of my nose before tilting my head up to his. "Hello, Trouble."

My body shivered at the sound of my nickname.

Other Fjord Fae swam and floated nearby, but in Øyvin's arms, it felt like we were in our own world. A place I never wanted to leave but only add to. All we needed was Espen.

He pressed his fingers to different spots on my body, the rough pads brushing against my skin. "You're hurt," he grumbled.

"Can't feel them."

"That's the adrenaline."

"I'll feel them when we've won. We don't have time right now."

"We really don't," he agreed.

"Reuven can be trusted?"

He nodded.

"Truly, truly trusted? He's not going to flip on us? This isn't a trap?"

"It's a trap," he replied, and my breath caught in my throat. "But not for us."

"What?"

"They've been preparing to flip on Veigar for a while."

"Reuven and Salka? You mean she wants to kill her own dad?" What was it with these fae and killing off their own family members? Sheesh.

He nodded again and trailed his thumb across my cheek before pulling me against his chest once more. "The deception was all part of their plan."

"And they've been working on it for years? Knew this was coming, but didn't warn anyone? Seems like a great time to send a text, letter, or even carrier pigeon."

He stifled a smile. "Veigar thinks he's the chosen one. Believes the ancestors told him not long after his wife died that he would be *the* fae leader."

I snorted. "Has no one told him? I'm the chosen one around here. I even have my own advertisements on store windows."

Øyvin grinned, and my heart sang a little victory.

Something moved beneath us, and I stilled, curling my shoulders and drawing my feet up. "Is that the scaly thing?"

He glanced down and then back to me. "It won't hurt you."

My eyes widened as the *something* moved to my left. Gripping Øyvin for dear life, I slowly turned in its direction.

Staring back at me, with a head the size of the firetruck and a long-ass body like a dragon without wings, was the fucking water snake we'd spotted the other day.

I screamed.

46

LENNIE

Øyvin hoisted me onto the dock as I'd forgotten how to swim thanks to the giant *THING* in the water that looked like it ate fishing boats for breakfast.

I scrambled over the sodden planks and flopped onto my back, droplets pitter-pattering against my forehead. "What the ever-loving fuck is *that*?"

Øyvin pressed his hands against the edge of the dock and hauled himself out of the water in one fluid movement. He crawled over to me and pulled me into an upright position. "That is Jörmungandr."

Yelling and fighting sounded behind me, but I couldn't focus on that. My eyes were glued to the surface, waiting for the beast to slither out and eat me. "Please tell me it's vegetarian."

Øyvin snickered and my heart fluttered at hearing the sound again. His chortles were so few, whenever I got one it felt like I'd won a Hasselblad Award for the best photo of my life.

"It follows Reuven's orders."

"And how long has it been in the fjord? Have you been throwing me in there knowing full well it was down there?"

He opened his mouth to respond, and his eyes blew wide. "Shit," he said, shooting his arms out and using his body as a shield. We crashed back against the dock and a bubble of water formed over us just in time to take a hit from a jet of fire.

My eyes rolled and my head thrummed from being smacked against the wood.

"Sorry," he said. "Stay down. Reuven!"

The fire hissed against the bubble and vanished a moment later. Someone must've taken out the launcher.

I wriggled underneath Øyvin and peered back at the village. A wave of panic washed through my veins and my body trembled. Fire, stones, and smoke were everywhere. Arrows of all kinds flew in every which direction—some smashing through windows, others lodging into victims. Wolves dashed back and forth, snapping at foes. And, in the middle of the melee, stood Espen. His torn police jacket fluttered around his waist like the capes on fae uniforms. Ominous green magic wove between his fingers and power pulsed from him like a steady heartbeat, quaking the ground where he stood. A Fire Fae bolted past Fisken, and Espen unleashed his magic like a whip. A green tendril wrapped around the soldier's throat and yanked. He crashed to his knees, and the ground opened beneath him, swallowing him whole.

My eyes widened.

Espen was death and destruction made real.

"We need to help," I said. "But steer clear of Espen's magic."

Øyvin brushed his nose across my cheek. "Agreed."

We pushed up to our feet and ran back down the dock. Wood gave way to asphalt, and I rolled my shoulders, shrugging off a spell of exhaustion. How long had we been out here? With the cloud cover from Reuven's rainstorm, it was near impossible to tell what the time was.

Battle like I'd never seen before raged around me, with Espen, Reuven, and Salka standing in the middle of it all. Together, they launched an onslaught of magic at the invaders. Salka served up balls of what looked like lava, launching them right at Fire Fae stomachs like a tennis champion. Espen worked in tandem with her, ripping the street beneath her targets open and gobbling them up. Reuven stood beside his wife, half-protecting her from incoming volleys, half-spearheading his own campaign of assaulting soldiers with boiling water. This wasn't my first experience with the Fjord Fae strategy after Torsten was hit last year, but I cringed at the sight, nonetheless.

Øyvin pulled me through the crowd toward the trio, one arm free to shield with me.

We did our best to stay out of the way while helping what forces remained. I crafted boulders, raising them to protect our archers, while Øyvin swirled water around our soldiers, dousing any errant embers.

"All down!" Reuven's voice echoed through the downpour, and Øyvin yanked on my arm, drawing me to my knees.

The Fjord soldiers around us followed suit, encouraging the Forest and Fjell soldiers around them to do the same as the ground rumbled beneath our feet.

"What—"

My question was lost to the wind as the water in the harbor burst upward like a geyser and Reuven's pet snake emerged like a hungry beast set free after its winter slumber.

Jörmungandr sailed over our heads, water dripping from its watery scales as if ancient mythology had come to life before my eyes. I shuddered as the thing that looked like a snake had merged with a really, *really* big dragon rose high into the sky with a deadly roar.

Reuven yelled something unintelligible as the street-sized serpent crashed into town square beside Espen.

A squeal caught in my throat, but Espen didn't even flinch, a renewed battle cry ripping from his throat.

The sea creature's head swung toward Espen, shared a look with him, then slithered toward the Fire Fae that remained, all of which took one glance at the oncoming threat and barreled past Fisken and into town. The beast hurtled after them, Reuven and our forces not far behind.

Øyvin tugged on my arm and helped me to my feet. After the shock of what I'd just seen, I appreciated the help.

We traipsed after them, listening to the battle rage once more. Screams sounded up ahead as if the beast was enjoying its meal.

My hair stuck to my face as the rain poured, putting out the fires that dotted the normally pristine streets. Now, water, soot, and lumps of sludge surrounded me, and my heart beat faster, my feet slowing.

Everywhere I looked, buildings had been bruised, windows shattered, and scorch marks marred doorways. Other structures hadn't been as lucky. Blackened frames of former houses smoldered, several looking more like opened dollhouses—entire sides missing and their contents laid bare to the elements. Rage-fueled tears filled my eyes, but I brushed them away.

"Why would he *do this* to our town?"

Øyvin sighed. "He isn't in his right—"

A flash of red shot out of the camping and hiking store, and Øyvin shoved me behind is back. A Fire Fae raced toward us, his hands raised as flames sizzled in his palms. Øyvin charged, I called forward a tiny dagger, and, within seconds, we had the guy pinned against the building.

Øyvin growled in his face. "I don't think so."

His fingers wrapped around the man's throat, and steam rose from our captive as water trickled out of his mouth. His black eyes blew wide as he scrambled, clawing at my partner before latching both hands around Øyvin's wrist.

A hiss sounded and smoke rose from Øyvin's arm, forcing him to drop the Fire Fae. Øyvin yanked himself free, stumbled back a few steps, and put himself between me and our attacker with a menacing growl.

"You picked the wrong side," Øyvin rumbled.

"I doubt that," the man replied. "Veigar is more powerful than all of you combined."

I huffed. "Then why is he hiding behind his troops? Where is your big, strong, ferocious leader?"

The Fire Fae's top lip curled, and he took a step toward us, flames igniting in his hands once more. I flipped the blade in my hand and prepared to launch as a snarl sounded from our right.

A blur of gray-and-white fur hurtled toward us, latched onto the Fire Fae's leg, and pulled him away. The man screamed as Marius bit at his leg and the unmistakable sound of bones crunching reached me. Not wasting the opportunity, I stepped out from behind Øyvin and threw my dagger. All of Halvar's weapon training came in handy as the blade lodged in the man's shoulder, eliciting another scream as he tried and failed to remove the canine. Phantom pain shot through my own leg, remembering just how painful those wolves' bites were, but this asshole deserved every bit of our wrath.

Øyvin and I rushed forward, and together, the three of us brought down the Fire Fae. He slumped against the broken asphalt, but I retrieved my blade from his shoulder and jammed it into his chest, just in case.

Eyelids fluttered shut. Water dribbled from his mouth. Blood seeped from his wounds.

Marius nuzzled at the Fire Fae's neck then turned to us and made a chuffing noise.

Dead.

Thank fuck.

A howl sounded from somewhere nearby, the eerie sound sending a shiver down my spine. Marius's head whipped in the direction of the noise, ears twitching.

"Thank you," I said.

The wolf looked back at me and his tail wagged once as another howl pierced the air.

"Go. Help them."

He didn't need to be told twice. The wolf bolted, leaving Øyvin and I with the dead soldier.

Yanking the blade from the Fire Fae's chest, I turned and found Øyvin staring down at me. His eyes were hooded, rain droplets resting on the tips of his lashes as a hint of a smile twisted his lips while he scanned me. A wave of heat followed his gaze, my heart beating wildly under his inspection.

"What?"

He shook his head and that smile grew.

"No, really. Do I have blood on my face?" I collapsed my blade and spun to the window in hopes of finding my own reflection.

Øyvin grabbed my arm and tugged me away from our kill. Tucking me against his firm chest, he swept his finger across my forehead, brushing aside errant strands. The touch was so delicate it was just shy of a whisper. "You're perfect."

My knees turned to Jell-o, and my hands pressed against him.

"Are you saying my violent side is a turn on?"

He shrugged and looked down the street, but the twist of his lips gave him away.

"Save it for later!" Espen yelled as he jogged toward us, Salka and Reuven right behind him, the serpent nowhere to be seen. "Back to town square," he added, barely out of breath. "Regroup."

We nodded and followed, my steps faltering here and there, exhaustion starting to set in.

"Are you okay?" I motioned to Øyvin's reddened wrist as we jogged back toward the harbor front.

He grumbled. "Might need Espen's help."

"You know he'll gladly heal you."

Another grumble.

"No point in going on with the rest of your day with what looks like a nasty sunburn."

"Fair."

We regrouped with the other fae leaders in the middle of town square like heroes assembling to avenge their home from the big bad that had shown up and stomped all over their town. Soldiers milled around us. Some attended to wounds, others prepared more shields and blades. I smiled at the sight of all three factions working together.

Øyvin held out his injured wrist to Espen. "Could you help me?"

"Of course!" Espen placed his hands above and below the red marks and his brow furrowed. A translucent energy wrapped around the burn and a wince slipped from Øyvin. The skin shifted from red, to pink, and finally back to its normal state. Espen retracted his hands and bounced on the balls of his feet.

"Thank you," Øyvin muttered and tugged at his sleeves.

"Any time," Espen replied. "Does anyone else need healing?" He looked around the gathered fae. Everyone shook their heads.

Reuven took a step further into the circle and cleared his throat. "We need to implement next steps."

"Which are?" Øyvin and I asked at the same time while Espen listened like a good little school boy.

"Expect another wave of Fire Fae," Salka said, her voice smoky and hoarse. "The next one will have lava."

"How do you know?" I asked.

She wiped the back of her hand across her forehead. "It's father's strategy. Send in the infantry, then batter what remains with swells of lava, with soldiers following after that to dispatch any stragglers."

"Any idea where your father might be?"

"Usually orchestrating from a distance."

I somehow hated him even more.

"Well, I can handle the soldiers in town," Espen said then pointed at the burning Forest. The line of fire had slowed thanks to the rain, but still snuck closer and closer to town. "I can't control that, though, and the barriers we created will only hold for so long."

Reuven straightened. "I'll take care of the wildfire. Please protect the village and fjord."

"Of course," Espen said. "Thank you, Your Majesty."

"We're allies. Call me Reuven."

A quick smile tilted my lips. Even more camaraderie between the factions.

Reuven gave Espen a few sentence run down of their plan and Espen agreed, but asked him to warn the Fjord soldiers of his powers.

"They're well aware," Reuven replied.

Espen's gaze slid to Salka.

"Even in Iceland we've heard tales of what you can do, Espen," she said.

Espen toed the ground. "I'd still prefer any soldiers remain behind me. Seems like when my power is angered, it... Well, things escalate into a rather ugly form of magic."

I eyed my husband, wondering how much *uglier* his magic could get than burying people alive. Was that what the green stuff was?

"Noted." Reuven turned to his Fjord Fae soldiers and barked orders before focusing on his wife. Their fingers intertwined and he leaned in, whispering something to her ear before planting a kiss on her temple.

A flush of pink swept across her face and her gaze softened, adoration shining through. They nodded to each other and then he was running, soldiers following him as he rushed for the forest south of the fjord.

"How many soldiers do we have left here in town?" Øyvin asked Espen.

Espen peered over his shoulder and took a quick tally of the thirty or so soldiers still standing. "Not enough. We're spread thin due to the other fires around the country, but the Fjord Fae will be a massive help."

Looking back over the town square, we still had a decent contingent of soldiers. Many of which leaned against plant containers or sat on what was left of benches, trying to get a moment of rest between the skirmishes.

A lot of them had reddened skin—what I could only assume, from this distance, were burn marks.

I turned to Salka. "You said lava was next? Where will it come from? Who controls it?"

"My father does. He'll likely be at the back of town, trying to usher it through the streets."

"Put a chasm of fire between him and us," Øyvin said, his voice heavy with thought, like he was calculating every move in a chess game.

The quiet queen nodded. "That's always been his tactic."

"Then we need to be more strategic than him," Espen said before sliding out of our circle to a group of nearby soldiers. He knelt beside them and started healing various burns. My heart fluttered and pride welled inside me. Even in the midst of chaos, my dear husband would always help those who were in need.

"We need to get Espen back there," Øyvin said, drawing my focus to the conversation. "Get him behind the lava line and close enough to Veigar to kill him."

"I have killing powers too," I added. "I used some earlier today. Wiped me out a bit, but I've been holding them back to use on Veigar." I turned to Salka and mouthed, "Sorry."

She waved aside the comment.

"Let's get Espen in there first," Øyvin replied. "Then have you slide in behind him with the attack."

I nodded. It was a decent plan. Simple, yet effective. And far from the harebrained idea of me climbing a nearby roof to zap the king from above. Would I be risking slipping on wet tiles? Sure. Would I be playing and winning a real-life game of *The Floor is Lava*? Yup.

"Can you do the lava thing?" I asked Salka.

Her lips quivered into a ghost of a smirk. "Not quite on the same scale, and not like he can. He can get it going and walk away, watching it tear through everything in its path. My powers aren't nearly that strong."

"Better than nothing, babes," I said and winced at the moniker. "Sorry, Your Majesty. Blame the waning adrenaline and exhaustion."

Her delicate smirk flickered again.

I peered over at Øyvin. He grimaced as if he wanted to slap his hand across my mouth. And, honestly, he probably should. I was running on minimal sleep and zero caffeine. Who knew what shit would come out of my mouth.

Salka bristled and a deep groove formed between her onyx eyebrows. As slow as a cat stalking its prey, she turned and faced the street we'd just run back down.

"Brace yourselves," she said, her voice loud but calm.

A shock wave of heat blew across my face and through my ponytail like someone had opened a gigantic oven. Soldiers stirred from their perches, rising to their feet, and drawing their shields. Espen hurried over to us as another wave of heat blasted past and a new plume of smoke rose from somewhere behind Fisken.

"Keep a distance between yourselves and the flow," Salka said, eying the street.

Øyvin stepped beside me, Espen taking the other flank but putting himself slightly in front. An action so different from his usual request of always walking beside me. It was like this would be the only time he'd step in front of me—when a danger presented itself.

Øyvin, meanwhile, would always have my back. And thanks to our height difference could keep an eye on attacks coming from any direction.

Red and black lava crept past Fisken toward the town square, orange bubbles bursting and sending specks of molten debris into the air.

"Holy fucking shit." The words tumbled from me.

"Soldiers! Cannons!" Øyvin yelled. Fjord Fae fell into line and blasted the oncoming flow. The water hissed as it made contact and steam blended with smoke.

"Spread out and divide!" Espen commanded, and fae from all three factions split up, trudging cautiously down side streets—weapons drawn, Fjord Fae leading the way with shields of stone protecting them all.

Salka and Espen stalked forward, the Queen waving her arms in some ethereal pattern that looked more like a witch casting a spell over a cauldron than a fae drawing on their powers.

I moved to walk after them, but stumbled, catching myself on the arm of a bench. *What the fuck was that?*

Peering at the ground, I searched for what had tripped me up. Was there a random rock I'd missed or had I tripped on my own goddamn foot again? Rain-soaked asphalt stared back at me like it had just played a prank.

Something in my arm spasmed, and I clutched it to my chest.

"Lennie?" Øyvin's voice sounded like it was yards away and under water.

A wave of pain and fear washed through me, bringing me to my knees. The lightning-shaped scar on my left arm pulsed like an erratic heartbeat.

"What's happening to me?"

Lightning cracked out of the forest on the north side of the fjord and shot through the sky.

Air caught in my throat. "Something's wrong."

47

LENNIE

I stared at the spot where the lightning had crackled through the forest as a wave of fatigue washed over me. My butt met the ground, and a shaky breath left my lips.

"What's wrong?" Øyvin's voice changed frequency like it was coming in and out of range on a radio. "Talk to me."

"What the hell?" I mumbled.

A stitch formed in my side like I'd run a marathon, the pain spasming at regular intervals. I hunched over, feeling for injuries, but found nothing. Still, something within me felt off.

I took a deep breath and focused on my magic. The mass of energy was still there but... not entirely. It was as if it were curling into a ball to protect itself. What the hell was happening?

Magical lightning shot out from between the trees on the north side of the fjord once more. My head whipped in that direction, and I narrowed my gaze. It looked like it was coming from the clearing where I'd photographed the illegal magic transfer last year. The spot that had been left scarred, like my arm, by the misuse of power.

Another torrent of electricity forked into the sky.

"Hey guys." My voice trembled as a wave of anxiety overtook me. Since Reuven had run to the southern hillside to ward off the flames, there were only two other beings that could possibly be behind those attacks. "I don't think Veigar is in town."

"I'm more concerned about you." Øyvin brought his finger and thumb to my chin and tilted my head toward him. His lips sat in a firm line, a crease knit between his eyebrows. "Tell me what's happening, Trouble."

"I'm not sure. I think—" I gasped, pain lancing through my body again as thunder rumbled. With a shaky finger, I motioned toward the mountainside. "Veigar found Halvar. I think that's them fighting."

That had to be what the lightning was. Those looked like killing attacks, but stronger. Something otherworldly. And there were two men in the area that I'd classify as not of this world.

"I'm not worried about Halvar. I'm worried about you."

Another pulse of pain ripped through my side as if protesting his statement, and a wave of concern washed through me. "I think we might need to worry about him."

"Doubtful," Øyvin replied. "And I'm not letting you out of my sight."

"Agreed," Espen said as he appeared beside us. A thin layer of rain-soaked ash clung to him like sprinkles on a cupcake.

"I have to do this."

"You don't *have* to leave our side," Espen said.

Øyvin shook his head rapidly.

"You both know I'm the only one here who has that killing power."

Espen's gaze dipped to his hands before looking back at me. "I have destructive powers that can decompose people."

"What!"

Øyvin and I stared at him like he'd grown two heads. Maybe that's what the green stuff was? The stuff that had been weaving around his fingers earlier.

Espen shrugged. "I don't like it. It feels like death, but I could use it."

"Then use it on the lava stuff and whoever might be lingering behind it," I countered.

Øyvin looked as if he was still trying to wrap his mind around Espen's revelation.

Another wave of discomfort ran through my bones, and I stifled a wince. We didn't have time for this. I needed to get to that mountain.

"We'll discuss that news later. I need to get up the mountain. This was always the plan. I have some extra magic juice in me from Freija that could be used against Veigar." At least, I hoped I had. I was pretty sure that was an accurate interpretation of her tale from the Temple, but either way. I had royal killing magic and my partners didn't. *I* had to go.

A rumble sounded from Øyvin's chest, and Espen let out a huff through his nose before pulling me into his arms.

"Lennie." Kiss. "Louise." Kiss. "*Solbakke.*" Kiss. "Martin." He kissed the tip of my nose. "Don't you dare get yourself killed on that mountain."

I grinned.

He nudged me into another pair of arms which spun me until I faced a broad chest. Øyvin pressed one hand to my lower back, the other cupping the base of my head. "What he said." Then he kissed me like it might be the last thing he ever did.

My heart pounded and I felt like a feather drifting on the smoke-filled breeze. Safe, protected, home. This was home.

"Just know I don't like this," Øyvin added with another rumble of displeasure.

"I know." I brushed the tip of my nose against his. "But you're needed down here."

Another crack of lightning lit up the north side of the fjord and shouting sounded from behind us.

I reluctantly pulled back. I didn't want to leave them. But I had to.

The mountain needed me.

Halvar might even need me.

And the town could be protected by my partners. They'd do everything they could to protect our home.

Espen tucked a strand of hair behind my ear as Øyvin let me slip from his hold.

"Follow me when the town is secured." I moved without further thought, my focus locked on the spot where I'd seen the flash of lightning.

With stitches in my sides and a constant tremble of pain through my bones, I bolted through town, ducking and weaving through the streets I now knew as well as the scar on my left arm. Ash-filled puddles lined the edges of the road, some appearing more maroon than others. Plants in window boxes sagged under the weight of the storm and soot, while rainwater rushed down gutters and spouts.

Sweeping through the edge of Skolvik, I barreled down the path past Solveig's house. Boulders glistened along the edge of the fjord and the little bushes that defended the homes looked like they'd been doused in gray icing sugar.

Another flash of lightning ripped across the sky, thunder rumbling in its wake, and I increased my pace. The path may have been slippery, but if I fell, I'd just get back up again.

Reaching the trailhead, I darted into the forest, jumping over logs and rocks, avoiding patches of moss that had grown slick with the downpour. Errant tendrils of hair glued themselves to the side of my face, sweat and rain acting as a natural adhesive. Something moved to my left and I ground to a stop as a fae with pitch black eyes and snarling lips stepped out from behind a tree.

Flames danced across his fingertips.

I didn't have time to think.

I launched for the Fire Fae, pulling on that killing magic that was a necessary evil to protect the mountain and village. Power seared down my arms and I aimed at the guy's head. He reared back at my advance, but it was too late. The magic wrapped around him like a vice and squeezed the life out of him. His body dropped to the forest floor with a dull thud.

"Don't fuck with my family."

I continued up the trail, ignoring the way my thighs and calves screamed at me, refusing to give in to the guilt of taking another life, however necessary. Magic swirled in my chest, slower now, like it needed to recharge after that death. I'd need to be more judicious with its use. Careful not to wear myself out. But most of all, I needed to get to that clearing. I needed to help.

Twigs and mud squelched beneath my feet, rain pelted the trees, and the sky darkened even more overhead as the storm intensified.

Reuven's magic, no doubt.

The sound of a branch snapping had me spinning on the spot, raising my arms into a fighting stance.

Another Fire Fae appeared, and I narrowed my gaze at his his hulking form. This one was bigger than the others in town. Thicker neck. Broader shoulders. And hands that looked like they could stopper a volcano like a cork in a wine bottle.

I drew a sword and settled into my battle stance. "I don't have time for you, Handsy."

He growled and launched a ball of fire at me.

Ducking and swinging, I swerved away from the hit before another orb flew at my face. I spun, but the fire caught my left arm.

"Not again," I huffed as I dodged yet another volley. This guy wasn't letting up, and he'd put me on defense. Football games may have been won with good defensive lines, but I needed to be on the offensive here. I needed to be the one who walked away from this fight.

He lunged, and I swung for his stomach.

Pulling to the side, he sidestepped the blade, but it delved into his arm. A roar of pain echoed around us, and I stutter-stepped as he wrapped his uninjured hand around the sword and yanked.

I flew through the mud and crashed to my knees, pain zinging up my legs. The sword fell to the ground with a muffled thud and panic ran through me. I scrambled through the dirt reaching for the blade. The number one rule Halvar had said when using a sword was to not have it used against you. I couldn't lose it. Couldn't let it fall into enemy hands. Especially hands that big.

Crawling across rocks and mud, I reached for the stone sword, pulling the magic back inside me, the blade disintegrating—

Fingers wrapped around the back of my neck and hauled me out of the dirt. A high-pitched yelp sprung from me and the man turned my face to him. His snarl was all I could see. I grasped at his arms, digging my nails into the stab wound I'd given him. He didn't even flinch. A bubble of hope burst inside me as blood and water sluiced down my back and around my neck where his thumb pressed.

My lungs screamed.

Vision blurred.

This was it.

But if I could... If I could only push some stunning... Magic into...

A ball of light flew over my head and smacked into the Fire Fae's face. The pressure around my throat loosened and I pushed out of his hold, stumbled back, and gasped for air.

"My eyes!" he screamed and pressed his palms to his sockets.

I whipped my head to one side, turning my body sideways so I kept the Fire Fae in my peripheral vision. Torsten stepped out from between two pines, his chest heaving, tawny hair hanging around his chin, eyes locked on the fae he'd just hit.

"I didn't know you had royal magic like me."

He shook his head and mouthed, "I don't."

"What? Then how the hell…"

Oh no, wait. He'd always said he didn't have royal powers, just royal-like light magic. My shoulders fell. "Shit."

He nodded, and I put myself between him and the angered Fire Fae who was now blinking and banking a bunch of fire in his now bloody hands. Both balls of flame flew at us, and I barely got a shield of stone down in time. The thick board of rock thrummed into the mud, shaking the ground beneath us.

Torsten leaned into the shield to reinforce it as a gigantic orb of flames shot at us. The shield exploded with an almighty boom. Rock flew in all directions and we went flying off the trail and into the forest. My head cracked against a tree trunk. Air whooshed from my lungs and my ears rang like I'd just been punched. I groaned and my favorite swear-word slipped from my lips.

A pained moan sounded from my right, and I glanced down toward the noise.

A blurry Torsten came into view—his gray uniform dark and mottled with black, shards poking out of his hair, and blood seeping from his nose and left ear. My stomach roiled.

No. Not Torsten, please.

The Fire Fae roared and circled back as if goading me to try and attack him now that I knew what he could do. It was a wrong move on his part, though.

"I might not be able to save my friend," I yelled and pointed at the fae in red, "but I'm going to fucking kill you."

I was losing friends today. People who'd welcomed me into their lives. People I cared about. My family. I wasn't losing another one.

Rising to my feet, I launched blade after stony blade at the Fire Fae. Magic, stone, and demi-fae worked as one. Launching, creating, and launching again. One hand and then the other.

Handsy was nimble for his size, but I still landed some shots between his own flurry of fire. All I needed was a few seconds, an opening to launch more of that death magic—

Something whizzed past my ear and a knotty branch sprouted from the soft flesh beneath the man's Adam's apple. I didn't bother to look behind me to see which Forest Fae had saved my ass. I took the split second of opportunity and finally launched a wave of my death magic at the beast. The power seared through my aching arms and wrapped around him like thick ropes. They pulsed and tightened. His eyes bugged out even more as he grasped at his neck, mouth opening and closing like a goldfish. He dropped to his knees, then fell on his face, lodging the stick further into his own throat.

"Fucking finally," I huffed.

Turning around, I found Leif on his knees, leaning over Torsten, his own uniform mottled with dark patches that looked alarmingly like blood. He draped his green cape over his husband's abdomen and clutched his hand in his.

I scrambled over to them and knelt beside my fallen friend. "He'll be okay," I said out loud, hoping I was right.

Leif's dark green eyes met mine, and worry struck through me.

"Trygve is at the boathouse. He can help. And Espen. Espen is in the village."

Leif gave me a thin-lipped smile so brief I might've imagined it before he turned his watery gaze to Torsten. "He'll survive. Won't you, my love?"

Torsten's head moved gently as if nodding, his eyes hooded and glazed, scarlet running down the side of his face.

Leif delicately examined Torsten's injuries and wiped his hair off his forehead. He'd turned pale. Too pale. Sweat mixing with rain at his temples. Another dark stain bloomed on Leif's green cape.

I swallowed hard.

"Thank you for saving me," I said, motioning over my shoulder to the dead Fire Fae.

"Not the first time one of my arrows has saved your behind, baby fae."

I furrowed my eyebrows. "What are you talking about?"

"Last year. When Kjetil captured you. My arrow was the one that took him down."

"What? I thought that was Espen."

Leif shook his head. "He was busy. I was watching his back."

"All this time I thought it was Espen who'd saved me."

"Do you really think I'd let the love of Espen's life get killed on the battlefield?"

My chin quivered and my stomach twisted into a mass of knots as I looked to his husband. If I'd made a stronger shield. If Torsten hadn't leaned against it. If he'd let me... Fuck, he needed to survive. But the blood. There was too much blood.

"You need to get that looked at too," Leif said, drawing my attention away from Torsten and nodding at my arm.

I peered down at what was left of my uniform. Large holes had formed in the wool and the skin below bubbled like a severe sunburn. I winced. I couldn't deal with that now. "I have to get up the mountain. I need to get to the clearing."

"Then go, and be more careful. Let the forest serve as your shield. Listen to her, let her guide and protect you."

Sounded like some mumbo-jumbo to me, and yet, I understood what he meant. I needed to put more thought and strategy into my movements, watch my own back, and use the terrain to my advantage. This was my home field. An area I'd photographed countless times. I knew it better than the Fire Fae.

I nodded to Leif and gave him my thanks.

I can do this.

Focusing on the forest, I rose to my feet and stepped toward the trail.

I dared one more look back at my friends. Thick pine branches hung over them like nature's umbrellas, protecting them from the steady rain. Leif lay down beside Torsten and wrapped his arm over him, pressing his hand to Torsten's chest.

My heart shattered as somewhere, deep within me, I knew he wasn't going to make it. Leif may have saved Espen's love, but I hadn't been able to save his. My chest tightened as a tear spilled from my eye. I batted it away. I should've stopped Torsten, should've protected him. Had the power to do so and fucking failed.

Leif's gaze met mine and he shook his head as if he could hear my self-loathing thoughts.

"Go," he mouthed.

Wiping away another tear, I turned back to the trail, stepped over a fallen tree, and continued up the mountain, leaving another piece of my heart behind.

48

LENNIE

Silent tears streamed down my face as I trudged up the mountain trail as fast as possible. I listened for any other footsteps or noises, following Leif's wisdom to tread lightly and watch my own back.

Leif.

Poor Leif.

Poor Torsten.

If only he hadn't stepped between me and the shield. If only I'd killed that Fire Fae straight away, avoided this mess entirely. A lump lodged in my throat. Head wounds like that were hard to come back from, and with the amount of blood pooling around him, I doubted I'd ever see his teasing smile again.

Another round of tears rushed over my cheeks, mixing with raindrops. I wiped them away as I tucked behind a thick evergreen. I didn't have time for sadness. Didn't have time to mourn. I could do that later. Right now, I needed to focus. I had a mountain and people to protect. I wasn't going to fail again today. Not a fucking chance.

A branch snapped up ahead and I stilled, bracing my back against the tree trunk as moss reached around from the north side to tickle my neck.

Footfalls thumped at uneven intervals as if someone was searching. My heart thrashed against my ribs, breaths sounding too loud as they puffed from my nose.

A Fire Fae slunk down the trail past where I stood.

I stopped breathing.

He scanned his surroundings, hands curved and ready to use his powers.

If he looked over his right shoulder... If he turned even forty degrees in my direction, I'd be caught.

Lightning clattered once again, and thunder rumbled from overhead.

He twisted.

I moved.

Catapulting from my perch, I threw a ball of stunning magic at the soldier. His limbs twitched, body convulsing, before he fell to the ground like a rag doll. Without checking on his condition, I conjured a camera-sized rock and smashed it over his head.

"Sorry, buddy." I threw aside the bloody stone. "You came to the wrong town."

Another flash of light blitzed from the woods up the mountainside and I ran toward it. There was no time to waste. Exhaustion clawed at me and my body ached, but I had to keep pushing, keep moving. I didn't have time to deal with the emotional trauma of killing other soldiers or the bile churning in my stomach.

Dispatching two more Fire Fae in the same way on the hike up, I eventually made it to the clearing where we'd first discovered the scars of Balder's illegal magic transfers.

A battle cry had my steps faltering and my ragged breaths stilling as I ducked behind another tree.

Halvar stood on the north side of the clearing, Veigar to the south on my right, dense pine trees surrounding them on all sides. The land between them looked like it had been torn apart by a massive, scalding rake—soil overturned and flora singed. New marks of royal power slashed through the trees, the silvery light glowing.

Halvar's cape was missing, and his uniform was drenched and covered in woodland debris. A thin cut marred his left cheek, his knuckles bloody and raw as he gripped a monstrous rock axe in one hand while the other wielded a circular stone shield.

Veigar's lips curved into a slick smile. Gone were his sunglasses and suave suits. Instead, his fae uniform, a majestic ensemble of red and black material with gold buttons and epaulets, clung to him like armor. All he needed was a crown and he'd fit the bill for a fairytale monarch.

Shame this wasn't a fairytale, though.

Veigar swung his fiery sword, and a jet of flames shot out of the tip.

Halvar raised his shield, buffeting the blow. His feet slid in the mud, the force of the onslaught enough to shift him backward.

A gasp lodged in my throat, and I crouched behind my tree. Holy mother of Satan, Veigar was powerful.

Stones flew into the air and twisted into a tornado of destruction, churning toward the king. Veigar dodged Halvar's counter like a ballroom dancer, only one rock crashing against his shin. He winced, growled, and unfurled his free hand, launching another barrage of fire at Halvar.

The beast of the mountain crouched beneath it and slammed his axe into the ground. Soil ruptured and the fissure ran toward Veigar. The King's fire stuttered and burned out, and he tumbled to his back.

Yes.

Veigar flipped and rolled to his feet again.

No.

They both stuck out their arms and aimed at each other. Royal power shot from them and crashed in the middle of the clearing. Lightning crackled from the point of impact, stretching toward the clouds.

Fuuuuuck.

That's what I'd seen in town. That was the royal fae powers at work... And Halvar only had a fraction of the royal power Veigar had, yet he could still do that! Was he actually a fae or a god who was really good with rocks?

A boulder sat at the edge of the clearing, branches draping over the top of it, moss clinging to crevasses. If I snuck closer and hid behind it, I could get a better look *and* be nearer should Halvar need back up.

The lightning onslaught ended, both parties' chests heaving.

"You won't last long, Head Guard."

"Fucking try me."

Halvar bellowed like a bear and Veigar cackled, both distracted by each other's new attacks.

Now was my chance.

Dropping to my hands and knees, I crawled over to the recliner-sized rock and pulled my cape over my hair like a gremlin to hide the blonde strands and blend in. This probably wasn't what Leif meant when he said to use the terrain to my advantage, but I was trying my best here.

I crouched behind the boulder, keeping my gaze locked on the two men in the clearing.

Veigar launched a beam of crackling and pulsing royal magic at Halvar. I squinted at the bright light, while Halvar launched his shield like a discus. The stone disk cleaved the bolt of lightning in two before shattering halfway across the field and sending splinters of stone and magic into the air. I turned my face away and narrowly avoided being pelted by the pieces.

Peering back at the fight, I found Halvar with an axe in one hand and a stone hammer in the other. He looked like a Norse god reborn. If any human saw this, they'd think their mythological gods were real and that Halvar was a silver-haired Thor with pointy ears.

The two men continued their dance of death, gliding around the clearing like gladiators. Their steps assured and measured, their movements confident and clear, like they'd been preparing for this fight for centuries. And maybe they had.

A boulder materialized between the two men and a moment later, Halvar's hammer struck it from the top. A massive *crack* pierced the air. Shards broke off the rock and shot toward Veigar.

The King waved his arm in front of him and a surge of heat washed over the clearing. The shards stalled in the air and turned molten. Glowing like deadly fireflies, the fragments hung immobile.

Halvar swallowed hard and grimaced.

"This is the best you can do?" Veigar sneered and waved his arm again.

The lumps of lava flew back toward Halvar.

He batted them away with his weapons, but not without taking a few to his arms and chest.

Shit that had to hurt.

I pressed myself further against my boulder, hoping what was left of my gray uniform camouflaged me. I didn't want to interrupt Halvar or cause him to lose focus, but if there was a moment for me to jump in and help, a moment where I could finally use these killing powers and whatever bonus-ancestor-juice Freija had gifted me, I'd take it.

Halvar's sky-blue eyes scanned the clearing, sliding around, pausing on my boulder for a nanosecond, before continuing their assessment.

Had he seen me?

He swept to his left, cris-crossing his steps. Veigar matched him, coming closer to my hiding spot and giving me his back.

My shoulders curved inward, and my heart raced as sweat and rain soaked every inch of my clothes. *Don't look behind you. Don't look behind you. Don't look behind you.*

"Come along, Halvar." Veigar's voice was filled with malice, goading the man. "Can't you protect your precious mountain?"

Halvar gave the king a death glare that would land me in an early grave if directed toward me.

The earth vibrated and gigantic rock spikes pierced through the soil. Veigar twisted and moved as one of the points jutted up where he stood. The edge caught his arm, tearing through his sleeve as it rose to the sky like a tree, and left a stream of blood in its wake.

The King's chest heaved as Halvar continued his attack.

More spikes retreated and re-emerged.

Balls of fire flew around the field.

Arrow-like stone shards filled the air.

Flashes of royal power shot from one man to the other.

The fight was like a clash of kings. Two powerful beings that refused to be torn down. Halvar raced toward the King, axe raised above his head, hammer across his sternum like a shield.

He swung.

Veigar roared and a blast of fire exploded all around him like a firework.

I sheltered behind my boulder as flames licked around it, heating the stone against my back. Wincing, I breathed through the onslaught and temperature. It felt like I was going to be burned alive and served up as steak.

Mercifully, the flames banked, leaving behind the smell of singed wood and grass.

I peered around my grilled rock.

Trees creaked, threatening to fall.

Pine needles curled.

Halvar staggered back, and I clamped my hand over my mouth to hold back my gasp.

Singed pieces of wool hung from Halvar's arm and leg, the skin beneath red and raw. Burns covered his entire left side as if he'd tried to shield himself from the flames. He groaned and fell onto his back, and my understanding of the world tilted upside down.

"Your dedication was always commendable, Halvar." Veigar's authoritative voice carried around the clearing like a Roman conqueror as he walked toward Halvar, dragging his fiery sword through the battered earth. "You'll be remembered for your bravery and sacrifice."

Remembered?

"Do it," Halvar bit out. "Kill me, and see what happens."

"I'm inevitable, Halvar son of Harald. The ancestors foretold this. Willed this into being. I am to lead the fae to a new dawn." He raised his sword over Halvar, aiming for his chest. The ground quaked.

My eyes widened, and my heart thrashed against my ribs.

Over my dead fucking body.

I launched from my spot and threw stunning magic right between Veigar's shoulder blades. The ball of crackling light landed perfectly and he spasmed, throwing his arms out wide. The blade of flames disintegrated as my own broadsword appeared in my hands, power zipping down it.

He turned on the spot, magic crackling in his palms.

But I was already across the field, already in range, and nothing could stop me.

A roar of anger ripped from my lungs, and I threw all my weight behind my swing. The blade sunk into Veigar's neck, met momentary resistance, then kept going all the way through. His head lolled to one side then popped off as his body dropped to the ground. Empty black eyes stared up into the rain, mouth hung open in shock, and blood streamed from the decapitated head.

Bile raced up my throat and my limbs shook.

"Holy fuck," I muttered as my sword slipped from my grasp. "I just killed the Fire Fae King."

49

LENNIE

I raced over to where Halvar lay on the sodden ground. Welts and scarlet slashes covered his left side in a gruesome tapestry of destruction. His chest heaved, tearing at the delicate wounds, and he winced through labored breaths.

"Oh my shit, I saved your ass!"

He grumbled.

Kneeling beside him, mud caked my knees and water sank further into my already soaked pants. "Holy fuck. What can I do? How can I help? We need a healer. We need Trygve. No. Espen. Espen is closer."

"Well—" Halvar inhaled sharply and groaned. "Well done."

"I'd make a joke about compliments, but now isn't the time."

The big guy rolled his eyes, and my fear of his untimely demise banked... slightly.

Blood seeped from more wounds I couldn't see beneath his tattered uniform and stained the soil underneath him. Injuries I hadn't seen him get. They must've been fighting each other long before I got here.

My hands trembled as I pulled off my cape and pressed it to one of his open wounds. It wasn't clean material, but we needed to stop the bleeding. "Tell me what to do."

Halvar opened his mouth and the ground trembled. His eyes widened with fear and my stomach flip-flopped at the sight.

"What the fuck was that?" I asked with a quick look back at the dead king. "He can't do shit from the great beyond, can he?"

"No. Look at me, Lennie."

I glanced back at Halvar.

"Leave me. Protect the mountain."

"What are you talking about, big guy? I can't leave you here to die. Who would run our Council meetings? Who would scare off the crazies?"

"You'd do fine."

I scoffed, fear nearly choking me at the thought of losing him. "We both know that's a lie."

The ground shuddered again, and an almighty cracked rent the air.

Halvar's lips quivered, his eyes focused above my head, and I slowly turned toward the noise.

It wasn't coming from the clearing. It *was* coming from the direction of the fissure. The one we'd been worried about. The one Veigar had visited the other day.

I sucked in a panicked breath.

"No... This can't be happening."

I'd known the fissure felt off magically, but what if Veigar had shoved lava down there? Salka said he could create lava and walk away from it, letting it do its thing—whatever that meant. My eyes darted between the mountaintop and the town below us, my heart racing wildly. The magic in my sternum curled further in on itself.

Halvar's hand reached up, turning my face to his as another crack sounded, the trees shaking.

"*Run.*"

"But you—"

"Leave me! Save them!" Halvar roared.

Spinning on the spot, I didn't hesitate again, running like lives depended on me.

I bolted through the forest, dodging between trees and over moss-covered boulders, the sodden soil squelching beneath my feet. Rain slashed at my face and my breaths came hard and heavy as I pushed myself to run faster than ever before.

The ground shook again, and I grabbed a tree for purchase, before pushing myself harder. I had to get there in time. I had to do something. Had to somehow stop the land from falling into the fjord or the resulting wave would drown the village and the loves of my life.

A few Fjell Fae soldiers emerged from behind trees up ahead, their gazes flooded with panic. "Ma'am! It's cracking!" One of them yelled, waving his arm above his head.

I careened toward him. "Clear the mountain!"

"But—"

"That's an order!"

What the hell had come over me? Maybe it was the trauma of the number of people I'd killed today, including Veigar, or the volume of adrenaline coursing through my veins. Or maybe the fact that I'd just left Halvar to die. Either way, I'd somehow flipped a switch and activated a new *boss mode*.

The soldiers scrambled and dove back into the forest, heading in separate directions.

My feet slid through the soil as I came to a stop at the tree line. The land before me vibrated and small rocks rolled past like tumbleweeds, bouncing down the steep incline. A large groove opened by my feet and I took a step back. "Shit."

This thing was coming down. Now.

I hopped over the cracking soil and ran out onto the middle of the cleared slope, joining the five soldiers huddled there.

"Do you have a report?" I asked the closest one.

She wobbled and readjusted her footing. "The northern watch guards reported significant heat coming from the fissure this morning."

My brow furrowed.

"They think a Fire Fae set an explosive down there," she continued.

"Was that what the cracking noise was?" I asked, putting my back to the fjord and looking up the hillside.

A tall fae with the build of a marathon runner raised his hand. "No, that was the land splintering after the suspected explosion."

"I think it's lava," I said. "Salka mentioned Veigar can walk away from it. Or could."

Five confused gazes stared back at me.

The ground quaked again and we wobbled, holding our arms out to regain our balance.

"Veigar is dead." They smiled. "But his daughter told me he could set off lava eruptions and walk away."

The woman next to me nodded as if a light bulb had turned on in her head. "Like his volcanoes. He can set them off and hide."

I snapped my fingers and pointed at her. "Exactly. I think that is what's happening here."

Soil above us detached from its perch and started sliding toward us.

Two male soldiers dropped to their knees and planted their hands in the ground. Translucent magic ebbed from them, caressing the mountainside as it wove upward, trying to fix the breakage.

"We need to figure out how to secure this," I muttered.

"I don't think we can," another soldier said. "It's almost half a kilometer wide."

I blinked. *Fuck if I knew what a kilometer was.*

"From this tree line to that one," the female soldier piped up, her eyes locked on my face.

Roots snapped, stones skittered down the hillside, and the purple and pink heather vibrated. Something in my sternum spasmed and my left arm tingled. My magic pulsed like it was under attack. Which was weird considering I'd already dispatched Public Enemy Number One. I rubbed the heel of my palm against my chest, hoping to alleviate the pain, but it was useless.

Something was still wrong. That exhaustion I felt in the village hadn't... "Fuck. I'm an idiot."

"Ma'am?"

"Get everyone off the mountain right now."

"We cannot leave—"

"You can and you will," I replied, my voice stern and unyielding, which was kind of new. I turned to the guys with their hands in the ground. "That includes you two, as well."

They lifted their fingers from the dirt. "What about the mountain?"

"Halvar is injured and dying in the clearing down the hill by the scarred trees."

Everyone's eyes went wide.

"Thought that might get your attention. Now, go save him!"

All five of them scrambled off the hillside and back into the forest. Thank goodness. If this went wrong, if my hunch was pure lunacy, I wanted them as far away as possible. Them getting the big guy to Espen would be helpful too.

I turned my focus back to the weakened hillside. The crack yawned open at the top.

"Hello, old friend," I said.

It wasn't Halvar and his fight I'd felt. Our magic wasn't connected to each other like some movie juju or fairytale fate thing.

It was the mountain.

My magic was tied to the mountain.

It always had been. Freija had said so herself. She'd asked the ancestors for more power to save her weakening mountain and passed that along to me.

This. This was what I was meant to use those powers for. To uphold my promise to her and protect her mountain while also protecting what I loved the most.

Another massive crack ripped through the air and the ground started to slide. I teetered and fell to my knees, pain smarting up my legs from the impact.

"All right, Freija. Let's see what you gave me."

Hold. I shoved my hands into the wet ground, pushing underneath the grass and rock-riddled terrain. Stones poked beneath my fingernails and plants tickled my wrists. The magic in my chest rumbled and unfurled like a bear waking from a long hibernation.

Hold. I willed the magic in my sternum to obey, to flow from me like it was the tide itself. That swirling mass of energy cascaded through my arms, painfully zapping my skin as it went.

HOLD.

The mountainside groaned as power seared through me, arching my back and splaying my fingers until it felt like they were being torn from my hand.

"HOLD!"

My vision flashed silver, the ground beneath my fingers shining back at me like a camera's flash. A scream tore from my lips, and I pushed harder. Lines of silver magic crackled out from where I knelt, shooting up the terrain like a spiderweb and pushing the land back into position. Back where it belonged. Back where we needed it to stay.

Muffled voices sounded around me, but I couldn't let my focus drift. I needed to put this piece of mountain back into place before it fell into the fjord and wiped out everything I loved.

Something wet dripped down my cheeks—rain or tears, I couldn't tell. It didn't matter.

I pushed and pushed and pushed. Giving all of myself, all of my power to the mountain.

Everything turned silver. Silver ground. Silver plants. Silver sky. My head lolled forward, my breaths ripping from my chest. The ground shook and moved upward like a puzzle piece returning to its spot.

Good.

My heart beat faster than a camera on sport mode.

My arms burned.

My head was about to split in two.

But it was working. It had to be working. "Please..." The word blended into the ringing in my ears.

If I pushed a little bit harder. Gave a little more.

"HOLD!" I screamed. Power seared down my arms and into the mountain. My hair broke free of its tie and whipped around me in a frenzy. Lightning crackled out of me and thunder rolled through the valley.

"Trouble! No!"

"Lennie!"

A thick wave of exhaustion washed over me, drawing my hands from the soil. My body collapsed backward, rain pelting me from all angles as I tumbled, and silver turned to darkness.

50

LENNIE

A blanket of darkness wrapped around me, but I could feel something… Hand. I could feel my hand and a gentle pressure against it.

Weird. Why couldn't I feel my body?

Weirder still. What the hell kind of dream had I just had? It was strange as fuck. I'd found magical creatures called fae, moved to Norway, and got married. If anything, that was my mother's dream—

"You're not dreaming, Trouble." The voice was muffled, like I was underwater.

The pressure against my hand tightened, and I squeezed back.

"Lennie? Lennie, can you hear me?" another voice said. Male. It was definitely male. Both of the voices were. Low and warm.

My elbow came back online, and I moved my arm.

"She's waking up."

"Stand back, let me check her pulse, please."

"I've had my fingers on it since we got here."

Someone growled.

"Oh, all right. But I wish to examine her when she wakes and has had time to process." A lighter, more old-fashioned voice said. Had I been transported to the 1800's? Doubt I'd do well there. Had they even discovered coffee yet?

"Don't give me that look, Espen," the old-fashioned voice said again. "You may examine her first, but as a Fjell Fae and my friend, it is my duty to check on her."

A door bumped shut.

Espen... I knew that name. It was the man I'd married in my dream. "Was I still dreaming?"

"No, you're not still dreaming, Trouble. Time to wake the fuck up."

Warmth filled my shoulders and chest. I could feel them again. Slowly but surely, sensation returned to my body along with enough brain cells to compute that the life I'd been living in my dream was real.

I peeled my eyes open and squinted against the faint glow of magical lights. A cavern-like ceiling loomed overhead, magical sconces flickered against the walls, and thick wooden chair backs surrounded me like pixies sent to worship their god. Cool stone brushed against my free hand, and my brows furrowed. Stone walls, glowing sconces, big slab table...

Wait a second.

"Did you guys put me on the Council meeting table like an offering?" My voice croaked and I peered at where Espen held my hand. "Yup."

"We got you changed and cleaned up too," Øyvin said from my other side.

That would explain the airy feeling around my body.

Hold up. What clothes?

I glanced toward my feet. They'd put me in a white tunic, billowy pants, and my favorite pair of fuzzy socks. My gaze slid up from my toes, and I flinched.

Halvar stood at the head of the table, arms crossed, eyes locked on me. Scars littered his left side and mottled his face, and part of his beard was missing. The other side had been shaved short to match.

"You're alive," I said to Halvar.

"As are you."

"Thank the ancestors," Øyvin muttered, and my attention fell on him.

The stubble on his chin was scruffier than usual, his hair in disarray like he'd been raking his hands through it, and those eyes... Those oceans looked down at me with a degree of sorrow that wrapped around my heart and squeezed. He'd been worried. Really worried.

I swallowed hard and turned to Espen. An air of hope clung to him and his lips curled into a gentle smile when he caught me looking. But I wasn't fooled by the visible relief. Bags hung heavy under his eyes, and he was still in his police gear, his shredded and scorched jacket slung over the back of his chair.

They both looked like they'd been holding vigil at someone's death bed. *My* death bed.

I wanted to reach out and wrap my arms around them, hold on and never let them go.

"What the hell happened?" I rasped.

"Wait," Øyvin said and disappeared for a moment, reappearing a second later with a pitcher and glass of water. Espen pulled me into a seated position, keeping his hand on my back, as Øyvin handed the drink to me, condensation cooling my palm. "Drink."

I didn't need to be told twice. I tipped the glass against my chapped lips and cool water sluiced down my throat. Saliva returned to my mouth, and I downed the whole thing before passing it back to Øyvin. He set it at the end of the table and turned his focus back to me.

"Thank you," I said. "Now, what happened?"

"What do you remember?" Espen asked.

I opened my mind and recent events came flooding back to me like a river that had breached its banks. The torrent of images and memories—happy and sad, terrifying and jubilant—washed through me. I shuddered and a whimper slipped free. Oddvar's burned. Ylva dead.

Forest scorched. Torsten injured. Halvar severely injured too. And, holy hell, I'd killed Veigar.

It was too much. I needed to bury my head in the sand again like an ostrich and ignore my emotions. But I couldn't. Ylva didn't deserve that. The soldiers we'd lost didn't deserve that. The people I'd killed…

I swallowed the hard lump in my throat and let the onslaught in. Let it fill every part of me. From my pinky toes to the top of my head. We'd been through hell, and I had to acknowledge that.

"I remember everything," I blubbered as a tear slid down my cheek.

Espen stroked his palm down my spine, and Øyvin sat down, taking my other hand in his.

"How long have I been out?"

"Two whole days," Espen replied.

The room swayed. "What?"

"You used a lot of magic on the mountain," Øyvin said.

"Did it work? I mean, you're alive, but did it fall into the fjord or not?"

Øyvin shook his head.

Espen rubbed his free hand across my lower back, easing out the tension that had settled there. "You put it back in place. You saved us all."

"Well shit," I muttered. "I definitely tried."

"And you succeeded." Espen bobbed his head from one side to the other. "But there are always consequences to using that amount of magic."

"Like taking a two-day nap?"

Øyvin cleared his throat, and Espen winced.

I narrowed my eyes and looked between the two of them. "What consequences?"

"Try stunning me," Halvar said from the end of the table.

"Umm, what?"

"Stun me."

"I could flash you my boobs. They're quite stunning, just ask Espen. He's really fond of leftie."

Halvar rolled his eyes, and Øyvin muttered something about definitely being awake.

"Use your royal powers, Lennie," Halvar ordered.

"Fine."

I focused on the well of magic in my sternum. It felt different. Weaker. Like it'd been depleted and was trying to refill itself, only reaching a quarter tank so far. Calling on it and picturing a simple ball of light, I flexed my fingers and waited for the magic to skitter down my arm.

Nothing happened.

I tried again. Scrunching my face and closing my eyes, willing the telltale tingling sensation to result in a sparking ball of light in my palm.

Still, nothing happened.

My eyes flew open, and I let out a frustrated sigh. "It's broken."

"It's as we suspected," Espen said. "Try your Fjell powers."

Reaching inside myself, I pulled on a tendril of power and pictured a pebble in my hand. A tickle ran down my arm and a second later a small stone appeared. The royal magic wasn't working, but the Fjell power was still there and healing based on the feeling in my chest. "So, I'm partially broken?" I asked, setting aside the rock.

Halvar grumbled. "Indeed. The royal magic is gone."

My eyebrows hit my hairline. "*All* gone?"

Øyvin examined me with concern etched across his forehead while Espen pressed his fingers against my upper stomach, examining. I didn't complain. I didn't move. I stared at Halvar in shock. "How?"

"You used it all on the mountain," Halvar replied.

Espen's fingers delicately poked and prodded at me. "I still don't feel any changes. She feels fine—" He tapped on my left ribs, and I winced. "Well, except for the bruising."

He pulled back his hands and I raised my shirt, careful not to flash Halvar. A purple bruise bloomed across my left side like lilacs on a summer's day. I'd fought a lot of people, but I couldn't remember anyone getting a hit on me, especially in the ribs. Unless it was from when that stone shield broke against me and Torsten. "How'd I get that?"

"You fell," Øyvin said. "Tumbled a few meters before we could safely get to you."

"What do you mean *safely*?"

"We didn't dare touch you while—" Espen waved his hands beside his head then motioned to his eyes. "Too much power."

More memories flooded back. Painful ones. Silver ones. My vision had turned silver, and a web of power had shot out of me, sailing up the mountainside and hauling it back into place. Protecting everyone.

I huffed.

It was Freija's gift. The magic she'd asked for. I'd transferred it all right back into the mountain. Back where it belonged.

"I think I did my own magic transfer of sorts," I said and looked at the men in the room.

Clear eyes stared back at me, and they all nodded.

"That's certainly what it looked like from the sidelines," Espen said.

"It definitely felt that way too. Ten out of ten, do not recommend." I looked to the silver-haired fae. "Do you still have yours?"

He opened his right palm, and a small ball of crystal-white light appeared.

"Show off," I muttered.

Halvar scoffed and extinguished his magic.

"So, you're the only one with royal magic now?"

He shook his head. "A new light fae has been chosen to take care of the mountain's lighting needs."

"Who?"

"A young Fjell Fae by the name of Sofie."

My stomach flip-flopped as the fact settled in. "Wait, if there's a new light magic Fjell Fae then…" Then Torsten had died. That magic was passed on to another when the former died. My bottom lip trembled, and I clutched my partners' hands. "Torsten?"

Halvar grimaced and another lump formed in my throat. The need to cry creeping closer to the edge of my emotional cliff-side. I'd known it was coming. I'd seen his injuries. He'd have needed a miracle to survive those lacerations.

"Lennie," Espen sighed, his voice sounding heavy. "Leif died too."

"What? He was fine when I left them." Or, at least, that's what he'd claimed. There had been an alarming number of dark patches on his uniform.

Espen brushed a hand over my hair while Øyvin gave my fingers a squeeze. I didn't like where this was going.

"He succumbed to injuries a day after the battle," Espen said. "Too much blood loss. There was nothing I could do."

A whimper slipped out of me. I ripped my hands free and pressed them against my eyes as a sob wracked my body.

"I will leave you now," Halvar muttered and a second later the door to the Council chamber bumped shut.

I don't know how long I cried for. A minute, an hour, a day. But when the tears finally ran dry and Espen stopped rubbing my back, I crossed my legs in the middle of the table. I felt like a wrung-out washcloth—out of magic and out of tears. I'd poured them both on the mountain.

The emotional toll was too much to bear. I'd lost loved ones, failed others, and led people to their own deaths by giving orders while fighting against the Fire Fae.

"I'm a shitty leader," I mumbled and sighed.

Espen pivoted me and pulled me to the edge of the table, letting my legs hang over the edge. He clasped my hands in his. "Look at me, Lennie."

My gaze drifted to his warm amber eyes and the steadfast kindness I'd always find there. Out of the corner of my eye, I caught Øyvin coming to stand beside us.

"You're not a bad leader," Espen said. "Look at everything you've done."

I sniffled. "The café is gone after I promised Oddvar I'd take care of it. Øyvin was captured. My crazy, harebrained—"

Espen squeezed my hands tighter, dislodging my words and train of thought. "You saved people's lives by pulling them from a burning building. You gave them shelter in your own home. Earlier this year, you protected an heir that was about to be murdered. You may not think you're a good leader, Lennie, but your actions say otherwise. And I, for one, am proud of you."

I rested my forehead against his chest. "I barely recognize myself anymore."

"Really?" He tilted my chin with his finger to meet his gaze. "Because I see a woman who went from valuing nature and its beauty through her photographs to protecting it. You haven't changed. You've grown."

I swallowed hard at his observation and leaned into his touch.

"Leadership is so much more than words, Lennie. It's about action too. It's being willing to learn and do better when things don't go right the first time. It's about giving up pieces of yourself to better the lives of those you serve. It's using the tools you have to do the best you can."

"He's right, you know," Øyvin added. "You did everything in your power to save and protect people. That's what a leader does. Something we should all strive to do."

I blubbered and sniffled.

I'd tried my best. Done what felt right. Protected those I could. "It doesn't feel like I did good."

"It won't." Espen tucked me against him, cradling my head in his hand. "Not for a little while."

Øyvin closed in and rubbed his hand across my back. His eyes shimmered with a thousand words he didn't have to say. He was proud of me and loved me more than he could ever put into words.

I sniffed again and pulled back from Espen.

I loved them too. So very much. And perhaps it would take time to wrap my head around everything that had happened and what I'd done. But at least I'd have them to lean on while I recovered.

Sliding off the table, I stepped between the two of them and grabbed the front of their shirts. I pulled them into me and wrapped my arms around their torsos, forcing them into a big group hug. Øyvin huffed, Espen sighed, but they acquiesced and melted around me.

They were both right in their assessments of leadership and the things I'd done. From the inside looking out, it didn't appear like leadership. They were just things I did to help. But, coming from their perspective… Well, I guessed they had a point.

I let out an extended sigh and buried my face against their chests.

Espen pressed a kiss to the side of my head. "Let's go home."

51

ESPEN

The day had come. The day I'd been dreading for the past week: Ylva's funeral.

There was nothing to bury. Her ashes had disappeared into the wind after Herja burned her alive. But it was Forest Fae tradition to bury a soldier killed in combat, and her mother, Gunvor, had requested a funeral. So here we stood in the stave church graveyard, wearing black and shades of dark green, watching over a coffin covered in flowers. It wasn't empty though. I'd placed a wooden sword inside to represent the sharp woman we'd lost too soon. The woman who'd fought bravely until the very end.

Ylva's burial plot sat at the rear of the graveyard near the forest, verdant trees dappling the ground with shadows. It was the perfect spot for her.

I laid a bundle of purple blooms among the other flowers atop Ylva's casket and turned to the gathered crowd. Sniffles and tears filled the air as the mourners watched on, the stave church looming over their backs like a bear ready to attack. Nobody cared though. The sorrowful faces all focused on the coffin beside me.

My gaze found Lennie's and she gave me a gentle nod, willing me on.

I nodded back and cleared the lump lodged in my throat as the group waited for me to start the ceremony.

"Thank you for being here today," I said. "Ylva Nygård was a great friend, fae, daughter, and commander. With a wry sense of humor and unyielding love for the forest she swore to protect, Ylva was the best of us. Someone the young looked up to and the old revered."

My gaze shifted from the mourning masses to Ylva's casket.

"We will miss you more that you could ever know. You were a light that couldn't be tamed. A mind so sharp and strategically inclined. A soul that yearned for peace in an evermore complicated world."

A tear welled at the corner of my eye, and I inhaled sharply.

"A protector through and through. One who made the ultimate sacrifice for her friends, family, and fae-kind. A soldier who wouldn't have wanted to go in any other way."

However much I don't want you to leave. Not so soon. Not now. Not ever.

I took a deep breath and clenched my fists at my sides. "Thank you, my friend."

There was no reply. There never would be. She was already gone.

"Thank you for all the memories. For the laughs and the joy you brought into our world. F-for the—" My throat tightened around my words, barring them from leaving. Leaving like she was. I swallowed hard as a tear tumbled across my cheek.

I can't do this. Flashes of her demise blazed through my mind, reminding me of the end. Her end. Her final moments on this earth.

My tear-filled eyes found Lennie's. She gave me another gentle nod and a loving expression that buoyed me.

With a final look at the casket, I whispered, "Thank you."

I shuffled to the crowd and stepped up beside Lennie and Øyvin. The former looped her arm through mine and pulled me against her side, offering comfort and stability.

More sniffles filled the crowd.

Gunvor stepped forward, having traveled all this way for her daughter, and raised her hands to the trees. They bowed to her as if they were offering their own condolences. Perhaps they were. Gunvor, a tree-speaker, had a rare ability to speak and command the trees. She never spoke of all she could do, but her power was incredible, even at her great age.

Gangly limbs groaned and reached forward as roots rose from the ground and wrapped around the casket like long fingers forming a lattice. Slowly, the tree tendrils lowered the coffin into the hole in the ground.

"Ylva Nygård has served the forest well," Gunvor croaked, her voice carrying through the solemn silence. "May her soul be transported to the ancestors and her power re-bestowed to the woodland she held dear. Trees aid me."

The pines around us swayed, their creaking limbs composing a somber requiem I'd never forget.

Her casket disappeared into the ground and the roots spread out over top it, pushing it further. The Forest and Fjell Fae in the crowd raised their hands and I followed suit, coaxing the soil to fill and cover. Small handfuls from a nearby mound of dirt slid into the hole, eventually filling it to the top.

It was done.

She was gone.

This was the end.

This was goodbye.

My gaze drifted to the stone marker with her name on it.

Ylva Nygård.

Commander and Friend of the Forest.

"Goodbye, commander," I whispered. "You did well."

Another wave of tears streamed across my cheeks and dripped from my chin.

A warm hand cupped my face, and I turned into the heat. Lennie brushed her finger through the tears. "Come on," she whispered. "Let's go home."

I nodded, and with one final look back at Ylva's grave site, uttered, "Goodbye, my friend."

52

ØYVIN

A week after the battle, the village had been cleared of rubble and bodies, humans slowly trickled back into town, and the final fae memorials had concluded. Skolvik was doing its best to revert back to a new normal. Myself included.

Today, I found myself in the mountain, back in my old role, on a diplomatic mission. Light orbs bobbed around the rocky ceiling like glass floats on water, and thick pillars held the mass of stone above us. Where the Fjord Council chamber was made of polished walls and carved furniture, the Fjell meeting space was a rugged show of power with little nuance.

Seated around the Fjell Fae table were representatives for each of the factions: Espen and Marius, his new second-in-command, representing the Forest and wolves. Myself, Reuven, and Salka representing the Fjord. Lennie, Halvar, and a man named Bodil for the Fjell Fae. And, at the far end of the table, flanked by two male fae with sharp chins, was Embla.

Looking like a harsher version of her onyx-haired sister, Veigar's eldest daughter and the new Queen of the Fire Fae was a formidable presence with a surprisingly genuine smile. Ever since she'd arrived in Skolvik a few days ago, she'd listened, observed, and been amenable to any discussions. Including this one.

The Fjell was putting a lot of trust in Salka vouching for her sister, saying that she wasn't at all like their father, however imposing she might be. But that was the whole point of our meeting together. All four factions needed to reestablish bonds that had been severely broken and could only be rebuilt by trusting one another.

"Thank you all for coming," Lennie said from the head of the table. Pride grew inside me like a wave about to crash along a shore. "I know this is unconventional, but unusual times call for crazy antics. At least, that's always been my philosophy."

Half the room chuckled, and Halvar rolled his eyes.

"I think we can all agree that working together and pursuing our purposes is in every faction's best interest. We don't need one leader; we need a diverse group of leaders who promise to always work in the fae's best interests. *All* fae."

Heads bobbed around the table.

"We have drawn up an agreement we hope you'll agree to. The Skolvik Accord. It's not super long, but details how we should proceed and establishes a Monarch Council with three members from each faction. You should have received a draft prior to the meeting." Lennie looked out over the assembled leaders. "Does anyone have concerns?"

No one spoke.

Reuven cleared his throat. "We, The Fjord Fae, agree to sign the Accord."

Lennie beamed, her body brimming with energy to the point where I could tell she was doing everything she could not to bounce up and down.

"We agree too," Espen said, drawing our attention to him. He smiled. "We promise to always work for all fae. Whatever anyone needs, we are here and willing to help."

I wasn't surprised in the slightest. He'd also told us this morning how the Forest Fae Council had unanimously voted to support the measure.

With three of the four factions on board, that left only one more.

All eyes turned to Embla.

She clasped her hands together and rested them on the edge of the table. "It has been a long time since we've been part of a greater whole, but I do believe we are overdue. The Fire Fae will sign."

I let out a breath of relief.

"Thank you, Your Majesty," Lennie replied. "That means a lot."

The Queen bowed her head in a sign of respect.

A large piece of parchment was passed around, ink and quill provided for each leader to sign. When it circled back to the Fjell Fae, Lennie nudged it to Halvar. He grumbled and nudged it back to her, motioning for her to sign.

"Halvar Haraldson, we talked about this. I will forge your signature if you don't sign it yourself."

He grumbled again and relented, adding two jagged *H*s to the bottom of the page before handing it back to Lennie. She held it up, smiled, and set it aside on a nearby table.

"Now, is there anything else we need to discuss?" she asked, holding her hands behind her back the same way Halvar normally did.

"We have no interest in unchecked power imbalances, nor a retreat from our purpose," Embla said, her voice scratchy and firm. "The Fire Fae have plenty of work to attend to in Iceland. With the tectonic plates moving more each year, we need every Fire Fae we have helping us relieve the pressure being built."

Salka nodded.

"Is there anything you need from us?" Lennie asked.

"Just the Fire Fae shard returned so we can commune with the ancestors and complete my coronation ceremony."

"Of course," Lennie replied.

Halvar silently rose from his seat. He crossed the room and opened a chest near a side door before returning and setting a lump of blue stone in front of Embla. "This is the real stone. You have my word."

Embla brushed her fingers across its jagged edge. "Thank you, Halvar. I trust that you have not been duplicitous."

I did too. No man would dare give her a fake in such a confined space. It would also undermine everything we were trying to do here.

Halvar returned to his seat and Lennie smiled at him like a teacher proud of their student, before turning back to the Fire Fae Queen. "If you ever need access to the Temple, please let us know." She faced the others. "That goes for the other factions too. We can keep the pieces in place or return—"

"Keep them," Espen and Reuven said in unison.

Lennie nodded. It was the best course of action. They'd be safer here and we'd be able to access them if needed, further solidifying our alliance.

Espen straightened in his chair and looked across the table to where I sat with Reuven and Salka. "We would like to discuss aid against the current ground conditions. We were wondering if the Fjord Fae might be able to conjure more rain to help soak the roots while still being cautious around the burn scars?"

"We would be happy to help you, Espen," Reuven replied with a nod.

Amenable conversation continued without any grumbles. In a way, Veigar was getting what he wanted: a united fae. Only difference was we were choosing to work together as separate entities, not one group ruled by one man.

I looked to Lennie. She caught me and smiled.

She'd been right too. All along, she'd said we needed to work together, and here we were doing just that. I returned her smile, proud of all we'd accomplished.

Together.

53

LENNIE

I traipsed up the hillside, camera slung over my shoulder and my rain jacket zippered up tight, protecting me from the cooler temperatures and the damp breeze. Morning had dawned and brought autumn with it like a reminder of seasons and lives ending.

The wind rustled the trees around me as it danced between the pines and muffled the sound of our footfalls against the steep terrain. Espen wandered beside me, surveying our surroundings and searching for spots that might still need healing after the battle a few weeks ago. Meanwhile, Øyvin hiked behind us in his navy jacket, watching our backs like normal, just in case something might jump out and try to kill us.

Everywhere I looked sat reminders of the fae we'd lost in the Battle for Skolvik—as it had since become named. Dozens of Fjell, Fjord, and Forest soldiers had died in the skirmishes, most of them burned to death.

There'd been losses on the other side too. Fire Fae had littered town square, some with severed limbs, others with severe damage to their skulls, others still with arrows sticking out of them like hedgehogs. Apparently, Forest Fae arrows had been doused in so much poison that they could fell a thousand-pound Fjord Horse on impact.

All the bodies had been removed from the village. Some taken into the fjell for burial, some to the forest, and a whole slew of Fire and Fjord Fae had been pulled into the inky depths of the fjord as part of the clean-up efforts.

Mass funerals and memorials had been held, with smaller ceremonies for immediate family to congregate and mourn. I'd attended them all, not in my official capacity as Deputy Head Guard, but out of respect for what I'd asked so many people to do and the orders I'd given that day. Each event had left me feeling like an empty shell.

But the worst ones. The ones that hurt the most, were the ones for my friends.

Ylva's had been first. Facing her mother, Gunvor, had been gut-wrenching, but with a pat to my hands and a hug that reminded me of my own grandmother, she'd said that Ylva had died the way she'd always wanted to: protecting the forest. I'd lost it. As had Espen. We'd held each other for hours after we got home that day.

The next day we'd gone to Leif and Torsten's memorial. I could barely stomach it. They were laid to rest together in a specially made tomb on the side of the mountaintop, near a small patch of flowers, where the forest and fjell converged.

The last few weeks had been hard, but, as Espen and Øyvin had both reminded me: death was inevitable. And those who'd lost their lives had known the risks, yet given themselves willingly to protect what they loved. I couldn't argue with that. I'd done exactly the same.

I'd protected my loves, the place I called home, and the mountain.

The crack was healed, but the humans had been informed that the storm had shifted the earth into a more stable position. Police officers and some geological surveyors had been out to check and deemed the crack and land mass no longer a threat.

I still couldn't wrap my head around the fact that it was my powers, my actions, that had made it so.

"Don't think too hard there, Trouble," a grumbly voice said from behind me.

"What if I was coming up with new ways to suck your cock?"

Øyvin choked on a laugh.

Gosh, I enjoyed delivering shock and awe comments like that. Sometimes he'd respond in kind, other times I'd catch him off guard, like this. It was one of my favorite pastimes.

Espen grabbed my hand from beside me. "You'd better be thinking of ways for my dick too."

I wiggled my brows at him. "Jealous?"

"Sharing is caring, remember?" He winked, and something inside me fluttered.

"Oh, I do."

"So, why aren't we still in bed?" Øyvin asked.

I smiled. "Because the lighting is too good not to be outside today, and we all need a break from town."

It was true. We'd been helping with recovery efforts as villagers slowly moved back in. Oddvar's had been my main focus. The proprietor himself was back and had brought his sons with him when I'd informed him that a lightning strike had caused a fire on the street. Together we'd worked on clearing debris and preparing for the rebuild. But all that work was a constant reminder of what had happened, and honest to hell, I needed a mental health day. A moment of reprieve to do something I loved with the people I loved.

So here we were on a morning hike instead of lying in bed doing unspeakable things to each other.

"Where are you taking us, wife?" Espen's usual pep-in-his-step attitude was slowly returning after the battle, and I knew this hike would do him wonders. It was a chance for him to reconnect and traipse through the woods where we'd spent some of our first days together.

"A little spot Halvar showed me once upon a time."

"When was this?" Øyvin asked as I clambered over a fallen tree with the grace of a potato.

"You were busy. Espen was poisoned"—the man in question quivered then hopped onto the moss-covered log and jumped back down like a freaking gymnast— "and he'd mentioned it was a good spot for a photo."

The big guy hadn't been wrong. It was an epic spot, but a bitch of a hike though.

"Hmmm."

"I know," I replied to Øyvin's noise. "Sometimes the bossman has surprises."

"I think I've had enough surprises for one lifetime," Espen said. "Don't need them from Halvar either."

I snickered and pivoted off the trail, the guys following in my wake. "This way. Just a little bit further."

"Oh, I know where we're going," Espen said as the rocky field turned into a copse of trees.

I wiggled my eyebrows at him.

A few minutes later the trees parted and revealed a view that was surely made by gods. A piece of rock jutted out from the cliffside, looking west down the length of the fjord. Thick, tree-covered slopes rose from the gray-blue water on either side. The sun hid behind a thin layer of cloud, perfectly diffusing the light and casting a soft glow over everything.

I stepped toward the cliff edge and tilted my face toward the sun.

Standing out here with the wind tickling my cheeks and the two loves of my life beside me felt like a breath of fresh air. If I closed my eyes tight enough, I could picture the cobwebs being brushed away and the grief of loss tiptoeing out the front door.

Arms wrapped around my waist, and my eyes sprung open.

Espen glanced down at me. His amber eyes hooded, those soft lips curving slightly. Whenever he looked at me like this, as if I were the most valuable thing in the world, it melted my insides. I swept my hand across his cheek and beard, and he leaned into the touch, his lashes fluttering. The way this man made me feel warm and fuzzy with a single smile was everything I hadn't known I needed in my life. And I'd be grateful for every second I had with him on this earth.

"I love you," I whispered.

He leaned down and pressed his mouth to mine. Our lips moved together, separated, brushed, teased, and nipped in a dance that was all our own. My pulse hummed and my muscles relaxed, content with being here in his arms and enjoying every ounce of sunshine he poured into me. When it felt like I was about to sway and stumble, Espen pulled back and set his hands on my hips. "I love you too. More than you could ever imagine."

"I can imagine every single drop of it," I replied.

"Me too," Øyvin said, and I peered over my shoulder.

Øyvin opened his hand and made a come-hither motion. My body lit up like the Fourth of July in response and I trundled over to him. When I got close enough, he pressed his hands against my lower back and yanked me flush against his chest. I ran my hands over his jacket and settled one against his heart. Its steady rhythm was the perfect soundtrack for today—a reminder of the life we had ahead of us.

I tilted my head up and brushed my lips against his. He breathed into it and reminded me of everything he'd done and everything he would do to keep me happy—even if that meant challenging me from time to time. As our lips moved together in a passionate kiss that would be etched in my mind until death, there wasn't any doubt in my mind that he'd always put me first. Espen too. We were his family now. The fjord had its place in his heart, but the two of us were where he'd always belong the most.

With a satisfied sigh, I wiggled out of his hold and stepped back toward the cliff.

"Don't go too far. We can't have you falling," Espen said.

I smirked and gave them a wink. "Way too late. I've already fallen."

The biggest smiles I'd ever seen beamed back at me, and it took every ounce of willpower not to launch myself into their arms.

"Focus, Trouble," Øyvin said like he could hear me mentally warring with my own desires.

I waved my hand at him, edged out onto the spit of rock, and peered down the fjord toward Skolvik.

There was the mountain that I'd saved from falling, the village where I'd fallen in love, and the hillside where I'd taken that first fortuitous photo and missed my cruise ship. This was home. My home. A place I'd photograph and protect for years to come... Or, at least until we had to move because people were getting suspicious of our lack of aging. There was only so much makeup and miraging could do.

Maybe we'd go to Alvdalen and be closer to family. Maybe we'd head down south to one of the fishing villages. Wherever we went, though, we'd go together. Our little trio. Our little family. The one I'd found in the most unlikely of places.

I drew in a breath and pulled my camera out of its case. Taking off the lens, I shoved it in my pocket and zippered it up. One could never be too careful.

Turning on the camera with a few clicks, it beeped to life.

Peering at the scenery, a smile twisted my lips. I angled the shot, adjusted the focus, and clicked.

EPILOGUE

Lennie – Two Years Later

I strode into Heidi's Viking-era hut in the forest after lunch, the smell of herbs and oils bombarding my senses like a camera flash run amok. "Honey, I'm home!"

Heidi scurried over from the sink, frantically wringing her hands in a piece of cloth, her eyes blown wide. "What are you doing here? You're not supposed to stop by until this evening."

"We closed the café a little earlier today seeing as cruise season is over. Didn't Espen tell you this morning when he dropped off Bjorn?"

Heidi swallowed hard and readjusted her long skirt. "He failed to mention it."

"That's all right. I'm here now. Did he behave today? Didn't get into the blue tinctures again?" The staining last week had been a bitch to get off his little hands even with Øyvin's Fjord Fae magic.

"He... um..."

I tilted my head to one side and narrowed my eyes are her. Why was it quiet? Too quiet. My pulse quickened and my hands grew clammy. Whenever it was this quiet in the house, there was a hundred percent chance my son was up to no good. I furrowed my brow and looked around the space. The only things that stared back were shelves full of little glass bottles, herbs drying upside down from the rafters, and a surgical table with dubious stains. No little one in sight.

"Where is he?"

She clasped her hands together and let out a breath. "He isn't here."

"What do you mean, 'he isn't here?'"

Her lips pursed together.

"Heidi... Where is my son?"

"Now, see here, child." She yanked her cloth-come-tea-towel out of her apron and waved it about. "He is a very persuasive man."

No. Please no. I clapped my hand to my forehead. "You didn't. Tell me you didn't."

She shrugged and held up her hands like there was nothing she could've possibly done. Which was a damn lie. If there was anyone other than me who could stand up to the big guy, it would be Heidi.

"How long?" I asked. I'd bet my new house this wasn't a one-time thing.

"Don't be angry, it's bad for your health."

"How long has Halvar been babysitting Bjorn?"

Heidi sighed. "Every Tuesday for the past three months."

"Three months!" I exclaimed. "Do Espen and Øyvin know about this?"

"Øyvin was informed the first day and said it was all right."

A breath whizzed between my clenched teeth. He'd fucking failed to mention anything to his partner and mother of his child. Fantastic.

I stomped to the door.

"Where are you going?"

Spinning in the entry, I replied, "To find my baby!"

I stormed up the hillside and into the mountain, moving like I owned the goddamn place and would steam-roll anyone who got in my way. After coaxing a terrified soldier into telling me where Halvar was, I barreled toward the throne room. Rough stone walls turned to crystalline blue quartz by the entrance where two soldiers stood guard. Their eyes went wide when they saw me. I ignored them. They weren't responsible for this. The big brute with silver hair was.

"Halvar, where is—" I drew to a stop just inside the room, my heart lodging in my throat. "What have you done with my son?"

Halvar beamed from ear to ear, which itself should have knocked me on my ass. But it was what he pointed at that had panic swirling through me like a tornado.

"Look," Bjorn said, brandishing a sharp, toddler-sized stone sword. He waved it around and made a few stabbing motions before holstering it like a soldier... *Where the hell did he get a mini-holster from?* More importantly, why the hell did he have a sword!

I frowned. "Halvar, he's not even two!"

The Fjell Fae snorted at me like I was being ridiculous and swept the tow-haired boy into his arms as if he were his own grandchild. "Bjorn has exceptional Fjell Fae magic. It will not be long before he joins Brokkr and the fae in the forge."

I planted my hands on my hips, careful to keep my tone firm but not too authoritative as I didn't want to scare Bjorn. He wasn't to blame here. It was the stoic beast holding him that was. "Again, he's not even two. And he's part Fjord Fae. Do you really want his unchecked water powers down there too?"

Halvar's mouth fell into a firm line. "We're working on that."

A deep and long breath pressed through my lips as I stared at the rocky ceiling. How was this happening? Being mother of one demi-fae was hard enough, but I was pretty sure I was expecting another. My guess was Espen's considering how much fun we'd had during his birthday yoga session. But honest to hell, how was I going to keep track of two of them when the first was being secretly babysat by a fae who only knew how to raise Fjell Fae soldiers?

"He is doing exceptionally well, and no one has been injured," Halvar said.

"Good, Mamma."

My heart crumpled a bit at the pride emanating from my boy. He was good. As clever as his fathers and a bubbly little thing too.

I knelt and opened my arms. "Come here, sweet pea."

He wiggled out of Halvar's hold and the man set him down. Toddling over to me, he lunged into my arms with a big smile, and I wrapped him into a hug, careful of the stone sword hanging off his hip. Peering over his shoulder at Halvar, I said, "If you put this kid in a Fjell Fae uniform before he turns five, I will personally castrate you."

Halvar rolled his eyes.

Bjorn freed himself from my hug and pulled something from his pocket, proffering it to me.

"What's this, hun?"

The light-blue wool was silky soft against my fingers and— My breath caught.

"Hat," Bjorn said, and my heart stilled. He'd been given a hat. My eyes lifted to the Fjell Fae watching us, wrinkles forming at the corners of his sky-blue eyes.

Bjorn gingerly pulled his hat from my limp hands and yanked something else from his other jacket pocket. "Mamma hat." He passed me a matching hat, only much larger. One that was exactly like the baby fae hats I'd been joking about since I became a demi-fae.

My breaths shuddered as I accepted the simple, knitted hat which rolled up at the brim. Lips curving into a smile, I slipped it on. Bjorn rakishly pulled his onto his head, messing up his hair in the process.

I glanced to Halvar. "I've been waiting a while for this."

His lips turned up at the corners and, for the first time since I met him, Halvar gave me an unfiltered, beaming smile. His cheeks flushed, his eyes crinkled, and warmth radiated from him in waves. "You finally deserved it."

I scoffed and swept Bjorn into my arms, positioning him on my hip. "Say thank you to Halvar."

Bjorn mumbled his thanks between a yawn and rested his head against my shoulder. His long eyelashes brushed across his rosy cheeks. He'd probably fall asleep on the walk home.

I turned toward the exit and Halvar cleared his throat, drawing me to a stop.

"I will see him next Tuesday," Halvar announced, and I spun on the spot. "He needs the training. The sooner he is trained, the safer it will be for him and everyone else."

I bit my bottom lip to keep from grumbling. He had a point. But dammit, I was still bitter that I'd been hoodwinked and left out of the loop on this.

However...

If he so desperately wanted to help us train Bjorn, then I wanted something in return. I wanted the kernel of information I'd poked and prodded people for, searched and questioned for the past few years. Information, it seemed, only one fae had.

"I'll let you train my son every Tuesday on one condition."

Halvar's nostrils flared as he inhaled and crossed his arms. "Name it."

"Tell me how old you are."

His brow furrowed. "That's it?"

"That's it."

Halvar shook his head and sighed. "I'm 964."

"What the fuck!"

Bjorn clapped his hand over my mouth.

THE END

REVIEW

Thank you for reading! I hope you enjoyed Lennie's story and all of her unhinged chaos. If you did, please consider leaving a review on Amazon, Goodreads, or social media!

Reviews are extremely helpful for indie authors, and I'd greatly appreciate your support!

Best wishes,
Elle

THANK YOU

Thank you for reading! I hope you enjoyed Lennie's story. This series meant so much to me and has truly changed my life for the better. I hope it has brought you some joy too. While this is the last book in Lennie's saga, it is not the last book in this world. Halvar and Freija have a story to tell too, so keep an eye out for that and a few other fun Nordic tales.

To Riley Jo: Thank you for beta-reading this entire series for me! Your feedback and suggestions made this story into what it is today. I truly could not have done this without you. Especially that question about Fire Fae. That sent this story in a whole new direction. Hugs forever.

To Rosie: My dear, dear friend! Thank you for having my back and for helping me complete a final eyes read on this beast. Hugs forever to you too.

To Aimee: Goddess of Punctuation and Chaos! Thank you for helping me make Lennie's left tit look ah-may-zing for the past few years. You da best!

To Carl: There are no words for the amount of gratitude I have for you. Thank you for holding me in the dark. I love you.

To River: Thank you for being the cutest (and sassiest) little floof that has ever graced the streets of Boston and for hanging out with me in the writing cave.

To my readers and supporters: THANK YOU. THANK YOU. THANK YOU FOR READING. Thank you for supporting me as I continue this journey and dream. This is only the beginning. I can't wait to show you what's coming next.

About the Author

Hey! I'm Elle Thrasher, an author of romantic fantasy books.

My books are filled with relatable heroines, swoon-worthy heroes, lots of laughs, and locations that will give you wanderlust.

While I'm originally from the UK, and lived in Norway for seven years too, I now live in the US with my husband and one very fluffy dog. When I'm not writing, I can usually be found drinking a cup of tea, staring at my never-ending tbr, or taking a joke waaaaay too far.

Follow me on Instagram for updates and don't forget to sign up for my newsletter to receive behind-the-scenes info, bonus material, and details about upcoming books!

www.ellethrasher.com

ALSO BY ELLE THRASHER

The Cerulean Lazulum Series
(Urban Fantasy)
Cavendish
Hawke

<u>The Nordic Fae Series</u>
(Romantic Fantasy)
<u>The Fae of the Fjord</u>
<u>Christmas on the Fjord</u>
<u>The Fae of the Forest</u>
<u>The Fae of the Fjell</u>

www.ingramcontent.com/pod-product-compliance
Lightning Source LLC
Chambersburg PA
CBHW020324010826

48973CB00005B/1118